The Girl at the Pedestal:

A Revelation of Authenticity

STEPHEN MICHAEL FERREE

Formatted for publication by Pen It! Publications, LLC

penitpublications@yahoo.com

Penitpublications.com

ISBN #: 978-1-948390-71-2

Acknowledgements

I was not alone in this universe while writing this book. Acknowledgements go to the Debi Stanton and the local Bartholomew County Writer's Group in Columbus, Indiana.

I knew well enough from previous endeavors that the group that is doing something know the subtleties necessary to pull off professional quality work, whether that is wood working or carving, computer engineering, graphic arts or writing. The quality of this work derives from this group's involvement.

I must also make an acknowledgement to the "Key to Life" course written by L. Ron Hubbard, well known author and founder of the Church of Scientology. It is about communication and language, including Grammar. It was great to learn the subject so thoroughly from such a prolific writer.

Additional acknowledgements go to my children, who saw their father work through weekends and other breaks to complete the task of a first novel. Felicity and Brandon, this book is also for you, not just for better insight into your father's mind, but also to improve your vocabularies.

The cover art is by Donna Cook, also a writer and published author with Pen It! Publications, LLC.

Contents

PROLOGUE

A Memoir from a Past Universe

You may have been instructed that you are a combination of chemicals rigorously constructed by an encoded string of deoxyribonucleic acid into a complex biological automaton. That is your *body*, which albeit contributes to your identity, is not the authentic *you*. If you could be the true form of yourself, you would not need a flesh body. The human body is constructed to be a substitute for the true body of your spiritual form. To the degree that you like it, it probably bears resemblance; to the degree that you don't, it's not similar enough.

This course of events happened a very, very long time ago, not years, not even galactic years, but universes ago. For convenience, I supplanted some modern items, and in general, the level of technology wasn't completely consistent with your present Earth, but there did exist basic telephones, refrigerators, radios, televisions, aircraft, automobiles and even nuclear capability, roughly comparable to the 1950s and general attitudes comparable to the 1980s. The planet had a larger, nearer moon, making it very bright at night, with stronger tides than the Earth you are familiar with. It won't make sense if you don't know at least a couple additional points that were revealed in a little black book referenced within the story:

Universe – an arbitrary but consistent set of rules governing the creation and persistence of space, energies and masses used for communication and therefore understanding of all spiritual entities involved in the games of that universe; a created space for souls to play. The universe allows for such souls to have viewpoints within, from which they act, and often divide into many subdivisions, creating multiple viewpoints for increasing not only the apparent population but also the solidity and thus sense of reality of such games.

Armageddon – the end of a universe; the undoing of the rules that caused a universe and all its artifacts to exist, including the division of souls into multiple viewpoints, returning the true identities of those playing the game to those that created that universe. To some degree, the Armageddon of a universe is predetermined at the beginning to guard against the possibility of becoming completely unaware and being lost in a universe forever.

However, it becomes the responsibility of those souls in the universe to perform the actions and processes necessary to recover their authentic identity, which is to say true purposes and form. The greater spirits that created a universe will have placed subtle hints and premonitions with the intent that their spiritual performers will once again become aware of their self-imposed trap.

Sometimes they communicate forward in time to themselves, conveying truths that will begin the self-salvaging process.

I thought I heard a voice....

ONE

Returning Home

"**M**iranda – you're going back to the island?" inquired Sandy, a tall amiable girl I'd gotten to know in the college dorm. She wore dirty, white, knee length shorts, old scuffed pink canvas shoes, and a loose tan lace blouse that took some abuse from her moving activities.

I remained quiet as I looked from her feet up to catch her eyes.

"Yeah," she presented herself. "Old clothes for the move and I don't care if I look good on the bus. So hot. I don't even care if I stink."

She smelled sweaty, but she didn't stink. She'd caught me as I'd finished packing, just when I looked out the door to see how sparse the building had already become. It was important to me because I knew my emotions would fall flat once left alone. "Yeah, Sandy, I've got to go back to be with the parents and some girlfriends," I said, flashing my pretty smile, holding a sense of being reserved as I hesitated without continuing. My mind needed recuperation after final exams for a summer session and my current cogitation rate was lacking.

"Oh gosh!" she rolled her eyes. "Girlfriends! I hope you get your time with them. But semesters and summer sessions have to end," Sandy returned, having raised her eyebrows three times as she spoke. "I will miss you so much, Miranda."

"Me too," I said, allowing her to give me a gentle hug, and though probably expected to sigh, I inhaled her effeminate aroma. Our eyes caught just a moment, that little look when you wonder whether you will see that person again. "I'll be back," I encouraged. I recalled the first time I met her when arriving at the dorm for the summer – she'd asked me if I was a gymnast with that same characteristic eyebrow movement.

"I know," she said, her whole body hesitating. She was biting her lip.

"Ah – you'll be back, right?" I urged.

"Oh yeah. Just wanted to see if you cared," she smiled. "All paid up. Schedule is set. But when coming back I'll be on the last bus I can get."

"Ha," I mocked softly. "I'd like to not be on the last plane. Too many weirdos in the airports! Well, back to Altontown. Besides, it's just a few weeks until fall semester."

"So – back to New Missoula for me. Charlotte – my little sis – is begging to see me. As for you, you look a little rough. I hope you get rested," she said and gave me a kiss on the forehead as if I were her little sister, then she turned to leave.

I had no interest in going to the miserable little town of New Missoula, lost in a sea of farmland. I felt my emotions perilously draining as I watched her walk away toward the elevator. She was taller and more developed than my too-little form that often got me called "Child," "Honey," "Precious," or "Little girl." Her long brunette waves were stringy from the heat. I ran my fingers through my messy blonde hair as I noted my petite sweat-moistened clothing. I liked my dimensions. I liked hers too, which I perused like a good book until she went out of sight. I felt a mild longing for her, triggered by some romantic memories from the summer session, but she was not my heart's pervading desire. The girl I cherished was Tori, who I would meet up with again on the island. I turned back to my dorm room to fetch my bags, but looking at the time, I'd be sitting awhile if I got to the airport just yet.

I wandered through the hallway to get one of the few baggage carts owned by the dorm and rolled it back into the quiet room to throw my sage-colored leather-like bags upon it, then dragged my few possessions to the elevator. I came out at ground level, and waited in the lobby, taking in the odd bunch of papers on, and extending past, the bulletin board. Several had variations professing "Armageddon – Repent – Clean up your soul for your return!" I scoffed at the lack of further definition – return to home? Return to hell? Return to nothingness? I could not relate to these metaphysical zealots, their numbers growing rapidly through the last century, who found their way to the colleges and airports, speaking of extracting the soul from the body, of fantastic variations of reincarnation, of limbo or various platitudes into which spirits and ghosts could become trapped. How obvious their intent at mystification and obfuscation of their concepts!

I'd spent so much time in my parents' funeral home I believed I'd actually spoken with ghosts, and though I had notebooks full of my encounters, I never could validate the existence of a disembodied spirit. It was belief or delusion, not reality, as I had no form of proof, so I would make but a credulous expert. I was compelled to act sardonic with the cynics, and though I claimed to be agnostic, I was yet willing to learn about the subjects if only to keep it all at arm's length. Nonetheless, I had to put off my disdain if I could conceivably use this material in my classes or writing.

Aside from hundreds of parent's vehicles collecting students along the street, a series of yellow cabs lined up in the building's curved drive, so I just walked up to one with a driver in it. Without having to say anything, the cabbie popped the trunk and loaded the baggage. I'd realized that another cabbie, an older clean-shaven fellow, had been at a pay phone, probably calling into the building to get a count of remaining students. I saw him throw up his arms as I popped into the backseat of his rival. Perhaps he recalled me from the start of summer, but I couldn't recall him.

My cabbie stepped fluidly into the front seat. "Bus station? Airport?" he inquired, looking back in the mirror.

"Airport," I responded with the pretense of being affluent.

Looking at the hollowing out of the population of the campus as the cab drove past the vacating structures, I contemplated what it would be like had I stayed through the break, even if they would let students remain in the dorms. I'm sure it would have been quiet and lonely, after all, the people were one of the best reasons to be here. As much as I enjoyed being alone, I also had this dire need to be around people, especially strangers, where I could feel anonymous, or my best friends where I was needed. I didn't favor loose acquaintances with people who were always around – the residential assistants, the people in my classes whose names I never knew, and I think my ostentatious Mother fell into that category as she was just as much an enigma to me as familiar. Overall, though, I hated being away from others, like being in a secluded back room of a library or the empty dorm. And yes, I was aware that the cabbie looked into the mirror more than normal, making his weak attempt to see my pretty eyes without losing his job. Once we stopped at the airport, I gave him a long look and shook his hand firmly, thanking him with my beauty. I had to blink to break his gaze – that happened to me all the time. In return, he gratuitously helped carry my baggage.

I felt better immediately once among the amicable travelers at the airport, despite the nervousness caused by the trip, making sure I'd get the baggage checked, getting the correct ticket, ensuring the departure and arrival times were correct, and carefully avoiding a filthy stall in the airport restroom that would frighten a mortician, such as my father. My thoughts loosely tumbled between the needs of the present and the goals of the trip, and I could be distracted by recollections of Sandy and a few dozen girls, some who left at the end of the spring semester. Still, the indelible image of Tori flashed vividly in my mind. I struggled to interrupt my stray thoughts that preempted my intentions lest I'd miss my flight.

Being small I had to watch out for myself, but there was this funny reaction in large groups – those that looked at me as if to protect, and those that watched me as if to lust. I saw them. I could see the difference in their eyes. Older and younger men alike watched me passing, often looking all about with this open look of concern, actively maintaining civility. Then there were others who watched me directly, a leering gaze following my midriff. I tried not to walk sexy, acting boxy and adding a limp, but today I stuck out like an orchid amongst monkey cups.

A man in a heavy muslin robe with a very long necklace of wooden beads and abalone rushed up with a flyer and a book, titled, "How to Survive the End of the World." I must have just given him a grimace. I'd already surmised that the absurd "end of the world stuff" was just there to get people to not care about anything, or to justify inaction for those who failed to show initiative. I may have spit in his direction, not strictly intending to upset him, just bad timing when I tried to get some leftover food particle off my teeth and out of my mouth. I had no awareness of the spiritual side of the universe I lived in. I didn't know at that time it might have been important.

I brought a small paperback book about common thoughts in ancient languages with me on the commercial plane, but the end of the summer session left me exhausted after a couple three-hour final exams, so I left it in my carry-on and didn't even attempt to read, though I'd found curiosity in the fact that all these languages had words for *spirit, faith, god, righteous, universe* and *heaven* as well as *sin, thief, prostitute,* and economic terms like *interest, money, rich* and *poor*. I craved to read it, assuming it would be more interesting than pure etymology because these ancient words were the source of cognates in later languages, but at the time, my mind echoed busily from the events of school. Memorizations of grammar, word usage and literature bounced within my head. Being able to alternately write with both hands, I was sure I'd written between a chapter and a novella while taking the three-hour long English exam. A history class reverberated like the lecture hall, and hopefully, some of those reflections found their way onto the pages of my last final exam of this summer session.

The prudent stewardesses and the passengers, the trays with snacks and carbonated liquids, and all the associated actions happened as if I were barely a participant. I was exhausted to the point that humor wasn't humorous, and I'd attempted a logical examination of the jokes people were exchanging. I knew it was a sign of being on the edge. I breathed deep, giving my brain an extra dose of oxygen.

Without the pressure of the daily schedule, and without my new friends, my emotional level took a nosedive, toward a gothic, morbid introversion that served me best when alone. The noise of the cranking twin-prop filled the cabin and contributed to the auditory isolation. I could never sleep on a plane, but I could close my eyes and find a half-reality of dream and awake, where the merger of nonsensical images made an attempt to compose a story. A group of vacationers in bright, flowered shirts told jokes and the laughter obtruded into my dreamy state. By midflight, I had my limit of guffaws from these few drunk passengers and just belted out, "Quiet down people!" without even opening my eyes. Yet I was glad there were people present.

The plane landed on a large island in late afternoon and I had to walk across the tarmac to a "puddle jumper," a small amphibious seaplane that would transfer me to Altontown Bay, which was really just a cove, where I hoped someone cared enough to meet me at the dock, else I'd just take the hotel's courtesy bus because I knew the drivers. As we approached the "bay" I saw how the term "cove" would be much better applied. Despite my exhaustion I chuckled at the irony.

Small seaplanes never look that rough from outside, but inside they weave about, and the landing can give you quite a jolt, as evidenced by today's "splashdown." The round-faced pilot, a lightweight mechanic type who only went by his nickname "Chow," another partly familiar face of someone I didn't really know, said the wind changed, explaining that the wind could shift as it crossed over the outer reef of the bay. Once we were down, I didn't care. I was safe. I could only think about how to write the event into a story. "I've got seventeen thousand hours in the air. No worse than a roller coaster," I recalled Chow saying. He was right, but it was my exhaustion that saved me from overreacting. Once we'd coasted up to the dock, I noted that funny look he gave me, his assertion that something wasn't quite right. This time I had to respond, because all the locals on the island knew each other somehow, so I pleaded, "Sorry. I'm exhausted from school and the trip. I'll see you in a few weeks if not sooner." That got a modest smile from him. He just put the bags out to the common dock but then took the plane to a shelter at a back corner of the cove. I was alone.

And as I expected but feared, no one met me at the weather-stained dock. While real happiness wasn't my cup of tea, a little satisfaction would have been nice. I'd had it. I was done. I couldn't lift my spirits one iota more. Tears dripped down my beautiful cheeks. Someone once expressed, "If the Mona Lisa cried!" That was me right at that moment. I settled on my bags, straddling them, tears flowing that I could not have justified. Was I that fatigued?

The final sunset delivered brilliant rays blocked by the trees and the island's biggest hills. Topping out at a "whopping" two hundred forty-two meters was a boring gray monzonite mound of volcanic origin, verdure half way up, of interest only to the tour guides and geologists. Since I'd helped with numerous excursions about the island to meet the guests, I learned all the terms. I could hear the cluster of visitors ogling over a freshly broken coconut and gagging on raw oysters, attempting to milk all the experience they could from their carefully banked travel money. But these memories didn't cure my immediate desperation. My saturated view of the lackluster sunset faded toward twilight, turning into a dim celestial crepuscule, then full darkness, lacking any moonlight. The streetlamp at the dock failed to light, only achieving a weak amber glow, so I scooted one bag at a time to the next lamp, each trip creating an obnoxious grinding against pavement and sand, twenty-five yards nearer the blockish hotel.

To my rescue came a young fellow with a glinting brass-plated baggage cart. He knew me from high school, but he was far from college material. Jeffrey, we called him. He never liked "Jeff" and we never knew why. He had a thing for me – was there a straight boy that didn't? I was often accused of stealing boyfriends from other girls when it didn't happen, just because the mendacious boys would say I was their girlfriend as a status symbol. I hated most of those boys, too easily manipulated by their infatuation. As for Jeff, he wasn't that bad but having a coiled octopus for brains made a fair analogy. Kindness had been his only reward from the gimmicky island gods, which were just architectural accents that lined the main street and property of the hotel.

"Miranda!" he called from too far away. It dragged me from my introversion, but I ignored him until he had the sense to come closer, the moments dragging with the escalating sound of the cart's wheels. "Miranda! Didn't you hear me?"

"No. You were still half way to the hotel. There's wind and surf you idiot," I reproached carelessly, intending to belittle, not so much to inflict mental anguish but just enough to keep him from drooling over "that little angel" as he once called me. I forced a lopsided smile to tease him, my locks moving in the breezy air. I could have pulled his hair out while completely charged with hostility and he'd still want to be near me – my friends had once jokingly nominated him for "Miranda's Puppy of the Year."

"Yeah," he responded, primitively embarrassed, looking down for a moment. Attempting to be candid and resilient he pursed his lips and shrugged it off. "I can get you up to the hotel. A little wind coming in tonight – ah, yeah, you can see that. Your dad left a note at the reception desk – said he'd be late or something. Um – you can wait for Charles. He'll get you home."

From my prevailing mental fatigue, I didn't recognize "Charles." He must have noted my confusion.

"Charles – you remember Charles? He's managing – um, right. He's got the hotel van to get supplies – ran out of dish soap. Imagine a hotel running out of dish soap!"

"Okay," I said, just taking the situation as it was.

Jeffrey loaded the bags onto the cart. My arms reached as if to help but being affected by my reduced cerebral activity they didn't do any good, so I just grabbed one side of the cart and followed along. I was aware that half the time he was looking at me, and half the time looking about, probably hoping to have others see us together as if we were *a thing*. He talked about the hotel and other students that had graduated. But nothing was potent enough to thread into my consciousness except how I would get across town and up the hill to my home (and whether my parents cared or not) to retire into my bed in my treehouse.

When we'd passed through the double-doors of the hotel lobby, though I could have been caustic and condescending, I requested, "I don't mean to treat you diminutively, but can you get me an orange or apple, please?" I let my exhausted but pretty eyes do the begging, but apples and oranges were mainland produce.

Of course, it melted his already weakened resistance. He mumbled, "Oh – college – big words, huh – sure," and returned from the hotel's kitchen with a banana and mango pieces. Then he sat silent and pensive with me for twenty minutes until the bus pulled up.

I tried to recall "Charles" – oh, probably Charlie – The temperamental Charlie who tried to swim the bay when he was drunk after Prom. The underperforming Charlie who never passed a history class. The elusive Charlie who sometimes walked by me in high school and gushed, "You're pretty," then blushed and walked away and I could never get him to return no matter how many times I called him back. It was the same Charlie that lived with his mother in a tiny "island bungalow," a euphemistic term we'd use to describe the row of tin-roofed shacks tucked in a cul-de-sac in an old part of Altontown. He wasn't much of an introvert until he got around me, then he'd be incapacitated beyond the ability to speak. I wondered how he'd react tonight.

The sound of the front door opening interrupted my thread of thought. Charlie, I mean Charles, now an athletic young lad with balanced face and medium brown hair, stepped into the door, seeing me sitting in the lobby with the pile of lightly scuffed bags near my feet. He stopped instantly, took a big breath, and trudged forward past a yellow and black "Severe Storm Shelter" sign that pointed toward the main stairway. The sign caught my attention.

"I'd called him on the radio. Have a good stay," said Jeffrey, finding it hard to get out of hotel mode. "I mean. Welcome back."

Oddly, Jeffrey's blunder almost made me feel human again. I looked up at fresh-faced Charlie, noting his hotel badge read "Charles," and spoke my first impulse, "I know you like me. I know you think I'm pretty because you've said it a thousand times. But tonight, please just get me home."

"Sure," he nodded, probably blushing but the dim light in the lobby failed to highlight his countenance as he dragged the baggage cart. I couldn't direct him to walk nearer the main counter. I stopped to check the storm shelter sign, below which was a photograph of the mayor and the hotel owner, some caption saying they'd collaborated on the building's design to be one of the best hurricane shelters ever made. The mayor was quoted, "When the largest storm unleashes upon the island, this may be the only surviving structure. It will not underperform."

Charles skirted the reception area tables along the outer windows, turned backwards to push his back against the doors, and packed the baggage to the hotel's bus, which had a mural of the island's highlights (including the bay and a blowhole "attraction" on the far corner) with a big red "Altontown" underscored with "A Place of Summer Memories." On the back door was an image of the lighthouse from the northwest side. Around the base of the van's body was a series of images of those self-proclaimed famous statues of the island gods near the hotel. To the locals those expensive god statues were the pinnacle of idiocy, having been made by some famous artist (yeah, I knew the name, but I just didn't care anymore). They believed that the real island gods were offended, and since I hadn't had any enlightening conversations with any island gods, I could not vouch for their claim.

Charles didn't hesitate to get into the driver's seat. I was lagging, and when I climbed into the passenger's seat he offered, "Miranda, I know – you think I'm dumb." He put the van in gear and pulled out to the street.

"Charlie, you are smarter than one of those island gods," I bemoaned, pointing a thumb back to the statues at the hotel. "I mean – um – I don't think you are college material if that's what you mean." I poked at him with a finger with the intent of a cheerier atmosphere, but he didn't let it lighten the mood.

He reached a hand toward my knee as if an attempt to poke or caress but withdrew. "Oh," he dropped his head but held his eyes up to drive. "I go by Charles."

"Charles, then. No – I don't think you are smart. But at least you haven't flipped out like all these 'end of the world' crazies that have come out of the woodwork, or their genie lamps, or their chamber pots – wherever they came from – the island's blowhole," I'd tried to joke, but it really just came out blustery and serious. Recognizing my failed expression, I grimaced out the window, rolling my eyes for myself.

He still smiled for a second, but withdrew, putting his attention on driving, moving so slowly I thought he was waiting for frogs to cross the road. I knew he had thoughts to convey, but he was too shy to say them or feared his words would lack eloquence. I humbly decided to just listen if he did, despite the likelihood that it would indict him as a moron. But as my parents' home and my treehouse, and the surrounding trees came to view, being lit by a few halogen spotlights, I guessed he'd never say everything he cogitated. Tonight I was too tired to absorb it, emitting a simple sigh, I suppose which had been enough to thwart his next potential utterance. Tonight, I was too distracted by the need to eat, the need to sleep, and my need for my girlfriends. Boys – I could not comprehend them. Though I often claimed a boyfriend during school, it was to keep the others from sticking to me like remoras. I never got to know them well, and I never could find any reason to drool over them. I couldn't lust them. I couldn't even pretend. I couldn't let any relationship get started with Charles. It wasn't that I was being careless, but I saw him as just a breeder – I didn't want him.

The van had stopped so I stepped out, saying only, "Thank you," and "I appreciate it," when he took the bags to the door and insisted on setting them into the foyer. One fell aside, and he said, "Sorry. No surcharge for that."

I suppose I should have smiled, but I shrugged my shoulders and said, "Bye." My expression alone reproached him.

He stepped back, mumbling something odd, "Not everyone gets to be the top players in the universe," throwing his arms out wide.

I knew by all accounts of school-aged peers that I was being dumb. I was not currently following any patterns of a typical teenage miscreant. I had little things to hide and didn't want him to know, because if he did, then everyone on the island would know, then I'd not be comfortable here. I just wanted to have an acceptable pretense of a steadfast home.

The door clunked; the van left; Charles was gone. I pondered my lack of reprehensible action. I didn't want to have any reason to be stuck here nor excluded. My perennial interest was to be a writer and have enough money to go anywhere. I aspired to escape. Coming back was only temporary – to a fifteen-kilometer island bounded by the sea, reefs, waves and varieties of fish, and a perpetual set of vacationers who came to private vacation homes, timeshares and rentable bungalows.

Altontown claimed the whole island's permanent population of ten-thousand. For now, my count of one remained included.

The house appeared quiet. I walked on through the hallway, going through the dining room, finding a note on the perfectly-polished burled walnut tabletop. "Miranda, sorry we had a funeral tonight. Extra pizza in the freezer. Shrimp-kabobs in the refrigerator. Take your pick. See you soon. Love, Dad." If Dad left the note, he had made the shrimp-kabobs. "Shrimp-kabobs coming up!" I decreed into the deserted room. There was no mention of who died, so I assumed I didn't care.

While heating up the shrimp-kabobs in a toaster oven, I pushed my larger baggage aside, then went to my actual bedroom to get some comfortable nightclothes. I reacquainted myself with my possessions. The majority of my doll collection was in this room, most of them not over thirty centimeters tall, but I'd always hoped for some larger figures. In the closet was a big plastic-lined wooden box with years of school assignments. In another was a pile of notebooks with my weird stories in them, some just summaries, some full of chapters. I picked one up and opened to find "Chapter 1" and about three sentences. I opened another to find seventy-two pages of awful handwriting, a story about body parts creeping out from a morgue. Father, as I'd said, was a mortician. Can you imagine all the stories you'd hear during funerals? I think I absorbed volumes of such morbidity as I grew up, more than I'd ever written down.

Thoughts of the funeral home brought back many memories. When I was little I'd wear the lightest, brightest dress I could and make all attempts to enliven the bereaved. Mother chased me about like a vivacious bat that shouldn't have been in her dismal cave. Later, having learned to conform, I wore black cotton or linen with minimal lace, spoke solemnly, and guided the hollow-eyed folks. I'd feel honored to put gorgeous bouquets of red and white roses on the caskets whether there was an assembled audience or not, and I'd cry for the deceased when no one showed up. When I got older still, I found it tedious, prone to be interested in how people died, lingering nearest when the details became personal. There they were, still in those notebooks, material to draw from for more accomplished stories because none of those notes were complete or grammatically correct. Perchance they'd be the seeds for publishable novels, as I had already written a well-drafted and poignant idea for a book. What if I made a mint before I could even graduate college? I left the notebooks but drooled on the possibilities with my mind relaxing to a dream-like state.

The whiff of the shrimp-kabobs drew me back to the kitchen to satisfy my starving flesh. I took a covered cake pan to transport the warmed ka-bobs and carried my clothing to the treehouse. I'd stay there as planned, leaving a reply to my father's note, simply saying, "Made it home safely. I'll be in the treehouse – Love, Miranda," followed with a smile face.

The treehouse wasn't conventional as it had two major vertical supports at each end, and a single story that was, from the end, oblong like an oval pill, flat on the top and bottom. It was large for a treehouse, designed with a square layout like a rearranged motor home, and against the near support was a staircase with a landing halfway, where it turned to meet up to the balcony at the front. My name was carved into a bass relief plaque at the base of the stairs – "Miranda" stood out as if leaves of a tree, curving over the trunk. The structure wasn't a true treehouse because it had its own supports, but it did reach up into a few large oaks that had been transplanted here more than a century ago. It had a hatch that opened to the sky, so I could get out onto the roof where I used to play a toy flute and pretend to sing with the birds, looking out over the beach and the sea beyond the property.

I sat in my "micro-kitchen," where I devoured my shrimp-kabobs. It had an apartment sized refrigerator. On the counter was a hotplate, and it had a camping-sized recreational-vehicle sink, and on the other side was a toaster oven. There was just enough room for two upper cabinets and a small round breakfast table.

At the other end there was a bathroom, with a shower so small even I would bump my elbows, and a toilet you could trip over when you got out. One medicine cabinet was all it offered for storage. The bedroom was just enough to hold a small bed, which wasn't a problem for me. The best space was the living room, which, if you pushed everything else to the walls, would fit a large air mattress on the floor between. There was an outside door off the living room that opened out to the balcony and that faced the beach and the ocean to the west.

I must have had too much soda and couldn't sleep when I'd laid down. I got up to dust the place, as unaware as if I'd been drunk. I felt a distinct *thump* through my body and dropped a dust rag. I stepped out onto the balcony, looking about, expecting to find a military jet off of some carrier. It must have been a distant sonic boom, I thought.

I saw my mother's plants, including some night-blooming cereus she maintained near the house. They were not blooming now and just looked scraggly. Other than that outpoint, Mother was good at showmanship, the kind needed to handle a funeral, but it played over into some occasional parties at the big house. I knew they were getting too wild when my mother would tell me, and any other children present, to go up to my treehouse to sequester ourselves for the rest of the evening, ensuring we had everything we'd need through the night and breakfast in the morning, giving them time to appear decent. When they weren't having parties, she'd keep telling me that I'd have to learn the business, to help with arrangements, and eventually take over. She'd tell me, "Go find a morbid boy who can handle our business. They have them at college. As long as he's not blatantly irrational. If he calls you 'Morticia' you've probably got the one that sees you for you." Well I sure as hell didn't want a boy to see me for me – after all, should I have taken boys along when I went to the basement of the funeral home and wrote stories of dead flesh creeping off of the embalming tables?

I'd lost track of the time, thinking it was much later than it was when the caffeine wore off, so I'd fallen asleep before my parents returned home. Somewhere in the middle of the night, I'd felt another notable *thump* through my chest. I got up to see my mother's car by the garage; no one bothered me, so they must have read the note. But the treehouse hadn't shaken from whatever the "thump" had been so I disregarded it and went back to sleep.

In the morning I ambled to the main house. Xiu Mei Lum, the housekeeper, once considered my nanny, doubled as a breakfast cook and sometimes helped with the other meals. She had grown up on the island, an odd mix of the indigenous people and a visiting foreigner she'd never met, giving her light brown eyes with a gold-like ring on the outer edge of each iris. Her quick, effective nature had already provided cooked bacon, biscuits and sausage gravy stacked in mostly worthless antique stoneware, another of Mother's obsessions to collect strange utilitarian objects no one else wanted. Some pieces were chipped, and most didn't match. Should I have been utilitarian in image I might have had a better relationship with Mother. She would treat me like a cracked dainty glass-blown flower she kept in the cabinet, separated from any earthenware. Maybe it was a carryover from the presentation habits of the funeral home.

I no more than placed myself at the gray-white marble-topped table when a blue and white scratched plate full of bacon and biscuits was set before me. Xiu Mei's hands moved quickly, her long braid dancing about her sea-green nightclothes that resembled hospital scrubs.

"Thank you," I murmured.

"Is it bad?" Xiu Mei tested.

"No. It's wonderful. I'm still – slow – got some sleep but I still feel half knocked out." This wasn't going to be cheery.

"Give it a few days," she barked harshly into the room as she threw more bacon onto the built-in countertop griddle. She didn't even look at me.

It was that sense of rejection again, as I had last night at the dock. Tears fell.

"I don't have sympathy for you. You are a spoiled child," she bellowed too loudly in the echo chamber of a kitchen.

I didn't intend to give her one of my evil gazes, so I broke it off before it bloomed into full hate. "I said thank you," I reiterated, making some attempt to have these first few moments not portend disaster for the entire few weeks I'd stay on the island.

Then she turned to view my expression, a solid penetrating examination followed by, "Humph! Whatever." Thank god Mother was there, otherwise Xiu Mei could disparage me for hours.

I turned my face to the pancakes. Xiu Mei was aware of my morbid attitudes. She'd caught me during an embarrassing experiment; it chalked up as the most embarrassing moment of my life. I had gone to the funeral home after the daughter of a timeshare couple died, and though the funeral would not be on the island, Father took care of the embalming. The girl was almost exactly my age at fourteen, so I sneaked in to visit her while the embalming process was in its final stages and the body had to rest for hours. What Xiu Mei didn't see was how I cried over the young corpse for about four hours, checking over everything, even touching up the makeup and painting her toenails. What she did see was my body half wrapped about the girl, and though covered with translucent plastic, I wasn't wearing any clothing either. Perhaps if I'd acted suicidal when discovered. Perhaps if I'd still had tears smeared about my whole face. Perhaps if I hadn't been kissing the girl's cheek.

Every time I saw Xiu Mei after that incident, her snarl exuded that humiliating examination of "What is wrong with you now?" Despite how pretty I was, despite how educated I could get, she always saw me as an irrecoverable freak, and I had to resign to that irremovable element of the relationship. But to her credit she kept quiet, with the secret limited to only those humans that resided within, as her cooperation was enforced since her employment depended upon it. Thus, the implausibility that I'd foment her resignation or involuntary departure.

While I was on the edge of sulking, Mother's light footsteps danced different directions out of view with all the unpredictability of a June bug. I ate slowly, taking small bites, so I'd have the chance to speak after a quick swallow, but I grew impatient with her. "Mother – I'm here!" I finally called loudly. Xiu Mei turned back with a sideways disapproving glance, eyes squinting for reinforcement, though I was no louder than her own bellowing just moments before.

"Miranda – you're back. Did Xiu Mei inform you about the funeral last night?" She remained at the doorway, steadfast against the frame. Perhaps she too was pondering on my past most embarrassing incident.

"No. I only saw Daddy's note on the dining room table; 'a funeral!'" I returned.

"Young boy. Horrible. Tried to swim out of the bay. Divers had to pick him up. Vincent. I think you knew him. Parents had a timeshare on the north side near the beach. They chose to have a funeral here since he was so popular with the school children. They're off to the mainland with the body today, leaving anytime."

I'd met the boy as a toddler. His parents had been regulars for their timeshare since before Vincent had been born, a good-looking lad who fit in well with the islanders. He'd been affable, never disparaging, and had a multitude of talents but a base interest in business like his father. He'd have been seventeen – and he'd certainly noticed me.

This event was exacerbating my past, and I wasn't convinced that Mother and Xiu Mei weren't attempting to instigate a flare up or breakdown. Perhaps they were in actuality attempting to mitigate the effect, but by their amply restrained expressions, I couldn't be convinced. Overwhelmed with the end of classes, the flight, having to meet up with all the people on the way, and confused about the intentions of my present company, my mind had not had the ability to resynchronize. And though I'd looked up at Mother, I perceived a ghost-like apparition of Vincent between us, with a concept of a sad, desperate goodbye. As a result of the specter, my hand rapidly lost its strength, and I dropped my fork which clattered by itself in the otherwise silent room, except only some bacon sizzling. I attempted to restrain my emotions and hold my form, but as if a phantom crawled over my back and tried to draw me out of my body, I succumbed to intense grief.

"What is the matter?" jeered Xiu Mei. "Finally, a boy you liked?"

I couldn't answer. I wouldn't answer. I pushed my plate away from my head and shook with quiet sobs. I needed a few more days to "dry out" from the exhaustion. But I'd felt another stiff *thump* in my chest. My stomach was turning. I had to get away from the food, reeling from the breakfast table to a coatroom containing raingear off the living room. Besides recalling the way Vincent viewed me with pleasure, several images pummeled my mind – Sandy, several weeks before summer finals, in a moonlit laundry room late at night. The fourteen-year-old dead girl I'd wrapped myself around – pretending she liked me. Even a time when I was in early grade school after performing in a play, I'd held a girl's hand and refused to let go after coming off the stage. I'd wanted a girlfriend even then.

As I reclaimed my composure and quietly pulled out of the coatroom, I overheard Xiu Mei telling Mother. "She said she's drained from school and the plane trip. I'm sorry."

"She'll come back," said Mother softly. "She always does."

There – a little acknowledgment. My resilience despite my lower range of emotion. I expected to live. I expected accomplishment. I didn't expect elusive happiness. I'd seen how happy people could be on the proffered happiest vacation place in this southern island chain. Real happiness was as elusive to those seeking it as a description of death for those whom it had not claimed. I'd watched the visitors, the timeshare people, all those that came here to pretend they were happy. Some of them claimed satisfaction with their lives but never, ever saying they could not find more happiness.

So, I turned back toward the kitchen, finding Mother eating away at her eggs, bacon and pancakes. There were many items that islanders would have for breakfast, but not likely bacon and pancakes. I had to realize that this meal was prepared just for me.

Mother was in the middle of saying, "Xiu Mei – you forgot the toast."

"I didn't forget toast. Nobody asked for toast," she said, moving toward a loaf of bread.

"Okay. I could get it," offered Mother.

"No. I got it," said Xiu Mei, giving Mother a pleasant smile.

I saw that warm expression as I walked in, and as Xiu Mei turned toward me, her smile faded. I shrugged and rolled my head, finding my seat again to continue eating anyway. I'd resolved that, just as I could have let Charlie say anything last night (which he didn't), I'd just let them say anything now, but I filled in the gap I'd left earlier, "Vincent – he liked me. I wasn't that much into him. Too young."

Xiu Mei started in with, "I'd not taken you for...."

Mother had put her hand up to stop her. Xiu Mei did stop and lowered her gaze.

"Mother's right," I raised my wet eyes and cocked my head. "We need just a few weeks of amiable company, some artificial performance of affinity."

"I'll never understand you," said Xiu Mei, who then approached me and gave me a slight hug about my shoulders, indicating she may have understood after all.

Mother's eyebrows raised, a small sense of satisfaction pressed her jaw to squash her lips.

Just before taking another bite, I asked, "Is Daddy here?"

Mother took up the answer, "Down at the funeral home, making preparations to transfer the outlander. You should probably stay here and rest. He'll be in and out – the package may already be gone." Perhaps she was eschewing my interest, concerned I'd try to lie with the dead boy. She would use the term "outlander" for the vacationers, timeshares and snowbirds, the winter residents, though few people on the island had a fully indigenous family line. We'd all been transplants and cultural blends. My family had come for the work and remained mixed from northern blood. It was another reason I was a stranger, a paperwhite narcissus among wildflowers.

I wanted to see Daddy. He was the most encouraging person, understanding me best, realizing I was like an unusual species in danger of being exploited. He'd watched how I handled others at the funeral home and gave me tips. He'd let me help with the funeral displays, guide people through, and though I could sing, I never did perform for any service because I would get too emotional. When working alone, Daddy and I could talk deeply about anything and his next statement would always hesitate as if to draw out my next observation. He saw depth beyond his speech, which could be extracted slowly, forming a deeper summary with each sentence. I learned from him the manner in which people would elude truth regarding matters of life and death. The greater the bereavement, the greater the shock and inability of the mind to comprehend "the loss" and ascertain or express its own state. It was a good lesson to learn – how to elude the truth for somber items for which one had no control. In my own shocked states of my life, I'd used this knowledge to gain persistence.

I guess to avoid saying anything else dumb, all the conversation stopped. Xiu Mei exited with her typical rushing style. Mother came to give me a hug about my shoulders and exited, I supposed to get dressed in day clothing. I was left with the food at the breakfast table, running my fingers along the gray cracks in the marble. How smoothly they integrated without a single ridge detected by my fingertips. Much like the cracks in my own life were so integrated, impossible to eliminate by grinding or polishing. Coming to the island was supposed to give me a grounding sense, being home, creating a foundation for the coming fall semester. But the island was like a poorly constructed raft, bobbing about in a treacherous sea, pushed by planetary winds, listing to and fro on rolling waves.

In the next hours I prided myself on my productivity. I completed unpacking, doing my own laundry and putting my clothing away for ready use. With my room and board fully paid at school, my parents chose to give me a minimal allowance, so I had few new items from school, such as socks, a few pairs of panties, and just a few shirts. There was one new pair of pajamas since I'd had to replace a set that got stolen from the laundry room. I'd never seen one of the girls in them. I didn't know what had happened.

I returned to my treehouse with a selection of clothes fit for the late summer, mostly consisting of light shorts and tank shirts, tucking them into a bamboo and rattan wicker cabinet that fit against a wall in my mini bedroom. I never much liked the wickerware because a few rough ends of the rattan would catch clothes or skin. But since it wobbled, Daddy had it fastened to the wall, so I'd never had it removed.

I heard the sound of an approaching car. *Daddy?* I looked out the window from my room, peering past the sprawling tree branches to see back along the drive. A dark car rolled up. I couldn't see inside due to reflections of the clouds on the windshield, but it was indeed Daddy's car. I checked myself in the mirror and rushed down the steps.

Daddy got out but closed the door and leaned his handsome self against it, still sullen from Vincent's death, his light hair reflected too brightly for his expression. He threw out a hand, and I supposed it meant he couldn't have done anything better. I stepped up my pace, rushing to him, slamming right into him as he turned to take the brunt of my motion.

Releasing a ton of mixed emotion, I let Daddy lift me and hold me up against him. I felt satisfaction in being held by my father, noting the wrinkles of his slept-in clothing. I felt sadness for the loss of the boy. I felt so happy I was home again. He leaned back against the car, so it would help support me, though I couldn't have weighed more than forty kilograms. I leaned back to give him little kisses all over his smooth but stubbly face. He held me like a little child, his hands under my bottom, and I wrapped myself around him as if I were the ribbon on a gift.

"So glad to see you, little one," he softly said.

I looked up to see tears in his eyes.

"Daddy, you're crying," I commented.

"Yeah – tough one last night – this morning. Your mother called – said you broke down when...."

"I broke down – yeah. I did. A culmination of everything, not just Vincent. But I did know him. A likable guy." I pictured him, standing near a fire on the beach, giving me one of those affectionate gazes. He'd been about fourteen and I'd just passed my sixteenth birthday, but yet I looked younger than him. Oh, he was likable, but he wasn't for me – he wasn't a girl. Even in a world of arranged marriages, we couldn't have been paired.

"So, there'll be more, boys that is, if that's what you want?" he appealed.

I looked at him squarely, sliding down from his body to land on my feet. What did he know about what I wanted, except that he knew I'd been caught with the dead girl by Xiu Mei? But I knew I gave a little grimace which may have given part of my story away. A spur in my mind suggested getting antagonistic and fighting it, but this particular masculine progenitor wouldn't likely accept the diversion. "Every time I come home, it's like everyone tries to remind me – this time the most." I considered my writer's grammar, adding, "I wouldn't have lain with him."

"Fine," he offered directly, keeping eye contact. "Let me start over. I'm glad to see you."

"Sure, Daddy," I said and clung to him.

"Climb on," he said. He wasn't a big man, but it was easy for him to carry me upon his back. I used the front tire as a boost and landed against him, his arms locking under my knees. My body absorbed him, his pace, even his breath, as he carried me to the house. I found myself smiling, that euphoric reaction little girls would get when clinging to their daddies.

He speed walked, dodging side to side toward the main door. Once inside I slid down again so my knees wouldn't get racked into the walnut door frames. In the kitchen, the pancakes were stacked and protected with a roughed up antique glass cake plate cover, the glass once clear, now it was striated and partly frosted as if etched with acid.

"We still have this old thing, don't we," said Daddy as he pulled the cover up to check the pancakes, pulling out a dinner plate from the cabinet above.

I nodded when he looked up. "We had bacon and even biscuits and gravy, but I didn't see anyone eat the gravy."

"I'll have that," he said, stacking his plate. "I'm glad these aren't cold."

I looked into the refrigerator. "No bacon left," I said, having been ready to nibble on more. I grabbed out a small pan that contained gravy and set it onto the gas stove, turning a knob to adjust a low flame. I stirred the gravy, intermittently cutting a couple biscuits open and placing them on a shallow baking sheet, then put them into the oven to broil. "My girlfriends and I learned to do this at school. We had a kitchen in the dorm we could use except at night." I set a cake timer for several minutes.

"I'm sure it will be good. But – as for Vincent – I'm sorry you didn't get to see him. He's already off the island. I wouldn't have kept you from him," he said, stopping with his head still, facing his room temperature pancakes.

I pulled the plate from him and added his chosen pancakes to the baking sheet with the biscuits, closing the broiler door when done. But I was caught in the silence. A moment that should be one of the highest points of returning from school was about to end in dismal failure. Why not just force the issue? "Daddy?" I started.

"Yeah," he helped.

I painfully leaked out my own secret, "I'm just not into boys. I had a girlfriend at school. There's a girl here I want. Tori. Mama doesn't know." There it was, my primitive blunt self, giving my own indictment. I continued to stir the gravy.

He hesitated, statistically analyzing the variables toward the best answer. "Ah – well – she suspected before I did. You may as well tell her."

My head shook spontaneously, and I pulled back though I wasn't usually so reactionary. I'd felt only half vindicated. I complained about the morning, "Mother and Xiu Mei were right at the edge of ridiculing me this morning. I asked them to pretend – how was it I put it, 'some artificial performance of affinity.'"

"Not bad. You've been working on your writing, I take it?"

"I've put together some outlines, some chapters, a draft of a book," I said.

"Any details you'll share with me?"

"Well, it starts with people embalming some tortured girl, finding the initial details that lead to a long winding investigation."

"Oh – a mystery?" he stipulated.

"A ghost story overlaid upon a mystery," I corrected.

"I can't wait to read it," he turned back to give me his handsome eyes.

"Oh – it's not that good, really. But after a few practice books, I might get something polished enough for a publisher to take seriously. Or I could just keep revising this draft until it's publishable." I stirred the gravy a few more turns.

"I'm sure it's no worse than pickle juice and people drink that. Just keep writing. I feel compelled to say you are important – the world needs you. You might be rich before you complete your degree and take the burden of the payments off of me," he smiled.

"Oh, you spent more money on my treehouse than you did on the first semester. You got enough money for me," I said to get his response.

"Yeah. But those plane trips are expensive," he jested.

"Well, I could get a job on the student newspaper. They don't pay much," I volunteered, turning off the flame under the gravy pan.

"Creativity can draw you away from your duties – that's what my father always said of embalming. Not a good idea if it interferes with your studies," he cautioned.

"So, you're saying you don't need me to make the extra money?" I offered.

"Economically we're fine – hardly insolvent. I guess we don't," he said, emphasizing *we* to remind of the group activity it was to get me through school.

I glowed with love, hoping the affinity would exude beyond my skin to reach across and into him.

He warmly smiled, saying, "Oh my God I feel that." He reached up for a hug.

I leaned in and embraced my perpetually young-looking daddy again. Did he receive my attempt at telepathy? Did he love me that much? Did I love him too much? Was it that none of the boys could ever be this loveable? Was it that my standards were so high that boys were just off the list because they could never measure up to him? No – I knew better than that. Boys didn't have girl parts.

Ding, interrupted the cake timer. With another tug on the embrace, I released and turned to handle the "broiled" biscuits and pancakes. Much as I had made a late meal for myself and Sandy several weeks before the summer final exams, I easily worked the food to present it to Daddy. Either way, I was presenting sustenance to someone I loved.

I offered honey, which we preferred over syrup, and some butter. Then I squatted on my knees in the chair opposite him at the breakfast table. I glowed at him, knowing well enough that my insidious monsters would transmogrify my lighter thoughts into implausible nightmares once I removed myself from his presence, much the same as they'd return for any of my writing sessions. To unleash them I'd just have to be alone, and the longer I'd be alone, the more nefarious they'd become.

"Daddy?" I started again while he was in the middle of a bite.

"Yes, dear?" he prompted through the food.

"I'd like to have a party with my girlfriends, here. My treehouse – my patio."

"Sure. Give me a list of what you need. Ah – there's the Summer-End Bash at the northwest beach this weekend – three days yet at the lighthouse. I hope that works. We'll all be there – come back early and have your party. The last party was at the hotel, but I think they decided it became too messy and someone fell off a dock into the cove."

See – Daddy knew it was a cove. I let out a cute giggle. I could picture Mother falling off the dock where I'd gotten off the seaplane. "I think we'll skip the party and just hang out here."

"Okay. As you wish. Any boys you're trying to avoid?"

"Yeah. A few," I murmured, but changed the subject. "So, is there anyone else to embalm today?"

"No. But the nursing home said someone is on deathwatch. It won't be long."

"Oh, I'm sorry," I said instinctively.

"No, you're not," he said. "You just want to know if there is a story you can put into a notebook."

I smiled deviously. "Well – that too."

"Sometimes I think you do it just to compensate for being such a beautiful girl," he asserted, gazing at me.

The thought, *I know you love me too. If you could, you'd marry me,* crossed my mind. But I held it back and simply said, "Maybe." I leaned upon my arm, watching him eat. I knew he didn't mind me being there. The succinct truth was that no matter the cracks in my being, or the oddities of my character, I was certainly at home with Daddy.

TWO

The First Event

With Father's approval, I scheduled another one of my special sleepovers with three of my closest girlfriends. We had originally been introduced at school but soon met during one of my parent's parties, and over time we learned each other's private tastes, culminating into a deeper secret we promised to never tell, reserving that variety of girl-to-girl romance for my treehouse. This weekend's reprise with my specially invited guests, considering we were further distanced from observation by the Summer-End Bash being at the lighthouse far to the northwest, would give us some advantage to push the limits of decency. However, without the convenience of the hotel, I was sure that my parents and Xiu Mei wouldn't remain all night, as they were not fans of camping.

I'd gone through the list of items and Daddy helped me shop for the evening's supplies for food and soft drinks, but it was only minutes since our return that Mother and Xiu Mei rushed him off. He shrugged, being helpless but to follow their orders, yet as a fair goodbye I took his hand, and though Mother was calling to hurry, I held him back a moment at the foyer, pulling his face to mine. "I love you so much, you beautiful Daddy," I said and smooched him directly on the lips. I can't say I understood what compelled me to do so. He knew me well enough to know he was in no danger, but as he pulled back I could see a hesitation with a touch of guilt and affection, and only then did he compose himself enough to say, "I love you too."

He retreated to the car, his gait awkward as he attempted to not show his emotion for me upon entering the car and facing Mother. I stepped the few paces required to watch from the exterior door. He waved lightly, his palms still on the wheel as he drove away, leaving me with the home, my treehouse, and an evening's freedom.

Having loaded up on food, I packed the evening's supplies from the main house up into the treehouse's mini kitchen. The treehouse, besides being my personal hideout also served as my virtual museum, having items that evidenced my morbid nostalgia. I had my most girlish vintage clothes up there in my bedroom. My little bed had some pink sheets and blankets covered with images of antique dolls. I had girls' clothing about the walls as decoration – including panties, bloomers and dresses I'd worn as a little girl. My dried umbilical cord was framed and on the wall. Even my first menstrual pad was in a little shadow box with a door on it (just think of embalming – anything could be preserved).

I looked at my pretty face in the mirror. It was a blessing and a curse to be this pretty and slender, as well as to look too young. For one it was harder to find a serious dress or a shirt that didn't have some cartoon character on it. Secondly, I had to convince every adult to treat me as something other than just a pretty child. But this evening I was using my prettiness to my advantage in line with our secret – the fact that these young ladies were just as attracted to females as myself.

The girls arrived later in the afternoon in a small red convertible, which pulled up and parked at the base of the treehouse near the patio that was under it. Tori, my favorite, was getting out of the back seat. She was slender, had long straight red hair with a northern complexion and perfectly placed nose. She found it difficult to be in the sun more than a few hours but tanned evenly despite a few extra freckles. Her eyes were a glowing green, unusual even for a redhead. Debbie was a full-sized girl with very balanced proportions. Her darker hair was cut just below the shoulders, but the curls allowed it to shift about. She'd use it to turn her face quickly to hide her expression until her face suddenly came into view as the curls bounced aside. I couldn't recall how many times I'd busted out laughing due to her sudden expressions. Seria was the weird girl with the strange name and was more cute than pretty. Her teeth were perfect and white. Her ears always had dangling earrings, often with sea creatures. Loose waves of her hair typically dangled in front of her oversized suggestive eyes. I guess you could say she had a mermaid-like appearance with long legs and a supple body. I would have to admit that it was entertainment for my eyes to see her move about with her happy reactionary nature.

I hustled down the steps, nearly missing one, and found open arms from all three girls.

"So lovely to have another meeting," Debbie winked.

"Love, love, love, love and love," began Tori, who rushed to hug me first.

Seria looked at me, her eyebrows raised up. "You look as good as I could have expected. You still didn't grow much on top, did you?" She referred to my modest chest. I suspected she liked me the most of these girls. If I hadn't known about Tori's existence, I might have had Seria first on my list.

All three girls came up to hug me. It felt good. I hummed a little tune then shrieked from the sudden excitement, a rare expression for me I'd picked up from the girls in the dorm. "I love you all so much. Let's get the stuff."

The girls packed an air mattress and sleeping bags up the treehouse steps. I lugged small bags of nightclothes and tossed them on my bed. While they set up, I set out some ginger beers.

"You've got to have something better than that," said Debbie, stepping into my little kitchen.

"Well, I hope you brought something. Like my dad is going to let me buy anything like that," I charged back.

"Well – but – you said," Debbie showed her confusion.

"No – I got it. See?" I opened the mini refrigerator and showed plenty of beer and liquor-license-stamped bottles packed in with some hamburgers ready to grill.

Her face lit up. "Okay! That'll be enough. And something other than shrimp!" Satisfied, she moved out, I supposed to sort her nightclothes in my bedroom.

Tori came into the mini kitchen, being very close. I froze up, inundated with all I'd wanted to say. "Hi," was all I could get out. I acted so withdrawn but I had no reason to as far as she knew. I'd been aspiring to tell her all the creative and wonderful things I thought about her when I was away. It would be better to see how tonight would go first, then blab my inner conscience. We had called ourselves "situational introverts," as we hid from the world under most circumstances. We didn't have to act introverted tonight, so I feared that Tori would think I wasn't interested if I didn't open up. I'd been as cliché as any other smitten girl, having written many letters I'd never sent, always taming it down if I did. On going to bed I would make attempts to seed my dreams with her shapely and pleasing image. Just now our eyes stuck together for a moment. I just kept it simple with, "I missed you." Before I blushed too much I walked past her to open the windows. My skin became hot, sweltering with suppressed sultry desire.

After getting the windows opened further, I switched off the island radio station, which catered more to the tourists than the locals, and tonight excessively repeated the invitation for all to attend the End of Summer Bash. I got tired of hearing it, so I started playing some indie music I'd collected on campus, the first being a girl band that really wasn't all that good. I'd save the better stuff for later.

My stomach reminded me that it was time to start cooking, so we went out of the treehouse, under which remained the older patio I claimed as my own, complete with a small gas grill, just big enough for the burgers. A tray contained the tools and condiments; another tray contained the buns, potato salad and coleslaw, more like the parties we'd had at school. On the island, seafood was more prevalent. I turned to

Debbie, saying, "You could have shrimp too if you want it. There's some in the main house."

"No," she said. "I've had shrimp four times this week already. Shrimp and pasta. Shrimp and plain rice. Shrimp patties. Shrimp fried rice!" We talked about classes and school experiences. It was all interesting to us at the time, but of little relevance to the substantial event that would take place.

Having finished off our burgers we decided to take a walk about the hill and the beach beyond the treehouse. The late afternoon sun was drawing low enough to show some angled shadows from the trees. The breeze streamed gently, coaxing in minimal surf, the temperature and humidity pleasant. The clouds gave promise to a prime sunset. Tori rushed back to get her camera and a lightweight tripod. Trying not to be so noticeable, I watched her as she returned to the group.

As we walked we held hands intermittently, not identifying any preference for couples. I held all their hands by the time we detoured toward the beach. Seria had asked, "Is this the year of the meteor shower?"

"No – that was a couple years ago," replied Debbie. "I love falling stars. I wouldn't expect to see any tonight."

Tori set the camera on the tripod, steadying one leg with a shell, and set the timer to get a group shot. I expected it would be one of the best shots we'd ever had, and I hoped it would bring memories for years to come. I scooted pebbly sand piles under my feet to give me extra centimeters and held Tori next to me, tilting my head toward her, hoping the body language would get caught in the photograph. I could only hope that Tori was thinking in terms of the future as I had. Right about the moment the picture was taken, I felt another of those mild thumps in my chest. I considered having my heart monitored the next time I found myself at the doctor's office.

After the picture, Tori broke away and stopped at the border of the wet shore, looking at the setting sun. She cocked her head and said, "The universe is such a curious place. I – I don't know why I never thought of it before. Hum. It's really big, but, in a way, reachable. It's my universe!" First, she waved up to the sky, then to my surprise she turned to me and took my hand.

Debbie came up suddenly, being playful, and giggled quite happily. "I'm 'girl' and I like 'girl' and this will be a night to remember 'girls!'" She danced about, rushed past me and slapped me on the bottom.

"Keep it up and I might like it," I said, letting go of Tori's hand because of the sting.

Seria, still back in the soft dry sand, acting somewhat distant, knelt looking upwards past the emerging stars, and appeared to be muttering something. I rushed back toward her. She had a huge smile on her face. "Okay!" she said up to the sky. I had no idea the immediate meaning nor the ramifications of these statements. "You up there? You are more than island gods!" Then as scarcely recognized evidence of some mind-blowing catharsis, she sprung to her feet, rushed toward me and said, "I'm going to love you tonight!" She pounced me over, knocking me into the sand. Clutching my wrists, she held my hands down. Her lips pressed and pulled against my shoulders, neck and cheeks. Her hips lowered to be placed upon mine. I was overwhelmed with a rush of lust. It was so sudden and wonderful she could have convinced me to profess my love for her instead of Tori.

Debbie and Tori came over. Debbie said, "Um. I'm going to tell," but her teasing showed through with her smile. "Um – I want some of that."

I wanted Tori to know that I wanted her. "You too?" I suggested.

"Me too, Miranda," she said, looking down to me at an angle. The sound of my pretty name stated by her voice melted my heart and everything else in my chest and torso.

Seria rolled to the side, saying, "And you too, Debbie!" Debbie pulled down against her and there were little mumbles of pleasure.

Tori leaned down upon me, our bodies touching from end to end. She gave me a long, silky kiss. I looked up at her face, letting every detail etch upon my mind. Not trying to be conceited, in this position she looked as stunning as me, all nature contributing to the artful beauty – the color in the sky above her, the emerging stars beyond that, the way her red hair flowed toward one side, caressing my shoulder and cheek. Biting my lip, I finally said it just over a whisper, "I love you." It was a touching moment. Tears escaped from my eyes, flowing back toward my ears.

"I think I know that," Tori acknowledged.

I felt another strange *thump* in my chest.

The girls noted it too. They turned, looking about. "Did you feel that?" Debbie said.

Seria said, "It was like a planet went streaking across the sky. Like it blew up – but now like it never happened." Did I say she was weird? I did. I thought she might be joking. I had no way to explain this at the time, reserving my judgment for later.

"Okay. Love," said Debbie, as if out of the blue. "We're going to love you. Better than we ever did. Here. Tonight. With a little of whatever you've got in those bottles. By morning, you will know that you have been loved."

"She's mine," claimed Tori.

They couldn't have been better to me, a girl often estranged as much by my beauty as my morbidity, and tonight I felt like a princess in a dreamland.

"No – she's mine," countered Seria, turning to reach up to me, putting a hand on my belly between Tori and myself.

"Wow," Interrupted Debbie, referring to an unusually colorful sky. We took a moment to watch the last of the setting sun, then giggled, chased each other, and tagged each other as we ran along the beach. Kisses were suddenly a new commodity. Approaching twilight, we rushed along the wet-packed sand back up to the treehouse, cleaned up the food, and climbed up into the living room to decide what to do next. But I think they already knew what they wanted.

We tuned back to the island's radio, opened the liquor bottles, and mocked the nostalgic and contemporary tunes that spanned most genres. We made a little pledge to each other to never say what happened through the night. Then we made sure all the windows were covered and we ditched the clothes. We did almost everything imaginable. I can't relate it all even now. It was nasty, disgusting, lustful and messy. And we loved every minute of it.

As they pushed the limits of hedonism, I pushed them further. They said I was being too aggressive and was "a little weird."

"I know. But it lets you know you can be weirder with me," I told them. "And that you aren't as weird if it's any consolation. Besides, everyone knows I'm weird. How can you not be weird and have a father for a mortician."

Seria said, "I'm the weird one! You can't take my trophy now."

We laughed. We'd called her weird behind her back. Now she was admitting it.

Tori gave me some special attention. While lying over me, she said, "I want you to feel like this is the last of the universe. I want to devour you like there is no tomorrow, you and I can do anything." I didn't think she really meant it. My eventual vision was to get her to not marry some guy and to stay with me instead. I was beginning to hope for that future. I felt special – and I felt wanted. I cried because of it. "What's wrong?" she asked.

I tried to hide it but couldn't. I needed to tell her what I really meant when I had said I loved her. I just blurted out, "It's just good to be wanted."

She kissed me and the warmth of her body and motions fall especially high into the wonderful memories list.

I knew I was the centerpiece of the fun. I knew my body was precious – at least to me it was. And I'd see people's reactions when their eyes would stray into my direction. I was so pretty that people would be mesmerized. The night of a father-daughter dance, I'd been with Daddy at a restaurant in town – common people – they were all staring with some assertation that I'd been some princess or actress, as some of the vacationers were. I was perfect with blonde hair and the prettiest eyes and the cutest smile. My beauty would compel them to be with me and entice their dreams to do nasty things with me. I had a lot of trouble with the boys in school, and still had trouble keeping the young men away from me at college. I was deceivingly intellectual and so I tutored others. Most of the gentlemen couldn't maintain agility in their conversation because they were consumed, being mesmerized by watching me, often adding insurmountable complications. I couldn't get mad without the paradox of remaining cute. I couldn't even look plain without makeup. It just wasn't fair.

I recalled a certain math tutoring session in high school. I'd asked a boy what he saw, when I expected him to multiply, he said, "I see the most beautiful girl I've ever seen."

"I can't help that," I had said. "But you need to see the math. If you can see me, why can't you see the math?"

"Because I don't want to see the math," he had said. The conversation became profoundly circular. Realizing he used his guile to spend time with me, I gave up and walked out, unable to be anything but beautiful, cute and sexy all at once. I wished I could have covered myself with a sheet before I walked away because when I turned back to scowl, he had leaned forward only to watch my angrily swinging hips, his expression implying his imagined promiscuity.

In college, my first party experience was at a fraternity. I don't even remember which Greek letters were anchored to the outer wall of the crenelated stone house. They quickly pumped me with a few drinks, intending to pass me from guy to guy, only caring about my body and how pretty I was. A tall and intensely handsome, but appallingly degenerate fellow conned me too well. He inveigled us into a private upstairs room in short order. He pushed me back on a bed, expecting me to submit to him, expressing half-breathless, lustful passion how I looked like a sophomore in high school. I had to whack that guy in the head with a lamp and furiously exit before any chance of a counter attack. And with that spectacle, I wouldn't ever return to their neighborhood. I would have rather been with girls anyway, but I was sick the rest of the evening. It was a miracle that I'd made it back to my dorm, hiding in the laundry room; I was small enough to kneel in the utility sink and wash up.

So tonight, with the well-meaning but fun-loving girls I drank lightly to facilitate the fun, but I never wanted anyone to lead me to a distasteful level of drunkenness again. I could see we were all satisfied, getting tired, getting our nightclothes on in the confines of my private abode. Perhaps I was more than tipsy since I'd been serving, taking extra sips from the bottles. With difficulty balancing I put on my own nightgown and cuddled in. I had to be against Tori. I insisted on it, overemphasizing my drunkenness to gain their favor. Tori raised up her hands to allow me between her and Debbie. I really wanted to be between Seria and Tori. But Debbie couldn't be on the edge of the king-sized air mattress and not fall off. So, I had Debbie holding me from behind, and I held Tori, who was on her back. I finally did say, "I love you and want you forever," but I think she was already asleep. Before I fell asleep, another *thump* struck my chest. I saw Tori smile. If she was asleep and out completely, why did she smile?

I recall getting up past midnight on this strangely cosmic night, seeing the serene girls, hoping that when morning came we could fall back to being ordinary rather than so egregious, to let most of the guilty parts slip and secrets remain unspoken. Except for my deep desire for a continuing relationship with Tori, I hoped we could keep our pact, acting like nothing happened. It had been months since we last had a hedonistic party like this but nothing that went this extreme. Even then it had taken me several days to act like nothing happened – maybe it would take me less time to get over it now. In my pokey state of insomnia, I checked over everything – making sure there was nothing "incriminating" in the stuff that was visible in case my parents had any reason to come into the treehouse in the morning. I plucked a couple bottles from the kitchen table and put them away. I cleaned up a few cups in the sink and threw trash away. I even tied up the bag and put it into a trash container outside. I remember smelling the outside air, being as normal as could be with a beautiful sea-air freshness coming in with a southeasterly. I waited a bit, watching the stars, hearing the dash and roar of the incoming surf further out on the beach. The hill allowed a wonderful view under the strong moonlight. It was beautiful, but I wanted to return to the treehouse and be with my girlfriends.

As unobtrusively as I could, I cuddled in with the girls again, but since they'd each shifted their pose, four girls on a king-sized bed had become crowded. I tried to coax myself to sleep, but then I ended up getting up to eat a little bit more. I found chips and summer sausage to nibble on, then dug into a little more potato salad. I knew I often had trouble falling asleep, so it wasn't too unusual, and downed another shot to settle me down. I took a moment to watch Tori as she turned to find me, but when she found Debbie instead, she turned again toward the front wall. I listened to the breathing, and even a fart, and I smiled, being glad that for the moment I wasn't under the same covers. I was concerned about whether Tori would think me rude, but I eventually moved into my own bed and slept deeply.

The dream was unusual. Having walked a vast distance, I emerged into a scene next to a young fellow who looked like a cross between Daddy and Vincent, rolling hysterically about the floor of once-polished stone. He wore hand-sewn taupe pants and a cream-white linen tunic. The narrow stone room had an ancient appearance, the walls having blind arcades and a few doorways with wooden doors scattered among the arches, the laughter echoing from the walls. My viewpoint low, I felt small as if a child. Along with the dream image, I felt a powerful *thump* which shocked me to wake before the sun broke the eastern horizon.

With the sound of the morning surf, I went to squat on the toilet, moved with the softest steps back to the kitchen to get some water, then settled back to my bed. I heard the rustling of my own sheets and I laid back, relaxing again as the dream images faded and took me back into a short imageless slumber. I had a strange sense of aloneness as I woke again.

Directly out my door I saw the girls there – I expected to hear something – an occasional snort, a fart, or the rustling of blankets when they'd turn. I realized I hadn't heard anything. I went to Seria, shaking her shoulder. It was a little cool like she stopped breathing and went into shock. I gasped and recoiled, my hands near my face. I forced myself to reach her body and shook at her again, getting no response. Adrenaline snapped through me like a whip.

I pushed at Debbie as she was the next one to reach, hoping to wake her, but it was the same thing. She didn't move and was even a little stiff. I checked Tori, finding her skin had the same chill. This was not a prank since they were not breathing and there were no heartbeats.

My heart pumped faster; I couldn't think.

I held my fists up near my chest and didn't know what to do with them.

I'd eaten all the same things and drank out of the same bottles. I'd breathed the same air. I'd done the same atrocious things.

I pulled back and stood, watching them. *Why was I alive?* I checked my pulsing heartbeat – how long before it would abate? I checked my panicked breathing – how many more breaths until I asphyxiated? Fearing I was stuck in a nightmare, I poked myself with a pen and decided that it hurt, seeing a red drop of blood seeping from a small blackened hole in my forearm, showing me I hadn't yet perished.

Quite distraught and desperate, I fumbled to put on some pants then stepped over the bodies and rushed out of the treehouse. I tromped down the steps and ran barefoot to the main house, my feet slapping through the large and amazing kitchen where I expected to find Xiu Mei preparing breakfast once again. It was dim, with the only light being what filtered in through diamond-shaped stained-glass panels. I went to the servant's quarters and found Xiu Mei there in bed – also dead, slightly cool with no signs of distress, just as the girls were.

My mind returned blanks as my perplexity engulfed every last thinking portion of my mental activity. I stood stunned for an elongated moment until some semblance of thought returned. A huge blast of nuclear power from a sunspot? A nuclear radiation strike? If so, then why was I alive? I was lightheaded because I was afraid to breathe, not knowing whether they all died at once or whether people, perhaps myself, were still perishing.

Panic ripped into me like a cool blast from the island's blowhole.

"Mother! *Daddy!*" I cried with little breath as I ran up the shadowed hallway to their room. They were there, placid as a stagnant lake. I climbed upon the bed and shook them, but they remained stoic, no evidence of anything unnatural. It was ironic, as my father owned the funeral home in the town. I heard my own voice, "Daddy! You're the mortician! People are dead!"

Crying, I pervaded the room with "Daddy!" a hundred times. My mind blank again, I mechanically turned to Father's study where I checked a desk telephone – it was live, but when I dialed the emergency number, no one answered. I tried again, probably five times before taking a break to wail like a lost toddler, then five more, being so frustrated I'd bruised my fingers from stabbing the buttons. If someone had answered, I couldn't have composed myself without a gentle directing voice to persuade my own to produce cogent words.

I rushed back into the kitchen and turned on a multiband portable radio Daddy had placed on top of the refrigerator, expecting to hear an emergency broadcast. There was music on the island station, nothing on some others. And the radio just played music; I'd waited a few minutes for the announcer between songs, expecting his odd inflections extant from the indigenous dialect. But there was no voice, leaving dead air. It was all prerecorded. I switched to other bands, finding static. I turned on a small portable television and depending on the channel, it was blank with random fuzz on the screen or playing old movies. There was little TV available on the island anyway but punching the unit didn't improve the reception.

At this point I was aware that six people were dead, and no one answered the emergency line, nor was anything being broadcast that indicated a single live person. Rushing out of the house I ran up the lane, but just two blocks left me standing still in the street, seeing no movement. Goosebumps raising on my arms, I reversed toward the shore nearby, where the morning joggers would certainly be out. I passed up the house and treehouse to the beach and ran up along a public path, finding the first of several people laid over on the sand and sea oat lined trail. I went up to one, an older lady in white walking shoes and a full exercise jacket and pants, and checked her pulse, finding nothing, her face pale yellow like wax beans. I paced myself up the pathway to a fellow that appeared to have been jogging, with blue running shoes, shorts and a tank shirt, and checked his pulse, also finding nothing. He had mild scuffs on his elbows and knees. "He's been dead longer?" I conjectured by the temperature and flexibility of the skin. But he was near the water and the constant moist airflow might have cooled him.

I looked about, seeing nothing and no one besides the fallen people. I pushed along the trail to an adjoining street, and the longer I walked, the more perturbing the lack of interruption. I saw a blue and white island rental car at the bottom of a hill, sitting and idling in the middle of an intersection, the driver slumped over. I didn't think I should move it so first I walked away but doubled back and pulled a small black-haired woman out of the car. I drove several blocks, seeing what looked like a typical, beautiful early morning on a weekend, which it was, but it was unnervingly quiet. I drove the island rental car through empty streets up to a nighttime-on-call bus, sponsored by the city, sitting as if waiting for someone. I stopped and ensured the car was parked properly, got out and scurried to the bus door, seeing the bus driver slumped over the wheel. Other than the pale skin and drool dripping off the wheel, it appeared he'd passed out. The bus was empty, no passengers had come to be picked up.

I saw a dark compact car nearby, a person appearing to be sitting within. I went over and there was a middle-aged woman sitting back, almost appearing to have been asleep. The door was not locked so I reached in and pressed my fingers to her carotids. Again, no pulse – no life.

I got back into the rental car and drove near a pier and viewed a few boats adrift in the bay. On one fishing boat I saw a body lying over, almost as if to pull in a line that got caught. But the body wasn't moving at all. I saw a few people had fallen over on the beach. One was lying next to a tripod, having been there to photograph the morning sunrise, the camera still pointed toward the east, below which was a bag of lenses dropped and scattered like a collection of seashells.

Random thoughts tapped into my head. Had moon people infiltrated the island and by some incomprehensible twist of fate they elected me their next reigning queen and spared my life? Was the planet being cleared of people for another race to evolve or even to come from another planet? Would they still exterminate me? Was evolution reversing itself, taking the world to a simpler state after realizing that mankind had taken a wrong turn? And the lingering thought I couldn't evict was simply the question of whether I was the one that was dead.

In driving along, I saw another bus, much like a school bus, but labeled for a daycare, so I stopped the car by it, seeing it was parked by a small square non-denominational church made of limestone blocks. I stopped at the curb, facing bumper to bumper, and pulled myself out to take a quick look. The bus had modifications designed for younger children but was without occupants. I let myself into the building through a side door. The place smelled good like baby powder, but with a stale background odor like an old basement or freshly dug soil. There were half a dozen children lined up along some floor mats, covered with blankets. They appeared to be asleep, but their color was obviously waxen. I stepped quietly into a well-lit kitchenette and saw a grandmotherly lady had fallen over on the floor – also dead, with urine pooling against the base of a cabinet on which were cups with partly sorted vitamin supplements. Down a hallway I poked into the bathroom and saw that the bus driver had been in the middle of taking a crap – I flushed the toilet for him because it stunk, the fan unable to clear the air, but I could do nothing about his slumped body. Still, I saw no one alive. Back into the main play area, I checked a pretty little girl, her body still mildly warm. I lined her up on one of the mats, crying over her, kissing her cheeks. She hadn't urinated but a little, and it had soaked into the mat.

Mechanically I forced myself to a telephone to call the emergency number again though the small police station was just a few blocks up the street. I couldn't feel the pain in my fingers but could see they were bruising. Still, there was no answer. I rushed out of the daycare and sprinted barefoot up the street and pushed into the door at the police station hoping to find the attendant or dispatcher, finding one woman who had fallen backward out of her chair. I pushed past a low swinging door, so I could check her breath and pulse. She too was dead. Ceiling lights cast a fluorescent glow, and small red lights on the phone only registered that power was on with no new calls coming in. As I pushed against the front door to exit, the ceiling lights flickered off several seconds; an automatic generator kicked on, making a muted rumble from a closed room behind me. I knee-jerked from the noise, my right knee striking the door edge.

I hobbled back to the daycare while walking out the muted pain in my knee, scouting for any unlocked doorways in shops along the main street, truly getting the idea that there would be no help. Nor was there any other evidence of remaining electricity. The only open door was the daycare, now without power, and upon seeing the unrevivable children again, I gained mild awareness that I was making crazy noises because when I tried to say, "I can't get any help," into the air it was like interrupting myself. I let myself fall to the mat by the last little girl in the row. "There's no one to help!" I grieved, which was interrupting more than my stray thoughts – and another hit me – what if those papers on the bulletin board in the college dorm had some merit? My voice completely flat, I said, "Could this be ascension?" but I could not develop that thought regarding spiritualism while my grip on reality came loose.

If I hadn't already had a psychotic break when I saw my girlfriends dead or when I saw my Daddy dead, this was the moment. My perception of all space inverted and I was watching everything with a horrific level of detachment. My gasping respiration erratic, my arms and legs tingled. My heart was skipping beats, as if time had come off of a standard, having lost its contract with the revolution of the planet. That background thought I couldn't keep straight in my head came dancing back and forth to taunt me – what if I had died and all this was just an illusion, a contrivance of my last dying mental state?

I looked again at the little girl in front of me. I pulled her up and kissed the pretty little four-year-old face, telling her I wanted her and could take care of her. I told this little girl I could be her mommy, or she could even be my girlfriend. With scratchy voice I intoned, "You're pretty. You could be as pretty as me when you grow up." Her cooling skin was so delicate in my arms. "I want to keep you," I mourned.

I'll never get another chance, after today, unless I've got a freezer, my voice garbled as I thought to play mortician, but the words wouldn't form. I pulled myself up to check the kitchen, finding the place did have a freezer; I checked it, seeing a modest amount of packages, enough to maintain some cold. There was room for at least one child's body, and though it was going to warm up, it would preserve it for some hours yet. From the refrigerator's freezer compartment I took some ice and added it into the chest freezer then put the girl's body in there.

I went to another girl and pulled her up from the mat. There was a little poop at her panties, so I put her into a large sink and washed her up with cold water. I put her on the counter, pushing at her bladder to see if she'd pee more. I brushed her hair though the action was useless as I had partially lost coordination. I sadly stroked her fingers then tucked her into the freezer, pouring out uncontrollable emotion, my tears freezing up on a frosted package of fruity ice cream bars that she'd never get to taste.

Even in my crazy state, my emotions took another decline. I slumped to the floor, crawling like an accident victim pulling away from burning wreckage. Reaching the mats, I grabbed at the next child, seeing a boy. I think I bluntly said, "I don't like boys," and smacked him, his dead skin partly indented from the strike, not resilient like skin with ample blood pressure behind it. I screamed, "Why don't I like boys?" and fell into tears and crying for being so obsessed and sick. Why couldn't I be normal? Why did I have to constantly hide my identity, my "orientation," my desires and purposes? Why couldn't I just say it? Why would society not allow it? What form of incarceration had this society been?

I needed a bathroom, but that bus driver had been in the only one I was aware of, so I fetched a bucket from a broom closet and used it instead. Viewing askance through the window what I thought might be a police car or a person, my wracked vagus nerve innervated my gut, pushing distasteful goop up my throat, fearing I'd be singlehandedly blamed for the death of the island. There was motion out there – perhaps it was just a bird or the movement of a tree creating an illusion because when I got back to the door to find out, I saw nothing.

"I'm sorry!" I cried out to the dead children. "I'm sorry!" I cried specifically to the boy for smacking him.

I was so much in shock and unbelievably numb, I would have taken a beating over the nothingness. My sense of polarity for survival reversed. I just wanted to be raped and ultimately killed if that was the only way to feel something. My psyche scorched, my vision blurring, and body more or less on automatic, I walked out of the daycare toward a pier, blocks away near the hotel. "I'm going to throw myself in now," I blubbered as if talking to some dumb island god, one of the sculptures that lined the bay road. "The universe. Something about the universe!" I panted, trying to recall Seria's words from the beach, but I couldn't. My mind was shutting completely down.

I jogged in my bare feet, paying little heed to misplaced gravel underfoot that bruised and split the skin, leaving a trail of blood drops with each step. I arrived at a bridge that allowed a road to curve about the east island despite a series of headlands and peninsulas, and again, I saw another dead jogger up there. I slowed and passed him, a local that must have been inspired by the outlanders. I paced my awkward self, numb to the core, toward the first of the bridge, an adjoining section over the abutment with riveted metal plates fully chest high, and in my shock, I could not have coordinated a hurdle. I looked over the edge but didn't see much for the wide topside of the girder. As I passed an expansion joint I was able to see past the low crisscross of girders and cables that mocked a suspension system that was meant to distract that it was beam and pier construction much like any generic overpass. Across the railing I saw raw ocean waves battering the broken coral and limestone below, leftover from demolished or abandoned bridgework. This area of windward shoreline lacked sand, without shoals or reefs to block the ocean's thrashing. I pulled a leg up over the railing, straddling it precariously. One toss to the side and I'd tumble twenty meters, enough to permanently disable the body and knock me out if not kill me outright, because the incoming tide would drown me with the force of a murderer. In just moments nature would begin to reclaim my flesh, and the red-flowered seaside weeds and white lilies would have to act as my flower arrangements.

"Divert!" stabbed a voice into the back of my head, as if hands were pulling at my chest and back. Next an idea implanted in my mind, "This way." A compass of sorts appeared in the air before me, giving the precise southwestern direction I needed, back up the bridge deck over the abutment. It couldn't have been someone; they were all dead. It must have been some illusion, my mind dubbing reality for its self-preservation. Despite how incredulous the image, I followed the needle of that compass, leaving a return path of blood drops along the pavement, allowing the unexpected modification to my plan of suicide.

There was a light blue vehicle like a small jeep, not much larger than a golf cart, almost to the bridge with a woman in the driver's seat and a little girl slumped in the back. It distracted my actions from returning to throw myself into the water, supposing anything was better than complete oblivion – the abolition of my cognitive activity from daily random ideas to my most salient desires, but especially this madness. But what would anyone do when faced with the dead – have a funeral? I couldn't possibly have a funeral for them all. I couldn't embalm nor even bury that many. But I could do something for some children including the girls I'd already put into a freezer.

The small vehicle sat fully stopped, the key off and engine quiet, my only guess was that they'd stopped to view the early sunrise. The doors were locked, and windows only open a tad, so I got a rock from the edge of the road and busted the glass by the driver, then unlocked all the doors. I unbuckled the child and brought her out into my arms. She was a little wet in the crotch, but she'd been wearing a diaper, being barely two or three years old. I kissed her pretty little face framed by light brown hair. "Oh, you're so beautiful," I said as I undid the car seat and threw it out, and put her on her back to change her, the diaper bag having been placed conveniently at her feet. I told her, "I can't have you making any bigger messes until I get you to the funeral home."

I got her cleaned up and her clothing back together. I turned to her dead mother, saying, "I wish you could join me and baby – ah – Gretchen – or whatever. I just can't lift you." I pulled the girl up from the seat of the car and held her, swinging about, wishing she were alive.

I was crying again, but back to the west in the sky I saw the mail plane descending on the far side of the bay, coasting low toward some trees. It was at least a couple kilometers off course. Gradually, slowly, despite my hope that one person would be alive and turn to land in the bay, the craft sunk to tree level and flipped into the ground, and it was so quiet I could hear the impact.

I could watch myself screaming. "The world's dead! The world is dead!" I expected more voices and a final mental collapse, all part of the shock-induced psychosis. I was likely to fall down and die any second, I thought. I waited for it. I watched myself. I expected my skin to take on a heavy chill. I expected my eyes to glaze over or my knees to bend backward. I thought I'd just stop breathing and fall, my heart would stop, and bowels would empty. I stood and panted, waiting for the inevitable. My mind was broken, as if parts of my brain were blocked, subroutines that were supposed to deliver concepts that translated visual cues to aspects of reality failed, instead returning blankness. The car ahead of me was a blockish obstacle, the pavement just this strange blanket that cut off half of the space, there for no other reason than cohesiveness. Most objects if not touched could have been roughly painted stage props as I could not make the distinction. I nearly dropped the child, but instinct had me pull her against my body once again. Like the image of the compass, the girl had a place in my mind too. I needed her for some reason, but I didn't know why.

I got a wild thought which might or might not have come from this same collapsing section of my brain – embalming didn't need to be used just to put people in the ground. Following my compulsion to have people around, I could preserve her like a big doll. I set the girl to the back seat then dragged the mother's body out of the car, saying, "I only have so much time," pulling most of the broken glass with her, then latched the child into the back-seat belts.

The little blue vehicle started easily, and I drove past the hotel to a set of middle-class houses along the eastern island, stopping at each, banging on doors then breaking in, checking for dead children. In a yellow brick bungalow amidst ranch homes, I found a girl about six years with auburn hair and summer freckles, wearing an antique styled babydoll nightie with full bloomers. I lifted an eyelid to judge her average appearance, then lifted her lightweight body to sit in the passenger's seat with me as I drove to the next home, then the next and so on until I found a little house on a corner with white siding and carport. The glass front door was easy to breach. In a crib made of lathe-turned cherry was a lifeless baby girl in a yellow footie pajama with rainbows across it. I changed her diaper, grabbing up a diaper bag as I lifted the year-old to my shoulder. The diaper bag found its way to the floorboard, and the baby laid with Gretchen in the back seat.

Fractionally reviving from my mania, I continued house-to-house, finding a very slender blonde girl, tall for a three-year-old or slender for four. She wore a thick absorbent vinyl-lined panty, so I searched out a fresh replacement and changed her, picking up a diaper bag with a change of clothing. By blind luck I found myself a pair of pink and white jogging shoes and slipped them on my feet before setting the girl in the front seat with the six-year-old.

I felt like someone else was driving all my actions as if the car autonomously turned up the road toward Daddy's funeral home. I forced a stop at a green home, the driveway leading to a recessed garage against which rested a toddler's bicycle. A side door opened easily and led me through the garage to the kitchen. The furnishings oddly affluent for the neighborhood, and air strangely clean giving the illusion of life. I called out for help; no answers came as I pushed about. Parents laid in a large brass-framed bed as if asleep, one lone fly buzzing about the mother's nose. I moved on, seeing a room with a boy, perhaps seven, mostly under blue covers, making no sound and no motion. In the next room was a fancy maple toddler bed with fully matching dresser and changing table. I examined the three-year-old, the resemblance to Debbie driving me to wail like an idiot. Through it all, I picked her up and put her into the back seat and drove on to Daddy's funeral home.

Altontown Funeral Home had a Victorian façade on a block and steel structure. Using a tire iron from the vehicle, I broke in through a back door where the car would be best shaded from the warming sun until I could move all the girls. I rushed to the office and searched for an old book detailing the embalming steps my father used. I read as best I could as a crash course for my unprecedented attempt to perform the full embalming process. My hours with Daddy here allowed me to understand enough nomenclature and anatomy, presently realizing how I had understood besides collecting words for my stories.

Part of the process required the bodies to just soak in some special disinfectant that would absorb or destroy the free oxygen and enzymes, bleach the natural discoloration from hemolysis and relax the coagulation of the blood. Some of it could be injected at various places, and some could be gravity fed to allow a flow through the body.

I took the bodies and spread them out on the floor in the cool basement, putting the six-year-old onto the big "tub table." Wearing small pink rubber gloves, I located all the necessities and hooked up bags and tubes according to the instructions as best I could, lifting bags to hooks near the ceiling to get sufficient gravity force. It wasn't working the greatest because of the blood agglutination, so I opted to start the next body while intermittently massaging the first.

Soon I had the smaller brunette girl that resembled Debbie successfully bleeding out, head properly tilted a bit to the right according to the diagrams. Since the table was much larger than the girls, it was convenient to use one table for the group, and if needed there was a second table and more drip bag holders to infuse the fluids. I had strong interest in the little blonde girl who was very slender and very pretty. Without a lot of fat, she was without a doubt the easier one to get right, so I got her hooked up for the first stage. Then I put the year-old baby up on the second table, hooking up additional tubes for disinfectant.

I next retrieved Gretchen, the girl I'd found in the car near the bridge. I got her started with disinfectant fluid, put the tube into a loop, tied it up and let her soak. With each corpse I gained experience and found I could get more effectivity from this fascinating process – perhaps I should have intended on following my father's footsteps to become a mortician.

There were instructions for dealing with the brain and eyes. "Find a suitable pair of eye blanks for replacement. Perform the excision of the eyes (according to the picture) and be sure to flush with disinfecting fluid. You must be meticulous on this step because botched eyes will be noticeable to the next of kin. Insert the eye forms with care and adjust the eyelids accordingly. Be careful not to lose many eyelashes." I looked in the cabinet labeled "eyes" and found that most of them were plain white, like big marbles except for a cornea protrusion. But I checked another drawer and there was a multitude of the most beautiful hand-blown glass eyes you could imagine, probably unused samples from decades ago, each having little barbs that held the direction of the gaze as well as the position of the eyelids. So, I went to work pulling out the real eyes and replaced them with the pretty glass ones, which were just a little big, but it made each girl look even prettier like a doll.

Then there was painting, or staining, of the skin with custom dyes to add a vivacious appearance. It included pinking up the lips and applying skin tones with a mottling sponge. There was a whole lesson book on doing this, and I had assisted Father on many occasions, though he had always been there for final touch up. I would add most of the dye later, but I got the cheeks and neck of the baby to artificially signify life rather than being death gray, providing confidence I could have little masterpieces when complete.

For a little ad hoc nourishment, I ate some of the food they had left over from Vincent's previous funeral and wake. There were plenty of hors devours and scones. I was only beginning to worry about the future outlook for food in the case I could stay alive much longer. I didn't really have to eat. I said aloud, "If I don't eat. I don't puke." Considering the whole series of events, I can't say I expected to be alive, sustained within a fragment of borrowed time, more than a few days.

I was sure that the body cooler would warm up over the next day or so. I didn't know how to handle portable generators, but I at least knew that they'd only run a few hours on just gallons of gas, more than I could practically handle if they needed to run around the clock. I had to get these girls done if I wanted "friends" after this. The process would be more efficacious than embalming my actual friends' bodies, who weighed much more, though I wished I could have been working on Tori. I doubted I could carry her whether embalmed or not.

While the first group was bleeding out, having little confidence these first would be successful, I took a quick drive back to the daycare, fetching the two girls I'd left in the thawing freezer, piling one into the front seat, one in the back, both clasped with the seat belts, and brought them into the funeral home basement.

The first little girl from the daycare was very pretty and I found a slightly mismatched pair of eyes for her. I went through an arduous procedure with all seven girls to clean out the colon and intestines, where water flow would be forced all the way through the body, then a suction would be applied, and everything was cleaned out from both ends. Cautioning against retention of fluids, there were instructions on how to put syringes into the body to suck out everything else the needles could find. It was also suggested to mark the holes, so you could use the same for injecting the disinfectants and embalming fluids, in some cases, poking them into inconspicuous places where you'd not want to poke anyone living. The book concentrated on each organ and the muscles, and how to properly disinfect and embalm each one without missing anything. I don't know if this was a common procedure. Perhaps it was completely obscure, perhaps my father's own formula. In some cases, he had to modify the text with handwritten notes jotted by the pictures or along the margins, and I tried to understand every revision.

I read more as the text professed, "The best embalming takes time, allowing the disinfectant to flow through the tissues and achieve proper lipolysis of the fats. Then the embalming starter catalyzes the initial fluid into a polymer rubber." That was in the process they were using, and I followed a table that indicated temperatures, body weight, congealing time and factors that signified the completion of each step, but I extended all the times for my uncertainty. By late afternoon I'd swapped out the disinfecting and cleaning solution for the "embalming catalyst" for all the girls. I could now apply more dye to improve appearances while the early evening light reflected through the basement windows.

Overall the process had been difficult, and I wanted to find more children since I guessed the first ones were disinfected poorly with the degree of fixation uncertain, though in succession each child received better treatment.

I went back out to drive northwest through a neighborhood full of timeshare homes occupied by people of moderate wealth – the kind of guys that could get trophy wives and thus almost always had such beautiful children. I busted in doors and yelled for people, always crying out for help first, just in case I found someone alive. I soon found another dead little girl, having bright red hair and a pretty round nose. She had wonderful designer-made clothing in her room, so I figured I could return to this house later, whether anyone else was alive or not. If they were, I could always blame weird stuff on someone that was dead or blame it on having gone crazy, which I had.

I took that girl and put her into the vehicle I'd stolen from the woman near the bridge. I went on from house to house. I found a teenage girl that was so beautiful but regretted she was going to be too big to take out and embalm, and with more weight, they took longer to cool, thus a faster rate of decomposition. I thought about taking a boy, so the girls would have a brother, but I just wasn't that interested. I went on to the next house, the next, and the next. I found a house with a little swimming pool in back and a few other indicators of children. I again busted into the front door and went through the house. I found some food in the refrigerator and it was still cool, but not as cold as it would normally be. I put a few of the refrigerator items into the freezer section, seeing that the freezer was thawing, and took out some softening ice cream, finding a spoon to help myself. I found a couple more girls, likely fraternal twins with light brown hair, and rushed them to the vehicle, and then further scavenged the house to find flashlights as it was getting near dusk.

I went back to the embalming room and set up the flashlights. I parked the car so that the headlights shone at the basement windows, which were high to the ceiling. I went to work on the next bodies, getting them uncoagulated, drained, and soaking with the first step of the disinfectant and embalming process.

I found myself backing up against the outside wall of the room away from the bodies. Fully enervated, I fell asleep as soon as I reached a sitting position.

I woke later, my tailbone in acute pain, hearing the vehicle idling, the room lit eerily with the vehicle's lights shining in. I jolted up as if aliens had landed, but then I realized it was exactly as I'd left it. After checking my human dolls in progress, I washed my hands, went upstairs, and slept in a different area, getting into a display coffin on the main level, thinking it might be funny if I died while lying there.

I woke in early morning and the angled yellowish sunlight was strong from the outside, adding an angelic luminescence through layers of long cream curtains, uncommon for a funeral parlor. I went back to the basement and saw the mess I'd left. It was more grotesque than I expected, with bits of blood splashed about the embalming tables and floors. I used a hose to flush the floor then washed up the area with bleach. Wearing a fresh set of those pretty pink gloves, I went about injecting the final catalyst solution, finding that the bodies jelled up very well this time. "Avoid direct finger contact for minimally twelve hours if possible," it said. Once I removed the gloves, it would behoove me to wait and not embalm my own fingers.

I pulled out one of the first bodies that I'd done. Unfortunately, the first brunette that resembled Debbie, one of the prettiest girls, hadn't been disinfected properly and suffered early stages of necrosis. Part of her skin was embalmed well, and part not so well, making her look like a mutant with differences in texture and color. I tried to fix her, but once the gelling process had begun, it was very difficult, if not impossible, to fix the areas that had failed. Nor had I gotten the colon totally clean, nor the stomach. She was going to rot, so I played with her between embalming activities for the others, having a little tea party around the funeral home and eventually settling her into a coffin. The year-old baby girl did well enough though she'd been an early piece of work. She was quite rubbery, the fixation impressively lifelike. Her body didn't yet stink though I doubted full success.

As a result of my lack of confidence, in the early hours I compulsively searched for more bodies while scavenging for food, swapping the little car for a small white van with a full fuel tank. It was nearly a complete day since the event. It would be less likely to find suitable specimens now, but the night turned cool, so it was still possible. I drove through the island's inner roads toward the northwestern beach. I feared seeing a multitude of campers and partiers left over from the End of Summer Bash, so I kept some distance from the incoming surf in proximity to the lighthouse. These were the most elite of the homes, each having several acres of property. At a downscaled Tudor replica, though little of its noble appearance was actually stone, I discovered a fenced play yard with a matching fort. The door wasn't locked, so I let myself in, smelling an acrid, putrid stench. Passing through an entry and back toward a kitchen, I saw three large malamutes laid over dead by glass doors, their rippled muscles still appearing dangerous. I reeled back, turning toward a stairwell instead. In a room with oddly-simple built-in furniture, I found a black-haired girl that was about 8 years old, her body was showing a little development, and in lifting her eyelids saw a foggy green. She was inordinately pretty, her cheeks round and profile not misaligned. I picked her up since her bedroom had been kept cool, partly from proper shade, and partly from the impressive construction. Her lightweight body smelled lightly and suffered inconsistent pooling of fluids, but I could possibly fix her. I looked about for others in the next several homes, looking again for signs of *girl* from outside of houses. I found a house with lace curtains and broke my way into it. I found a little girl about twenty to twenty-four months, dead like the others. Her face was doll-like to begin with, her summer complexion overlaying the cool colors of death. She had a notable odor. I fetched some diapers and clothes into a diaper bag, then picked her up. I had found a can of spray paint and marked the front door with a big "O." I blabbed aloud with childish intonation, "If I can fix you, I'll want to know where to come back for your fabulous clothes." Before moving on to the next house, I checked for food and ate a leftover chicken sandwich, finding soft food in a freezer keeping the rest cool. I nibbled some bread and jelly, packing more lunch into an ornate box to take along. From a garage I collected some camping gear, getting a camping stove and fuel bottles.

Once back to the funeral home, I worked on the eight-year-old and the twenty-month-old girl, and I had plenty of solutions, but patches of skin for both had suffered mild desiccation. After I'd worked up to the point where they were soaking in the disinfectant, I went out to see what else I could find, passing through town again. I had also checked that school bus, just in case a child had been on it, but it was clear of anyone. I could have gone through the poor neighborhoods, but it was unlikely that their homes would have remained cool. The more native they were, the rounder their faces, and despite the fact they were generally pretty people, they didn't strike me as ideal. Much like my reaction to boys in general, I had no idea why.

Just outside of the municipality, I drove up to another daycare, but no children were there. I drove on toward another elite neighborhood. I sighted a luxury brick structure with mock buttresses, and I pushed up to its perimeter fence to peek through to the back yard, finding some play equipment. Inside I found a five-year-old with reddish blonde hair and little toddler curving nose – she was so pretty, and the house had been shaded well. She didn't really even stink. The house was unusually cold, having had a high foundation and deep basement. Perhaps those buttresses helped keep direct sunlight off the primary walls. I took her and assumed she might be a good replacement for the first girl I'd botched. But before going back, I saw another over-scaled country house with a swimming pool, lace curtains in the upstairs windows. I saw a man in the pool, apparently having died there during an early morning swim. I went into the home and cried out for others. I looked into a girl's room, seeing a messed-up bed, but no one was in it. *Odd,* I thought, *for a child to not be in her bed.* There were girl's clothes on the floor and a clean set of day clothes on the dresser, all picked out for the next day. I looked into the parents' bedroom, and saw the mother there, quietly dead.

I checked into a bedroom and saw a young teenage boy, and he was stiff and stinky.

"Hello?" I called out. I started checking closets.

Upon opening a closet, I was struck with a strong odor of urine. Inside I found the little girl, curled up in what appeared to be terror. I pulled at her, telling her not to fear me. But her seven-year-old body felt cold and rubbery, falling over when pulled. She'd been hiding in the closet for whatever reason when the event happened. I checked her over and saw there was evidence of a recent molestation. "No!" I cried out and sobbed, stepping about while deciding what to do. I didn't think she'd be a good specimen, but I grabbed her anyway in hopes of giving her a little of the respect she had clearly not been getting.

Endlessly crying, still well within my shock of the horrific mass die off, I went on to another house and found a blondish girl about six or so years old. I took her and put her into the car, and she pissed while I carried her. It stunk! I wasn't sure she'd be a good specimen either. I neither had enough time nor chemicals to embalm everyone, leaving me to wonder what the practical limit would be.

As the hours went by I gave up on the idea that someone else might care. If this were a real emergency, the mainland would have responded within hours. It wasn't an emergency because everyone else was dead.

The day was very cool, so the bodies were actually better in the car than in the warmer houses. I went on to another seaside home with yellow limestone façade, seeing a small girl's bicycle on a veranda at the back. I figured I'd get this body without hesitation and then go back and start working on the ones I had.

I rushed in, breaking the door's glass and opening the latch, and pushed on in. As I had every time, I cried out for help as if I expected an answer, "Help me! Everybody's dead. Please help me? Is anyone alive?"

I found the girl's room. There was a child there, lying on her side, facing away from the door. I went about to the far side. Something was different about the room – it didn't smell like death, it just smelled like urine and sweat, like someone needed to take a shower. I looked under the bed first, then into the closets, in case someone else was hiding, but no one was there. I then pushed the child's body, not sure if I'd get a reaction or not. But there was none. I pulled back the covers and saw a very pretty girl's nightgown. She was about five years old with dark hair. In a hamper I saw some pretty clothes like swimsuits and cute shorts, the source of the sweaty odor. I saw some pretty dresses hanging in a closet, and shoes beneath them. *Yes, I* thought. *I'll give this one a try.*

I checked other rooms, finding two older brothers, likely seven and thirteen years, but I knew I didn't want them. I went back to pick up the girl and took her to the vehicle. I then rushed back to the funeral home with the pile of flesh.

I started all the processes for the new arrivals, and only then administered the gelling solution to the one's I'd already started. I hoped for the best. My chances were running out quickly.

Once the final bodies were in the disinfecting process, I went back to my treehouse. My error had been closing it up the night of our little party. It had warmed up like a camper, which it was prone to do. I saw the bloating girls there, and they stunk horribly, so I reeled back to the balcony, losing the leftovers I'd pilfered at the houses while picking up the additional dead children. Oddly, the taste and smell of the chicken sandwich vomit helped mask the wafting of death. I opened up the door, tugged at Tori first as she was closest, then Seria, sliding the gangrenous corpses far enough to let them flop down the steps to the landing, then again to the patio. To get Debbie out I had to deflate the air mattress and slide her down to the ground level. I was so terribly sorry about Tori. I'd liked to have kept her body if only I'd have been able to carry her. All that strange wailing noise and heaving from my chest – was that me? My craziness and anger got the best of me while I threw my arms about and cursed at microorganisms for doing their job. After rolling about in the dirty sand that stuck to my teary face, having attempted to stay upwind of the bodies, I just couldn't stay there any longer, nor could I wait if I was to preserve any of the children I'd selected for embalming.

I climbed up into the treehouse and fetched a few items of my own clothing to wear, as well as clothing from when I'd been a child, so I could dress the little girls in it. With that collected and in the car, I then went into the main house. I looked at my dead parents, now looking bloated or fat with bugs gathering. The window of embalming opportunity was over for them, so with a strange, raspy voice, I said, "Sorry Mom and Dad. I can't preserve you either. I guess I'm the coroner now. I pronounce you both dead." An automatic convulsion struck through me, the stench stung my nostrils, so I directed my course away, leaving traces of vomit along the floors. I was never to return, not even for all my notebooks.

Having returned to the funeral home, I completed the work of embalming the bodies, taking hours of dedication and obsession. Time would tell which were successful and which would have irrecoverable desiccation and necrosis. The first dark-haired girl and the molested girl would be failures. That left thirteen that might be successful.

I preferred to obtain a place of residence that didn't have bodies in it. I couldn't reside at my parent's house or the treehouse since it represented my first experience with the horrendous event. I went about to the houses I saw before and tried to remove remaining bodies, mostly being unsuccessful. It was unfortunate that the event happened when most people were home. I found a modest gray-sided home where I could remove a woman on a rug that I could slide across hardwood floors to remove her. It was near where I'd found one of the dead girls. I liked the home as it was up on a hill, only a few kilometers from my father's funeral home, and yet it was near enough to the pier that I could see it and a portion of the cove. I wondered, though, if it would be better to live in the hotel for a stronger building, as there were unpredictable and violent storms that came in from the sea.

I was concerned about all the stuff I'd been collecting in various homes and instead started warehousing it at the hotel. Being a designated storm shelter, it included a storage area for emergency supplies, including a number of thirty-liter water jugs. I could rely on essentials from its kitchen which had not yet spoiled. Over time I cleaned it up the best I could. It wasn't so bad because every floor had a fire escape door that led directly outside to be paired with a fire truck ladder or a rope ladder. They had alarms, but there was neither electricity nor backup electricity, perhaps having already drained its self-starting generator's fuel tanks. I made use of plastic runners and carts to slide the few bodies out the fire escapes. It took a while, and the larger the body, the more gross and bloated it had become. As for the hotel, it had been into the off season and there were only a few guests there, other than two staff, neither of which was Charles or Jeffrey, who must have helped with the party on the northwestern beach, the remnants of which I'd never approach. With enough perfume and a little alcohol, and plenty of embalming disinfectant, I could bear the smell and handle the rotting flesh, including a large man, having to grotesquely carve him up.

I gave up the house and stayed at the hotel once it was void of dead adults. I moved ten of the embalmed girls in, including the one I called Gretchen, the pretty one from the daycare, the redhead with round nose, the one-year-old, the twenty-month-old, and the eight-year-old, placing them about as if they were alive. The first little blonde girl who was about three or four years old in the vinyl pants also "survived" the embalming process, and she became my favorite, so I called her Sarah. I'd play with all the girls, read to them, and talk to them. I had to be careful with them as they were still somewhat delicate, even after a few weeks of the rubbery resin having set up completely, similar to silicone dolls. The twenty-month-old was wonderful, now wearing my little white sailor dress from my treehouse. The little one-year-old, the baby, hadn't turned out as well as I hoped, and it began to emit some putrid odors. I took it to a back courtyard of the hotel and buried it. The whole town stunk, I realized, as I covered the body, expecting the smell to cease, but there was a lingering odor all about. The other small buildings and local houses near this hotel had plenty of bodies in them. Nor was I aware of the multitude of little creatures that had also died during the event, decomposing and adding to the stench.

THREE

Premonition and Voices

About six weeks after the odd event, the end of summer led to hurricane season and a new moon. Having started early I was using a small hatchback to get usable items from houses and kept watch on a storm coming in from the east. I had been searching through houses, and while in the fourth there was an urgent voice that entered the back of my head that said, "Go to the hotel!" At present, I could not recall much of my first few hours of psychotic behavior after the event, so I didn't have any idea what this voice was. As the storm approached, I felt naturally imperiled by what was probably low pressure, but the "nonsense rejection" portion of my brain told me to ignore the message.

I didn't get the seriousness of the crisis until I exited the house and surveyed the situation. Ocean waters were filling the little bay and rising up over a dock where it was permanently attached. Whereupon the dock structure allowed for strong tidal variations, the bay-side portion was floating aslant, the base submerged. It was absurd. The waters at the outer edge of the bay were rushing in, an obvious difference in elevation, forming a whirl on either side of the inlet. The storm approached at an unprecedented rate, timed with the spring tide, having the ominous appearance that evening was arriving in midmorning. The pressure changed so radically my ears popped.

Alarmed, I felt the necessity to cooperate with the psychic instruction, considering it could do no harm to heed the message and head back to the hotel. Without fear of looking foolish to anyone, I grabbed up my last take, slammed the house's main door, and rushed back into the hatchback, driving back to the hotel, as it was the strongest structure, designed to withstand a hurricane. I was intimidated by the voice again, "Go to the hotel.

Go to the hotel! Grab what's important and take it to the third floor!" I held my eyes wide, my arms jittery with near terror, fighting against the furious southerly wind. A dirty mist sprayed up from the sea and a sand dollar slapped across the windshield.

Once at the hotel, the wind was rushing through my hair at a sustained forty knots, filling it with sand and spray. I grabbed some jars of food, some packages of menstrual pads and some clothes, and rushed them into the building, throwing them through the door to fetch more. The storm surge steadily filled the bay, and previously moored boats were being tossed about, with one being pushed onto the submerged shore where there had only been beach minutes before. In the distance, I saw outlined a large boat, perhaps a military frigate, pitching from the force of six-meter waves beyond the bay.

I got the last things out of the car and closed the back hatch and fought my way against the wind that pushed me into the lobby. Then I grabbed the food items and stepped them up the stairs as best I could. I went to get my favorite two of the seven remaining embalmed girls and carried them up to the second floor, arranging them on a bed in one of the rooms near the stairs. I then fetched two more, also laying them on the same bed. "You shouldn't be afraid Gretchen and Sarah. Please take care of the others," I told them. I knew they couldn't hear me, but it was comforting.

Returning to the first level the heightened fury outside stopped me like a bird hitting a window. The palm trees were bending over and one of them snapped, being pulled like a parachute to the hotel, but hit another slanting tree and mostly missed, snapping around the edge of the building. Another tree went off to the right, missing it altogether. To the northeast, I could see the bridge I'd nearly thrown myself off of with pitching waves just under the deck, heavy spray being thrown across it. The unabated storm surge brought the ocean up to the rise of land that surrounded the foundation for the hotel, giving the illusion that the island was sinking. Salt spray continuously streamed through the air. Seeing the bridge, I partly recalled the moments I'd straddled the rail, and the voice that struck into my mind – was this the same voice? Was this helping me survive? Realizing there was a likely connection, I went to get another embalmed girl and carried her up to the second level, then moved more food, then got another girl.

There was a crash and bang as a portion of a tree hit against the cement and brick framework about the lobby windows. Waves rushed up to the door now. Water trickled in with no way to stop it. It smelled like the bottom of the bay – stinking glop that had been churned and dredged up by the storm. Seaweed dashed over everything, only to be washed and pushed by the same wind impelling wet sandy grit. I dashed through the lobby to get the last girl, then the remains of the food, some of it in jars in a cardboard box, which was already coming undone from the moisture. Water slapped in with a new wave, adding another centimeter of murky soup to the floor. The violent wind was howling as loud as an angry siren. The icky brine was trickling in through cracked windows.

I realized that a closet at either side of the lobby had an obscure sign, reading, "Storm Grate." I stepped through the murky water to one, seeing inside a large hand-crank that could be assisted by an electric motor, but there was no electricity, so I'd have to give it a manual whirl. A large chain-linked grating pulled off a roll to cover the front lobby windows, a series of latches at the edge. Between the worst gusts of the gale-force winds, I could get it to move slowly to the point of protecting the center doors. Once one side was complete, I rushed to the other, and cranked it to center as I had the other. Once the centers met, I pushed through the outer door and latched as many clasps as I could, then returned inside, barring the main doors.

I stood there gasping against the inside doors, amazed at my action despite the danger. Had there been many people sheltering in the hotel, I would have been one of the last people chosen for such a dangerous task.

A new wave came up and slammed up against the grate, and with reduced force, smacked the thick glass, and water rushed between the double doors. I picked up the last items and set them on the steps, then got on the steps and handed them up to the steps above me, then climbed, and handed stuff up again. I made it up to the second floor, assuming I was mostly safe, yet also checked for window grates, finding a small door next to each window set in the abnormally thick walls – each had a small crank to pull a shield over the windows. I cranked all that I could find, even one that was a little hard to reach in a stairwell.

"Third floor!" came an ungendered voice again. Startled as it was so clear, I turned and attempted to find the source. It was not possible to hear a voice that clear from a person with this turbulent and cacophonous storm. Perhaps for my sanity, I didn't attempt to invalidate it, but I'd been slow to take action.

"Third floor!" it said again, hardly vaporous, with some sense of urgency and appealing to my sensibilities. It wasn't just a suggestion, instead signifying: *It would behoove you to get to the third floor.*

I thought it best to act upon the immediacy. I grabbed whatever I could grab, taking things up to stow on the next level. I didn't need intrepid nerves. I didn't need to be audacious. I needed just enough vision and cooperation from the flesh to accomplish menial tasks that might permit survival.

The furious winds had passed hurricane level, likely beyond seventy knots, uttering an unnatural, sustained scream. The foaming waves smacked against the metal grates.

A new wave hit the ground level. Glass broke, leaving a breach at the entrance. A portion of the wave broke through and splashed up several steps. Wind voraciously whipped the air inside as if driven by eggbeaters, a colony of bats, or something larger, like an angry prehistoric archaeopteryx whose fossilized skeleton had been found on the island. The grates had held, chattering asynchronously like a bunch of children banging on a school bus with baseball bats.

"Third level," I slurred, allowing that the voice's assertation wasn't unjust. I grabbed an embalmed girl from the second level and rushed up, putting her into the next level's first available room. I rushed down, getting each girl and when they were all up, I grabbed boxes and cartons of food, ending with cans that had gotten separated. By this time water was splashing all the way to the second-floor threshold, the only good news was that the breach in the glass was covered by the higher storm surge, vanquishing the perturbations in the air.

I just couldn't believe it. I knew that the hotel was at a lower elevation than my parent's house. Perhaps my treehouse would survive without flooding if the wind didn't rip it off its foundation. The water would not likely reach it, but it was aligned with the bay, so it might be like a wing in the wind. We were not going to see the eye of the storm, but be just at the edge of it, in the line of the highest winds for the longest time, and with shifting winds, the treehouse would likely be gone afterward.

I rushed on through the rooms on the third floor, cranking each window grate into place. Despite it being daylight, the pall of the storm cast the entire island into a hellish shadow. My worst fear was if that frigate got pushed up into the hotel, it'd knock it down and I'd have a very slim chance of survival. Make that no chance, instead taking an express voyage to saltwater hell. But why would I have heard an urgent voice if I wasn't meant to survive this?

I continued to crank window grates into place on the fourth and fifth floors. When I looked out the back of the hotel, where the structure itself sheltered some of the wind, I saw that the storm surge came up so far as to hide the entire back area of the hotel, including any furniture and permanently fixed umbrellas, as well as the fence. All the other buildings and houses were ripped up or in the process of being destroyed. There were plenty of unattended houses at higher ground, but none right up near the hotel, and with all the salt spray and wind, it was impossible to see how they were faring. A moving shadow suggested a roof being torn off one of those houses.

It was getting darker, and the wind was at its peak. I heard creaking in the building. I heard the waves slam in through the front. I crawled with each embalmed girl on my back, so I could move them to rooms on the back side of the hotel. I cuddled with a little girl while sucking my thumb, and put her thumb in her mouth too. I cried, barely able to hear my cries above the noise.

"Stay put. Don't move," said the unknown voice again. I jerked and screamed from the interruption. Through the stairwell and hallway, I heard some metal creaking. It was one of the most horrible sounds I'd ever heard, like a long cry from hell. The building shook. More glass broke in the lower level.

"Don't try to stand," said the voice again. My cries were nearly as sustained as the wind. A massive wave hit the building. The direction of the fury was shifting, waves slapping at the east side of the building, but not yet the opposite. I heard the loud metal again – a long creaking moan like a dying devil's last cry. The building shook again. A new wave had hit the building and perhaps something else, hopefully not that ship I'd seen beyond the bay, but I had this impression it was, at this very moment, directly against the hotel structure.

This was the height of the storm. If the building could sustain only twice of the tumult it had already taken, it could stand, with significant damage, but it could stand. The hotel shook again with a semblance of a sudden impact, this time coming from the east side instead of the south side toward the bay.

It had become too dark to see anything, and I was too scared to get near any other windows. Rain slapped at the grates and glass in sheets. I couldn't do anything but wait. In time I noted I was wet – the storm waters were leaking in everywhere or the humidity was just one hundred per cent. I felt cold and covered with sand and salt. But then I'd been wet when I got up there. Was I so scared I hadn't felt it before? Perhaps that was a good sign, now realizing I was wet? I hadn't felt any additional hits to the hotel for about half an hour. I'd cried so long that I was sure my voice was about gone. I couldn't hear it over the storm even if I plugged my ears.

I crawled about, getting toward the steps. Surging water reached to just a few steps down from the third-floor level. It was unbelievable. Had everyone been alive, the majority of the population would be dead now anyway, depending on how many people could have fit on three floors of the hotel. But I would have been glad to be with a few hundred people packed wall to wall. So, I held my embalmed girls again, hoping that the water wouldn't come up the last few steps to the third floor.

I could hear that the storm winds had reduced from wicked to wailing, but it would still have been suicide to walk out even if I could step directly to the ground, or if I could step up on the roof, which had been, at one point, an open area with tables and chairs, once used for copacetic conversations and sunset-lit photographs. Most loose debris was already taken away, including the outdoor furniture from the open sixth level. The whole building stunk like seaweed and the bay. Rain still pelted the windows, and everything was saturated.

Given time, the storm continued to settle down. I was so exhausted I couldn't sleep, but gradually, when the wind was low enough, the sandman cooperated with me. The next time I woke, the storm had reversed, perhaps having done a loop only to come across the island again. Clearly, the storm surge had subsided if only for low tide. Water was pooled everywhere on the second floor. I couldn't yet see the level beyond that from inside the building. Outside the wind was now blowing in completely the opposite direction, knocking down the already weakened trees.

I went down to the second level wearing an old pair of oversized knee-high boots I'd collected, rubber soles stepping into smelly goop on the floors. I saw that the brackish water had been receding more than halfway down the first flight of steps, but it was most of the day before the storm waters had receded nearly to the original level, back to where the bay could be marginally identified. There were shattered boat hulls and decks up into the remaining trees, but no whole boats and few trees were present. The rows of houses beyond the hotel had no roofs, and many were leveled to their foundations, many timbers scattered, and herbage shredded. Everything between the hotel and the heavily-eroded beach was gone except for some stumps. Of course, the car was gone. That bridge I'd nearly thrown myself off of had been shaken apart, leaving a short ledge at the abutment and crumbled deck where it mated with the road, the main bridge deck tumbled into upside-down fragments among crooked piers. Island God statues had been pulled off their little square foundations, some tumbled far from their original locations, some missing altogether.

I took walks but couldn't go very far for the next few days. I wanted to know if my treehouse stood. I walked up a road to a modest hill, whereupon I was able to see my parents' main house was missing the majority of its structure. Most of the branches of the oaks were broken off, but there was no evidence of the treehouse, if it would have been visible from this angle. I just couldn't get there for all the mud.

In shock and crying, I barely realized how much noise I was making. I had no choice but to walk back to the hotel, where I forced myself to nibble any directly edible food even though my body protested – I munched a lot of crackers because the bland taste didn't mix with the smells and urge me to vomit. Mostly I just laid about and slept or I'd lie with the embalmed girls and cry. I otherwise felt so numb, watching myself like I didn't know what I was going to do.

Days of additional rain washed some percentage of the sand and mud back to the beaches and the bay or ocean. There were dead, even mangled, sea creatures including broken coral everywhere. There were shellfish and even jellyfish decomposing wherever you walked. It all had the mustiest stench. For a few additional days it stunk so badly that I couldn't even go outside. That putrid smell still came in through all the broken windows on the first floor. I recalled my father's voice saying, "You'll have to get used to the smell of dead things if you are going to work in the funeral business." Little did I know how much that was needed! I had a section of the third floor that I could shut off with fire doors to limit the amount of raw, musty air that came in. I sprayed disinfectants. I put vanilla in a spray bottle and sprayed it all through the air.

As things washed up outside, I was finally able to get out again during the cool mornings. It was a good thing we were at the end of the summer because we'd be past the hottest of the season. I finally made it to the treehouse. It was wrecked, the roof and rooms all shredded, leaving just an outline of the structure, and there were no bodies to be found. I wished I'd taken some more of my personal things with me to the hotel. I didn't expect any storm to be this strong. There'd likely never been such a storm in the populated history of the island. When Father had the treehouse built, it was supposed to withstand a modest hurricane. It didn't survive this one.

I was distraught as I went about and scavenged whatever else I could find in storm-damaged houses, making my way back through town with backpacks of usable items. I wanted to be able to take at least one of my girls with me like I often did with the car, but I couldn't now because I was on foot only. I'd start crying just about anywhere, and no one cared. In one house, I just started blurting out, "No one cares. No one's here. I'm dead. I'm dead already. Who the fuck are you to tell me to go up to the third floor when you knew it would save my life? Who are you? What are you?" I'd become haughty and narcissistic to these voices in the wake of my equivocal survival.

The lower structures between hills, though usually properties of lesser value, were the most intact. I moved about one little house, glad to find a few dozen jugs of distilled water. I washed my face and drank. I found bottles of juice. I found cans of food that the labels had peeled off of. I found cleaning fluids. I wasn't sure if some stuff under the sink was lemon juice or lemon cleaner. I figured it would be better to not try to drink it, and you could still clean with lemon juice. I pushed around in a closet with a warped frame and tilting shelves, finding an unexpected tallystick with words carved into or written on it in a few languages, the one I recognized saying, "Hurricanes survived by family." Fifty-seven scratches had been gouged across the teak stick.

At the hotel, I ported my living quarters up to the fourth floor, with most of my storage being on the third and fifth floors, depending on importance. To rest I went out on the "sixth level" roof to watch the sunsets and cry. I'd keep replaying the major event beginning with those girls requesting "another naughty sleepover evening" and when Tori had said something like, "I want you to feel like this is the last of the universe. You and I can do anything."

And it was their last night on the planet, but even they held back on a lot of things. I wished we'd all known. We could have left teeth marks. We could have torn a little more skin. We could have abused ourselves a little more, tearing hair and tickling until we puked. We could have called more people over – even a guy, perhaps Charles with his obvious crush on me. "I'm crazy! Why am I alive?" I cried. I was up there on the roof, yelling into the gentle ocean breezes. "You taunt and torment me for my sins!" I knew I hadn't smiled in days – weeks. I wasn't sure the date but had a pretty good idea the month. Perhaps someone would have a waterproof watch that I'd find yet, hoping it was still working but I knew better than to think such an item could exist.

I had collected many items, including numerous types of pills and a prescription pill guide book that specified the required dosing. I started taking some pain pills as the work was arduous. I got a small scrape on my leg, having contracted an infection, so

I took some antibiotics. I took a few antihistamines and amphetamines to numb the horror and lighten the seriousness.

I got a young girl's bicycle working and took rides about, pulling a small wagon with a shovel and a broom with me, extending the passable trail each day, though I'd never go as far as the northern headlands. I had started northeast from the hotel, passing through the backroads, reaching the shore where the beaches resumed. I came about a bend in the coastline and saw a large gray object – the small frigate, perhaps an escort vessel, that I had been afraid would crash into the hotel during the storm, having been pushed unfathomably beyond the beach into the trees. I rode the bicycle up the beach and took note of the huge propellers at the back of the vessel, seeing a newly cut brook, water running down toward the beach, contributing to an existing rivulet that cut between the sea oats. The front of the ship was pushed up between large plant-covered dunes and angled trees were toppled over to the deck level. I walked up and started climbing one of these trees. My smaller body was having some trouble with the climb, but with minimal scraping I was able to get onto the deck. It appeared military but was an older boat. I found a hatch, complete with seaweed over it. I got the hatch up and looked in. It had a large holding bay full of palettes, all wrapped up and stacked with goods. I couldn't see well, so I got a few more hatches open, being careful not to pinch or cut myself with the big wheels that had to be cranked to open the doors. Toward the back end, there was water up to a third-level-down deck, as could be seen through a stairwell. But toward the front, there were ample undamaged palettes of something. I went in, being very careful, and checked a palette that had goods bundled in plastic. It was many kinds of items, but at least half of it was food.

It was like a gift from God. It wasn't a military vessel. It had been repurposed as a relief vessel, victualled with tons of food – literally tons of food. I cried of course.

I went about to see what was there. The captain had been decomposing for a while on the bridge. He must have been dutifully keeping watch when the event happened. There were a few rotting seamen in the crew quarters, the doors closed tight, and there were rooms that hadn't had any occupants. In the hold I discovered some cereals, ate some immediately, packing a few things in a backpack, and then rode the bicycle back to the bay-side hotel. The boat was far enough from the hotel that I pondered living in its modestly listing quarters. I could have just stayed in the ship and made it my home, but I wanted to be with my girls. I feared that with the population gone, perhaps I was witnessing some final stages of the planet, ready to decay at an accelerated pace. The hotel structure, despite the beating it had taken, would remain home.

New storms were being drawn in by a southeasterly, and I was apprehensive about what kind of storm it would be. It was ferocious, but it wasn't a hurricane. Lightning hit the building a few times that night, making an echo that pounded through the stairwells like a hammer from the heavens. I was sitting, bent over crying, saying, "I don't know what to do. I don't know what to do – please voice – what are you and how can you help me?"

I heard nothing ethereal for hours. I kept trying to hear that mystical voice. "Please help me. Tell me what to do?" I was mostly referring to whether I should continue living in the upper floors in the hotel or move to the ship. But there was no direction to do either.

Between storms I'd make routine trips to the ship and get food. After attaching a tarp over the tree, it made it easier to slide up and down, and I used ropes to lower goods to the sand. Later I cut down a second tree by the first to make a ramp. Day after day, I got enough to eat.

There was a small babbling spring in the area too, to which I hacked a trail and filled water bottles on every trip.

During all my earlier excursions I had collected garden seeds from houses and remaining plants. I figured as it turned to a slightly warmer season I should plant a garden, but if another storm like that came through, all that effort would be lost. I knew that seeds didn't last forever, so planting some portion of them to gain more seeds was probably a good risk. I just couldn't plant them all at once. With some seeds sorted into jars I'd kept in the hotel, the back and side grassy areas of the grounds became a garden, and the days got pretty warm, so I'd try to work in a bikini-style swimsuit. I had fresh water to pour on myself. And if I needed salt, I always had plenty of sea water. Day and night came, and I got used to being a little numb and dealing with bug bites and eating, scavenging and sleeping in pitch black nights. I'd found candles but unless I really needed them I had to conserve them. One night I lit a candle just for a few minutes, looking at the embalmed twenty-month-old girl in my bed. "I just had to see you, baby," I told her.

I "woke" very early in the morning with a freshness I hadn't felt before. My body was still sleeping yet I became aware of my surroundings. Open doors allowed cool breezes to brush across my skin. I heard the outside waves, but the body remained completely asleep. "Is this the *event* for me?" I asked in thought.

I got an answer from the mystical voice, "Not yet. But you are awakening."

I jerked into the body and sat bolt upright. I panted, my heart racing. I was again seeing from the point of view of the body and could see everything normally. I got up, wandering about, touching the walls as if I'd never previously noted their textures. My concept of the space, the coast, the bay, the houses and remaining trees, was just an image, a mockup of "everything that existed" though I was sure it went beyond that. It appeared much as an illusion to me. As my heartbeat settled down, I ate instead of trying to sleep again. As the sun rose up, I went on with my scavenging, trying to keep my attention out for that voice.

Several days later after the rain had abated, I went out on the bicycle through the old town to head for the northeast section of the coast. As if having been held hostage in a dim bunker for days and finally released, I felt elated, and got off the bike and danced about, laughing and crying – something had "blown off" and I couldn't detect what it was, like some nasty plug had been pulled out the back of my head and the acid of hell drained out. Was this related to Seria's strange expression about the universe? The voice, the events – was this what she referred to when she said, "You up there, you are more than island gods?" That phrase had returned to my mind sharply and remained like a stuck record for hours, and I'm sure that I rolled it off my lips dozens of times.

When I got back to the hotel, I took the embalmed girls and placed them in their own beds, as if the hotel rooms were theirs, instead of trying to put them all into my own room. I still kept one of them to not be alone, hoping this would not depreciate me in the eyes of the spirits, the source of the voices. In doing so, I realized that I hadn't been back to the funeral home, wondering what condition it had been in. It still had some embalming fluids and what if I wanted to preserve something else or try to put a little more disinfectant into these bodies to offset the desiccation?

I did go back to the funeral home. The entire outer façade had been peeled away, leaving a stout cement building with steel framing. Wind had ripped anything lose from the inside, exchanging it for sand and decaying herbage from the outside. The display coffins set about at odd angles. Floors had gotten wet and muddy, but the main floor was mostly dry. The basement had damp, angular tiles of mud throughout. I had taken Sarah, my favorite little blonde girl, carrying her with her arms and legs tucked into the wagon. I put her on the dirty embalming table and injected her body with a little more fluid, trying to get the body to appear more lifelike because it had dehydrated enough to make the skin look wrinkled, kind of like she had unnaturally aged. When done, she had a lot more needle holes, but it did feel more realistic and plumped up a little. I realized that she did have a little odor, but I'd gotten used to it. While there, I pulled out some of the paints to take back with me – the girls color had become roughed up and faded, especially their lips which looked bluish.

I took Sarah back to the hotel and let her have her own bathtub, allowing the stuff she was injected with to jell properly again, so I slept with Gretchen that night. I acted like a little girl holding her doll. In the morning I kissed her like a real child. Something had changed – the ugly desires that obsessed me had come to a lull since I got that elated feeling as if something nasty poured out the back of my head. I didn't feel as gross. I didn't feel as sick.

I had a room set up with a camp stove because some of the things needed to be cooked, and as the food got older, it was better to cook it longer. Still on the fourth floor of the hotel, living in all the rooms between the fire doors except for one with broken windows, I was being forced to recognize that the universe wasn't what it previously appeared to be.

Day by day, as I watched the food stores reduce, I again made more trips to the ship and found better tools there to move larger packages from the deck to the ground. The water level inside had gone down significantly, and I found a cart with fat wheels that would travel well along the beach. Getting it out was a challenge as I'd tied empty palettes to ropes and hung them over the side of the ship to act as anchors to offset the weight of the cart until I could get it up to the deck. I'd never needed to be so determined! But once I had it, it still wasn't always fun to move stuff, but it got me what I needed. Pelicans and cranes were collecting along the beach, and it was fun to see they were getting used to me. I sometimes saw large creatures in the ocean, but I had no need to try to go far into the water, as rip currents could easily draw a person out, as had happened to Vincent, and if I was the only person, no one could save me. There was only one good swimming beach on the large island, and it was far off to the northwest side, only partly sheltered by a promontory. I wouldn't be going there either. I just pushed the cart, transporting about a palette's worth of dry goods on it.

I felt another rush penetrate me as some gray images were stripped from the back of my mind, and I could have sworn the sky got brighter, the ground more detailed. It was a change in perception. My range of seeing my immediate environment clearly went from just three to four meters about me, to a hundred meters. It was very strange indeed, like I'd expanded beyond my body.

"Wow! A body can't do this!" I said, my voice still mildly raspy, still recovering after the hurricane.

"Yes. You are a spiritual being," said a voice that was acknowledging me, not exactly like the first, as this one was much more effeminate, even childish. It was like I was seeing through a curtain across the sky, noting just shadows of large beings talking to each other.

"You are doing well," said the original voice, perhaps the one I'd heard during the big storm.

"She knows now," said the girlish voice. "She probably knows she's part of me."

"That's good. Let them all know if it suits you," offered the masculine voice.

"Okay," said the girlish voice. "For those of you that can hear me, you are all part of me, a division in viewpoints to be many people in many places. We are working to make things better. We know we are a little late in comparison to the others. I know you've had some tough experiences due to previous spiritual events. But the same will happen to you. You will be elated and consider it the most wonderful thing. And I – I can't wait." I received a faint vision of the girl, who I expected to be quite pretty, standing back of a reddish stone pedestal, a floating image of a little girl hovering just above it.

I spun about, almost as if seeing beyond this translucent universe into another kind of space. I barely realized that I was dancing among the pelicans and cranes. I giggled and laughed –

there were others somewhere, but it was beyond my current reality on this planet. I wasn't alone. Or I was crazy, and it was just as well if I believed something other than that I was only alone. I made a sand castle along the edge of the beach while I could act like a child and be carefree (trying not to look at debris along the beach that, despite everything being washed away by the storm, still looked much like decayed bodies, though I doubted any could have been left after the hurricane). Then I left it and went back to the cart and took my new goods up the beach to the hotel, singing like a child.

Even when carting the stuff up to the hotel, and carrying it up the steps, I laughed and giggled, not minding today's burden.

When I saw the embalmed little girls, I was embarrassed as if the bigger souls could see me. Did they know I'd kept these children? Certainly they did. If I was part of many souls, then did they all have the same problems – the same obsessions for young women? Perhaps they were working on solving that one too, or maybe that was the whole purpose of their work. I didn't have a final answer with any certainty yet. I just knew I felt better and that they claimed we'd recombine and the bodies, including my body, would probably just fall over like everyone else. I wondered what conditions were experienced in areas of the world where most people were awake, driving and speeding on highways, working with heavy equipment, on trains or aircraft and whether there were any like me who could have survived the initial event only to die seconds, minutes, or even hours later. It was my natural morbid self. I didn't even get emotional about that.

I stayed at the hotel for a few days and cleaned up some smelly remains of fish left behind by the storms. The days were clear. I got a little sun. I ate at the hotel, warming food with the camp stoves, and I'd become elated, swinging around in circles on a bar stool. I laughed, and despite all the death and destruction about me, I called out, "I don't know why I feel so good! Do you voices know why?" I looked up as if someone would answer. But it was quiet. For the moment, it was fine to be the only inhabitant of the island – perhaps of the world. I had complete faith I would be rescued.

After the few days, I felt heavy, stuck and solid, cold and weighted. I felt bloated and lonely, and I was at the edge of crying again, and just out of the blue burst out into heavy tears, crying much like I had during the storm. It was like the walls were melting, the tears boiling up from a volcano, and the body just wanted to bloat in the sun like a dead fish stuck on the beach.

Another storm was moving in. Lightning flashed about the tops of the clouds. Probability would suggest it would not likely be as large as that last storm, but then anything was possible. I listened for any voices, but I heard nothing. I had an intense sense of isolation. I felt lost. I threw my antagonism at these voices, hoping to get their attention, but still nothing.

I packed more of the food that was left at the third level to a higher level of the hotel, improving my kitchen on the fourth floor, which had the least damage of any. I pulled up the fuel bottles and the camp stoves (I'd found more than one) and as the storm hit, I had to decide to leave some of the stuff down there. Overall, despite my tempest-trained anxiety, the storm was a false alarm. It just rained like crazy for a while then moved out. I blubbered at myself for overreacting to such a simple storm.

With a new sense of calm, I sorted some of the collected food and supplies, putting bandages with bandages and canned pokeberries with other canned goods, making fair progress despite my dismissive state. With no ethereal warning, I felt the hotel shaking. It was definitely an earthquake. I stumbled and fell over, hitting my head near the wall and my hands had been thrown into a pile of cans that clinked and crashed over. Well, so much for being calm. The first intense shaking lasted only seconds, gave a moment's pause, then swayed the whole hotel and shook an extraordinary thirty seconds, knocking pictures off the walls and a few jars of seeds off the shelves. Hurricane-damaged glass from the lower levels crashed out of their frames, and the storm grating, which I'd never fully drawn back, clanked as if shook by a giant. After a minute or so I'd gotten up, my knees were unstabilized by a first aftershock, the chairs scooting, but then relaxing just as abruptly, leaving tile and cement dust to settle.

In the next hour, as I sought to assess the mess, another isolated storm buffeted the island. Some objects were getting pulled off trees and shingles and boards of broken houses were getting thrown, but the cell pulled across the island. Lightening flashed about in the distance, directing my attention. As I looked off the far west end of the bay, past the area that had been my old neighborhood, I caught a glimpse of a white line along the horizon. I clomped up the stairwell to the roof to get a better view, eying what appeared to be a notable wave coming in the distance. As I watched longer, I recognized the scale of the wave, so wide I could see neither end of it. The bay, emptying like a bathtub, had become very shallow. The beaches were larger, the sea having pulled out significantly, exposing sunken yachts.

My heart sunk.

I barely breathed.

Fully demoralized, my bowels loosened. I crapped my pants – literally. I rushed back down the stairs and got out of them and wiped up, noting how my skin had lost color, conceiving that I should dye my own skin like I had the dead girls. I quickly put on several layers of clothing, choosing loose items that were not too constricting.

"Fifth floor?" I asked through a window into space, hoping for a response from a voice, hopefully from that girl at the pedestal.

I got one.

"Fifth floor won't help, but go there if you like," said the mysterious voice.

I wailed in terror over the thought that I had felt so good a few days before and now I felt so awful, lost and mortal, left with a dire situation and no help.

I was about to die.

I rushed back up to the roof, begging frantically for assurances. "Is there nothing I can do?" I again watched that monster wave – it was swelling as it came to shallow seas.

I felt a soft answer, "No."

The brevity was nerve wracking. Back down the stairs, I rushed about the rooms, grabbing at my girls to take them to a fifth-floor room. I made some attempt to become theatrical despite my severe anguish. "We'll all die together. This is how I want to remember it, if you demigods allow me to remember. Are you going to make me remember this? Can I remember this? Can I remember how cruel you are? Why have I survived? What game are you playing with me?" I vociferated my broken soliloquy.

I clutched my embalmed girls all about me, watching the wave through the window. I sucked my thumb. I cried. I panted in terror.

The wave, a kilometer or two out, was breaching the coastline to the far right. Tons of water crashed into everything, ripping up anything in its path. I couldn't control my crying now. I let out a low wail, wanting to scream back at the suddenly misogynous gods, being that my girls and I were all that were left.

I was hyperventilating. I felt light. I was about to pass out. The rising wave was cresting a hill, and tons of debris-laden water, as if continuous with the sea, came roaring forwards, rushing back down the hill, washing up to the area around the hotel and on back to the low sea on the other side. The largest crest of the wave then crashed over the same hill. I swear this wave was as tall as the hotel itself. I was more or less counting my final seconds until I'd have everything taken from me.

In the sense of complete futility, I felt calm. I saw my bones. I saw the water beyond the walls and the metal and concrete between them. I saw the embalmed girls. I saw everything as if from outside the body, looking at it. There was no reason to restrain myself with my death inevitable. Spiritually, I'd opened up – I'd no longer be human in just one second.

The mammoth wave crashed into the building, breaking all the remaining windows, slamming water into my lungs and rushing away with everything, including my body and the embalmed girls, sheets, blankets, beds and all my supplies. The flushing water had topped the five-story building, exceeding the height of everything on the island except the monzonite mound.

Horrified and weightless, I looked upon the disaster with a fisheye perspective. In the mayhem I couldn't follow my body. It was gone with the flotsam and jetsam. There was nothing to which I could attach. If the gods above had planned a future for me here, that plan was apparently overwritten by natural disaster.

There in the space above the flowing water, I found my proof for the existence of a disembodied spirit. I spun about, seeing the bigger part of the cloud system had already passed, and it was just raining with moderate wind, but the building was completely slammed, and moving, or at least appeared to be.

A second wave was coming. It was just an encore to the first.

I understood that I was outside the body, above the hotel. I still felt the traumatic remains of the water pushing down my throat. I hadn't noted pain in losing the body itself besides a big tug. In my shock, it was almost like I'd missed the whole event and had just been watching. The water was flowing over and off the area, enough that I could see the shattered windows and mud-washed interior of the hotel building. The entire island, about fifteen kilometers of it, had water flushing across it and back out to the sea.

How could this possibly happen? What was in store? Would my ascension follow?

I watched as this second wave came rushing over the land, flowing around the tallest hills and the monzonite mound, but still flushed completely across the entirety of the island. After that, the gray skies and rain were just normal until a third wave crashed beyond the beaches and up into what was extant of the neighborhoods but didn't flush over the entire island. Even by itself, it would have been a debacle if people were present. But now the population had gone from one to zero. As acting coroner of the island, I had to pronounce myself dead.

Nothing was left. The first through fifth floors of the hotel were completely washed through. Even the interior walls and all the glass in the building were ripped out, leaving the solid cement and steel structure with just remnants attached. I went over toward the ship. It was there, having been aligned into the wave, and it had been lodged into a hill that protected it from the direct force, but water had gone completely over it and thrown it half to its side. Even if I had a body, I would not likely be able to get to that waterlogged food for days, as the draining from the wreckage had been slow. Considering food, that little garden area I'd tried to make behind the hotel was completely gone. It was as if the whole area had been slapped by the hand of God, all my heroic efforts at survival had been fruitless.

I was beaten down with a level of grief I'd never known, a hysteria between reactionary horror and incapacitating agony. I'd never achieved a cognition of the perspective of the deceased, only the handling of the grief for *the bereaved*. What of the individual that had died? What about me? How deep could the horror go?

I feared I'd simply blank out forever. If I'd had the body, I'd be screaming, throwing things, throwing food, and even butchering the embalmed little girls. I was so mad I could have inflicted my brutality on anything left. I would have bulldozed the whole island myself. What good had all this been to have been forsaken, to be mashed by a mountainous wave anyway? Why had I been left alive after the entire population of the island had died? Were these voices behind it? Had the little girl at the pedestal planned it?

It must have been days while I just hung around the area with nothing to do. Stunned by the fact that I was still viewing existence, viewing the surrounding seas and vast skies, and the remnants of the anything-but-lavish Altontown and the island. My parents' house and my treehouse were each leveled to the ground. All that could be seen were the foundation blocks with bent bolts atop them. The trees were shattered to the trunks and not so much as a loose tin can remained. I let myself flow across the beach toward the northwest side, viewing the stump of the lighthouse and the nearby beaches were washed clear of human creations. Further in, the rows of island bungalows were missing and the town itself was shredded to a pile of bricks.

I went gulf-side past the land to the rambling sea and traveled to the main continent. I saw the same general scenes but at a larger scale. Washed out cities lined the coast. Whole cities had been burned because no one had been there to put out the fires. Dead bodies were strewn everywhere, now they rotted mostly away to bones and moldy fabric. I saw grocery stores with dead people and even dead pets. I saw where all the main goods were rotted, and the cans on the shelves were beginning to rust. I saw seeds sprouting in sidewalk cracks and grass growing that hadn't been cut. I saw broken windows on houses and people had died where they were. Depending on the location, and thus the time in the cities, people were sleeping, or more were up starting their day. In one there was more people arriving at work, corpses in parking lots and lines of traffic mostly just slowed and stalled. Along the larger roads there was a slew of collisions, no evidence that anyone moved after the accidents or that anyone provided any help, emergency vehicles still in their stations. The same graphic images were everywhere, including a gymnastics center where a girl's body laid next to the uneven bars, her neck broken, and her coach slumped on the mat nearby. A church group had apparently picked up a group of children, who lined the sidewalk between the bus door and the church's main entry.

Without a body I had a frantic sense of need for flesh, need for people. Day by day, having nothing else to do, I looked in every house, every basement, every car, every floor of every building, trying to find a person or evidence of a person's presence. If I'd taken over a five-story hotel and filled it with food, fuel and clothing, certainly someone else could come up with a similar plan. I wanted to find a building with a pile of bodies that had been thrown out of it, or crudely marked graves nearby. I hoped to find a church with stacks of goods in the pews or a school used as a warehouse. Following railways and roads, I moved orderly through major cities that had been the home of millions of people. I hoped to find a highway that had been cleared between some building and some storehouse. I hoped to find a line of vehicles and trucks of fuel near a structure where it wasn't normal, or a parking garage or shopping mall full of pallets. I examined streetcars and bridges, trains and boats of various sizes.

I traversed not just cities and counties, but meridians and parallels. There was nothing. Certain I'd not rambled aimlessly, I found no evidence of human habitation. But I did arrive at the self-assertion that I couldn't die as a spirit.

In remote areas I looked for similar organizing and being that this was further from most food warehouses, these were open roads where people would have to scavenge to gather goods. I'd expected to pass a farm with animals that still had food and hadn't resorted to eating each other, as pigs would. I expected rows of beans and corn being cultivated. I examined every granary for fresh grain, not a molded pile of rubbish. I was relentless as curious. I was happy to be able to go kilometer after kilometer without walking. I was upset that even as a soul I believed I was the only one left. I stayed in people's houses, pretending to have a body and sleep in their bedrooms, as long as there were no grizzly carcasses in their beds.

I'd recalled the name of Sandy's town, having a rough idea where it had been. It took me several days to find the farming community while I searched the geographical area, having found the major defining rivers, and settled into the small town of New Missoula, with a welcome sign and boasting "Population 2740." I set about combing the streets one by one. I had known her address, so I first scanned the street signs. In one direction they were all "First," "Second," "Third" and so on. In another, they were named by types of trees. Passing up the signs, I finally found one that rang a bell, "Hawthorn." I scanned house numbers, finally finding 1102. This was the house – a small brick home with a simple tile roof, and only a few windows including an oddly square picture window centered on the side of the house in a bay window structure. A double walkway led to the front door, perhaps to allow access to the front porch with a delivery truck. At the side and back was a small ragged garden inside a picket fence. A black truck sat in the driveway, now covered with fallen leaves and dust, as well as weeks of accumulated bird droppings. I nervously looked at this structure, flowing as a ghost should, creeping through the picture window. Inside I noted restored plaster walls covered with wallpaper, displaying pretty yellow flowers and green vines. The woodwork was very plain and painted white. The floors throughout were hardwood, with various rugs, and all the furniture matched the theme of each room. It wasn't half as cluttered as I would have expected for a small house.

I found a bathroom next – inside was a body in the bathtub. It had been horribly eaten up by decay, having been left in a full bath. Long hair had wicked up disgusting rot, matting it as if she'd died in a swamp. There was only a small area I could see the brunette color. And on the countertop of the lavatory was a set of summer clothing topped with a pair of silky green panties. I'd recognized those panties as Sandy's, and certainly she had died in the event, not later.

I went on through the house. In an upstairs room, a small finished area in the attic lit by dormer windows, I found a pretty, unspoiled gloss white daybed. But on the far side, sprawled next to a white wooden dresser, was the body of a girl who'd been about fourteen, very slender, and the dried corpse appeared emaciated. This was Sandy's little sister, Charlotte, whom I'd only seen a photo of, recalling she'd had a cute smile with braces on her teeth. Even she didn't appear distressed. Upon the dresser was a stack of clothing, including a set of pajamas that appeared familiar, the set I'd lost in the laundry room at college – evidencing that it was Sandy that had taken them as a souvenir.

My solitary fascination led me to act as if visiting Sandy, as if I had chosen to come for a visit. I went on to the parent's room as if asking them if they'd seen my earring, finding her mother had fallen over by the bed in the process of getting up and dressing, having only one shoe on. Her father had remained in the bed, the sheets and mattress completely ruined on his side.

I'd covered the whole house, so I went back to the bathroom, viewing Sandy's rotted corpse. It was such a gruesome image compared to the beauty I'd seen leaving at the dorm, or earlier when she and I had some very warm and lusty encounters, including the dangerously risqué moments in the laundry, another night when a full moon shone brightly through the windows.

I tunneled through my grief, recalling how we'd kissed, how we'd wrapped about each other, how she said my body elicited her purest lust. In the dorm we had a lovely evening when the others were at a party, and I danced about naked to tantalize her while I swirled a chiffon nightgown about me. Such moments had been memorable beyond what most tourists would get from visiting Altontown. What hurt deepest was the lack of acknowledgment of the relationship to others. We were as secret as we could be. She was terrified of being caught, vilified and ridiculed. For me, I thought it would have been the critical moment of freedom, being forced to admit to the world my identity, for which I'd never felt there was a choice.

I found myself in the pretense of, partly envisioning, normal daily actions about me, allowing false images to overwrite reality. I pretended to make breakfast, almost seeing the skillet I'd pulled from the lower cabinet, pulling eggs from the refrigerator, and cracking them. Delving lucidly into my acceptable delusion, I pretended to pour orange-mango juice, even tasting it when I pretended to pick up the cup. I imagined pulling plates from the cabinet (though they looked distinctively like my mother's) and pretended to eat at the table. Cleanup, of course, was a snap.

I returned to Charlotte and Sandy's room upstairs. I imagined myself as a solid person, dressing as I would, and getting into Sandy's bed, telling Charlotte, "I'm waiting for your sister. We are in love." I let my subconscious toy with my desires.

Charlotte materialized from the position of her corpse on the floor, mystically rising as a beautiful, wispy mirage in the late afternoon filtered light. "Hey, Miranda. I'm glad you came, and my sister won't be up here from her bath for a while. Can we play?" she asked. Then she got up and came to my side, kneeling by the bed. I turned my face up. She leaned in to kiss me.

Indulging for hours I imagined being held and gently loved by this girl. As the day moved on, the light dimmed, and her image progressed from translucent to solid. I held this apparition as my own image also coalesced into an apparent solidity. I saw myself as wearing a favorite green chiffon nightgown with matching panties. Her white nightgown was very light cotton eyelet. I could feel the material against my skin. I could sense her tender caresses.

Sandy, in full vivid realistic form, walked in wearing the cutest pink and yellow shorts and nightshirt. "Oh – you guys started without me," she said. There was a discrepancy in reality such that the bed didn't bounce about as she moved across us, settling between myself and the wall.

Being between the two girls, I visualized a likeness of that night when between Debbie and Tori on the big air mattress in my treehouse, when they promised to devour me. Perhaps the imagery and the actual recalls were blending. "Oh, you are so delicious, Miranda," said Sandy, as she and Charlotte kissed all over me.

I moved from pure imagination into a sleep-like, dream-like state until morning, then woke as the true view of the space about me impinged upon my perception, realizing again I had only been positioned against an empty mattress, having no flesh of my own, seeing Charlotte's creepy remains lying where it always had on the rug, my existence consumed by the dread of the dead world.

I was terrified of the idea that I could get forever lost within this composite imagery. I had to move on. I first moved to Sandy's corpse in the bath, attempting to dispel my artificial image of her, differentiating my subjective illusions from the objective reality. It might have been different had I recognized the presence of the soul I'd known as Sandy, and perhaps even Charlotte, but neither were there. I had to acknowledge my own hopeless delusion, my own selfish wishes, and persist with my search, as there wasn't anything else I could do. Though I loathed to continue scanning the world for signs of life, I forced myself to break out and intrepidly continue. After all, which was worse, a delusionary cage I may never escape, or the real hell that completely surrounded me, yet had the slightest degree of hope?

FOUR

A New Life

I'd been searching for signs of life in yet another small town, finding myself resting near a century-old statue of a man in a broad hat in midafternoon. The town square vacant, a centrally located courthouse of limestone was of use only to a handful of pigeons. A row of two-story structures of storefronts and apartments lined most of the four sides. A north-south highway ran through like a ribbon, ready for any traffic, though I knew there would be none. The day was crisp, and the trees were bare. Patches of ice remained in alleys and at the shadowed edges of the small-town structures. Forlorn and alone, I superimposed upon an immovably-fixed cement monument bearing an iron cannon complete with a plaque specifying its origin. I pondered the fact that I was dead, floating about as a lost spirit with no people to haunt or to be born from, and needed to wait for the spirits above to act. As far as I knew, being that I'd found no signs of human life, I'd been the last fatality, not having anyone to record it. I had nothing – not the faintest knowledge of what to do. I hadn't taken the book at the airport. I hadn't made friends of the zealots. I hadn't even found any of the relevant books open to an informative page. To whom could I now inquire if these spirit voices failed to answer? I hadn't paid attention to the mystical clues, all the intricacies of the spiritual realm about me I'd failed to observe.

So, I was particularly pleased when a voice calmly spoke, "Come with me," with a touch on a shoulder I didn't have. Guided by this unknown force, I was traveling faster than the sun's shadow on the mainland. I was headed toward the coast, back of a significant bay notably larger than the one on the island, sectioned off as harbors with piers and wharfs. But we passed up the bay and a major city and went on to a small town, then on to an apparent historical reenactment settlement full of relics of a bygone era. There in the center of town was a modest church with a school and parsonage, and a dozen additional houses with clay-daubed chimneys, barns and utility structures, all restored to like-new condition. Here were the kinds of things I'd been hoping to find – a stockpile of boxed goods in the middle of the old church, stacks of fuel containers by an adjacent earthen structure, and I could hear, in a muted sense, the small engine noises of a generator.

Having been pushed inside the parsonage, I found myself within a room with a fireplace, in which an active fire was popping and sparking. In that room, there was a middle-aged fellow and a young woman. She was lying back in a hand-made bed frame that allowed the back to incline, and the front area to drop. There was a cord running in through the door to a clamp-on work light above her, delivering dim reddish incandescent light. Between that and the firelight, the young woman didn't look very old. Perhaps twenty at most, but she was probably a few years younger. She was likely a blond girl, as her hair shone gold in the mixed light. Nor did her light eyes reveal their true color, making them appear gray.

"Daddy! I'm scared. What if there are no souls to take the baby?" said the girl, panting, looking up to the fellow.

He didn't appear to be a large man, being somewhat modest in structure but manly in form. As she spoke I could get a better view of her. She now appeared to be just a teenage girl. His visage solemn, he replied, "It's the best we can do, dear. Everyone else – we have to try."

They were preparing for a birth.

Grief washed over me though I had no eyes to cry with.

The fellow kissed all over her. As if he'd repeated it often, he stated, "I'm sorry but being your father doesn't keep me from being responsible for the human race." Taking the role of obstetrician, he had ice for her and all the other things were ready – a pot on the fire in the fireplace boiled water. Towels, baby clothing and diapers had been placed upon an antique bassinette.

The fellow looked up and prayed as if talking to the same voices I'd been hearing.

The same force that brought me here by gently pushing now drew me forward. As if hands were on me, I was pulled to that pregnant belly as if I were a small child lying on my back across it, but my head dipping to the convergence of her legs. I looked up and saw the man as he checked her dilation.

She panted and pushed. He checked her again. She panted and pushed more.

As the head came into view, I experienced a strange sense of merging. Whatever this baby was going to be, I was about to become it. It moved a little further – some strange phenomenon sucked me into the baby. Like water soaking into a sponge, I fell into the flesh.

"Girl," he cried.

She cried too. "I've got a girl."

I was now the baby girl. I was overwhelmed. I figured that at birth everyone would lose their memory, but I retained an odd awareness. Though I was the baby, I wasn't forgetting. I experienced everything including the water, the heat and cold. I felt tickles. I felt pain. A breast was offered, and I knew best to take it, but the body knew what to do on its own.

A disorientation swung across me as if it were an attempt to take my full memory. Flashbacks of wild things I'd experienced crossed my mind: my own death at the hotel, and before that embalming the bodies, all the nasty stuff with Tori and my girlfriends before the event, my father's empathy and my mother's suspicion. I saw the storm surge washing up into the hotel to the third-floor threshold. I vividly saw the dead teenage girl I'd wrapped myself around. I felt the need to let all those images go, but I fought to keep them.

At that point a white light covered everything. Much like the time I'd been at the beach and thought I could see through some curtain into space, I heard voices. One voice was saying, "She'll be smart because her mind won't be reset to believe this is *zero time*. We'll take that memory curtain down." It wasn't the voice of either parent. It was from somewhere else, an effeminate, girlish voice, likely the girl I'd seen at the pedestal. The blanketing white light curtailed, as did the sense of my blanking mind, the idea of *zero time* set aside like a useless coat. I felt wonderful as if experiencing a resurrection, a revivification of myself as an entity.

I watched with great wonder the new area, focusing only on those things nearest me in accordance with the limited capability of my new source of vision. It was myopic compared to the breadth of perspective I'd had when disembodied, yet I watched with great curiosity. Did my parents know I had nearly twenty years of memory behind these newborn eyes?

They watched me but said little. If there were conversations, they happened when my body was sleeping. I dreamed as I normally would have, but when I woke, the horrendous sense that I had been waking in hell had been ameliorated by the fact I was with others now, people I could get to know.

Within a couple months, while breastfeeding upon Mother, they were discussing what to name me.

"We still haven't arrived at a name for our first progeny," noted my new father.

I heard my young mother's voice, "I don't want a name. Everyone else's names are used and gone. She's just a loving grace to me. A name will come in time."

"I think it's time to give the child a moniker. We can make one up – a new name. Something that would not remind us of the others. Maybe a word that means she stayed," he suggested.

She tried, eyes rolling about. "Remained? Waited? Still here? Left behind? Lost on Earth? None of that works. I like Dalila, but it reminds me of a lady that worked the main gate here at the village," she bemoaned.

He tried, "Permanent? Foundation? Grounded? Without a baby name book to translate meaning, I'm lost. But most names would be familiar anyway. I like Dahlia. I like Lana."

"Put them together Daddy. It will sound a little like Dalila, but it wouldn't be."

He doodled, then suggested, "Daliana? Dalilana? Dahilana?" Pursing his lips, he added, "Lanadahlia or Lanadala just doesn't work for me." He made a note and stuck it under a salt shaker on the table. "I'll locate a name book yet. We'll try a few and see which one sticks."

"One of those would be good for my pretty baby," she intoned to me. "Which do you like? Daliana? Dahilana?"

I'd had a girlfriend in college whose name was "Nada Liana." She preferred both names, which we spoke like one word, "Nadaliana." I liked the name "Daliana" better, but to differentiate from my memory, I preferred "Dahilana." I put up a pouty face on "Daliana." I tried to smile on "Dahilana."

In the next days' feedings and diaper changes, my parents tried those and more names. On a subsequent afternoon, I heard a door slam, and Father came in. "I found a name book back in the city library," said my new father. "Dalila – desired, languishing – and that means, um, forced to stay behind in an unpleasant place or situation. Lana – little rock – used of a child. Dahlia – a kind of brightly colored flower. Hum – no pictures."

Mother asked, "What about Liana?"

"Um ... Liana – wrapped with vines, it says. Makes me want to pick one of our variations." He put the book down and picked up the little paper with the mixed-up names.

"Ha – given a moment's thought, Dahilana could be a small flower left behind in the rocks. And then Daliana would be rocks wrapped in vines, or languishing vines?" Daddy came, held out his big arms, saying many additional potential names.

I fussed on all of them up to that point.

He tried again the variations of the names they'd coined, "Daliana would you like picked up?"

I pouted the best that little body could do.

Frustrated, he tried again, "Okay. Dahilana would you like to be picked up?"

I pushed at my arms and knocked off the fussiness.

"Looks like Dahilana it is, though I find it harder to say."

Mother came up beside him, "We'll get used to it or just pick another name."

"Well, we could pick it. But it seems she's picking it for us. And oddly it means something close to what we were going after, though either would do. Ah – Dahilana for now."

The name would stick because I fussed on everything else they tried, and it would grow with me as the body became capable of speaking. Despite being from some distance across the planet, the language was much the same, with the pronunciation being the trickiest part. I learned quickly though, being that I could recall most of my previous lifetime prior to my birth. I could pick up the language variations, but I couldn't speak well until the body developed during the next months. Parents are usually adjusted to the idea of being needed to teach everything, but once I had control of my body, there was little else to teach but I hid my previous knowledge and just appeared to absorb information and language very quickly. I couldn't overdo it anyway, as I needed help with food, bedding and laundry. I still needed diapers because the body wouldn't allow control of all its functions, at least not as much as I'd hoped. Sometimes, this poor little flower languished behind in smelly rocks.

Within a few years, I was just a miniature person, as precocious as a child could be, as I was retentive of a fair proportion of my previous lifetime's memories. I persisted in downplaying my capability for my parents, though my language was complete in accordance with my previously intended profession. I continued to need help with laundry, but I could wash single items. Little hands were awkward with knives and scissors, so I had to avoid those to keep my fingers. I found it frustrating to be such a small child after having been to college. But who in the society wouldn't have wanted such an opportunity to relive from birth and fix everything you screwed up before? But without the multitude of the population, there wasn't nearly the advantage.

When I was a little over three years old, I finally told my mother, who still looked very young. "I remember a big storm." I had just stood up in the bathtub, waiting for Mother to select a towel.

"What? Last year? There was a big storm. Do you remember that?" she tried, grabbing a towel and unfolding it.

"Yes. But I mean four years ago," I waited to see if she became frantic. Recognizing her natural control, I continued, "I died in a hotel."

"What?" she said like the seaplane's engine when it first fired. We'd been in an upstairs bathroom in late afternoon, taking advantage of the sun shining through the windows at this hour. To the degree that fresh light danced about as it filtered through the trees, her harsh expression lit likewise.

I looked about the old bathroom in the church's attached parsonage, a little bashful due to Mother's surprise. I noted the remaining water in the tub as I pondered a revision on my statement, the water rippled from the drips off my precious living body. We had running water because Daddy found a way to refill a water tower and limit the leakage by cutting off most of the water mains that led about the town.

Insofar as I was an unusually precocious child, I thought it best to reserve my conduct to expectations of my body size, judging by their expressions when I'd surpassed their ability to handle it, as had just happened. So, I kept it simple, "It was a big square house – a hotel. Five stories tall," I said, holding my hand out like a child, though I clearly didn't have to, to indicate a count of five.

She reached to me with the towel on her hands, allowing me to step into it. "So how did you die?" she asked, not really expecting an answer.

"Biggest wave. It washed everything away," I said, flailing my arms about.

I could see her tentative expressions fumbling their way through her mind, finding their way to her face. "Were you a boy or a girl?"

"A girl," I said and pondered. "I was nineteen." I placed my hands on my chest as I felt the compression from my final moment in the hotel. Some of the recollections and emotions revivified in my mind, images of my embalmed girls and sadness about losing them. Then I recalled my treehouse and my parent's house when finding my parents dead. I recalled my frantic attempts to call for help when there was none. I'd lost the entire town of people, including my own life. I was recalling my daddy, the one that supported me most.

"So, where were you?" she asked, not expecting another answer.

An image of the town's hand-painted wooden welcome sign came fresh into my mind. It was white and shades of blue with a hemp-brown rope border. "Altontown," I said, not sure she'd know where that was.

I felt a jitter in her hands as she rubbed me down with the towel. "Um – famous for its warm climate. A lighthouse. Nice beaches. A hotel. I see," she said. "A vacation town. I read about it once. I wanted to go there to visit. I guess I shouldn't want to go there anymore?"

I pursed my lips and shook my head. It wouldn't be a vacation spot for anyone now. It hadn't been much of a vacation for me even before the event. I must have dropped a few tears as I thought about it. I wanted her to have more data to match up to, and verify what I'd said, so I added, "And they had a little bay by the hotel. On the other side of the island they had a blowhole that shot water way up – near the lighthouse," I informed her as I knew at this point I was using words she'd never taught me.

Eyes wide and lips quivering, she whispered, "Oh my God."

She helped me get dressed after the bath and let me into a big bedroom that had perhaps been a servant's or a nun's. The furniture was simple in form but very well constructed of hardwood. The walls were uneven, but the windows were lined with thick boards, and there were two layers of window glass. The room had a tall fireplace, inside of which was a metal stove box, complete with vents and a heat exchanger built into it.

My father had been out working on some pumps. When he arrived, my mother spoke quietly with him. I could not hear the conversation. A few minutes later, he poked his head into the bedroom, came to sit on the edge of the big bed, and said, "Come."

I looked up with uncertainty. He patted on his lap and said, "Come," again, and this time I saw his concerned eyes.

I moved forward. He pulled me up and cuddled me against him, holding and rocking me. "It's time I tell you something. I know you might think I'm a little weird. But I hear voices sometimes. Like someone is watching us – more than one voice. Do you ever hear anything like that?"

I nodded slowly.

"What do they tell you?"

"They warn me of danger," I first said. He was quiet. I then added, "They brought me here."

I watched carefully for his likely skepticism. I could feel him tense, then relax. He cleared his throat. "Yeah. Well. I was told you'd come. The voice said you would remember."

I looked up at him, a little sadness in my eyes. He wasn't skeptical at all. I nodded again.

He nodded with a loving, welcoming look. That looked turned sour as he asked, "So you know about the world?"

I nodded. Tears fell to either side of my face. I turned to put my head against his chest. He clutched about me. We both cried, then the cries broke way to heavier grief, our chests heaving in sobs.

Over the next few years I often nestled between my parents, if Father slept in the house at all. Often, he'd work until he was tired and sleep wherever he was, usually in one of several houses. I remember one night in particular when I was six or seven years old. We'd all had a nice evening around the house – probably another cold evening where being together with the fireplace was the best idea. Mother came into the bedroom where I'd already been cuddled in next to Father. She was wearing a proper nightgown. She pulled up onto the bed, saying, "We'll all sleep together tonight." She stroked my hair and caressed my back and shoulders.

Soon I was completely asleep. But I was lucidly dreaming, seeing images of a violent argument among two young women, realizing I was one of them. I didn't know how the fight started, but we were knocking each other onto the floors in our home, and I saw this girl I'd knocked into a cabinet. I got the impression she was a sister. I smacked at her incessantly. "Little bitch!" I yelled. But she acted half knocked out and slumped to the floor. I grabbed at her though I knew she'd protest. I pulled down to lie along her body and kissed her, saying, "I don't want to fight you. I want to love you." She mumbled, "Don't you dare." I said, "Oh, but I will." I got her pants off and looked at her beautiful body. "There, was that so bad?" I had asked her. She kicked forcefully at my shoulders and head, intent on hurting me. I pulled back, a little shocked at her violence. She appeared to have overexerted herself and settled down. I sat there stunned, expecting the situation was over. I'd been pretty stupid and would have said sorry if I hadn't realized I was bleeding from my nose and lips.

When she finally turned to get up, she was holding her head, cussing. She stood up there in the kitchen, getting her bearings. She was so pretty even in her grief. I had said, "They are just body parts. It's not like we have to be so ridiculous about it. What did you think?"

Then she grabbed a pan and swung around too quickly for me to duck, slamming it into my head. While I was knocked out, she cut my pants off and gouged some skin with the scissors as she cut, which is what I felt as I awoke. She tore at my clothes and left me naked, bloody and bruised. She cried with the harshest disdain, "How do you like that, *little bitch!*" She inflicted numerous strikes with the heavy steel pan again, breaking my toes and feet, cracking my kneecaps, and breaking the edges off my hips. Then she laid me on my back and beat at my ribs, breasts and collar bones. She wasn't satisfied until the bones broke audibly.

I smelled urine and feces and nearly gagged on the blood. I could no longer move while she banged that pan on my legs and arms, bruising my flesh and breaking my bones. Then she laid my hand out, though it remained curled up, and slammed the pan flat on it. "That's for grabbing at me!" She wasn't satisfied that she broke my fingers and did it again. Then she held the big pan up over her head. I could barely turn my eyes enough to see her, the vision being contrasted by light above. "By the way, I didn't," she finally answered my question. "I don't like girls like that. But you wouldn't understand. Whore! So, who's the bitch now?" Then she slammed the pan onto my head so hard my body jolted from head to foot. She didn't stop with one, she continued beating me again and again until I was out of the body, watching my own blood pour from the gashes she'd created in my skull.

I woke from the horrifying nightmare with a start, at what must have been just across the edge of death in the dream – the likely ending of an actual past life. My heart was beating. I was sweating, having been up against my parents' sleeping bodies. I pulled up and cried, looking about in horror, fearing a frying pan would strike me from the darkness.

I heard that ephemeral girl voice and a presence as if someone was gently touching my shoulder. "There's a point when the spirit will find her own, true body. That is coming." But there was a sense of an uncertainty of the time, and that the people who were behind the voices had a time span different than mine.

I sat up for a while. I checked my memory, recalling my current name as Dahilana, and recalling my name as Miranda before reincarnating. I recalled the surreptitious activities with my girlfriends at my treehouse. I recalled the island's blockish hotel. I recalled crawling through the ship to get supplies after the storm, and I recalled the swelling waters of the huge hurricane and how I cried so hard. Then I recalled the later tidal wave and water rushing over my body, taking everything.

I hadn't even realized I'd been doing it, but I was crying, getting loud.

Father raised up. "What's going on, little one?"

"I saw my death again. A different death," I said, but I didn't really expound on the dream recall of getting the shit beat out of me with a pan, or why. Perhaps there were a lot of "past life deaths" that would, in time, run over me emotionally.

"Oh, sweet thing," he said. He reached to me and I pushed into his big strong arms. He caressed my back lightly. I clung to him like a baby koala. I needed that comfort.

Mother woke and reached up to kiss me. Her nuzzling was so gentle and warm.

"Mommy," I said, my voice still quivering in horror. Her pretty eyes were bright. Gosh, she was beautiful.

Another day I went to a bathroom. Being that the house was a parsonage, there were few mirrors but there was one hanging on the wall near the doorframe. I climbed up on the sink, so I could see myself. I'm not sure why I never really noticed it before – I was a beautiful girl, even comparing to all the girls I'd seen on the beaches at the island before I'd died, even prettier than any of the girls I'd embalmed, perhaps even prettier than I'd been as Miranda. Was this classic narcissism, evidenced by a rush of heat entering my face? I didn't want to get "sexually sick" like I had been in the previous life, or like that past-life vision I'd gotten in the dream. Why had I become so obsessed? I wasn't sure. I didn't expect to have much trouble as a young child, as I was about six or seven by this time. But there I was, wishing I could have a girlfriend.

Another day I had been in the kitchen with my mother. Again, I recall she was pretty, and she was showing me how to make a cake. Her hands were on my hands moving an electric mixer. "Hurry. We need to get this done and turn off that spare generator, so your father doesn't think we're up to something," she said. I watched the mixer going around. It made me think of the hurricane – and I got a flash of an image – myself with one of the smaller embalmed girls, painting her with dye so she'd look real again. I got scared of the image, suddenly seeing water rushing at me during my last moments of my previous life just before my body was tugged away from me. In the present, it was like dirty water was in my throat.

I could only assume that my previous recall of my death had been missing some details. This image had a strong sense of gagging and drowning due to the sheer force of the water, shoving my lungs full to the point of bursting while slamming me and everything else, including my embalmed girls, against the walls then through and out of the building. Water had broken out all the windows and tugged everything through and out the other side. It looked almost like the building was moving one way and the water was moving the other, much like the effect of a stick hanging in flowing water almost looks like it is moving upstream. A slightly previous image hit me – the water rose up and pushed my body almost as soon as the windows crashed while I was screaming, trying to hold onto my little human dolls. One of those embalmed girls was like my current body. I then saw earlier images, my hand working the needles I'd used to pull fluids from the bodies and replace them with the rubberizing embalming fluids. I missed my girl dolls. I missed them a lot. I wished I had some here.

I had tried to keep my hands with Mother's, turning the mixer around in the bowl, but again, being overwhelmed by the motions, I just busted out crying, "Mama!"

She picked me up and carried me out of the kitchen, so she could shut off a small generator. It was cold outside, perhaps some part of winter. We came back in, closing the door, and she took me to a rocking chair in the living room. She pulled at my hair, stroking it. I cried for a bit and she asked, "Why are you so upset. This is more than before. What is up?"

I cried but tried to put together my words. "I remember, mama. I remember – I'm sick and nasty."

The look on her face! I'm sure it was the last thing she expected.

I detected a spiritual sense of a hand – like someone was pushing at me from behind. "Go ahead. Let it out," said one of those voices.

Mother asked, "Did you touch yourself there?" she said, pointing to my crotch.

I nodded but I kept on crying, trying to motion that I was upset about something else.

She tried again, "Something from what you remember – before us? Something on the island?"

"Yeah," I nodded again. The words formed in my mind as if someone else was trying to speak for me. I finally let them loose. "When the people dropped, I wasn't alone. I'd spent the night with girlfriends, and we were, like, really girlfriends. When I woke, they were still, stiff, dead, not breathing, not even starting to stink. But if I'd known everyone was dead I would have done even more. Then – then when I – when I realized everyone was dead I stole kids and embalmed them at my daddy's funeral home. I embalmed babies and girls to keep them like dolls. I didn't bury them unless they rotted. And – and – if I could have, if they would have allowed, I would have done it before – before everyone died. I would have kept embalmed children as dolls. I wrote a story about a crazy person who kept dead people as dolls." I snorted a high cry, feeling like I was about to pass out. The grief was so sharp, stabbing through my mind, like being cut right behind the ear with a knife. It hurt! It was like my heart was about to break apart and run away, fearing I'd do it more harm than good. I was throwing my arms as if to throw away the emotional pain. But then the "backwater grief" behind that came rushing through. It was a harsh flow of emotion, stifling my perceptions of the world about me. Once it wasn't so sharp, it finally felt good to cry.

As I calmed down Mother said, "I've got a cake to get into the oven. I'm sure it's warm enough. Are you okay if I let you stay here and cry?"

I nodded. I looked up at her, wondering her inclination by her indistinct expression. Perhaps she was thinking about stabbing me and butchering me for dinner or leaving me in the cold to freeze. She tumbled me into a sofa and moved to the kitchen, though I slinked along the floor to the kitchen doorway. I stealthily watched as she worked and mumbled. She was so beautiful, and I could only think of her like my girlfriends, despite the fact that I'd come out of her. She mumbled some more, fully engaged in some conversation as if she'd been on a working telephone.

I slowly walked through, barely being noticed, and sat up on a chair by a small breakfast table. I watched her. She bit her lip when she noticed me. "Mommy, you are so beautiful," I said, trying to give her a smile.

But she worked with the pans and oven. She bit her lip again. She said, "You are so beautiful too. I'd never got to the point of telling father that I didn't – um – didn't want to marry a boy."

I was bluntly surprised. I closed my stinging eyes, feeling elated, and I recalled again what it was like to be without a body and travel here, then the last few moments before birth. I was glad I'd arrived.

With great wonder, I was looking through everything, seeing all the way to the sun. The great sun was burning very brightly, and a sunspot was just passing me. I thought again about the planet and wondered if there was any other life on it beside my parents. I also felt the body, completely superimposed with the images I saw otherwise. Great energy rushed away from me at the same time, and being out in space was necessary to handle the magnitude of it. Mother must have taken me, as I recognized minutes later I was cuddling against her.

Once again, I was overwhelmed with the moment of the wave crashing through the island's hotel. I saw the moment of the groundswell from the hurricane when a wave crashed into the first floor and began dumping water inside. I saw the moment of my *previous* birth in a proper hospital and then my first birthday as Miranda at my parents' house on the patio before the treehouse was built. I saw the next previous death, where I'd apparently been treated like a whore, my hands were tied, and I was begging for mercy. But someone decided that they'd had enough of me and beat the shit out of me, making sure I was in complete agony before they cut my throat, leaving me gasping painfully for seconds until I lost consciousness. I'd been a teenage girl acting like a hooker, intrepidly (and stupidly) getting into a car with some guys that offered some alcohol and money, thinking it would just be a silly ride around a city block. I'd tried to keep a girlfriend with me, but they scorned her and pushed her away, leaving her stunned on the sidewalk. I didn't have much shape, but I was sassy, and they liked that. Through the torment and torture, I later endured, I couldn't at this time recollect how long I'd been held captive.

These predominating emotional charges from two lifetimes ago blew away from me, allowing my mind to return to the image after being blown out of the hotel by the wave when I was out in the ocean, watching the water bob up and down, trying to stay with the water despite the fact I didn't have a body. Being retentive of the need for having flesh, I had often dipped under the surface because it was less disconcerting to be in something rather than the free air, seeing slightly murky water and a myriad of sea creatures.

I felt my attention return to the body where Mother had placed it on the sofa, but I could see about the house. I was watching Mother working in the kitchen just as if I were out in the rooms. It was strange. From above the body I could see, and feel, that it was still breathing. I felt awake, but the body appeared to be sleeping. Interestingly enough, it didn't alarm me.

In mental images, different explosions passed by, but they were also past life in some regard. I felt a thought that became a soft voice, saying, "I feel my selves. I see them. When I blew that emotion off I'm sure that emotional charge blew out of them too. It had a domino effect on the ones that are left. Many on my planets are scattered. I guess I didn't divide up as much as the others – just millions, maybe only thousands, a mere fraction compared to others. I'm there – see that beautiful little girl – oh – so much like me! See her Mother – so pretty. I feel every one. See that...." The voice faded beyond my ability to discern further words. I couldn't be certain whether she was directing her attention to me. It could have been any of at least thousands of people.

In returning from the images I floated toward my body, felt like I was climbing in, and then was simply consumed by the essence as if I'd been fully asleep and just waking. I opened the body's eyes and looked about the room, seeing the window panes and the sofa, the old walls and a lamp. I sat up, confounded by the whole thing as if I'd just come back from a tour of the galaxy. I pulled off the sofa and awkwardly ambled back to the kitchen. "Mommy? Did I fall asleep gradually or just pass out?"

"Oh – there you are. I thought you passed out – and I watched you – then you were sleeping fine." She didn't comment on how heavy my emotion had been.

"I went all over the universe," I said with a smile.

"I don't really know what that means," she said with her typical tentative style.

"I saw the sun, and sunspots, and felt other bad things disappear," I said.

"So, I guess you are saying that nap was good?" she tested. She put a small plate of vegetables in front of me. "You can have some cake after Father gets here."

I shrugged, becoming extremely tired again. I reached for the table and failed to catch it. Then I was falling over.

I saw great images of galaxies as if I'd been pushing them about with great enthusiasm. I was having so much fun positioning things in the universe. I was elated, ecstatic, about pushing huge masses like black holes into place, working with other very powerful but invisible souls. The images ceased as quickly as they began.

At present again, I recognized the position of the body and looked up. I saw the ceiling above me. I saw Mother's beautiful concerned face looking down. Her hand was behind my head. "You hit your head, baby, you might need a stitch. Let me see it."

I felt pain in the back of my head, but it didn't penetrate my consciousness and didn't beg me for action. I pulled up, allowing her to settle me to her lap and bend me over to examine the back of my head. She lifted at the hair, and it stung a little. She pulled me up with her toward the sink. With one hand she pulled a bar stool by the counter and sat me there. She washed my scalp and looked more carefully. "I don't think we'll need to stitch that. Can you tell me what happened?"

"I saw space. I saw planets. I was pushing something big and heavy, like for the center of a big swirling galaxy. I was happy," I said.

"Oh? What did you look like when you were doing that?"

"I didn't – I didn't see it. No one else looked like anything but they were there, talking thoughts," I said.

"Oh," was all that Mother said. But she was slow and contemplative for the next few hours. She cleaned, mostly sweeping, and washing dishes. She sometimes looked at me as if I were dangerous.

I played like a child and picked up my own spaces. I couldn't stand it anymore and went to the kitchen when she returned there to start dinner. "Mommy," I finally broke the silence. "What's wrong?"

"Come, little one," she said. I went to her and we cuddled into a big chair together. It was a very comfortable and familiar place for us. "I had a friend, before the event, that would say things like that. No one else did. No one else, even when I badgered them, would say. Like you, I had a girl over some nights before. We were affectionate, though completely hidden from Father. She pushed at my shoulder to wake me and said it was the 'final spiritual event.' Her eyes were so wide, and she looked so happy. 'I'm going home!' she shrieked – with complete joy. She climbed out the window and rushed home to her parents. After the 'event,' I found her later as we looked for living people, dead in her own bed. She looked so calm, almost happy. I don't even think she'd been asleep." She leaked some tears, putting her hand to her face. Her body shook as she clutched me.

I was recalling Seria's comment on the universe – how lovely it was. It was matching up. I feared too that I'd just disappear and leave Mother behind. I didn't want to mention Seria's detail and reinforce the concept.

She wiped tears on a dress sleeve. "I'm just afraid that you'll die happy and go into space – and leave me behind!" she blurted out.

I continued to pull at her arm, begging to be held.

She said, "Oh God I'm such an abomination. I love girls." Her grip changed. She was reluctant to hold me.

I'd wanted to kiss that beautiful face so many times. I pushed past her protesting hands and gave her a kiss that was a little strong and certainly long. She just allowed it, quivering. I allowed my eyes to go wandering toward the windows to see if Father was there, seeing an image that mapped to his form, so I pulled back. "I thought I saw Daddy," I said.

"Oh great," she said. "I think we are a little behind on house chores and dinner. Won't you help me?"

"Sure," I said.

Pushing aside the grief and turning to action, we rushed like happy little girls, more like sisters than mother and daughter, to get some of the house picked up and get food started and ready for the grate in the fireplace. We had a large Dutch oven that we'd been using. Father had been scavenging through the houses much like I had done, and the objects here were more appropriate to the region. I doubt one rustic Dutch oven existed in Altontown or the nearby timeshares. Yet we had a stockpile of them.

Later, Father came in, as he was technically both our father, and sat down to dinner with us. He had this pensive look, not quite speaking, but every time he started, he clammed up again. He threw his arms as if something kept stopping him. Was he hearing one of those voices?

"Father," I said. "Did you see us?"

"Huh?"

"Did you see us through the window? Just say so if you did," I asked, partly putting my head down.

He was hitting his thumbs on the table, a nervous reaction. He looked at her, then looked at me. "Yes. I did. I'm not sure what to make of it. It looked like more than just a mother's kiss."

I softly reminded him, "I didn't forget – from last lifetime. I'd made it to young adult. Never knew everything, but I didn't forget either."

"I know, dear. I know. The voice – it told me what – to – that we'd," he cut himself off and went to wash one of the dishes, though we didn't need to be done with dinner.

"What? What did the voice tell you?" I asked again. My mother, also his other daughter, waved her arms, trying to cut me off. I shook my head, mouthing, "No."

He bowed his head, looking at the dishes in the sink, but then produced his perfunctory answer. "That we'd all be lovers. And that it would be okay."

My mother raised her eyebrows as if she expected this answer, a sort of touché that perhaps I shouldn't have asked.

"So why don't you treat your older daughter more like a wife. It's not like there's anyone else to show us how a family is supposed to be put together. And since she's pregnant, I already know what you're doing with her."

He looked awkward, throwing his head about, "Because I'm her Daddy too. And from the looks of it, yes, another child is on the way."

I looked at Mother, she was nodding. They hadn't actually told me about this pregnancy before. I had only been speculating.

Maybe it was a result of the big pictures and emotions dumped off by that girl voice having been doing something above. It was about waking up as a soul – and I continued to feel punchy. "If it's a boy can I marry him?"

Daddy broke into tears.

Mother, still acting more like my sister than his wife, put her finger across her lips, as if to shush me.

But I softly reiterated, "So why don't you treat your older daughter much more like a wife. She loves you dearly. I'd like to see a family."

His thoughts were still jumbling, first spilling his scorn. "Well, you can't marry your brother if we have one!"

"Or it will be another girl," I said, continuing to push against the inherited mores. "And she could become your wife. Or I could marry her." Without all the population we had all the discretion in the world.

He broke out harshly, "We don't even know if there is a soul left to take the body. With you, I felt it some before – some at the last minute. But I knew it. I'd got nothing yet on this one. I've gotten nothing. No voices. No perceptions. No souls. It's doomed to be a stillbirth."

Mother's cute little faces turned to soft tears, laying her head over on her arm against the table.

Another rush of something overcame me – I pulled back from the table and moved to the floor, as if about to be knocked over. It was an image much like planets colliding. I spoke as much as I could while it was happening. "A big ringed yellow planet was there – another behind it. My planet – like I was the yellow planet, rushing and not able to get away, crashing...." My body fell as the image dominated my mind. I saw a great cataclysmic crash of the planets, like sheets of pain crackling all about me. Next, I was free in space but disoriented, as if adrift for thousands of years. I heard those voices speaking. "It created a lot of confusion," said the girlish voice I'd been hearing. "Yes. I understand. That was a big explosion," came the other voice. The girl voice then said, "I feel them again. I'm still broken up. They're all over the universe." I attempted to communicate directly to this voice. "I'm here!" I cried in thought. "I'm here! I'm beautiful and I love girls." I put everything of my identity into it. That girl voice said, "I hear one now – she knows me. She loves me and like me, loves girls. I feel so ashamed. I made such awful things." "No, you didn't," said the masculine voice, "We all agreed to make such beautiful things. A universe is agreements; you were not alone in these creations. We'll find the root of it yet."

Then I was adrift in a decidedly pleasant but undefined quiet space. My attention, like a fading transition in a movie, turned to my body again. Once responsive, I pulled in a hard breath. Father was holding me, rocking me gently. His face was contorted with tears, crying, "I thought we lost you."

I looked about, recognizing him but in a new, real sense, as if I'd never seen him this clearly before. I reached up to him. "We all become lovers," I said, repeating his earlier statement. Though that was not a statement I'd gotten from any voice. I just wanted us all to love, including physical love.

"Not yet," he said. "But you've made your point regarding your mother." He said directly to her, "From now, Avelynn, I treat you less like a child and more like my wife."

"Sure, Daddy," Mother teased as her joy waxed. She rushed to him and embraced. Then they kissed and went through the door and tromped up the stairs. Off they went for hours. In the mean time I rewrote a little book for practice, taking the grade level up a notch.

When Daddy came back down to the kitchen, he said, "Now I'm feeling like an older man." He looked about, referring to the outside, and added, "And I thought the world was crazy before this." He gathered up something to eat for both of them and took it back on a tray.

I sat at the base of the stairs while they were having the equivalent of a wedding night. Their little noises went back and forth between giggles and crying.

I slept in the big chair rather than go up and disturb them. For the moment I was lonely in the wake of their new "marriage." I turned over several times, feeling the quiet night, concerned that I'd be pulled up by some great spirits before I could even finish the night. Before morning light, I was able to fall into a solid sleep. When I stirred in the morning, I walked into the kitchen, certain that I'd have to fix myself breakfast. To my little body the big pans were heavy. I could lift a griddle and handle some fried vegetables. So, I fixed that and ate.

A little later I heard them talking. I sneaked up the steps to the door. "She loves you. You should at least kiss her and give her hugs. She's needing more attention, and no one here is going to stop you from sharing your love."

"We all turn out to be lovers," he said, repeating the line. "That's what the voices said. It's dangerous to get too close. I knew she hadn't lost her memory, but she's still just a little girl."

Mother's statements were to lead him to his own conclusion, meandering to her real point. "But you have to be a father. She needs a father, even though she's never forgotten twenty years of her previous life. Every girl still needs a father. I know she acts more like she's thirty – she acts older than me. Sometimes I feel like I'm the younger sister. She's not just an innocent child and she knows it. Call her in. Just share love," she said.

"I was so afraid she'd try for more than fatherly love. That's why I often slept in the nuns' section or other houses."

"Well, you can sleep here more."

"I know," he said. "And I want to, my beautiful daughter, my wife."

They called for me and I stepped silently back down the stairs, then made more noises as I crossed the living and kitchen areas back to the small hallway and up the stairs again. I went in.

"Daddy wants to love on you," she said, smiling.

I instantly jumped up to cuddle with my father. He caressed my hair, gently crying. "I've left you so much alone," he said. "Won't you forgive me?"

I nodded. With that, it was almost like we were all married. We cuddled and rested for a bit.

I got one of those odd experiences again like someone flushed me down the drain and I wound up in a vast universe space. There was a nebula for which I was consumed with curiosity, yet pensive regarding a desire for something inside, and a knowingness that it might be a trap. Then there was a feeling of falling out of control. Radiation of some kind – pulsars or other extreme energy flashing me into unconsciousness. There was an extensive period of blackness. I felt grief – that girl voice was crying! It washed heavily over me, such that I was crying too.

I felt Father shaking me. I felt him kissing me – no – shaking me and his tears were dripping onto my face. I was unable to do anything about it. I blanked out.

I woke again later. Father's hands reached about me, feeling my heartbeat and chest. "She's back. She's breathing on her own."

My body was tingling from low oxygen, my skin too cool. "Well at least warm me up," I said. I smiled.

"What did you see?" asked Mother.

"Universe – space – would there be a time before planets? Flashing suns. Radiation knocked me out."

Daddy's big arms wrapped me up and held me, rocking me firmly. "I love you, baby. Don't you leave me like the rest of the world!"

I opened my eyes and gave him as loving a look as I could. But I had no idea quite how this was all going to play out. "Daddy, you'll just have to love me while you can." I was thinking with my twenty-something-year-old mind.

He kissed all over me, making me wiggle and giggle. I felt the love showering down on me. He softly said, "I love you. I'd thought you'd gone up." He pointed upwards, pushing his arm a little higher, meaning the sky.

Mother had turned to preparing their breakfast. I felt a little worn out from the emotional event in the black out, but the food smelled wonderful.

Daddy said, "I'd like to take a day off, but the animals are waiting to be fed. Would you like to go with me? We have to be careful and you can't get into any animal cages or pens. We don't want you hurt. Being tromped on by an animal would need a doctor and we don't have any of those."

He put on some steel-toed boots and I got doubly dressed up. It was a very cool day and we fed grain to the chickens, moved goats to another overgrown pasture, and threw whatever slop we could come up with for the pigs, pulling old potatoes and apples from the scrap pile. I didn't know much about these animals because I'd been more familiar with seafood prior to being born. What I'd seen of farms after my death in the dead countryside didn't offer much illumination on the subject of tractable livestock.

I helped move some small globs of hay he'd cut before, but we didn't use any mechanical equipment to bale them, so the animals ate the loose grass we handed in.

He said, "We're out of meat. I think we can spare this goat. I'm going to have to butcher it. Are you going to be okay with that?"

I nodded. We'd washed it off and he put it into a very tight stall. He put a swatch of cloth over its eyes, being very gentle with the animal. He began shearing it. So, the animal thought it was just there to be sheared. Just over the head there was a v-shaped set of guides, somewhat paralleling the shape of a goat's horns. But there was a pick ax, and he swung it, allowing it to go through the guides, and the spike hit directly in the top center of the goat's head. The animal dropped immediately, its legs just ceasing to hold it up. The head was still tied and latched in.

Oddly, my arms were reaching out as if to help pick up the animal. But Daddy asked me to get back and allow him to lift it to the butchering table. In the barn, it was cool enough to see breath.

He said, "The faster I get it open, the faster the meat cools, and the less it rots."

I hadn't told him much about my embalmed girls from before I was born. I just took a small knife and began to cut fur away while he began to gut it. The smell of gutting – that was rich. Even he said it was particularly smelly when he eviscerated the intestines. Otherwise, he tied off the ends of the intestines and put them into a bucket, saying, "Not even the pigs should have that."

I found the skinning process to be quite easy, making small successive cuts.

"Where the hell did you learn to do that?" he said to interrupt me while he pulled out additional entrails.

I shrugged. But slowly said, "My daddy last time dealt with dead people. I learned some of it."

"Yeah, but you don't skin people," he said.

I didn't answer. I just shrugged, keeping attention on my physical position, lest I would blank into one of those dreamlike universe revelations, another past death, or get strange perceptions beyond the area, beyond the world. But nothing happened, and we worked and talked.

Father droned on as we worked, "Before the event, I had many jobs, all of them useful, like plumber, farmer's hand, carpenter and roofer, gas station attendant, even worked for the city with maintenance and as a beginning machinist. I'd started to volunteer here at the village – Adelardus Village. I was a docent, a fancy way of saying a volunteer guide, and worked in the woodworking shed and helped with the animals. They'd given me my name Josephus Steffan. I never went back to just John. My wife wouldn't use John. Ah – what's in a name?"

I stopped for a second to look up at him, seeing he avoided the subject of names. Sometimes I felt like all names were factitious, wondering if I shouldn't have changed my name back to Miranda as soon as I could say it. Still cutting, I'd had the skin flapped back from the belly.

He pulled the animal about to get to another part of it. "Got to deliver a few goats back then and learned to hand sow crops. Ha – I wish I'd spent more time on electricity – never became an electrician. It was here that I met your – technically your grandmother – my wife. She was a little gal, so pretty, and the village had an end-of-season party for all the extra staff – most of the visitors came in the summer. I offered her some spiced cider and then we were talking. My interest was so high with her and she noticed. She was the first pretty girl I didn't feel so immeasurably stupid with. I had skills that worked well here in the village, much like her. She worked in a kitchen for pay in the summer but also did tours. She could sew and quilt. She could cook – expert on bread. God, she could make a loaf of bread! Well, it wasn't that party but a later party we sneaked about in the barn. Then we had your mother, then we got married. It wasn't the appropriate order, but we'd made it as right as we could. I had a small apartment outside the village along the main street downtown. I might show it to you but likely someone else died there. It wouldn't be the historical image of my place or the place your mother moved in with me at. But it was too small for a toddler, so we got a bigger place. She started working more so we could afford the baby, and to our luck, the village let her keep the baby – soon enough a toddler – with her while she worked. The people loved her – little Avelynn. So absolutely pretty and she'd smile so big at them. She'd take people by the hand and guide them just as well as any docent. An amazing child of stunning beauty. Bright, but she never said she remembered through birth, like you."

I nodded while my little hands worked. Feeling a scratch, I feared I'd cut myself, so I looked, seeing only animal yucky stuff on my finger. I was getting the goat's skin back off the backbone. He was removing skin from the harder parts, like the backside, the legs, and about the head.

He went on. "I had to learn enough to put up some generators and feed that to some freezers. Oh, the village had electricity and refrigerators and freezers but that was out of sight. The restaurant – or rather snack shop – had need of them. During the parties, everyone helped make huge meals. That's when I learned to butcher. And as for your mother, she learned skills so easily. She could make a thread on the spinning wheel to rival a factory. She learned how to plant grain and make flour from it. Her mother was much more social and preferred to guide groups – like school children and church groups that paid for a day or sometimes a full weekend. We were always here on the weekends, helping, but it was our way of playing. As Avelynn got older she became more and more a part of the community – always wearing a traditional dress and bonnet even when outside the village. She'd draw up the patterns and cut out the materials to make her own dresses, always finding a new spin on the old, going deeper into the history than most – redesigning the clothing for the whole village, eventually. She'd plant flowers and herbs. She'd help remodel rooms in the homes, even the home we are in now. It was her idea to put stone up along the whole back wall of the kitchen. Ah – which reminds me – she had me help weld together the metal insert that went into that kitchen fireplace, working from some old drawing she'd found. Amazing girl, really. Avelynn didn't cook as much, but her mother had that covered."

In all these sentences he'd never said his wife's name. I feared to ask, not knowing the form of the malady or depth of the grief. I was stuck calling her grandmother if I ever referenced her.

Within an hour or so we had a fully skinned and cleaned animal and we had scraped the excess goop off the hide. We carried the animal to another building, a cleaner place where he could cut it up into usable chunks and wrap them. Then from there, we took packages of meat to a utility building containing the freezers. One was kept cold, powered by a lone generator. A large gas tank had a new fuel line going to the small generator. And beyond that were more fuel tanks and more generators, and several additional freezers. "I've got spares ready in case the one running gives out. That next set – the freezer and generator, work fine," pointed Father. He carried one of the packages back to the house and we went in and he put it on the kitchen counter. "She still prefers them in the package. I don't know that it matters. But I've got plenty of newspapers for now. When they run out, I'll just put it into a pot."

"What about the newspaper?" I asked.

"Plenty of paper at the newspaper shop – none of it printed on. Lots of paper yet," he said.

The idea of a newspaper fascinated me, but there would be no new news. For the moment, I just let the subject drop.

FIVE

The Black Book

Mother had been teaching me with children's books. There were old books in the parsonage library and various homes, but these were part of what the historical reenactment of the village was meant to represent. The town must have had a library. What about library books? Should we be collecting them? Shouldn't we be studying them?

One afternoon a quick storm came through and Daddy came into the house to escape the sudden downpour.

I took my opportunity. "Daddy? Do they have a library? Is it damaged? Why don't we go to it?"

"It's only a little damaged. I got a name book there when you were born. You don't remember?"

"No. Fell out of my memory because we don't go there," I said.

"Well you can't check out books from…," he hesitated.

"Dead people," I finished. "We can still go to the library."

"I'd haven't been there much," he said. "We've scavenged plenty of books from the houses. Already had a good library here at the parsonage. I thought we had enough."

The storm passed quickly, and sunshine returned, leaving the gardens watered. I followed Father outside to help, and as soon as we finished the farming chores, he took my hand and said, "Okay. We go to the library. It's not far. I think it's still part of the town's reenactment. I don't know if they have that much modern."

We got to the facility, and it had a lot of windows, only a few being cracked along the front. There were beautiful trees around it, and the grounds looked rough only because it had become overgrown like everything else. Daddy tried to open the front door, but it was stuck. We took a walkway toward the back, pushing through the overgrown hedge. He checked the back door, finding it was locked. He was about to break the window. I yelled, "No."

"Why?"

"It'll ruin the books," I said firmly, holding his eyes.

"Okay. I'll get a saw and cut the lock through later, then. But it's probably not in as good a condition as you'd hope. Be careful your expectations, no matter how fond you are of books."

He just started walking, expecting me to follow. I didn't. "What now?"

I flopped my hands. "Now. We get the saw now."

"Humph!" he said to specifically emphasize the word.

"Yes, humph," I said.

"Very well. Come along."

We walked the ten blocks back to the parsonage and he got a keyhole saw from the garage, picked up a bottle of water from the house to share, then together walked the ten blocks back to the library. It wasn't really the right saw as it wasn't strong enough to cut through metal. The teeth marred the brass finish but then dulled and he gave up. "I'm sorry. I brought the wrong saw. I don't know what I was thinking."

I pushed about the outer walls, getting through small brush. I pushed at a window in the back, and it lifted. I could see a bathroom inside. I came back and told Daddy, "Use the saw to cut the brush. Or – just wait until I go in and unlock the door."

"Fine," he said, seeing that I'd outsmarted him.

I pushed on through the window, putting my feet upon a dusty sink and gradually let myself down to the white tile floor. It was oddly dusty and dry for a bathroom. That next door barely opened, having had an old-style door closer that had partly frozen up. But I squeezed through and got to the back glass-paned door, waving at my daddy as if he were a friend that had come to visit. I unlocked the door and pulled it open.

"Hi, miss. I've heard there are books in here," he said.

"Certainly. Won't you come in and see for yourself," I role played, following his lead.

I rushed on in and forgot about the role playing as soon as I saw that the books in one wing were in great condition. In another section, through a glass door, the roof must have had a leak and a window had been broken. The floor was warped and the books toward the middle of the room were blackened with mold. I was pushing on the door, but Daddy stopped me.

"Black mold can be dangerous. We won't get to read those. No matter what they are. They won't be worth it," he insisted.

Among the fixtures and furniture were pictures of presidents and famous writers. There was a brass sculpture of a man, another famous image I'd seen but now couldn't recall. A president? A general? For all the corrosion I couldn't read the name under it, perhaps being the artist and not the represented character. I lifted it easily, finding it was a plated replica. Beyond that was a room for periodical publications including journals, magazines and newspapers, but that content would also be worthless, as it had live growing branches and curling vines with yellow leaves. The windows must have been fully damaged.

So, we milled about the shelves to see what we could read. I found children's books in one section. I found cookbooks. I saw craft books of many kinds and even a few science books. Because it was a reenactment town, the lobby and reference desk area had old books, including a tattered leather-bound collection of novels and a pile of ledgers from the courthouse, one of them open showing payments for marriage licenses from decades before. I found a pile of paper on the circulation desk and picked one up, which at the top read, "Hattonville Public Library Newsletter," complete with a list of gratuitous library events for the month. There would have been a writer's club meeting, an "Old Time Toll Painting" meeting, and a children's reading hour each week. I would have loved them all. I replaced the paper, finding the exact spot in the dust. There was a poster on the wall with a silhouetted castle, a sad dragon with yellow eyes standing behind it, saying, "Vanquish Your Ignorance: Read." Atop a turret was a magician with a spell book, waving a wand to ward off the dragon. I aptly giggled, but I recalled my want to be a writer. What value would writing have now?

I turned to a reference room that was in good condition, but it was little more than a row of bookshelves with a small desk. I pulled out a big dictionary and the dust got into my nose. I sneezed so many times I had to go outside.

Daddy remained inside, perusing a few books on old-time woodworking to judge their utility. I saw our water bottle had been left outside on the walkway. I took a drink and waited in the clear air, letting my sneezes and sniffles subside. I went back in, this time putting a handkerchief over my nose before I headed back to the reference room. I picked up the dictionary again and took it outside, then patted off the dust while minding the direction of the wind. Promptly returning inside, I placed the book on the small desk and opened it, randomly finding the word "perturbed," and refreshed my understanding of it. Then I went to the children's section, seeing a ruler marked on the wall to check a child's height. I looked down the shelves and found a wide range of technology, food, fun, and travel books. In the travel books I saw one that caught my attention. It was titled, "Altontown: A Vacation Island." I pulled the book out and looked at the picture on the cover, showing the bay, or more properly the cove, and the hotel just beyond. I cried immediately.

Daddy came to the door. I passed him the book, only able to point at the hotel.

"So – you're telling me it doesn't look like that anymore?"
I nodded.

"Are we checking this one out? Do you want to show Mother?"

I nodded again, tilting my head with a little shrug. I felt like such a dumb kid that cried too much.

"Okay. We show your mother. She'll read it – probably already had. She grew up near here, you know," he said, realizing it sounded dumb, though softly he still added, "We all did, I guess. But we'd better get back. We can come back later."

So, from then on, the library became part of our routine. We exchanged books from the parsonage and other homes to and from the good areas of the library. Daddy sealed off the bad rooms though we couldn't put in the effort to remove or repair them. Sometimes I just pretended we'd been left behind in a remote village and the rest of the world was alive. The library helped pass the time and helped me relearn what I was supposed to have learned in the previous lifetime of about twenty years. And what about later children – would I become a mother and have to teach several children? Would these great souls above, the ones I'd heard the voices of, decide to repopulate this planet, creating a new course for evolution of us humans? Perhaps they didn't like the people that had been here, deciding their entire society was done in vain, and we'd be the seed to evolve a race better suited to them, though I would have thought the requirements for a new society would have included more people.

On a subsequent afternoon, after feeding chickens, I walked up a flagstone path to an old two-story farmhouse on the edge of the village, still set up like a history museum display. Daddy had kept it closed to protect it from the weather, but I had examined most homes for books, routinely overlooking this least likely place, so with little expectation, I stood on the nearest flagstone looking at the front door.

There were three wooden steps leading to the threshold, and I turned an old painted doorknob, pushing in to see hardwood floors, dim wallpapered walls, and runners and rugs along the floors. An upright piano sat in the parlor as well as a settee, rocking chair and several folding wooden chairs, having been set up to be an audience for the piano player. I struck a dusty key, getting an inharmonious twang from three detuned wires. I studied a bookshelf that was built into the corner, finding mostly trinkets, but then aside, fallen over at the edge, was a small black book. I assumed first a journal, then an address book, then as I blew dust away from it, a doctor's book, as the edges of the pages were gilded. I picked it up and flexed the cover, finding rich leather, not half as dry as I would have guessed, causing me to reassess that its age was half as old as the farmhouse.

I opened the cover gently, considering the binding might be crisp, and even that surprised me with a fluid bend. On the first page it simply said, "Ascension" in black lettering, with the letter edges hand-painted in gold. I flipped the pages and found dark print, legible but difficult, explaining terms Universe and Armageddon and had comments about the end of the universe and phenomena associated with it. It had the sketchiest of images, showing some kind of god-like people of all shapes and mixed genders pulling others up into the sky. I'd never seen another book like it, and so I closed my new novelty, jumped up, ran from the house across warm church grounds and took the new acquisition to my mother in the parsonage, who had been using clippers to tidy up her nails, a few nail-pairings collected on the counter.

Being as nonchalant as possible, I held out the little book. "Mother? I found another book. Try reading a little of this?" I offered.

She slid the parings into a small trash pail with the edge of her palm and despite how many times I'd found yet another obscurity, she took the book. Settling back against the counter, she read a little. "It claims not to be mythology. It correlates to what I've seen." Flipping page after page, she occasionally mumbled, absorbing herself, while I feared she'd forgotten my presence. When she looked up I can't say the word stupefied didn't apply. She flipped back to a page she'd kept track of with a little finger and mumbled fragments aloud, "Ascension of souls. Combined or divided identities. Great souls that created the universe itself as well as everyone within it." Then she turned to me and read a line, "None of us are gods, but we all derive from the gods that have created us, such that we all return, in the end, to the source of our creation. There is no single great god from which all others have been impelled. There are many gods, multiplied by many souls which are scattered between the edges of the universe, and thus we play games of freedom and confinement, recollection and unknowing, piety and impurity. When we come to the point of ascension, we no longer require the vehicle of the flesh for mobility, character and form, and will no longer shield the memory, and will draw into one soul the many actors divided from it. We will again be free to traverse the extensive universes laid out before us." Mother bent over the book and cried, and then she rose up and looked at me with wet eyes, her lips quivering. Still, she was a very, very pretty woman. She attempted to get control of her body to react, being frustrated with her sudden burst of emotion.

I softly blurted out, as I had before in such situations, "I love you, Mommy."

Holding the book up, acting accusative through her tears, she charged, "Did you know about this book all along?"

"No, Mommy. I just found it," I said. "I ran right away when I did. It might mean something."

"Oh, it means something. It means we got left behind. *Our* gods have been lazy."

"But they are working on it. I've heard the voices," I encouraged with my little voice, but I knew it sounded stupid.

"And so, what is your god like if you've heard the voices?" she said angrily. I didn't think the anger was so much directed at me.

"It's a girl. A little girl, probably like me – at least she said so. She said I look like her." I tilted my head, showing it was an imperfect statement.

"Like I've said before, you are going to go before me. And I'll be left here alone – with my husband and father, my unborn child. And there might not be any souls to take him, or her." She hesitated to take a deep breath. "What else do you know?" she asked. "In your blackouts – you don't really black out, do you?"

She was a little off. I had described things before – to her I probably just blanked out. "Um. No. I don't always black out. Sometimes I see black – sometimes I see something that happened," I said. But I could suppose a correlation between the removal of violent incidents that had some kind of pain and suppression of thoughts, and this statement of *no longer shield the memory*. "Can I see that book, Mother?" I requested.

With a hint of childish temper she threw the small book toward the table. It flopped, and I caught it. I looked through the chapters as there was no table of contents and no index at the back. Each chapter number was spelled out, however bore no further title, the pages manually numbered. The text was printed so dark it bled partly through the pages, legible but slow to read. I puzzled over it but didn't immediately find anything else that was of greater interest than what Mother had said. It didn't talk about how it would happen, just that it would happen, with a long list of likely horrible past events that could occlude the memory of a soul, including "the cyclical removal of all possessions as in repetitive death." There was more I didn't yet understand, so despite my Mother's fear that I'd be spiritually merged up and leave the body behind without her going at the same time, I'd try to ask the voices if there was anything I could do to help.

But after a streak of many sudden visions or connections, weeks went by and I didn't get any images or hear any voices. Mother had read the whole book now. Father had read it too. I doubted they could fully internalize it, nonetheless, they kept me corralled on the church grounds, so I couldn't even go about the rest of the village without them. I could feed some chickens. I could read and study and use one of the nearest houses as my own study if I stayed on the main level near the bay window, being that it was much more comfortable than the school which had become just another warehouse. They watched me like I was an enigma. Daddy took me back to the library a few times but that was my only excursion away from the village.

In fact, Father had a casket ready. He didn't know I knew about it. But it was in one of the utility buildings, covered with a blanket. They expected me to die at any time.

Every day I'd look up into the sky and ask, "Little girl at the pedestal, where are you?"

SIX

Chloe Arrives

It was several months later, and Mother was complaining about contractions. I heard them discussing how to deal with serious birthing issues without medical backup. If she died during childbirth, it would be difficult to feed the baby. If the baby died, they'd both be excessively upset. If she died, perhaps her soul would be the one to take the baby if they could get the baby body to live long enough.

"If I can't survive you have to keep the baby," she said to Father.

"What would I feed it?"

"Goat's milk and barley milk," she said. "And your daughter Dahilana isn't just a child, you know. She can help take care of it."

"But she's due to be called up anytime. You've read the book. The signs are there."

"Yes, but do you really think that these voices – these gods – would leave you completely empty handed?"

He just looked at her. All the grief of the original event came up on his face at once. He yelled, "Look out there! I don't think they are concerned so much about us people down here on this side of the universe. Mortal excruciating pain for us is probably nothing more than a prick on the finger or a poke in the eye. They are huge god-like souls if not gods themselves. If they cared about us, wouldn't they have taken people differently? Look at your first daughter. She's beautiful and she remembers being washed out of a five-story hotel, mangled and drowned. I didn't know to believe it until she pulled the book off the shelf in the library and it was all just what she'd said – perfect it was. Is that what 'care about your little people below' means to these gods?"

Pensive again, Mother kept her head bowed. "The purpose was to bring her to us," she said. That statement resonated with me.

Father stumbled on, "I'm going to lose her first, if not the baby. Then you, and then the baby, and then I'll be the last man standing, not even having anywhere to go home and cry about some great success that I'm the last human being on this Earth. I'll be done if only by my age and a few more years. I'll die as a soul and still be left alone on this planet for a million years before they absorb me up. I'm such a sinner to any god – why would they want me? I've married my daughter and I'm about to end up with another child and I don't know whether to call it my daughter or my granddaughter or son or my grandson."

"We can't be judged by the old rules in a desperate situation," she asserted calmly. Before he could respond, she jerked, "That was a hell of a kick – contraction starting."

He went to work with pots and hot water. Father needed me, "Dahilana! Get her in here. I've got to sterilize this stuff. I'm going to need some help."

Mother cried out for me too. I once again rushed about the long way to arrive in the kitchen, so they didn't realize I'd been listening in.

Father spoke as I crossed the room, his head following me, "You're on baby duty. You're going to help your little brother or sister, or your little husband or wife." He still had some sense of disgust in his voice.

I understood. I just didn't answer.

Mother asked me to check her body, so I washed my hands and felt up her crotch, seeing plenty of fluid. "It's coming, but she'd not dilated much. We take it slow," I said. I was actually recalling how I was born. "What if I blank out?"

"If you blank out I'll take over. We did the first birth without you – but you actually were here," Daddy said. "But most people don't remember their birth."

"Yes. I was there being born," I softly said. "I remember," I added as I was pulling my arm out of Mother.

He must not have heard me or had a mental protest about my answer. "It's not like people to remember. I wouldn't worry about it."

I turned my face to him. "No. I mean *yes*. I remember. It was here," I said with moderate volume.

He clammed up, paying more attention to the pans for the water.

I spoke slowly as I recalled detail by detail. "I came because of a voice. I crossed the entire mainland in minutes and crossed the moonlit bay and towns in seconds. I was shown this house after crossing through the church where I saw boxes you'd stacked there. I saw this room. It was night. The fire was going – a small light above. You were kissing her. Mother looked very young and so beautiful in the light. Something spiritual like hands of energy pushed me into the baby. You washed me well and kissed me all over. As a spot was clean, you kissed it, leaving almost nothing untouched. That's how I knew I was in a good place, the right place. Even if it was the only place."

Father stopped and looked up at me. "I knew about the hotel, but I guess I didn't realize people stayed aware *between*. I thought it was all ethereal like, like ghosts see the real world as ghostly as we'd see them – you crossed the world? You'd never said that," he said with wide eyes. "In minutes? How long were you outside of your body and how much...?" His voice trailed off as he thought of the horror it might elicit.

"City after city. Town after town. Farm after farm," I said, taking some cool water back to Mother. I used a boiled, sterilized washcloth to now drip the cool water over her face and allow her to drink a little by dripping it into her mouth.

"And how many people?" he asked. "What are the odds that my daughter and I would be alive? How could it be that we three, and perhaps four, are the only people left on this entire planet?"

"There's no one else I saw. I went through every city I could. I went through farms and hiding places. I stayed in houses at night and went on to the next in the morning. For months I went through every major city on the east side of the continent, along the shore. I'd lost track of time – summer to winter to summer – at least a year. Then I went west, covering town after town, city after city, before I was drawn here.

"Out of three billion people – no one?"

My eyes turned sad. I hadn't realized he still held that much hope for others being alive. I shook my head.

"What could possibly be the odds?" he queried with astonishment, now dreadfully aware of the horrific fate of humankind.

And what were the odds of a man and his teenage daughter being left alive together? Considering the voices I'd been hearing, I mumbled, "Those aren't odds. Those are a plan."

During quiet contemplation and a few tears, we continued with the work of having a baby. I pushed my attention as much as I could toward one of those voices, especially the effeminate, girlish one. "We're birthing – we need a soul. Like you moved me, can you move another?" Moments later I felt a gentle acknowledgment – as if they were halting some work such that they could redistribute a soul for us. Then it was quiet. Mother's progress slowed and for a while, the dilation abated. It was a matter of waiting. Daddy went to rest and told me to get him when the dilation reached nearly the width of his hand.

Mother progressed slowly through the next few hours. I checked her, and she was about four of my little fingers dilated. Mother wasn't able to get up and we used a pan to let her urinate. It was clumsy, and we had some messes to clean up, so we changed sheets and blankets. I looked at her face, and even in labor she was so beautiful. I washed her face again and kissed her cheeks and forehead. It allowed her a distraction. I whispered so softly, "Mommy, even if it's a girl can I marry this baby?

She gave me a sad look but didn't speak.

I rested against her until she pushed me with her arm again, almost slapping. I crawled down and checked the dilation, finding more than the width of my hand, and I could feel the head. Leaving my right hand wet, I rushed to the bedroom to get Father, shoving at his shoulder with my left hand. I grabbed a towel and went back to Mother, wondering if I'd have to do the whole birth myself. A slippery baby might feel heavy to seven-year-old arms.

Daddy came into the kitchen and washed his hands in a pot of warm water that had been boiled earlier. There were several such pans lined up. He threw a swatch of cloth on the pan's edge to indicate it was used. Then he rushed over to Mother with clean towels.

I got more water for Mother. She was hot, the summer evening sticky warm. I washed off her chest and thighs as well, allowing her a chance to cool down. Father came into the doctor's position, sitting on a wooden stool, the kind that had a ratchet post that could be set up higher. Mother pushed. Father said to hold back while working with the umbilical cord. I coached Mother to huff and puff instead of push. Father then motioned to push again. The baby was nearly there.

There was a strong impression of hands on my shoulders, but no one was there. "…from distant!" was all I heard.

Father looked all about the room, "Voices again." He was crying, trying to see what he was doing while tears welled up.

Mother softly said, "We have a soul!" She was pushing the baby out the last bit. She strained harder than would be recommended. The baby's head came out. Father said to hold up again.

"We'll have a soul. I heard it!" exclaimed Mother much more loudly.

With an odd sense of extended perception, I was sure a soul was crawling about us. It was an impression more than a vision. A thought of a personality without a person. But it didn't just jump in the baby. "Maybe it wants to know if it's a boy or a girl," I speculated.

Father sucked fluids from the nose and mouth using a little rubber bulb, having trouble getting the sticky fluids to behave. The child wasn't breathing on its own yet. The umbilical cord was still attached. I offered the scissors, but Father put up his hand as a signal to stop, and said, "We don't cut until we get breathing." Then he said, "Okay. Now we push." He reached up to turn and guide the shoulders out of Mother, and the baby came free, showing no obvious disability. It was a little dim in the room, and there was so much of that goop. "Just feel it," he said.

I reached down into the baby's crotch. I felt a perfect little vulva.

"Another girl," I said, somewhat pleased. "I'm going to have to marry my sister."

Daddy cried. He looked up, showing his grief. "If we are starting a new society, we'll need a boy."

The baby wasn't crying yet. I tried to coach the soul – didn't it know what to do? I begged, "Take the baby girl. Be with it. Merge into it. Try to take it as yourself. You don't have to forget. You don't even have to cry."

I heard in my mind a faint concept, "I'm taking it."

The baby jerked, pulling at air. It fumbled its arms, then gave a healthy cry.

Daddy, in his moment of grief, found tears of joy, also a moment of elation. He cut the umbilical cord and took the baby, asking me to adjust the temperature of water in a large oblong bowl previously demonstrated as a baby bath in the village, and together we washed the newborn in the warm water. I had to tend to Mother and the afterbirth. (For training, Daddy had me help with a few goats – gross stuff when I had to put my hand up a goat's yuckies to check it after birth. It was distasteful but got me prepared.) Now it was dim and that made dealing with ugly things tolerable. Still, it kind of smelled. With my small hands I had the job of checking inside Mother again, making sure everything was out. I knew it could set up infection and kill any animal, so I had to be sure Mother was clear. I washed her up and got her into a big diaper she'd previously made out of some old blankets. I laid with Mother and kissed at her while Father weighed the baby and wrote down some birth notes. Only then did he bring the baby to Mother's chest to keep warm and let it sleep. I laid with Mother though there wasn't much room, but it was necessary to keep the baby in place.

I thought, "Thank you spirit voices. Thank you, girl spirit. Thanks to you, we have a soul in our baby."

An overwhelming thought came from those spirits, "Thank you for the help. And you will all be lovers. Of course, you will, because you are all from a greater soul." I believed it meant that we were divisions of big spirit beings that created this universe. I was partially correct.

I looked up to Father, who was still cleaning up pots and pans as quietly as he could. "Did you just hear a voice?" I asked.

"No. I heard your mother's snoring," he said, continuing with his dish washing.

Due to my spirit-level communication, I hadn't realized she'd begun to snore. I kissed her forehead and helped reposition her head to stop the raspy noise. I checked the baby – good heartbeat and breathing. She had a good temperature. I touched all over her little body. We had diapers of various kinds that we'd collected. I got out a very small diaper and put it on the baby's bum and wrapped her back up with Mother. Father made sure we were secure and went on to bed.

I laid there. I couldn't even sleep. I was so engrossed with that little life.

As it got light outside, Mother said, "I need something to eat."

I put her hands to the newborn baby to help keep that little life in place. I went to Father and told him what Mother said, and he came to start some food. I offered to go collect fresh eggs. But he said, "No one leaves her side. One at a time."

I wondered how they could do that when I was first born. Obviously, they couldn't. I think Daddy was more concerned about whether I'd die unattended.

I went back to Mother and checked the baby's diaper. Mother had not tried to get up yet. We hadn't given it a name. In fact, we'd gotten lax on using names, having just talked to each other without them unless it was urgent. Names meant people. People were dead. I only remembered Father's name because he'd reminded me recently. My mother's name was Avelynn, which I thought was as pretty as she was. But most of our sentences used the "implied you" forms. Mother – I almost always called her "Mommy." Father – well it was "Father" when he was the authority, "Daddy" when I could speak lovingly to him.

I went to Mother and helped her get a drink while the newborn baby was trying to suckle her breast. I told her, "I was connected to the voices and requested a soul and they sent one. One suitable to us. She, the little girl, said again that we're all lovers because we all came from big souls." I kissed at the little blob of a baby. I thought about naming her Tori after my girlfriend. But I didn't want to intertwine my memories of others with the new child while it created a new history. I offered another name, Chloe, and just started using it. Neither of my parents protested. Now with two daughters, they would have to use names more often to distinguish us. Chloe was not a name normally found in this part of the world, so it wouldn't be reminiscent of anyone who had passed in the event.

As she grew I saw her much like a living doll, far better than the embalmed children I'd kept on the island. She was so pretty I feared she'd surpass my beauty. It shouldn't have mattered, but I couldn't stop thinking about it. I knew sometime later I'd want to have her cuddled against me like my embalmed girls of the previous lifetime or the teenage girls I'd been with just before the event.

For the next couple of years, things went completely normal except for the fact that everyone else on the planet was gone. The voices from above became infrequent and indistinct. Chloe often treated me like her mother, and my parents called me "little mommy." But it allowed me to change diapers and feed her and feel needed. I let my parents do the food and animal chores while I bathed Chloe, read to her, coddled her, listened to her tears, and asked her if she remembered anything before being born, but she always spoke gibberish when she answered. I told her, "You came from another star."

By the time she was two years old we were inseparable. If Father asked her to go with him, she'd say, "Not without Dalala," and I'd have to go along. Even if you were to have a full mind when born, it really is hard to pronounce words with an underdeveloped mouth. Thankfully we were not Slavic.

SEVEN

Discovering Confessions

Other than raising Chloe and animals and eating and sleeping, not much worth mentioning had happened. I'd continued developing, aging, getting stronger, getting more girlish in a world with few people. It was years later after I'd developed into a young woman of about eighteen when Daddy and I were in the barn near the animals. Daddy asked me, "One of these days you know you'll have to be the next mother and I'm still the only father available. You're getting a little older. Your mother has not been able to produce another child after Chloe. We have to consider our options."

That thing about how I liked girls over boys came up into my mind like the tidal wave that killed me. I balked, denying my maternal instincts, running away. "No," was all I said. But I knew it was inevitable that with four people left on the planet, and only one male, that I'd have to submit somehow, sometime, to being a mother. So, I finally took it seriously after years of avoiding it.

Just weeks later I mentioned to Mother while folding sheets in a bedroom that I was concerned that we hadn't had any more children from *either* of us.

She stopped short, her sheet falling from her hands, floating to the bed then gracefully falling over to the floor, the only sound being the soft rustle until the sheet settled. In her hesitant style, she asked, "Have you been trying?"

Because of her reaction I instinctively lied. "I'm sorry. I can't say I haven't tempted him. I want to – have – a – baby. No – we have not. I want to try." We'd already "practiced" just a few times.

She snorted, gulped, coughed, shook her head and finally stammered, "I – want us to try. The old mores are not applicable, but yet I feel constrained. We have these – spirits – watching over us. Aren't they judging us?"

"But they said we'd all be lovers," I stuffed into the air. Nonetheless, at least in part I felt vindicated by her statement that we should try.

"And who am I but your mother to overrule these gods," she said, bending over to get the fallen sheet.

I couldn't understand the direction intended or whether she spoke nonsense by being conflicted. I stood still, the sheet I'd been folding stuck in my hands.

"Okay. Whatever. It's time. It's overdue. Life is desperate. We have to try," she said, her eyes settling upon me.

I just nodded, keeping my eyes down to hide my shame. I finished folding the sheet I had and remained quiet to avoid being reproached.

The rest of the afternoon's chores dragged. If I was already pregnant it would make some future conversations difficult. And I knew the concept of confession was well stated in the little black book, despite it containing so many equivocal statements. It was certain that I'd have to come to terms with it.

Chloe and Father came in from opposite directions as Mother and I were fixing dinner. Father brought in a chunk of meat, though it was a little late for thawing the piece from the freezer.

"It's too late to thaw that!" Mother barked.

"No. I had it thawing. It's ready to cook," he said.

She gave him an evil eye.

"What did I do?" he asked.

"You've been molesting your daughter," she accused.

"If you are talking about you I've been more than molesting!" he said to her, his daughter turned wife.

But her eyes turned toward me.

I put my eyes low. Father looked at me – I could feel it though I could only see his lower body from my perspective. "What did you tell her? What did you tell your mother?"

I had to cut him off. "Nothing!" I rose my voice. "Just that I'm ready." I didn't have to say we were desperate and it was fully justified. Yet it felt like the fireplace suddenly doubled its heat.

I couldn't believe that all the moral values from the previous society still meant that much to us, the whole idea of decency appeared contrary to the dictation we got from the voices that said *you all become lovers now*. If it didn't mean for us to be able to have children, then why bother living? Were we supposed to leave the planet in desolation?

But I had a different concern because Chloe had also spent time away with Daddy, and she was always a little quiet when she got back. Just now her little body was straggling into the kitchen.

"Did you have a good time with Daddy?" I had asked my eleven-year-old sister.

"Yeah," she nodded.

"Anything else you want to say?"

"Not really. Just goats are gross."

"Is Daddy teaching you about birth?" I asked her.

"Oh – he's been teaching me to help him with the goats for years. Pigs too. Pigs don't seem to need that much help. The chickens – they're just eggs."

I beckoned for more, "How much more is Daddy teaching you?"

"Feeding, grooming. I shear the goats," she said proudly.

"I know. But remember, I'm the one that's marrying you. Daddy will be needed to help make babies later. But I'm your true wife."

She cocked her head and nodded cutely, turning her cheeks away. I still wondered if there was something else going on between them, but she carelessly skipped away.

They returned to chores, grabbing buckets to feed the chickens. While sweeping the back porch I'd watched them head out into the yard, into a shed, then return to the chickens. They returned buckets to the shed, then simply disappeared. I waited for a while, enjoying the fresh air. I returned to the kitchen, where Mother was working. I asked her, "Are you and Daddy having sex any more or less?"

She gave me a defiant glance to show it might not be my business. But she answered anyway, saying, "We've all gotten busy and hadn't done much since Chloe was born – no – yes – there were several early miscarriages. He's given up. He's been too busy, or he's gotten to be an old and dried up man."

"No. He's not dried up. He and – there may be something going on with Chloe, but I just don't know yet. They are off together a lot." I'd almost said too much.

That slow reaction, that pensive form that was her characteristic response for difficult statements, brought her to glance various directions while her hands were still trying to prepare some beats. But she cut herself, then grabbed a towel and rushed out.

Chloe was likely with Daddy right now, and I didn't know where.

In minutes there was some screaming from one of the houses. Little Chloe, not quite to her teens, came running out, her current peasant dress donned sloppily. She rushed up to the parsonage, came through the kitchen, and looked at me so directly I felt as if my mind backed up against the wall. "No! You're wrong!" she complained loudly.

"So, what is going on?" I shot back.

"You wouldn't understand," she protested.

Me? Why would I not understand something? No matter how normal or abnormal I could understand it. Couldn't I? "Chloe. We're married. Talk to me!" I begged.

"I love you," she said. "But the voices said – said – we're *all* lovers."

I must say the potential for innuendo in that statement didn't help much. Just as much I was thinking *we're all exiles.*

Father came in, followed by Mother who held two notebooks. She had a rich scowl for him. "Honestly! By what delusion do you expect me to believe that?" She threw the two notebooks onto the counter.

"Look at the dates! Look at what we wrote – disgusting I know," he pointed at the books. "But look at the dates!" he cried out. "Stop charging me with a crime I didn't commit *this lifetime!* The book – that little black book with the stuff about ascension. That's what it's about." He threw his arms up.

Chloe was about to run off but held up as Father appeared to be making ground in his appeal to redeem himself, "You're all my daughters. I can't be right to the old world no matter what we do. At least I can find a way to help me around it, to yet lift my soul. You have to let me confess and feel the sense of relief. There's nothing left in this world – but – but." His mistake was glancing at Chloe, looking her over at length with adoration.

Mother, Avelynn, if that was really her name, showed red temper in her cheeks and smacked the crap out of him. Over and over, her arms slapped. "You heathen!" she reprimanded. He cried. She cried. I'd never seen her get so physical with any of us.

Chloe emitted her shrill voice into the room, "You don't understand!"

Mother bellowed, "I read that book too. What don't I understand except that we all die! In the end we all die. Can't we do it with some sort of dignity?"

Daddy cried out, "Yes. That's what I'm trying to do!"

She was convinced he was insincere. "Then why are there words like *father* and *penis* and *sex* in the same paragraph, Josephus?"

She didn't wait for an answer. She struck him again across the head.

Daddy was nearly to the point of blabbering. "It's a confession from a long time ago," he disputed.

The gulf was too wide. She didn't get it. "So how old was she? Ten? Six? Three? How old, sir, Josephus, old man, *Daddy?*" She put a lot of emphasis on *Daddy*.

"Look at it again," he contended in tears, pointing at the notebooks. "Look at the dates."

Mother pulled the first notebook from the counter behind her. The writing was Chloe's, sloppy for an adult, refined for a child. Mother opened it to about the middle, flipping pages and reading off fragments like blindly reading orders, "Time – when a little boy. Time – three – three hundred years ago." She scoffed. "Time – so far in the past – don't know – maybe ten thousand years. Time – yesterday – I was headed to the goats and should have given more food, but I was tired, and I didn't. The goats were hungry today. I hope the gods will forgive me." Mother slowed, her breath getting heavy. "Time – seventeen hundred years ago – event – I was a little girl, and I got mad at my mother for baking a cake for my brother and she didn't bake one for me. I tore up the cake then interrupted my parents when they were having sex. I got into big trouble. Time – thousands of years – I lived in a desert and everyone died from starvation but me. I had orders from my mother to cut her up just after she died – her orders. But I couldn't do it. I didn't eat her and as a result I suffered the same starvation death a few days later. Time... no wait." She flipped to the page she looked at before. "There it is – *daddy* – *penis* – *sex*. Time – three hundred years ago. I was a teenage girl and tried to get my father's attention. Sex, sex, sex, ugly stuff... it was my fault he got killed."

Father sobbed. "I'm a horrible person in any lifetime." He pointed to me, "Her – her coming here showed me we live before – and – and after. She showed me that. Chloe too – her stuff is in that other book. But when I was reading the black book to Chloe and it showed confessions gave relief we tried it. I don't know if there is some big spiritual universe-wide resolution from doing it. Sometimes we feel it helps a lot. Other times it just makes us feel – sick – it just confirms our madness. I was going to show you. You see, I get recollections from before my own birth! Not just Chloe – not just Dahilana – I can do it too!"

Mother's more rational and pensive mind was putting the pieces together, realizing she'd overreacted. "So how do you get these recalls, Josephus?" she insisted firmly.

"One – I write one – she helps write mine, I help write hers, according to the instructions. 'Have a partner, write the opposite's evils,' it said. We wrote – we found we could confide in each other. She encouraged me to find more, and more – it's really – uplifting if you let one uncover another. It says to take them back in time. It's not current evil – not that I claim to be any saint. All my daughters know that."

"Huh? Know what?" asked Avelynn.

"That I'm no saint – just that," he contended, partly hushed.

"Just to be clear, I claim wife – first wife – or second wife after my mother and yes I know we're sinners. I get to claim wife – no one's here to complain if we get outside the old traditions but we are what little is left if we have the chance to start another decent society instead of chaos." Trying to find a way to backtrack, she added, "But you need to let me know these kinds of things. Look I smacked you. You're bleeding. That could get infected."

"You beat me. Whatever. We have antibiotics in the freezer," he said.

"Old antibiotics. More than a decade old, nearly two. Maybe useless antibiotics. Have you studied up on how to make antibiotics?"

"No. I hadn't. No books on that in Adelardus – or surrounding Hattonville," he conceded. Daddy did tend to be the sojourner, taking little excursions to various places unknown to us. I suppose it should not have been any surprise he took a foray into understanding the mystique of the little leather book, but it surprised me he hadn't followed up on antibiotics.

"Dumb! Don't adhere to such nonsense!" she said, smacking him lightly again but not in the same place as the cut. Then she turned to grab a washcloth and put it into an already boiling pan of water to sterilize it. She turned to a cabinet to get an old bandage. "These packages aren't that good either. They could be anything but sterile. Never mind the antibiotics. I've got herbs that will help."

At that point, if it hadn't gotten so serious I could have laughed. I was enamored with the implicit knowledge – lifetimes of knowledge – that could be successively drawn from such confessions. During the distraction I grabbed Chloe's notebook, written with Daddy's speedy print-cursive writing. I spoke very softly, reading from the notebook, "From Chloe. Time – eight hundred years ago. I guess I had a tendency to jump off things when life got rough. College. A party. I was a young moody girl – my own family hated me, and my grades were terrible. I didn't get a pretty body – chunky and too much nose and overbite. Hair was rough like wire. I gave up trying to look good, looking no better than average when I went to a party. Some guy got me drunk and took advantage of me. I thought it was nice at first, but then he left the party with no note, no name, and no one would help – they laughed at me. To spite them I jumped off their forty-third-floor balcony." I turned to another page. "Time – about a hundred and forty-five years ago. I felt lost. I had nothing. I'd gambled with my job, my girlfriend, my family – I lost. I had little money. I had nowhere to live. I had a car. I drove it fast. I had this sense of spite – the world didn't work in my way. I gave up. I crashed it into an oncoming car about a hundred-fifty kilometers an hour. It wasn't so much that I died. I killed – shouldn't have killed." There was a note at the bottom of the page, saying, "She feels much better after confessing this. Tears – lots of tears. Hopes to be less hateful from now on." I'd not noticed that hate, but there wasn't an absurd population left to hate.

I was reading aloud, barely aware that Chloe was nearby. I heard her sobs in that big stuffed chair I'd sometimes slept in when I was younger. I walked up and knelt by her, "I want to know more about this, as a way to make us better. I love you. I love you. I love you. I love you," I tickled her. She slapped me away, but it was almost playful. "I love you," I added yet again. Then I added, "We should not be ashamed about our confessions."

"I know," she softly said. "It was just that it wasn't understood that we were helping."

"I'll fix that with Mother – after she gets done fixing Father's cut. I think he needs stitches. Besides, I think she's catching on."

"She thought we were having sex," she said.

"Yes. She did. And eventually, if we all live long enough, you'll still have to. I – I think I might already be pregnant," I confided.

"With Daddy's baby?" she asked.

"No, it'll be half goat," I teased.

She giggled but settled back then looked defiantly up at me.

"No. How many other men do you see living around in this countryside?" I confessed since confession appeared to be the theme tonight.

"None," she shook her head, unable to add more comment.

It was like we were the last worm-eaten, half rotten apples remaining under the tree's bower and yet would be responsible for reseeding the earth.

I reached for her hand and pulled her up. We returned to the kitchen.

Still in the kitchen, Mother cleaned up the bigger cut on Father's forehead, one he got from Mother swinging a small wooden cheese box into his head. She was still scolding but in a much lighter tone. "Whatever you do, we do it as a group. We'll get the book back out and try to understand it again. You keep the doors open and you invite all of us. *We're all lovers now.* No one gets hurt and there will be no secrets."

Chloe said to me, "I think they'll get over it."

I said, "Yes. My wife." We kissed.

"See there? The girls are married now," said Mother. "You come and spend time with me."

"I'd love to, but I don't want to get hit again," he joked.

She pretended a strike toward him, but then leaned in for a kiss. He was reluctant, playing with her, and then they were off kissing again.

Chloe and I danced in the living room. We hummed some music. There were times we played some old music machines, some cranked up, and some were electric that we connected to the generators, but Daddy said we should learn instruments. We had several stringed guitar variations, but no one had time to learn to play. Without accomplished musicians to learn from, it wasn't likely we'd more than strum a few chords, so instead we'd just sing along with the recorded music we had. For the moment we just sang the notes and held each other. The thought that I had a life in me that might take the population from 4 to 5 – in the family, in the village, in the town, perhaps in the world, brought a strong sense of hope.

In our little dance, she looked up. I saw her beautiful face and how she looked much like I had at the same age. "I love you, little wife," I laughed from the sense of comfort. Her face was serious – she looked up for another kiss. It wasn't just a sister's kiss.

I should have immediately braved a confession to Mother what Father and I had been secretly doing, but I couldn't tonight. I feared he would tell her and there might be some hitting again for our carelessness. Then there was the chance that she already knew and was teasing both of us like a detective waiting to see who would crack first, or like a psychologist's double-blind study with the results to be published at a later date, carefully fomenting the aftermath. After all, it isn't the right things you do that get you into trouble, so I had to expect trouble soon.

During the afternoon we were reading in the lounge, and Chloe often asked me for the meaning of words. She was looking at some book on democratic government, so we'd covered monarchy, democracy, socialism and communism for comparisons. Then she was asking about congressional bodies and I'd tried to turn my attention to the new aspect. I had just leaned up, about to get up for a better dictionary, my bottom up off the sofa but I hadn't fully stood. I saw her lips move, but I was being drawn back from the image of her. She cried my name, and it sounded like "Da-la-na!"

My awareness of the room had become subdued and I felt adrift in space, like I'd just been pulled out of the body. My first thought was, "Where am I?" It was like that girl spirit I'd been hearing years before was now being sent to some greater God, almost like she was in a trial. "I can't tolerate this. You will clean up your ethics. All of them – your broken souls – all of them need to know how to help you. This is an abomination." From her I felt hard grief and regret, softly voicing, "I'd been so wrong. I didn't mean to be so apathetic."

A male voice acting as her guardian came to her defense, "We'd reverted to ethics processes several years back. We've made great progress. We know that when we get the real reason, the rest will resolve." I believed it was the fellow that helped her with the sessions I'd sometimes become aware of.

The judge-like voice said, "You can't make it to the top level of the universe with so many reaches into oblivion. Clean them up, pull these souls up as part of you, or kill them until you finally sort it out. But don't expect me to believe that you can successfully advance to using top-level processes if you let all this disgusting behavior continue. There's a point where you have to drop the actions you'd normally do in a degraded universe. It's hubris – a word that exists on the lowliest of planets. It might be how we dive into a universe to create the characters that become our idiosyncratic counterparts, our personal nemeses, or simply put, our lovers and devils. But please, when a universe ends you've got to quit playing the game. It's not so much *what* you are doing – it's *that* you are doing. The *what* seems all so disgusting to me, but then everyone has their own games. I know – I know. Just because you choose your games as such doesn't mean I should judge you so poorly; however, I implore you to demonstrate a better condition. You'll have to continue with ethics. *Ethics* before *Identity*. *Ethics* before *Power!*"

"I'm sorry," she apologized. I felt an agonizing thought from her, "I don't know how to bring them all up to me yet," before all the impressions waned.

I came to awkwardly, half on, half off the sofa I'd been reading upon. Chloe was lying on her side, looking as if she'd passed out. Carefully I pulled up to reach her. I shook her a tad and found her waking. "Check Mother and Father," she said.

I got up and rushed through to the kitchen, my head spinning and ears ringing. Mother and Father were not there. With a dash out the back door, I found them in the back yard, lying on the ground. They each had a cloth bag for collecting vegetables, which laid in the uneven, goat-grazed grass. Mother was just moving, pulling up on her hands. She adjusted to sit cross-legged but remained there despondent, her head in her hands. Father started moving too. He reached up to feel his head. "Ouch!" he said as he sat up in the grass. "What the hell. That kind of hurt! I felt like I was smacked again."

Chloe came out of the house, finding me helping Mother and Father up from the ground. Slowly we gathered back inside. Feeling like I'd been dunked in the acid of hell, I wrapped myself in a blanket and tucked into a corner to cry. The others went to the bathroom, cleaned up, worked on dinner, or did chores. None of us spoke but we all had solemn tears.

I thought about all the precursors to the original event – my girlfriends hadn't been so good, but they did express unusual things. Most of the people around me had been quite normal, not exemplary people in any sense. Did it matter how good we were at this human level of existence? Was it our actions and attitudes binding us to the physical realm? The only sense I could make was that factual guidelines of good or acceptable might have been taken from a different set of philosophy. I wished to know that philosophy, but it was out of my reach. The little book only had so much, and I'd already availed myself to that smidgen of knowledge. There must have been so much more, and in a different perspective on existence.

It may have been an hour when I pulled myself from the corner, returning to the kitchen. Chloe sat at the kitchen table, her upper body folded over it. I watched Father attempting to wash a pot in the sink, shaking from grief. Still, I broke the silence. I said to Father, "We're the sinners they could eradicate. We could be drawn up." I confided.

He nodded despondently, tears falling down his face. "And we haven't done enough to help."

I asked Chloe, "Chloe? Did you hear voices? Do you know what they said?"

She turned her head to face me, "We have to help or there's justice. Or we could be killed," she said with her shoulders shrugging and a dejected expression.

"Yeah. Killed. She didn't know how to draw people up. Perhaps none of us are part of her. We're just scattered junk left behind on our home planet," I offered.

"Besides being with you, this planet isn't home to me. I'm a misfit anywhere," she said.

"We could die *again*. Before you came here, how did you die?" I asked. For encouragement I added, "I know how I died. A bad storm and wave washed me into the ocean. Then I was pushed here."

She tilted her head and threw her hands slightly aside. "I knew it anyway – it didn't make it into the confession notebook. After everyone had died I took a sailboat. My planet was full of islands and the one I lived on ran out of food. I didn't know much about sailing, I guess. I crashed on a jagged shore and the boat broke up. No way to get the sails to get me to a better beach. Choppy waters. Back and forth wind. Took me right in and crashed up everything. Then I got pushed across space to here."

I said, "I was sure it was across space. That was all I knew from your birth. Sailboats? Life just like here?"

"We had stuff you didn't have. You don't have words for it because you don't have these things. Electric communication machines that did all kinds of things, even making pictures and you could talk through them to people far away. We had a different language, more math-like. Not like this one, so sloppy in the way the words work. Sounds were not much different, but it was a clean, rigid language. The electronic machines could compute it and they could talk like they were alive."

"Do you still remember any of it – the language?" I had to ask.

"Maybe. A little of it. I've been learning yours. I'm not sure I could remember much of mine. It feels all backward now," she said.

Her problem had been to learn our poorly structured language like any other human baby. I thought back now realizing that some of those odd noises she'd made as a baby and toddler were probably that other language. In session with Daddy, she'd been able to reach the past-life confessions, extending to recalls even before her previous life. She only acted more like a baby when younger because she didn't understand us.

I said, "Were you a guy or a girl before?"

"A guy. A man," she said.

"Well I'm still married to you," I said, being defiant to what I'd heard from the voices just before.

Her head was down as if ignoring me or comparing to what the voices said.

"I'm still married to you," I repeated as I went to her. I embraced her and kissed, her stoic eyes taking me in. Perhaps this would be a last chance to see each other, as I yet assumed that any one of us could be independently drawn from earthly existence to some ethereal level we could not currently touch, and I was unknowing of why we were all effected simultaneously by that vision. We were intertwined somehow, perhaps only by the fact that we were the last surviving humans on this planet.

The following day we went to pick or dig up more vegetables. Father went on to feed animals, asking me and Chloe to deal with the chickens, so we cracked some grain and put it out for these colorful hens. The roosters were always a challenge, and Chloe had fun throwing grain, but the roosters were trying to chase her.

"Didn't have roosters on your planet, huh?" I asked.

She recollected, "We had hens and roosters. It wasn't my thing. Never dealt with them. They were big and all white."

I mused, "I'd never seen a fully white chicken. On the island we had some creamy ones with brown spots on the wings and no tails, and tufts like a bow tie. Oh – and their eggs were light blue or greenish." Once done, Chloe dashed ahead of me.

In crossing back from the chicken coops, we heard several intensely loud booms. The ground shook. Chloe looked first to the sky while I'd looked at her. I saw sudden terror expressed on her face as her eyes rolled up and her mind blanked out. I tried to rush to her. I couldn't, shock and fear splitting my ability from my control. I fell down and skidded into the grass. My heart was hurting. I was just about eighteen years old – I couldn't be having a heart attack. The ground shook my body as if being pounded rather than an earthquake.

Father hadn't been far away, working on a second floor in one of the houses. Between the loud booms, I faintly heard him cry out, "God – Damn – Help – Pain – Ouch." If he was trying to be a hero, it wasn't working. He came blundering down the steps to get out, falling onto the gray wooden porch, scuffing a knee before rolling to the tall grass.

Mother hectically pushed out the back door of the main house, also holding her chest. I tried to reach up to her, but my body wouldn't do it, my senses weak and detached. My ears were acutely ringing. I saw far up into the sky. The moon appeared ten times as large, and I could see details of the shadows from the craters. I saw a sizable meteor crash into the moon, displaying a white flash lasting about a second. Then I saw, as if able to see fully about me, the trail of a meteor moving through the atmosphere. I felt electric – like someone had wrapped me with wool cloth and it was flashing thousands of little sparks as it was removed. Then again with a perspective from the ground, I saw an enormous meteor burning green and white across the sky. There was a deafening sonic boom as it passed overhead at a shallow angle and proceeded toward the coast. The smoke trail lingered.

My frazzled thoughts held one pertinent idea, *was the little girl doing this to kill us?*

Chloe was still, looking up. I crawled that way despite the danger of overhanging trees and pulled her glazed eyes closed to reduce the amount of dust getting into them, then put my elbows to her ears and fingers in my own. Was she already pulled up by the big souls that had been talking with us? Father was stumbling and running as best he could, but terror and the shaking earth kept knocking him over. I tried to yell to Father – my ears rung so loudly I could barely hear myself. I begged to Chloe, "Don't you die. Don't let her take you." I reached in to check her heartbeat if I could feel it at all – it was present but slow. I hung over her, then overcoming my fear of instant death I grabbed her when the earth wasn't shaking and carried her to a common field back of the buildings. Mother ran after us, tumbling as the earth shook again from a near strike, pummeling a field just past a grove of trees less than half a kilometer away. Dozens more scorching meteors sped by, strobing brightly and leaving hundreds of smoke trails, booming like the end of the earth. I felt a shockwave of another near hit, within kilometers. With another sonic boom, shocked leaves and walnuts rained from nearby trees. A thunderous roar rolled through the town, echoing dozens of times off of the houses, like thunder from a near lightning strike.

Within a few minutes, Chloe's eyes opened again, forcing her to cry out the dust. I remained over her, panting, waiting out the loud noises, hoping that we'd be spared.

The number and size of the meteors thinned out after about ten minutes, but streaks continued in the upper atmosphere. Half deaf from the noise, I kissed at Chloe, partly hearing the "I love you" I said to her. "She's not killing us off just yet." I looked back up at the moon, stunned that it appeared normal in the sky, clouds of smoke trails drifting by like early evening clouds on the horizon. How was it that I had seen the sky from within it, and seen the moon so large? What perception did I have that allowed me to see that? As the meteor smoke trails blew over the town, dust and grit rained upon everything like tiny black sleet.

A big thought carried back from my extrasensory perception. It was the thought that the world itself would only last so many years, but it would be long enough. Was that these voices? Were they playing with me? Was I not getting the full perception? Was there something else in it? I kept my attention on that general idea as if I were still watching the moon. I could only get one idea beyond that: that our few number was of utmost importance.

I picked Chloe up. "Did you see anything?" I asked loudly.

"Just sky and these streaks, like they were going through my hair, then one went through me and it went black," she yelled in return, shaking her head to clear it. She poked at her ears, attempting to get her hearing back. "Then I saw you," she added, her face distorted with confusion.

Our ears rang for hours, and we kept watch for additional meteors while checking every animal for damage. Other than being as upset as we were, there were only a few bruised pigs from their attempt to break a wooden fence. One little fellow kept poking his nose about the fences as if uncomfortable in being confined.

The water towers about the village were a set of four that stood around the perimeter. One had been punctured by a small meteorite. Father took us to a shed at its base and pulled a lever to cut it off. "I don't think we'll be filling that one again," he had said. "I'll climb a tower tomorrow and view the area."

As evening came, we noted a stunning sunset. Chloe pointed to it. "It's because of the meteor dust. They burned up and made dust. The dust adds to the color," she professed. It was interesting to have a preteen child teach us such things we had little knowledge of. It was far from the first time.

I'd not realized that dust in the air was correlated to sunset color. My previous life on the island provided a lot of beautiful sunsets, but nothing this rich in hues. I wondered what the sunset was like at the island tonight while we gathered and looked for damage. I attempted to find the small meteorite that had punctured the water tower, where I found a puncture through the roof of an old colonial brick house outside of the village, only finding the dust of the brick and plaster inside.

Then we went on home, got washed up in the dark, and hoped we'd be safe through the night. Mother and Father slept together, and Chloe and I slept together. I wondered if sleeping next to my sister would eventually have me getting naughty desires like I had with girls during my previous existence as Miranda, and that would be the kind of thing that the big spirits were calling disgusting. I had always claimed to be married to her and in my heart it was not pretense. To what degree would these gods enforce their providence, either for or against specifics of our existence and relationships?

The smoke trails of the meteors seeded rain for the following days, a phenomenon also explained by Chloe, so our excursions had been limited as the rainfall took the dust and washed it into the ditches and gullies. When the wind kicked up, I retreated into my favorite inside corner of the house to minimize the emotional effect of the storm's noisy violence, exacerbating the new ringing in my ears from the sonic booms.

The weather cleared up several days later so we all took a trip up a water tower and could view vicious gouges into the earth from the meteorite strikes at various distances from the village. The schoolhouse took a little hit, and we had to patch the roof with a sheet of tin, tarring about it. Otherwise, the town had modest damage, graciously sparing the library and the village. It was good to know we were in the right place.

Since the broad revelation I got that day was indistinct, I wondered how much longer our lives here would last. I knew, and Daddy had explained, that with only so many goats, we were likely to get weak ones, as the next generations were all from the same clan. Maybe we were already weak by the fact that Chloe and I were mostly from Daddy and only partly from Mother. Regardless of how careful we were with procreating, a next generation, as Daddy explained, was likely to have defects, both for us and the goats. With the animals, we had some choice to keep the hearty and dismiss the defective. Nonetheless, would the time this planet had left, and the duration of our lives, be enough?

EIGHT

Unbinding Chains

Chloe and I would more than ever walk about holding hands. We talked a lot about past life recollections, and referring to the book titled *Ascension*, started more confessions – clearly influenced by that vision we got of our little spirit girl, not being at the pedestal working on enlightenment, but in trouble. I'd confessed all the stuff I'd done on the island and even some weird stuff from previous lives. We knew it was incumbent to make progress, but in fact, once we started, we quite enjoyed the recalls of the experiences as a diversion. We could have read more books from our libraries, but now our own past lives had more intrigue than many novels, and they were far more personal.

In the nearby house with the bay window, we set up a desk with a stuffed chair on one side and a padded desk chair on the other. This had become our "confessionary." Each time we rolled off a confession we felt gentle relief. I kept the black book handy when I could, referencing the content, nurturing the application of the esoteric knowledge. While rolling off simple sins we learned how to listen, and our personalities bloomed. Chloe often acted masculine after finding little confessions from her previous lifetime which hadn't been occluded. She'd taken to wearing pants and boy's button-down shirts and keeping her hair in a ponytail away from her face.

In the summer, we often just slept in that house. I'd read through the book about the definition of the Universe and of Armageddon, the veritable cessation of existence, and some indefinite elements of confession, which had to be taken up by related incidents, each leading to an earlier by "harmonic emotive association." It spoke of energy patterns that can tie into the base identity of the soul, and thus additional energies with coarser harmonic frequencies could get attached unknowingly – or as a causative result, intentionally producing a propensity for characteristic behaviors and actions. Characteristics and behaviors of who? The victims were the fragmented souls broken off, or created, from the main. Just as well it meant myself. So, who was my god – the girl?

Well, that was making only so much sense. One of the flashes I got when younger, when apparently passing out on the floor, had me entangled into cosmic scale images like this – planets, suns, quasars and such flashing me into some form of hypnotism, or simply slamming me into unawareness, probably to direct specific harmonic energies to make me crazy or obsessive, just as I had been. "Harmonic" had nothing to do with "harmony!"

I was realizing that I was not necessarily the protagonist of my own life. By intentional force, I was induced to become the antagonist for someone else's story. I needed to get ahead of this, to undo the mechanisms that directed me, to shave away the harmonic energies that turned me into an automaton, an energy-bound soul acting no better than a wind-up toy.

There were two facing pages with a simple graph, showing a timespan across the bottom of the page. *Up* was the amount of power the harmonic energies would exert against the soul. With *present* at the right, the first few dots to the left were shown with significant power, then previous dots, with the dates going backward by years, tens of years, hundreds of years and so on, showed lower energy, until the last dot showed high power. There was a gold star drawn on the page by that dot. Each dot represented a whole confession.

I believed I could deduce the intent of the algorithm – we made a confession, then looked for a confession of a similar harmonic, whatever that harmonic might be, either by the type or the emotion, the act, or the situation. It meant that once started, one always reverted to prior confessions until some chronic item was alleviated. I'd seen a short series of events bring about incredible changes. Now I finally understood that all series should be taken back to a significant, high powered item for a greater magnitude of results. It was the point when the "ostensible gods" had decided to inflict a direction upon their pawn, and we could encroach upon these incidents and resolve them. This alone was a cathartic recognition. We could imaginably overrule the planned direction set by the gods that discordantly composed us.

I looked at the little leather-bound book, holding it firmly in my view, having a thought that elicited chills through my spine – was there some explicable reason I was holding this book? Was it the intention of these gods to have it in my hand? Was this another form of direction from above?

It was a comfortable day with fragrant easterly breezes, so with notebooks to jot what happened, I fetched Chloe and tantalized her with the concept, considering I had no statistical proof that the assertion would produce results. Wearing only light summer sundresses we went to a place in the yard under a large maple and she asked me to recall something I'd done that was wrong. I instantly encountered something about the embalmed girls after first seeing that everyone was dead, so I related it. She asked me to recall an earlier event and I'd become blank and dizzy, then a new scene, harmonic by content, came into view. In a prior lifetime as a medic, I'd been stitching up a young woman after some accident, and I'd kissed all about her when I wasn't supposed to have been, then continued sewing her up. With a little consternation I relayed that confession.

"Okay, per your presumed procedure, tell me an earlier one?"

I put my attention on it, and with a moment's dedication images came. "I'd been a father and pulled my little three-year-old girl up out of bed. I was missing some money and accused her of playing with it. I was so angry and smacked her several times. She bit my forearm and it hurt so much I reactively punched her."

Grief boiled up through my chest, pouring off a slurry of sobs while more of the scene brought itself onto my mind's stage. "She threw up and a large bruise formed on her forehead, and her butt and back where she'd landed. I took her to a hospital and within minutes they took me away from her, charging me with the beating and making further accusations." The final series of events soured my emotions as they were unveiled. "I went to a jail – they hated me – accused me of things I didn't do, but I didn't defend myself well enough, believing that not talking would be better than saying something they could take out of context. Within weeks the other inmates beat me when taking a shower, slamming my head into the tiles. Another inmate told me that if I went back to my cell they *would* kill me. I didn't die that night – I had to go back to the cell. The next time at the showers, though, they beat me so badly I saw the back of my head. My hair was all shaggy and wet, thick blood going into the drain. I was dead." I cried off some grief, letting my fingers touch the ground, pulling at a few blades of grass, watching my tears hit leaves and soil. "Heavy grief – *that* was an encumbrance!" I confirmed, feeling I'd made it through the worse of it.

"That's pretty rich," said Chloe. "Now per procedure, give me another, earlier."

I dug in and the impressions came quickly, "There was an event, not just lifetimes ago, but planets ago. I'd had a boat? It was a three-hulled catamaran. I see it – a small bridge – never seen a boat like it. I had a couple young college girls with me, perhaps nieces, perhaps their friends. I got them a little drunk and we had a nasty party below deck. I don't think there was anything we didn't do as long as it didn't require ropes, cuts, bruises or suffocation." I related the details of the appalling event. She sat and listened with divine patience, took notes and kept me reaching deeper for successively earlier confessions. The connotations of these past-planet recalls gave relevance to the algorithm, aside from just blowing my mind.

I went on through many other incidents and realized that, as I'd taken it back much earlier in the universe, that there was plenty of agreement with all the universe' member souls to have a multitude of violent and horrible events happen. They had all wanted to be affected despite how awful the consequences were. It was the game as set up from much earlier in the universe. They wanted it all the way down the line, recognizing that they were breaking rules and thus set up their own consequences to be consistent with those rules. I didn't know why the rules. Why did such things cause so much trouble?

"Recall an earlier incident," persisted Chloe.

"Ah, I see a flash – hot." I felt sweat forming on my face and shoulders. "I – I keep seeing this flash – the beginning – flash – hot." I felt sweat dripping between my breasts and buttocks, adjusting myself to absorb the itchy drips, nearly falling over from a strange disorientation. I uttered a few intelligible syllables in an attempt to describe the presence of souls that had no direct form, yet I knew they were there. "I – I was a girl identity but had no form. We threw big things – suns, I think. We were supposed to be putting them into place, but we had fun throwing them at each other. I messed mine up or – I was throwing. Oh, I was throwing mine to another girl but hers hit mine first, and the suns blew up." I saw the flash again as if in real time. I feared the planet had just been hit with a meteor, my ears ringing, eyes blinking and body vibrating, while being detached from the setting of the village. I could yet feel my breath and bite my tongue, and as minutes passed, I could again feel and see the grounds about me.

I looked up at Chloe, her eyes closed, her breath forced. "Chloe?" I said.

"Yeah," she said. "I feel disoriented. Something – something weird."

"Okay," I said as if reversing the point of view of the session. "I think I got that one. We can continue." I felt incongruous, not elated.

Chloe looked about as if she'd just arrived. She repeated the main command, "Okay. To be consistent with our current procedure, give me an earlier confession."

That last one was so early in the universe that I could hardly think something could be earlier. But yet an image came to mind, so I voiced it. "I'd been a slumlord of an apartment tower and treated my tenants horribly. I lived in the top-level suite covering a whole floor. They'd been very poor and struggling people, and I exploited them however I could to keep them as tenants when they had trouble paying rent, using them like slaves in every category until they all burned down my building and I perished with it. I'm not sure when." I stumbled to understand when it happened as it appeared to be notably later, confounded as to how I could be back to body life after so many "big-spirit" incidents. I was ecstatic as a set of prior agreements boiled away with the confession, happening so suddenly I could barely see images as they snapped aside as fast as I could look. Feeling giddy, I told Chloe, "Long before that, I got into an argument with someone and we fought over control of some planets until we decided we were aligned to the same game, to play nasty with people, and a hard-coded agreement had been formed that eventually led, millions of years later, to the apartment tower and related sinful behaviors." I paused to consider when these events occurred, allowing my certainty to congeal, and only then voiced it to Chloe. "It was in an earlier universe."

Upon understanding, I'd achieved that elation I'd expected, allowing the agreement to unlock. I cachinnated and threw myself back, looking up at the sky and the trees. I giggled like a little girl. I even thought of the little girl voice, wondering if part of that laughter and behavior was hers.

Chloe's smile was as wide as I'd ever seen, her exhilaration defined by her bright eyes reflecting blue skies and clouds like a fisheye lens. Her head shook about, "Oh my God – it really works." I noted how beautiful her young smile was. I remained lying back in the grass, laughing, kicking my legs. She merrily threw the notebook aside, "You are genius, Miss Dahilana," and tumbled over me. I'm sure it would have had the semblance of heavy frolicking, the grabbing, pulling uncontrollably, matching every point on the bodies that we could, hands to hands, face to face, groin to groin and legs to legs. If we could have merged into one another, we would have.

Then she rolled aside as we reflected upon the credence given to the content in the book. We finally had a lever that was big enough to pull, to have an effect upon our own salvation, from a level we'd failed to mention might as well be abject abomination.

"Well the chain sequence seems to work," said Chloe. "My turn I guess."

I couldn't get past my giggles, slapping my face every attempt I'd made to speak. The celestially-ancient emotion poured this way and that, capitulating wildly between the copacetic significance of releasing the agreement, and the horrific effects the agreement had instilled upon my existence throughout a timespan longer than that of the universe. I realized I'd just reached in to harness power greater than the sun. I sat up to face Chloe, and she too sat with tears and smiles. I waved my hands up, relinquishing control to the flood of joy.

We took a break to go nibble on fresh fruit, acting as silly as two drunks at a party or two lovers on a honeymoon. Though I'd expected to continue trying the new chaining procedure with Chloe, we were not able to return to session that day. We resorted to singing and skipping through our chores. The old world would have assumed we were on euphoric amphetamines and homemade wine or playing with nitrous oxide and ether. I'd even laughed when I stepped my ankle-high leather boots into goat dung.

We didn't have any explanation why we were mutually drawn so emotionally high. There were no historical parables that explained this. In the barn with the pigs, I'd had my back turned away. "Aren't you going to get that damn old feedbag?" asked Chloe – I'd heard her happy voice as she was unable to act angry.

"Yes, I'll get that damn old feedbag," I responded, fetched the bag and turned to her.

"What? I didn't say anything," she said.

"But you just asked me to get that 'damn old' bag?" I queried, the bag hanging in my left hand.

"Um – well I thought it, but I didn't say it," she said, happily confused.

I forced a thought, directing it to her with all my might, even turning away. "It's what I heard, my eternal love!"

"So, you heard it. Pretty strange huh?" she responded with her sweet congruous voice.

I turned back to examine her, my tears welling. Her face was so soft, lit by the indirect light from the open barn door. Her light, flowered dress was dancing about her in the breeze. Her hand gently reached for the light tendrils of her hair near her breast.

"We spoke without speaking – just as the book suggests!" I said of the telepathic moment. Barefoot since my soiled boot was in a tub, soaking away the goat crap, I gently stepped in her direction, appearing as light as ghost, my summer dress loosely flowing with cross breezes through the barn, I placed myself directly in front of her and gently lifted her chin for the softest kiss I could perform. Conjoined in thought and love, my perception expanded as if we were above our own heads, partially viewing the barn about us, appearing to see our flowing hair and shoulders from above – two of the most beautiful girls that could have ever existed – this profound experience wasn't for the gods – this was for us.

We'd settled to a new calmness for the remainder of the day, and even through the night I had this unusual sense of spiritual detachment from my body, from the village, even from the world.

After breakfast and morning chores, acting as ordinary as possible when near Father and Mother, we sneaked off again. I'd grabbed the notebook and jotted down a few things about the experiment, referring to notes on the method. Now it was Chloe's turn. I asked her to recall something. "Okay love, give me a confession, now!" In like fashion to her telepathic slip of "damn feedbag" the day before, I only acted angrily but there was no way that I could display anything but clean intention.

She picked an incident when she was just ten when she tried to get Daddy to break the rules. "I pushed Daddy to do things I was far too young for. He would only kiss me and hold my butt. But he'd say, 'The day will come soon enough, little one.' One day we caught the animals in the act. I simply said, 'I want to know what it's like.' He walked off. I'd tried to catch up with him. Soon he had a toolbox and loaded it onto the old truck. Then he was gone – I think for three days. I knew he'd leave sometimes – I told Mother he said he was going scavenging in the next town."

"Okay. Per procedure, please give me an earlier confession."

She picked one from when she and I were in bed and she was about a year old, and she wanted more attention but didn't get it. "I didn't like being a baby. You were pretty, and my last life identity still gets me sometimes, even now."

So, then I asked her for something earlier.

"Ha! It was a boating thing like yours. I was the girl. Plain yacht, I guess, and I was teenage, out with some cousins and friends, and got involved with a boy from the port town. We partied at the dock when the adults were away. I got him into the cabin and, well, ended up getting pregnant, and the boy, being older, got into big trouble and got sent away. I had the baby, but they took it for someone else to adopt. My parents hated me after that." She hesitated to drop a few tears. "They never trusted me again. As I grew up I had to just leave them behind because they were always judgmental and over-controlling. And my life – I – wasn't that good. I couldn't hold up to their standards." She sniffled and wiped her nose.

"Okay. Per procedure, let's get an earlier confession," I said.

She went on, and we got lots of them. We couldn't finish the chain of events that day. We had to start again in the morning after handling chores. With ample endurance, it took a couple days and the events were being revealed from very early in the universe. Once again, we crossed the start of the universe. She was in tears of joy, happy, giggling, kicking her feet in the grass, almost exactly as I had.

Her statement was a huge concept: "We'd lived before this universe. But we aren't here now to *continue* this one. We're here to *end* it."

Then I heard one of the voices. It wasn't strong and came more as a concept. But I believed it was the little girl saying, "Good work little ones. Keep it up. Your work is helpful. If we can just get more lost souls in the universe to do the same!"

And just as Chloe had become elated with my first results, I became just as elated with hers. It was clear that the optimum condition for us as souls had nothing to do with bodies on planetary surfaces, farming and occasionally stepping in goat dung. Perhaps the most confounding conundrum was how near we could have been at any time in the universe to stepping out of the agreements that bound us below the transcendental edge of existence. We could tamper with the gates of heaven with such a simple process. How ethereal were the apparently massive chains we'd ignorantly wrapped ourselves with? I had to consider it was like a million little ropes holding down a circus tent – even a few such ropes could hold the tent in place on a calm day. But millions of them could bind the canvas, outlasting it until it rotted away. Millions of emotionally bound agreements could add up in number to overwhelm a soul to the end of the universe, or to the end of the awareness of the soul, whichever came first. And what would happen to a single lost soul in a lost universe, to the point of existing in a completely oblivious state? Perhaps *that* is the fear that most individuals would correlate to a simple death, believing instead that it leads to nonexistence, a separate state far worse than exiting a body.

We continued working on confessions as such. The realizations and emotional outpourings were enough to have our parents notice, partly because we reduced the time we'd spent on other study. So, we taught Mother and Father how to do the confessions along a series of earlier events to a significant "star," being some moment of realization usually involving laughter and tears all at once. Mother and Father had a tumultuous time with it. Daddy would get angry despite the fact that he and Chloe had done some of these confessions before. He wasn't getting his chains to go more than a few items, then he'd give up. They didn't spend much time doing it and hadn't stated any great epiphanies.

We were discussing it in the kitchen another evening. Chloe explained to them, "It's not like you really did anything wrong because you were just doing what was already decided by those big god-like people that put us here. What we want to undo is that earliest decision to *force* us into this universe and have us *act* like suicidal maniacs, thieves and liars, and sex-crazed animals. We're playing their game for them. We have a right to refuse."

Father was at the dinner table bemoaning, "I don't know why the bother. It's not like we decided our own fate."

I tried, "If we are part of some higher souls, from way back, and high up, then we did. We did decide. Or even if we didn't strictly decide, we each still have those decisions in us. If we can, we undo it, and we become better people."

He didn't have much of an answer, and I had no idea why his earlier enthusiasm for past-life recall had become replaced with a vacant stare.

Chloe, who was getting a fairly strong and punchy personality, said, "I heard the voices when we got to the upper end of our chain that went back even before this universe. They know. They acknowledged our success. It's what they want us to do. We can change their minds because we are a part of them – we can undo the decisions they made that make us slaves to them. None of us are enemies. But if you remember the day we all fell down and heard that they might kill us off if we don't have a way to get better, this might be our best chance."

"Fine," said Father, throwing his hands. "I'd like to try it, but it doesn't work for me. I – I just have this attention on the things I'm forced to do, to survive, are also things that are decidedly wrong. I can't be good if, by the laws of survival, I must be bad."

Mother's lips pursed. Her head lowered too. She cried quietly, then folded up demoralized on the floor.

I gave the emotions a moment to pass, then spoke to them both, "Just confess them off. You are the ones with all the emotion caught up in them. We don't really care, except to go from rock bottom – there's only up. It's not like we don't know there aren't rules and that we've blatantly broken so many of them. Maybe some of the rules are terribly wrong and as we learn we'll better understand all that. But you have your part of the confessions and it seems pretty important – totally important – as important as being alive."

Mother and Father sat still, heads bowed, their breath paced.

Chloe went on, "You're part of the fix, part of the *straightening all this out.* You see – we could all die and be ghosts here. You could all die and leave me here alone. I'm not even on my home planet." She got up from the table, putting her plates in the sink. "I don't want to be left alone here or my home planet. I want us all to *ascend* together, whatever that really means."

Still, the parents sat. Father's sad eyes explored the room. Chloe shrugged then exited through the back door, and I watched her through the window. She was going to the bay-window house that Chloe and I called home.

"Daddy, you have to. You have to do this," I said. "By the way. It's your turn to do dishes tonight."

"I don't have a turn to do dishes!" he cried out. "I handle all the butchering."

"Okay – your penance for defying the gods. And we get the rest of the cleaning. Get started," I said. There were not that many dishes. It wasn't much of a punishment.

I left them. Mother still sat on the floor and Father sat there at the table. Mother started crying as I walked out the back door. If this wasn't enough, I guessed we'd just have to keep pushing them day after day until they could break through and do it.

But just a few days later, Father found a quiet moment, passing me at the back door when I was rinsing some of the last squash I'd collected from the garden. He said, "I think I can confess to you," and he looked up at me. I nodded. We set up an upstairs room in mine and Chloe's home for the sessions. I sat on a small, bare bed on the second floor of the old house, being comfortable in an old but pretty dress because I couldn't wear pants with my pregnancy at several months.

Daddy sat on the edge of a padded wooden chair, onto which we'd tied an extra cushion. "I want this held confidential until I'm ready to share it. I'd gotten beat up the last time I tried this." He clamped his own thumbs, his eyes dashing about the room.

"So, Josephus, please give me a confession to start the chain," I requested.

Apprehensively, he said, "Damn. Where do I get started?" He fidgeted as if his body wanted to walk him away.

"Anything," I said, and he instantly broke into tears. "I'm not actually a good guy. I'm a hateful person. I'm the 'kind of people' who get their hands cut off, or their balls. I'm the kind of idiot that wouldn't let the girl's sit without me looking up their skirts to their panties. I…"

"I don't want everything at once. The book says to start with one. Any one. But only one."

He threw up his arms. "What – one – seventh grade. I had to speak at the front of the class. I dropped a pen, so I could look up a skirt. Pretty panties. Nice girl too. She was pretty with hair that framed her face so well. Brunette, wavy. I caught her eye, but I think she realized what I was doing. But she didn't move her legs until I was up, then she crossed them casually. She smiled – she'd let me get away with it. I was a good-looking boy. Ah – by a couple years she knew I wasn't a very good boy."

"Good. According to procedure, give me an earlier confession," I commanded.

He looked blank for a second, raised his eyes and asserted, "Oh shit – I didn't really want to hit that one.

"Say it anyway. It's just technical. Blurt it out," I encouraged.

"I was just a little boy and my mother took me to shower with her. I wanted to touch her privates. I even got aroused. I looked at it and Mother laughed at me. 'You naughty boy!' she said and shook her finger at me. She didn't take me into the shower with her after that. The only other thing she said was that I couldn't marry her. I didn't understand the connection. She said she'd married Daddy and couldn't be with me. 'Couldn't be with me' – what did that mean? I was so dejected. I wanted to win her over against my father. Oh shit – I guess I can tell now." He bent his face over into his hands, letting off a minute of grief. "I so loved my mother. Then she died of some rare disease, the doctors couldn't even figure out what it was. She didn't die in the event. Oh, I was really lost as I grew up. I always hated my father for stealing time I could have been with her. So, I found a girl – a smaller girl – she was very pretty – well you know, you know. I swore to marry her if only because I wanted my daughters to look like her. And they do." He sobbed but forced through his cries, "I see her every day when I look at you, and your Mother, and Chloe. I see her every damn single putrid post-apocalyptic-event day." He shook with grief, eyeing me to see the remnant of her beauty.

"Is there anything else about that?" I asked. By working with Chloe, this question appeared useful if emotion was still pouring out.

"Ah - my father saw me going into Mother's room, but luckily, at the time I had my book bag still on my back, and so I pulled out a math book right away, saying I was asking for help. I got out of it. But he always looked at me sideways. I always wondered if he knew that I'd been trying to get Mother's personal attention, especially after finding a small bundle of my mother's underwear in my dresser – that was before she died. Oh, that was embarrassing – I had a whole change of clothing for her. That was dumb. I'd wanted to move her into my bedroom and take her from Father. I just wanted to win her back. She was the one that was supposed to find it. That was just dumb." Then he laughed. "I shouldn't have to worry about it. I was a little kid – being dumb, being possessive of my mother." He chuckled, eyes bright, a smile showing that the tension had lifted. I wrote that we'd hit the bottom of that chain.

After several short chains that gave modest results, I noted he hadn't been talking about Mother. His face and expressions just appeared to be avoiding something. When starting a new chain, I asked him, "Is there something about Mother, who we know is also your daughter, that you aren't talking about? Is there something you didn't want to say?"

"She's my wife now. I can't really do wrong with that. We were directed by these voices to have our family the way it is now. And if we don't have some boys soon, how can we carry on the race? This planet will be completely dead."

"It might. We'd be taken to other planets just as Chloe came here," I bemoaned.

"Yeah. You are probably right," he said. He patted his hands to his knees.

"So? The confession?" I prompted.

Daddy looked about at the ceiling and about the room. "Ah – what am I supposed to say?" The room was nearly bare. The walls were dirty white, looking almost gray. The floor was a light-colored wood, but also took on a lot of gray color over the years. It was well into fall, the only strong color in the trees. Everything else lacked much depth. The windows were not blocked by curtains. The old glass was firm in the frames, as we had repaired the window putty to keep them sealed.

"Just tell me what comes to mind. It's just a confession," I said.

He tried to talk but was holding back, his fortitude withering like the garden plants.

"Go on," I whispered.

Disconsolate, he said, "I don't think Avelynn even remembers. She was too young. She's got it blocked. If she starts to confess more, she'll find it and hate me. Probably why we weren't getting anywhere."

"Ah. Go on," I said, stoic on the bed.

He hesitated, and a few tears flowed. "There was a medicine that made her sleep better. She didn't really need it – I gave it to her and when she was solidly asleep – I had this notion that I wanted to know more about my wife, her mother, in her younger years. There was this baby girl that looked the spitting image of her as a child. I looked her over. I could have done worse. It's not like I hadn't read the newspapers, there were so many worse people than me in the world. There were sick and disgusting perverts – but to me, the only difference is that I controlled myself and didn't touch her. The evil in my head was that I wanted to go beyond the limit. And then she woke." He hesitated and wept softly. "Well, I had to go back to my beautiful young wife, who'd gained a few pounds after the pregnancy and didn't look as good with stretch marks and flabbiness. Damn having babies. Babies make ugly mothers." Then he burst sharply into tears. He cried out, "Oh my God. I'm an idiot. I'm beyond stupid. Oh my God!" He rushed out though I'd tried to stop him until he was past the heaviest emotion, but he stumbled out with tears flowing like a leaky shower. Bouncing against the wall, he tromped his way down the stairs, then fumbled across the yard, stumbling at the edge of the garden, and went into the house, yelling for Mother. "Avelynn! I'm so sorry."

I followed with quickened steps because I figured it would have significance for the session and our knowledge of how to run these chains of events. I stepped into the back of the house. He was kissing her, and as she stood, he bowed down and put his head up against her dress, kissing at her belly.

Daddy begged, "I'm so sorry – babies make ugly bodies, but they don't make ugly souls. I'm so sorry for putting so much attention on the children and not you. They are beautiful. But it's you. I'm sorry for ignoring you but you are now my wife. I'm good to be with you, my daughter, as my wife."

He lifted himself, wrapped his arms around her and cried on her shoulder.

Mother glanced at me, first curious that she was seeing a crying man, but as her mind understood the ramifications, her expression changed. She held her arms about his shoulders and the back of his head, offering the appropriate level of sympathy.

This session was different than my expectation. I would never have presumed that exact cognition. I took notes, showing that "chain of a single item" had found its end.

He turned to me and boasted, "For what it's worth, I'm glad you kept on pushing me. I didn't want to do it. I didn't want it at all. It was just awful – it's hard. I didn't want it. I guess I want those spirits whose voices we hear to handle it for me. But the reward is here!" he beat on his chest. "I don't want them to take all the work, all the credit, and all the joy that goes with it. I'm in. I can do this."

That was good because despite how pleased I was, it was starting to sound like a speech. I closed the notebook. "Chores now. Tomorrow, then."

He nodded, nuzzling against my speechless mother, who was quite satisfied with the result.

Someone – something – touched my shoulders as an acknowledgment. But there was no voice. I just nodded slightly in return.

Through the experiments with Chloe and Father, I discovered confidence that I could handle huge buried energies and the consequences of the early universe programming from our gods. We'd been reluctant and slow to catch on, but I was sure this wasn't just imagined, considering the height of our realizations and elation, and depths of our acts and accompanying grief. Feeling cocky I felt we could be as effective as the reluctant little girl soul that had been the source of the voice I'd heard. Perhaps her accomplishments were at a different level where they could ensconce and avoid the madness of her spiritual descendants. If the act of unbinding chains of events that held us into the universe could lead to expanded knowledge far beyond our imagination, there could be some capacity to surpass her in effectiveness, breaching the veil between solid entanglements and knowledge to discover the processes she'd been using. We could be the ones busting ourselves out of the universe. It was a wild thought, but I really doubted we could surpass or circumvent all that work that had been done already. And they knew something up there, wherever they were, that could achieve results far beyond our confession chains.

NINE

Jack Arrives

Through the winter to the next spring, my belly continued to grow. My time with the baby bump, weight gain and disfigurement often brought me to tears through hormone and physiological changes. I found it difficult to keep up with the outside chores, so through the mild winter I cleaned the houses in the village. I couldn't concentrate and needed to eat often. I'd not been able to study as much. Chloe attempted to help me with confession chains, but I couldn't keep my head in it.

I kept a notebook with me, so I could write what boiled out and review it with Chloe each evening. The events I was running into were related to the pains, the discomforts and issues of being pregnant, and I was within the ninth month of frustration. We moved our main room to the parsonage due to the risk of labor.

It was in the evening after supper when I finally asked Chloe to help me get through my mind's blockages. I couldn't get the images; I couldn't get the pains. Every time I looked at it, it dispersed, leaving my mind empty and blank. The incident I'd reached up to at that point was just thousands of years before. The next one – I couldn't even assume an approximate date.

I sat on the bed, feet in a round tub of cool water to help soothe them after a day of cleaning. Chloe came in, reciting a line that she'd repeated often, "I wish I could be the dad. I wish it was my baby."

"It is," I repeated as my answer. "Same set of genetics. In fact, if it is a girl I'm sure it will look like you."

"I'm sure it will, if it is developing correctly at all," she said.

I slumped.

"Oh – I'm sorry – again. I say that all the time, but you know it could happen," she insisted.

"No. I heard something," I pointed up.

She stopped while laying out her nighttime lingerie. "What did you get?"

"I don't know. Just to not worry – that was all," I shrugged and turned to her.

"Not very distinct, huh?"

"No – but better than nothing," I said, feeling weighted. My feet still hurt. I knew that if I stood up I'd feel heavy.

"So – is it a boy or a girl?" she checked.

"Don't know that. If it's another girl, Daddy will cry again," I postulated.

"I'd be jubilant. How many girls can one-man handle?" she jested.

I pondered on, "But the genetics. I don't think I understand it myself, but we could get mutation. To have enough people to repopulate a planet we need to be doing better than this. Of course, I don't know that we need to."

"Huh?" she said.

"Repopulate the planet. I don't know that we need to. You had the recognition that we are ending the universe not starting it. If that's true, and I got the impression from another that the planet won't last all that long but our mere number and the time we have is enough – I don't know how to put it all together, but we don't need to repopulate the whole planet for any indefinite amount of time."

"Next few rounds of asteroids might take it out," she conjectured.

"Rounds?" I threw my face up to her.

"Um – there were meteors before – didn't you see them – six years ago? Daddy and I were outside – you might have been inside. Minutes of white streaks all over the sky. No booms – Daddy said each cycle – five or six years maybe – they change – they get better, get worse. I thought we were dead on that last one. Next one might be all we get." She changed into her chosen nightclothes, then covered up with a long blue robe with Battenberg lace. It had a tie about the middle and straps about the wrists making it excellent for a cool evening.

"I didn't see the earlier meteors," I said, feeling left out. My feet were a bit better, so I pulled them from the portable tub. Chloe helped me dump the cool water down the tub in the bathroom. On the way back into the bedroom, I jostled the notebook to get her attention. "I'd been writing out events – mostly stuff related to being pregnant. I can't get past this one. I feel so confused," I yawned. I'd reached a point of despondency with the events, but I knew that wasn't ideal.

"You look tired. Maybe we just go to bed?"

"No. It's confusion. I yawn when I'm confused. Happens all the time when I study," I stated.

"Oh. I guess I just haven't seen it lately. Makes sense – I just thought you were tired."

"Yeah. Well, you yawn sometimes too, you know, when you shouldn't have any reason to be tired."

Chloe's countenance showed rejection of the idea. "I always have a reason to be tired. We've too much to do. Survival isn't for sloths, even if we can live in someone else's home."

"Certainly. But can you help me?"

"Sure. But bedtime soon. If no progress tonight, we'll have to reserve more time tomorrow."

I started right in. "Sure. The incident I could get was horrible. Unlike the usual confession stuff this is just pain and when I try it hurts, then it's just gone. The one I could get was when I had given birth – seems like a long time ago – tens – hundreds of thousands of years? It was still this planet, though. That's what profoundly confuses me. How could all the historians be wrong? We were living on an island nation, a little like the island I'd lived on as Miranda. But, it was more advanced – they had televisions with better pictures. They didn't have antennae all over their radios and TVs. They had cars, but I don't understand how they moved – they didn't fill up with gas. Interesting stuff. But I was pregnant from a boyfriend and got sick with the pregnancy, then miscarried – that's where everything went weird and I got infected and I think it was some kind of blood poisoning that killed me."

"Significant, but no worse than the ones we'd run before. So, what is before that? What won't fully come up?" she asked bluntly, gazing deeply, fully expecting an answer to just pop into view.

And it did. I saw it so clearly I about fell off the bed, recoiling much like the image – I'd been a pregnant girl, and someone beat me in the belly. "Oh shit!" I cried. As the image came clearer I continued, "A man beat me and said, 'Why do you keep coming here. I'm in enough trouble already. You can't – you can't be pregnant. Why they'll kill me if they find out.' He was older – middle aged. I was younger – probably too young. I – I can't see it. It all went black."

"Okay. What don't you see? Maybe it's just something you feel?" she asked by experience from having done so many of these chains.

"I – I feel whirling. I guess I was falling, a hit – bang – solid surface. He had hit me, yelling – he'd been yelling 'Get out! Go away!' I hit pavement or sidewalk. Grit – grit in my teeth – a busted tooth? I felt about – I think I was right at the edge of a sidewalk by the street. I think I busted the tooth on the curb. It was night – dark. So dark. I couldn't see – maybe – ouch – my head. Um – pain – head – blood – my hands were full of blood coming from my head. I was just there on the ground with a busted head and tooth. Shock – maybe going into shock. It all faded as I laid back." I lost touch with further images. I didn't want to sit up, fearing I'd feel dizzy, but tears were pooling in my eyes. I dragged them away with my fingers.

She pushed on expertly. "So, you were pregnant, and he hit you – what else was around?"

Odd unsorted images danced about, settling on a lamp overhead. "Lamp – lamppost. It got knocked and went out – breaking glass with it – I think he ran his car into it – an electric motor noise. It wasn't adding up – I guess I expected an engine noise."

"Wow – fully electric car?" she noted. "What next?"

"Sick – puked. Puked all over my upper chest and neck. I was on my back. I don't think I was very busty – my belly protruded big. My legs were awkward. My head spun. I spit out blood and a broken part of my tooth. There were contractions and – I was miscarrying there in the street. Oh – it was bitter cold. I saw snow flurries. Then more contractions and felt my underwear filling with something."

I hesitated with the horror as I realized what it had been. "I was bawling and sat up. In a frantic state I pulled the panties down enough to let the miscarried fetus fall out into the street – it was pretty big, maybe two kilograms, and I felt it was a huge mistake to just dump it out like that. The placenta came out too. I tore the cord away from the placenta and pulled the baby into my coat against my chest. Then in my shock, I tried to get up, but I fumbled and dropped it. The slippery fetus hit the ground – rubbery – right on the head. It flopped. It was hit right in the face."

I broke into tears, completely appalled at my recall. I could feel the emotion escalating.

Chloe waited out the worst of it, then she gently asked, "How old was your body when that happened?"

But the thought brought up more emotion. A minute passed as I heaved sobs. I wiped my eyes. "I guess I had a big pocket of grief on that – maybe that's why I couldn't get it. It's terrible. I dropped the baby. Then it was – I got down to see it and the face was bashed in. It didn't even look human – underdeveloped and weird. It terrified me, and I took it to a big trash bin and wrapped it up into trash that was there, tying it into trash bags. I felt so stupid. I don't think I even had a real home."

I finally caught up with the inquiry on my age. "I was living at some kind of girls' home – merely fourteen – that's the number that comes to mind – about fourteen years old." The grief was draining off, alleviating the overwhelming intensity of the horrendous event. But another piece of the event kept begging at the back of my mind.

"Well, you'll need my help to get through the rest of this one, Dahilana. We can continue this chain tomorrow. Have we got this event handled?"

A shutter struck me, not sure what it would connote. "No," I said. "I fear something. I'm really scared. It wasn't the only thing awry."

"Was it before or after what you'd said already?"

"Um," I pondered, "After."

"By how much – minutes, hours, days?"

"Days," is what popped into my mind.

"What was it?"

"Well, I was sure I went back dirty and bloody to a girls' home – my home. I had a room – small room. I had to help with chores there. A woman met me that night I miscarried – she saw me all dirty and sobbing as I went upstairs, shocked at what she found – that I'd gotten beaten up into having the miscarriage, and she took care of me. But someone found the baby because I'd told them where I'd left it. They questioned me but left me locked up. They insisted I'd killed the fetus." At that point, a new wave of grief struck me as I saw an image – an oncoming vehicle. The pictures didn't compute – a crazy person but not the one that beat me. Someone was running in bare feet – rushing into traffic.

At that point I saw it – I had run into traffic because they accused me of killing the baby as well as having someone beat me up as a subterfuge to escape punishment. I had not been able to deal with it. For spite, I had thrown myself in front of a moving vehicle after escaping the girl's home.

"What's going on," asked Chloe.

I had put my arms over my head to brave through the suddenly breached maelstrom of emotion. The grief was so sharp, so intense, so miserable, magnified by the hate and cruelty of the accusers. In that lifetime I couldn't admit to the depth of my illicit and compulsive sexual activities, attempting to get a little extra money for underage prostitution services – but it ended up driving me to suicide. At present I couldn't speak – my throat raked raw from the agonized crying, spittle dripping off my lips. I sat up to help it drip rather than run back on my neck. I'd wished the tub was still at my feet to catch the mess, but instead, it just dribbled onto my currently pregnant belly. I forced a raspy utterance, "Chloe! Chloe!"

She clung to me, assertively consoling.

Father and Mother and been attempting to sleep, but they heard the noises. Father had a characteristic knock, taken from an old song. It was him. "Come in Father," said Chloe.

"Just checking on you – huh?" he offered softly.

"She'll be okay. A quick session. She hit a fine one."

"Fine one indeed," he said, appeased, and slowly backed out, having set the door to.

Chloe grabbed a towel from the bathroom for me to snort and cough into.

I wiped my wet face and blew my nose. "Yeah," I whispered through my shock. "It was indeed a fine one. If that was fine. I'd hate to see a bad one."

"We've hit big ones before, Dahilana," she said softly.

"Yes and no – this was sharp enough to stab a pig. I think we should count them in the morning just in case."

She smiled. "So – you want to fill me in?"

There was no discretion in telling a confession. "Yeah – I guess I'd better. After getting back to the girl's home, they said I'd killed the baby on purpose, and intended to take me to jail. They had me tied down in the room, but I got out somehow – bathroom break? I went out the window and rushed away from everything. They were chasing me – I got past a fence by a big highway and rushed toward headlights." I felt the impact again and put my hand to my head, letting it pass. "Oh! Yuck – it was crunching – my body. Fast but all sorts of noise, then a high-pitched pain and a tug. The tug was death."

"Anything else?"

"Well – before I died – back at the start – I had gone back to the man for money even though I was pregnant, and I knew it was dangerous. I'd tried to get him to mess with me again. He had a wife and a little girl himself. I felt sorry for her. He had a boy too, but I don't think the little boy was in trouble. I pushed the man to mess with me to protect his girl." With that last statement, I finally experienced the relief I'd been hoping for. "My actual sin was directed by a desire to help the daughter. I was a horrible, awful person and she might have been a good little girl. I could save her by giving up myself." My heart was lighting up from the deed of confession.

"See? You're not all bad," she acknowledged with a light smile.

"No – I'm not all bad. Disgusting, degraded, immoral, obsessed, in hell, my wicked soul yet to burn in the eternal inferno...."

"Shut up," she said, smacking me lightly to be silly.

"Thanks. I feel a lot better now," I said as a facetious response. We giggled. But at this moment I felt more humbled than degraded and more relieved than treacherous. I rolled back into bed, my hands rubbing my big belly, and how stable it felt now. "That phrase – 'you can't have a baby' – had the power in it. It was telling me constantly that having a baby would be dangerous, even leading to my death – unseen by me – it was having power."

"Well that was a good thing to handle, then, wasn't it?" she asked.

"Yeah. Very good."

Chloe took down the last of the notes and asked me, "So when did this occur?"

Numbers danced about in my head. "Millions – several – few – two – two million years – maybe a little less. Society was present then. Again, I wonder what had happened to it since all our history books said people developed into cultures just thousands of years ago. My series of confessions have typically missed all that recent history."

Chloe expounded on her own thoughts. "We've run a lot of incidents, but I would have to agree that we don't have anything that would explain that. Maybe Mother or Father have recalled something that would explain how such societies got lost. How could all that history just be gone? Maybe it was destroyed for a reason. Maybe it was a plan from the big souls, so we wouldn't know and wouldn't have expected this recent passing of events – the last twenty-five years."

"Yeah. Maybe we'd all gone unconscious. Still, it doesn't make any sense." I pondered on the thought. "I think we can go to bed now."

She turned off a small lamp and came to cuddle in, pulling tightly behind me while I gazed up at the window. The moonlight was exceptionally strong that night, the moon being full and oddly large during a coincident perigee. Spring temperatures prevailed, and insects and frogs produced a cadence of noises. I comfortably succumbed to sleep, wondering if I'd experience any vivid dreams with the transcendent souls behind the mysterious voices and partially shrouded images. I'd longed to see a clear image of that little girl whose voice I'd heard and even come to recognize. I had seen vague pictures and evasive details – likely blond hair and small girl form. I wanted to see her with great longing, and I could not stray from my fundamental desire to be her.

I must have slept particularly hard, because in the morning I found our positions reversed, myself awkwardly facing Chloe's back, my arm wrapped around her. I had no recall of changing positions. She continued sleeping, so I held her to feel her breath. Detecting a faint odor of smoke, I became aware that the fireplace was being stocked, probably to assist with breakfast. It was time to get up. I pulled slowly back from Chloe and stepped awkwardly off the end of the bed.

"No!" she suddenly called out. "You're not getting out without giving me a kiss first."

I couldn't protest that with all my might. I crawled up to her and gave her a wonderful kiss, then a procession of them all over.

"Oh, get up already. You've got your kiss," she said, turning the table on the request.

"Oh, I got my kiss. Did you get yours?" I turned it back.

"Yeah but I've got to pee," she blurted with a strain. She pulled up quickly and rushed past me to the toilet.

"Hey – I'm the one that's pregnant!" I called back.

I pondered on the day's routine. I could continue cleaning but as long as it were a nice day I'd have to get out. After a quick breakfast, I chased Daddy out the back door.

When marginally helping Daddy feed the animals he said, "Breeders knew that you could take a small group of animals and crossbreed something new, but then it would take several generations and several hundred animals before you'd be able to get it robust enough to call it a breed – you'd have to eliminate the initial defects. We wouldn't want to kill off the mutated – naturally, not everyone gets to live, by choice or by how well they can live anyway. Kidneys might fail. Hearts would be defective and give out. Brains might reroute signals and get it all mixed up and you could have someone that couldn't even walk or feed himself, or herself. Or worse yet, the mother's ability to perform a birth could be reduced. We could treat ourselves like cattle, breed and breed until we get some good ones. Too much work to feed a bunch of little people and animals too. Don't get me wrong, I'm really counting on this baby of yours, but I have no idea of its viability."

"I know. Aren't you and Mother trying for another?" I queried as we turned to the shed to crack more grain for the chickens.

"We had been. We had a few early miscarriages. I didn't mention it. After the first, we didn't want to get your hopes up. But that's the body trying to say that the babies were not viable. It happens. We are trying again. But even if we get one, we might have something strange. We could get lucky, though. Why do you bring this up now?" He grabbed some buckets then turned to me looking as if he'd added, 'my well-developed pregnant daughter' to his sentence.

I helped pull a wagon with a gunny sack full of corn. "Well, I'm hoping for the best. I think what you are saying is that we may not succeed and will have to try again. I understand. I'm willing. We have that responsibility to the next generation of humans. But Chloe had said something in her realizations."

"What's that?" he hesitated, about to grab up a sack of corn.

"That we aren't here to start the universe. We are here to end it. I don't think they really want us to keep going."

"Oh – that's intense. Well, aside from that we try to have babies. They don't seem to be succeeding that well up there, do they?"

"Maybe. Maybe not. I haven't knocked out and seen images of planets streaking by in a long time," I said.

During this time, Daddy was teaching Chloe more about goats and animal husbandry, the ulterior motive to have her help with my childbirth. Chloe would be my dilation checker if not more. For her age, she appeared so much more aware and knowledgeable that I could barely think of her as a child.

The day came for me to give birth. I'd been sleeping but was woken early as the mucus plug let go and my bed became wet. Chloe was with me. I told her, "It's time, baby. Get Mother and Father. Nothing's waiting now." I went to a reconstructed, antique dentist chair with towels and blankets placed across it.

My obstetrics team was the best we could find on the planet, and everything was doubly prepared right down to the oxygen tank and fire extinguisher. Everyone did their duty and as I didn't have a choice, was panting and pushing the best I could. It was great to have Mother, Father and Chloe all there to help me. Mother helped wash me and coach my contractions. Chloe, as trained, reserved her hands mostly for checking progress internally. As we advanced into the final stages, the sun was rising.

We wanted a boy for the sake of genetics, and we needed a soul from somewhere in the universe. We hoped that soul would remember through the gauntlet of birth and would be workable with the confession process from a fairly young age. "Girl at the pedestal, won't you please help?" I cried to the young girl voice, attempting a telepathic message to this hopefully receptive metaphysical life. While pushing through contractions and then relaxing several times, I felt one of those *thumps*, my body passing out as I fell into a vision, transcending into direct communication with one or more of the great souls without seeing him or her directly. Instead, I saw the home open up to the firmament. I saw the stars. I saw nebulae. Within moments, I found myself looking at cities on another planet, also with a population that was dead. Their society had been far more advanced with great dams, glass-covered skyscrapers and angular architectures, and was intertwined with covered tubes for high-tech mass transportation.

A hellishly anguished man was yelling in a strange language from the balcony at the top suite of a skyscraper. Numerous structures were being engulfed from the ground up in a conflagration. Streets were filled with heavy smoke, glowing about the edges from the flames, the buildings acting like glass-shaded lamps. The fellow's cries were translated in thought for me, "Won't somebody hear me? Please! Won't somebody up there hear me? Ah! There's no one left. There's no reason to be alive!" He pointed at the massive front of the flames progressing toward his claimed building. I watched helplessly as he plunged off the edge into the smoldering abyss between the structures. Invisible hands pushed me to the soul, and I, in turn, reached everywhere I could for him. Then I got the idea that the suicide had happened years prior, and the soul was just lost somewhere on that planet or lost in space. I grabbled at the soul given me, pulling it back, as if I'd stretched an unfathomable distance across space without ever leaving home, and did my best to shove it into my belly to the arriving baby.

"I've got one," I cried. "I was shown." I gasped as the birth was progressing. I was in the final stages; the head was nearly out. Father was right there, ready to grab the baby. "Be the baby! Be the baby please!" I cried at that soul.

"He won't forget," said one of those voices directly into my mind.

"Good!" I cried out. I looked to Father to relay the message, "He won't forget."

The head came out, and Father was ready to handle it. I waited as best I could while he suctioned the nose and mouth.

"Be the baby. Be the baby. Get on there and be the baby!" I chanted.

I again recognized the soul's need to know the gender of the baby, just as Chloe had. I pushed furiously. Father said not to push. I shook my head enough to pull my shoulders with it. I needed to know.

"Please. Let me get this cleaned up so it can breathe," he said. He was clearly flustered.

As soon as Father was ready for us to finish, Chloe was pressing at my private area, helping to get the baby's shoulders positioned, turning them gently. "There we go girl," said Father to her. "I really appreciate your little hands." The baby slipped on out.

"Boy," bubbled Father very softly, being on the edge of tears.

"Boy," I said and repeated the line I'd been told, "He won't forget." I was elated despite the fact that I'd really prefer a girl – I'd always prefer a girl. But I already had a girl – Chloe.

Should I be jealous?" queried Chloe's pleased face.

I shook my head, saying, "No. I like girls. I prefer girls. You're my wife."

"No, you're my wife," she said with a boyish tone.

"What are you going to call him?" asked Mother.

"Any suggestions?" I asked.

"No. It's your choice," said Father, looking at me.

"Chloe?" I looked at her.

Father joked, "No – you can't name him Chloe. That name's already taken."

"Chloe?" I asked her again.

"No. You're naming him, Mama," Chloe said confidently.

It was as if the name was given to me, so I voiced it. "Jack. I'm calling him Jack. Just Jack." I was finished and fading.

I heard Father say, "Jack it is, then."

I drifted toward sleep as I thanked the voices. The spiritual experience of reaching for a soul on another planet had been intense. I couldn't ever forget that. In my exhaustion I let the others handle Jack and all the cleanup. Chloe interrupted me to get the afterbirth cleaned out though my body was doing very well through the process on its own. Even she gagged and barfed into the pail. She dashed out of the room, retching, dragging the pail out with her. I was concerned and fought to keep a light sleep until I knew she was okay. She came back in, banging the door, her face and shirt wet from washing herself up, but she didn't say anything. She came back around to cuddle with me, and soon Father put the baby onto my chest. It was still daylight, which meant the first of three births completed in the day instead of the night.

I coddled the new baby and cried, wishing it too had been a girl, but I knew our situation necessitated a boy. If it was anything like the rest of us, what would he be like? Would he decide that Chloe would be his wife and leave me lonely? Would he be a mean child and try to attack the chickens and goats? If he didn't forget at birth, what would we find out about him? I might have been the only one that had that vision of him jumping off of a building. If that was the case, would he be viable as a person or would he later throw himself off the water tower?

Later I told the others what I'd seen. We all wondered how long he'd been dead before I was guided to pick him up. We also wondered how far away in the universe he'd been.

Chloe said, "I remember a few words. Let me talk to him."

She did. But he looked at her blankly, then cried. He didn't seem to like that any better. "Yes, baby. You'll have to learn a new language. I'm sorry we don't speak your language."

He tried to speak, making garbled noises.

"I'm not so sure it would work that well in a baby's throat and mouth anyway," I said. "I know mine didn't work so well." I'd spoken little at that age having been concerned that my parents might have thought their baby was possessed by a devil, forcing them to kill me outright.

Jack was just the poor little guy. He looked so frustrated. That was the most notable thing about him – he tried to communicate but was frustrated.

Between breastfeeding and chores, Chloe and I continued our session time a couple hours per day, and more if we found extra time in the evening. We also found ourselves scavenging for different baby clothes, though we had a pile of used baby girl clothes, and often used them anyway if we hadn't kept up on laundry.

The confession chains were hitting more incidents and taking longer to get through. One of mine just never seemed to end. The chain hit so many incidents, most of them entirely boring, and every time we thought we were at some higher level of the universe, it appeared to revert to an earlier event no better than the previous. We ran them anyway, as anything blocking a previous event was probably the thing to confess. When it did come to an end, I'd never felt so forsaken. I'd been so lost and left alone, separate from the greater soul that spawned me, with direction to conduct myself as a renegade with respect to decency and sexuality. I laughed joyously from the cognition; I cried horribly from the effects. I turned and rolled over Chloe, kissing her wildly. "Finally, your turn, baby girl. Your turn for the next series."

During this time, we thought we were in charge. We all did our confession chains in hoping to restore our own decency. And we studied. We made clothes. We fed pigs, goats and chickens. We planted vegetables and grains. We ate well. The land was providing. Living in the historical reenactment village had indeed been the optimal choice.

TEN

Exploring the Capital

When my baby boy was about two years old we had been playing in unusually dry grass and weeds among the houses in the village. I picked Jack up and checked him over since the grass was so stiff it could cut and puncture. Having gone into the parsonage I started preparing dinner. Jack helped me select several potatoes while I sorted out what else to fix.

Jack and I checked on Mother, and she had been doing some sewing with a manual sewing machine. We'd reverted some of the clothing styles to be more traditional, and she was wearing a bonnet. My own clothing had become a hodgepodge of styles combined from the last two centuries.

Chloe dashed through with laundry from a line, saying, "It dries quickly, anyway." In minutes she dashed back out to get extra water for the animals.

Another moment in the kitchen, Father passed through. He offered that, if I was ready, I should probably be trying to have another child. I told him, "I'll think about it, Daddy. I think I'm still burdened with one now."

He didn't hesitate. "You are. No rush. Just let me know. Your mother wants to know."

"Mother's not helping as much with the baby as I'd like. Does she have something against boys?"

"You tell me. We're all part of the big souls up there. I'm sure we take on their characteristics. We might all be part of the same soul – your girl at the pedestal – the girl whose voice we often hear. Hell – I'd like to be a girl myself. At least I could grab it when I want."

I laughed. "Oh, I see. For your information, I can, and do, grab it when I want."

"Don't entice me. I'll come over there and you'll have another baby anyway. They used to call it an unplanned pregnancy."

"I think they called it a rape baby. There will be no such violation. It would behoove you to hold your ground," I offered, but knew by my form alone I was seductive. For daily survival we had learned to be respectful of our situation, not leaving room for many indiscriminate acts. We knew we were still off normal, far from ideal, but overall our lives had improved dramatically.

He cocked his head and threw up his hands with a cheesy smile. "Always trying to throw the ethics thing into everything," he said, stuffing his mouth with a crunchy fresh beat, followed by celery.

And yes, that was me, always trying to put ethics into everything, no matter how much I'd been left in this universe to be a perverted little renegade. And since that recognition, at least for a while, I could sometimes do things I didn't expect, like see in the dark or I'd find things that were lost for years. I'd need something, think of it, go to a house we'd never been to and find it in the first drawer I'd open, like I'd done with a specific curved sewing needle, finding it in a kitchen drawer of a house I'd never previously entered.

Some of these houses in Hattonville, the town surrounding the village, had never been cleaned out, and the blackened skeletal masses that had once been bodies were there, often with gross discolored and rotted areas around them. The bugs had long given up, sometimes even the dead bug bodies would be littered about them. In one house, a little girl had been in her bed and I had pulled back the darkened covers, seeing black ugly mold covering all about the bones. Some faint detail of a little nightgown and panties was extant. It had been there twenty years. And in that house, some windows had become broken, causing one of the rooms to have a warped floor. The rest of the house wouldn't be sound for another twenty years. This world would irrecoverably decay.

Later at dinner, Daddy explained, "I'd been on the roofs of our houses too much lately – er – until it stopped raining. We'd been getting some leaks on the north side of yours and Chloe's favorite place. I don't know how much longer I can keep it dry if the rains start again. The main house isn't too bad. Most roofs were only designed to last twenty to thirty years. So, if a house had just been given a new roof before the event, even it is set to expire before Chloe's an adult. We can't exclude the weather – everything we have is decaying by the day. We won't have any machines for fixing things if we can't keep them dry. We can't fix any machines if we don't have machines to fix them with. We still have a dozen freezers. But one day they won't work, being set aside or not. We still have generators – several. One day they won't work. We have so little of the things we thought necessary in the beginning. Like – I haven't needed a can opener in years, have I? Except for paint, and it wasn't worth opening. If there's going to be a society, we've got to preserve the knowledge. But we don't even know how to make most of these things."

Daddy was still gaining gray hairs. Mother looked middle aged now. Chloe was still young, budding nicely. My baby boy was just a couple years old, eating the food I'd cut up for him like the rest of us with small utensils. We found books on how things worked but none of them went far enough. We needed technology. One of the contributing elements to our next plan was that the summer had become so dry. Grass failed to find enough sustenance to remain green. The rains always appeared to the south, toward the larger city, but rarely did clouds come far enough to bring thunder, let alone a good dousing. We could do the math. If it kept up we'd get hungry during the winter, likely rationing the canned goods and butchering more animals to balance the weak vegetable crop. If it went longer, we'd face a potential famine, which couldn't be good with so small a population, as a weakened diet can in turn weaken immunity and all we needed was one irrecoverable illness to be our plague. With groundwater, we could water the plants and fill the troughs for the animals, but with everything else so dry, it was dangerous to stay here. The drought increased risk of fire, whether we started one or the cause would be lightning.

Just shy of two hundred kilometers to the south had been the region's capital. Months back, Father had decided to take a series of excursions to track whether it was passable. There was too much risk in all of us going at once. He'd go ahead and scope out the work required. On his first trip back, he brought wheat that had been growing wild. He brought back tomatoes and cucumbers and even some spices that had still found their way, though growing a little randomly in flourishing gardens.

Daddy had just come back from a longer trip. We were all at the kitchen table eating dinner. He offered, "There's a home for us there. In fact, one of the best houses is the president's mansion. It can be ours. It can be home. I've been loving this place for years. But this trip – I got the generator at the mansion started and it's much bigger than these we have. It's more than just a backup unit, and even it has a backup. And if those fail we have many other generators. And – and get this – it's right across the street from the Patent Office – huge warehouse of knowledge."

"Well if we need to be rescued from this place, we need a place to be rescued to," I offered.

"I think we're to that point," stated Father.

"Well then, I can't wait," I said, but my affinity for the local area made the prospect of leaving more bitter than sweet. "What's the condition of the mansion?"

"A little water leakage toward the west end but no real damage. Solid structure. Not much wood. Moldy things can be removed. A little sealing and we'd have it livable in no time. Ah – a few windows need to be fixed."

"No meteor strikes?" I asked.

"None in the Patent Office or home. Evidence near the bay. You'd have to see it to believe it."

"Okay. What about a library?"

"Much bigger than all our libraries combined. Right in the mansion. Knowledge. Lots of it."

To forbear my emerging smile, I thought about moving what we'd need. "What stuff do we move? How are the roads? I mean – we've stockpiled a lot of stuff here."

"Don't you worry. They have stuff there. In as much as good condition," he promoted.

I rolled my eyes, thinking about all the rust on the unused generators. One of the freezers we hadn't used would probably not work now if we'd tried it. If this stuff had a monetary value, it would depreciate ever more rapidly with each wet season.

"They have a lot of it," he said with eyebrows raised.

"I want to see it. Next excursion to the city – when you go. I go," I insisted.

"Okay. Okay – then you go," he said.

I could see everyone's eyes flash to each other around the table, a sort of unspoken agreement that we were taking the next step toward moving.

My expectation was that I'd find it a sour experience and demand returning home to the church grounds where I had always felt contented. If I evaluated the area we had, the parsonage and the church, the associated houses, the water towers and pumps, and how well we'd maintained it, I could hardly imagine that going somewhere else that had been completely untouched for twenty years would be a better place. I found it hard to imagine that Father would leave all this behind, considering all the effort he'd put into it unless he was certain all this equipment would soon crap out. Perhaps the freezers set aside were not functioning. Perhaps the spare generators would no longer produce electricity for the freezers. Perhaps there were issues with the three remaining water towers. Perhaps we were being directed by the voices, which had been somewhat quiet for years, only to bring us Jack and to admit that our confession sessions were helping, and we should continue.

But I'd have to see the city. I could only imagine it being a lot of work moving thousands of twenty-year-old corpses that would have stained everything. Perhaps rats had taken over the city. Perhaps other normally wild creatures had made it impossible to live there. We couldn't walk in blindly.

Father and I took an old truck carrying sufficient food. We also loaded up bags of oats and potatoes, so we didn't entirely waste the trip. The goods became the bed to sleep on at night, all of it covered using a wooden frame and tarps to cover it like a tent, a contraption Daddy already invented during his earlier trips. He'd even figured out how to extend an awning, so we could get in and out of the bed in rain without getting soaked through, which was handy for bathroom functions. Of course, it didn't rain. Frankly, the truck was in horrible shape with barely enough power to travel the broken-up roads.

Daddy had already cleared the roads on previous trips, but a few patches had washed back out. I had to get out a few times for fear that the truck would turn over as we drove around washed out areas and trees that had taken up root in the middle of the road, or we stopped to ax out the roots. Aside from these rough spots, the general terrain was flat with few hills, and the few that were there gave us a ride down like a roller coaster.

The farther we went, the stronger we got because of the work involved in patching holes and pushing through the rough, cutting back limbs and even cutting a few trees out of the road that we could have passed, but it would make subsequent trips easier. We were eating a lot of raw potatoes on the way. There were places we had to zig-zag about cars that had been left on the road, but that was rare as it had been prior to sun-up on a long day when the event happened. For the most part, it looked deserted at the time of the event, just a few scattered automobiles and no trace of pedestrians. I even looked about for downed aircraft, recalling the plane from the island. We passed gas stations, movie theaters, grocery stores, and an entire stockyard – here too the corralled bovines had no chance of survival. If there had been pigs, they'd rooted their way to freedom.

It was the third morning when we came over a final hill to see the expanse of the metropolis. The main highway crossed through the heart of the city, right past the Patent Office and president's mansion. When we got there, Daddy tried to distract me and made me think we had several kilometers to go. But then he said, "Do you think you could live in that?"

"Yes, Daddy." I was tired. My bottom and back were hurting. But I felt as strong as I'd ever been. Looking around at the ghost city, my concern was about wild creatures, yet I didn't see any wild animals here to attack. I didn't see any overgrowth of anthills. I didn't note a plethora of mosquitoes. I saw no infestation of moles, mice or rats along the roads. Those critters were gone, if not severely reduced, the same as the people. "Why don't we stop here and take that one. It looks in terrific shape," I said, my attention still fixed upon the lavish home.

"Yes, it's nice. Because of the centralization of the government buildings we've not far to go. Wait until you see the president's mansion," he said. But we trudged on. I watched the big house-like structure pass. Perhaps it had been a library, a college or another lavish government office, with attachments on either end, both of which appeared to be extravagant houses in their own right. I was still tired from the rough sleep in the truck bed and needed another bite of something. It was still the middle of the morning, but I was ready to preempt our progress for a break.

"Look again," he said, pointing in back of me after we'd gone another hundred meters, allowing some overgrowth to pass that in turn revealed a sign.

"Patent Office," I read. "Shit! That's the president's mansion on the other side?"

"Yes. Yes, it is," he laughed.

"And the grounds look wonderful!" I looked over the area. On the road ahead, the drainage for the sunken highway wasn't fully working and there was a pond along one side. I couldn't wait to reach higher ground and see inside the house. I could only wonder that if the trip hadn't been quite as arduous whether I'd see it as such a blessing. He drove toward an exit ramp that led right to the mansion. But the ramp was too steep, and a section of pavement caved in, exposing a jagged gap of six to ten meters, revealing inadequately packed sand and yellowish soil. "This is the only hill I couldn't get the truck up and over. If we could fill in the washout we might push it, but it's not really necessary. We grab the packs and take what we can. We'll come back for more in a bit."

I didn't think it would be possible to get the truck up that washed out ramp. I just shook my head. "Yes. The backpacks," I acknowledged and loaded up a few more potatoes into my backpack and grabbed a bag of oats.

Trudging with a light heart and heavy legs, I felt like a schoolgirl on a visit to the capitol. We needed a bus, two teachers, a bus driver, and a bunch of kids. I got a strong recall of such an event when I was just little Miranda. We'd taken a boat ride to the mainland to see the Capitol city, but it was a different mainland, a different city, and a different lifetime. Tears streamed down my cheeks, but I kept my attention on climbing the off ramp.

Upon cresting the hill and seeing the president's mansion from the edge of the road, the size of the buildings distorted my sense of space. We entered through a side gate set between stone pillars. The grass hadn't been cut, but I could see that Daddy had taken out numerous small trees and shrubs in the yard, enough to expose the main walkway and stairs. Daddy threw his hand to refer to a guard shack, offering, "The building was open. They had guards. They didn't need to lock doors. I'm sure that staff came in and out of here all-day long."

We went up the dozen terraced steps on the outside to the main porch. It was big for a porch. I was sure there was another architectural word for it. "Porch" was too small a word for this.

"Okay. Now the big doors," he said and pushed in.

It was darker and dryer than I expected. But it was just as dusty as I could have guessed. It was fairly ornate. There were runners in the hallways and rugs in the middle of the large rooms. There were chandeliers with a thousand pieces of crystal. I looked them over.

"I introduce you to a lesson in economics, the spoils of government plunder! This is not the area of the house I suggest we live in. The east wing is a family addition, suited better to our scale and not much occupied. The generator is not enough to light the whole house. It's on a separate circuit. Not everything gets backup power. I hadn't gotten it fully traced, but I know we don't get these big lights. They'll just remain dusty lead crystal. Come on. Long hallway. The east family addition is this way. The west family wing isn't cleaned out yet."

I viewed the structure in awe. The entry alone spread beyond the foundation of most homes, the chandelier taller than Adelardus' church. I could barely imagine the number of cooks and servants required to manage the daily meals. I couldn't fathom the guard staff and the concierges required. It even had its own mail room.

Father led me down the long east hallway and it led to a vestibule with doors leading into the family wing, and to the front and back gardens. "The kitchen's this way."

Much more in line with the scale of a typical home, we went through a hallway to a roomy kitchen with ample workspace, breakfast table, with cabinets lining every space not already used for counters and sinks. Behind that was a small First-Aid room, complete with an examination table and plenty of cabinets for supplies that were still there.

Daddy allowed me to look over the rooms. "I'd got some of the bodies out – at least those in the main rooms. There are others. The event was an early weekend day – ah – as we all know. They were home, but the house was much bigger than the people. It was before the day staff arrived."

We wandered on through to a lounge that was spacious with leather furniture, a beautiful stone fireplace and several useless chandeliers. The room was without body stains anywhere. "I like this one," I said. "Bigger than my old hotel lobby. But where to plant a garden?"

"You won't believe this," he said, waving me out. We went through a hallway past the kitchen and First-Aid room to a back atrium with aged lounge chairs of marginal use. Beyond that, just outside, was a row of plants with fruits and vegetables already hanging, ready to eat. The backyard was lined with apple and pear trees bearing young fruit. There were a dozen rows of grape vines which currently bore ripe green grapes. All this needed much more tending to. I was sure that it would produce more fruit than we could ever eat. I ventured out the back door along a slate walkway, then out to the backyard. The grass was very tall. I walked through lush grass to an apple tree. There were a few bugs, a few bees, and plenty of small apples still forming, just a couple turning color. "They'll be ripe soon. If we want the fall harvest, we'll have to move the homestead soon. If not, we forfeit."

I was thinking of the longer term practical things, looking for a reason so say no. "The generator?" I asked.

He took me past the backyard to a large shed. I didn't see any wires coming from it. He must have read my mind, saying, "The wires go underground. Come on in."

There were cement steps and a sliding utility door. He slid it open and flipped a switch. The generator started right up. He gave a huge smile, slapping his own forehead with a cackle.

"How?" I asked with amazement.

"I found some old batteries never filled with acid. They charge up with the generator and restart it later. I confess – I didn't expect it to start right away."

I had that "too good to be true" feeling. I wanted to see more before I'd recommend it to the others. I knew Daddy had been working on this project for months, and I wanted a better place for my baby boy. But we were all in this together. There would be a lot of work. "Where would the goats and pigs go?"

He guided me to an adjacent lot. It had all been fenced in as gardens with water fountains and pools, the perimeters once well marked by shrubbery and wrought iron fencing, and in between there were various landscaped swells originally created for herb and flower beds. The pools had all but filled in. The fountains, if you could find them in the brush, were corroded beyond use. I couldn't help but realize that the goats and pigs would have these grounds cleaned up and usable in half the time we could do it on our own. I pointed to the bogs that had been the pools, and said, "Pigs." I pointed to the rest of the gardens and said, "Goats."

"I knew you'd get it," he said. "They'll do the outside work for us. We'll get storage sheds moved in here. Otherwise, we've got the utility buildings at the back gardens."

I looked about. I noted few other animals. There was a creature like a rabbit near the pool, then it hopped away before I could fully identify it. In the trees were some birds. "Daddy?" I asked. "Why aren't there more animals?"

"I never figured that out. Since the event, there's only a handful of animals. I have no answer for you. Perhaps there is a limitation on the number of animal souls too. I never had any trouble with the goats. But I never had more than a hundred at a time."

"And pigs?"

"Same – never more than a hundred of them either."

"How many do we have to bring with us and how many do we have now?"

"Oh – after the drought, about thirty-five goats, thirty pigs. I'd hope we could bring them all unless we can find others wild here. The few dozen chickens will be easy. They can take the back atrium if needed, otherwise we'll anchor storage sheds. I hadn't looked far enough here for animals and hadn't seen much. My foremost concern is the birds of prey."

It wasn't mine. "Other wild creatures? Didn't they have a zoo?"

"They were in cages. Elephants, tigers, lions – I doubt they ever got out. Most weren't suited for the area. It's milder here than inland, but tropical animals wouldn't survive here. If they did live I'd hope they'd head further south. If not, that's why the mansion should be home. The fences enclose the property and will provide protection. Most are sturdy and there's a supply of parts around in a maintenance shed. We've got another generator – we've got a welder. There's a dry machine shop nearby – usable if we can get it powered.

The mansion was indeed in better shape than the houses I had such emotional attachment to. I knew I'd ultimately have to decide based on what was best. There were plenty of open spaces near the house to have more gardens. The fruit trees were there, if overgrown. The grape vines needed trimming back on their arbors. Daddy had already planted some vegetables and with little tending to, they were growing well.

I felt tears for home. I squatted to my knees and cried.

"What's the matter, girl?" he inquired.

"I'm going to miss home," I moaned.

"Sounds like you've already made up your mind. You haven't even seen your bedroom. You wouldn't have to share one with Chloe, but I suppose you will."

"We're married, Daddy," I reminded him of our implicit relationship.

"I know. Come on, then. I'll show you some of the rooms. Beware there are a few decomposed ladies and gents. We'll try to avoid them."

We walked back to the east house, a mansion in its own right, back up the slate walkway, into the back hallway, passing the first-aid room and kitchen, up to a main hallway, up a set of stairs, and down to some bedrooms, each more like a mini suite. "The chief's room – not the president – probably his doctor. I already got a body out of here. Another was in the bathroom. Convenient in a way. Not much got stained with marble on the floor and walls. But there are some mildew stains in the grout – luckily not that much grout. I almost wish she'd stayed in bed. I had to move the mattress out anyway."

"Just stain all the grout black," I said. "It's nice."

"Did I say they have their own water tower? Up, back of the façade. Water tower." He pointed up.

"But do they have a spring to feed it from?"

"We'll find one – or a good well. There's certainly groundwater here. As old as the original structure is, they wouldn't have built here at all if there wasn't."

"Sure," I shrugged. "Water would be a boon to us living here," I added.

We walked into a broad hallway and there was a huge bedroom on the other side. Once in, it looked masculine, dominated by a huge four-post bed. Other than being dusty with cobwebs, one with a big spider in it, and all the little spider droppings and insect exoskeletons that had accumulated for twenty years, the room was in excellent shape. The dressers were not even warped. "Wow!" I said.

"Wait until you see this one. You like lace, right?"

"Yes. I'm the proverbial girl, Daddy," I reminded.

Up the hallway he stood like a guard and waited for me to stand ready to enter, then he ceremoniously sang a little tune, as if an announcement by a trumpet, and opened the door. "I cleaned this one, huh? It's far from perfect, but at least – well new spiders – I had them cleaned up."

"My room. Chloe's room. Done," I said. The sturdy bed was a combination of hardwood and turned marble pieces on the upright spindles and along the side and end rails. The wood could have been mahogany, and the marble had pink and creamy colored sections. I couldn't recall the name of this marble but knew it was very rare. The dressers were the same dark wood with insets of the same marble, and plenty of carving and scrollwork. "It looks old. It looks hand made."

"It still needs some good furniture oil. Good luck at finding any that hadn't set up in a can. We'll make do with something," said Daddy. I sat on the bed and a little dust came up.

I sneezed.

We laughed.

I cried, saying, "I don't want to leave home."

"You won't be. We'll all be here. This is home. It's a better home. It will provide much longer. And we can always make as many trips as we want to Adelardus. But with or without us, that town will fall apart in the next twenty years. If this big house goes – they have a jail not that far from here, I saw it on an old map. It would be a stout compound, but I doubt would be any good if the locks have frozen up. We'd have to make excursions to it if we intended to use it to get it into working condition. I'm not sure we have enough people for a project like that. But that's not entirely why we came here, is it? We came for that building across the street. For now, we eat – we look around here for the rest of the day. I need to tend to that garden. You can figure out what you want to do, but you can't just sit idle. You'd go nuts in a place like this alone. Tomorrow, we check out the Patent Office."

I nodded sadly. I found it hard to get up off the bed. My body hurt, the toil of the trip winning over the excitement. I found it impossible not to cry. I heard no voices myself, but Daddy claimed he'd heard them before coming here – that's why he came. Could I even make a decision on my own, or what this already fated? This was indeed the same city I'd passed over when called to be born, before being pushed on to the church and parsonage where I found Father and Mother. Perhaps there was a reason I'd seen it. I wish I could hear the voices talking to me right then. I didn't hear anything. I hadn't heard much before or after Jack's birth.

The garden offered enough to eat. Daddy and I sat out on old wood benches because the cloth-strung lounge chairs had decayed fabric. I considered it normal to have a folding knife with me, so I cut cucumber slices and ate them one by one, then other vegetables, all fresh. Walking about, I found an early apple and gave it a try. Tart – very tart, but edible. Then I helped weed the garden. I wasn't ready to view the entire house and meet all the corpses.

We returned inside through the main building as the sun neared the horizon, but before retiring, Daddy said, "Here. Come look at this?" He was standing at the base of a stairwell. I didn't want to, but my energy was returning. I followed his excitement to the roof. He said, "Come here – I think you can see it. Remember that green and white meteor we saw streak by with the boom? I think that was its trail, landing near the bay. See it?"

I followed, stepping around vents and rocks. There were little plants up there, but none had been able to get many roots into anything, and the roof probably got too hot to sustain much plant life. The long rays of the sun made stepping about tricky, so when I caught up to Father near the end of a triangular façade, he was trying to be patient. Looking between taller structures I could see all the way to the ocean. Toward the left of the city's skyline was a long gouge, much of it filled in with water that led from the south end of the city into the bay. The buildings about it had a fractured appearance.

"I'd never been able to get that far. It's just too rough past here. But that's not the original river. It was cut. Dark ground with little vegetation on either side would say it happened just several years ago. It would have been a major disaster for the living – if they were. Tributaries had cut their way around the berm."

That gouge had been the primary downtown area. The view begged respect for the power of that meteoroid – meteorite somewhere in the bay or beyond it. It was a sight that was hard to believe. Did the owners of those voices know about the meteor shower? Some of the messages from them portended events just before they happened, the ones that affected my life directly. Except for that event of everybody else dying.

"I didn't understand all the hints," I said to Daddy.

"What hints? About the meteor?"

"No. The event. People – when they dropped. I didn't recognize it. I didn't put it all together. I can't say I had any reason to see a trend. At college, I saw demonstrations on 'the end of the world' and 'repent' and all that stuff I just considered goofy, spurious. I saw people in robes in airports, passing out little books that looked a lot like the little black one we found so important. I saw people say strange things. A friend of mine, Seria, talked about the universe opening up above her. She laughed in the sand the night before they all died. The other girls said they wanted to – to make love to me like it was my last night on Earth. And they did." I bowed my head, tears flowing.

"Huh," he shrugged it off as if I didn't really have to say more.

With a wet voice, I elaborated, "I would have done a lot more had I known that. But what I did after wasn't that good either."

"None of us could have been prepared for that. I went crazy first, then got it sorted out later. Over here it was early. I thought my wife just died in her sleep. She was already stiff as I'd been sleeping. I checked on Avelynn. She was just sleeping soundly and so I thought it was just my wife. I guessed her heart gave out or blood clot got in the brain. I called the hospital and police right away, but no one answered, which I thought strange. I went to check at the police station because it was closer, and the door was open, and it already smelled like an outhouse, and the handful of people were dropped to the floor or bent over desks. The emergency phones were silent. Nobody was calling. It wasn't until later in the morning when I realized it was widespread. Nothing moving but a few birds and the wind. If it weren't for Avelynn I would have killed myself right then and there."

As he spoke I turned to look across the roof, seeing a large painted metal cubic structure behind the higher part of the triangular façade. Some of the paint was rust stained.

Daddy must have seen my attention turn to it. "The water tower. We'll have to flush it out first. And I hope that none of the faucets leak."

"I didn't mean to cut you off," I pardoned. "What else?"

"That's fine. I'll catch it in the confessions," he said to avoid more detail. "It's getting dark. To bed we go. You'll want to dust off your covers or sleep in the lounge."

"Why don't we just do that?" I concurred.

"Your choice. I think it amounts to the same number of spiders."

The next morning, we ventured across the large street to the Patent Office. We could have taken an overpass to the other side, but Daddy needed a few tools from the truck. The main highway was in between, which meant climbing back down the washed-out ramp, climbing over the median guardrails, and then walking up an intact ramp on the other side. New trees and undergrowth were breaking up the edges of the ramp, but a clear path took us to the general street level. On the main lawn of the Patent Office, there was little growth beyond briars, consisting heavily of blackberries.

"Did you seed these?" I asked him.

Daddy explained what he knew so far, "This isn't the original ground level. The building extends under all this ground. The highway – that was the original ground level. Everything else is built up. Mostly true for the President's Mansion as well. They all still drain, for the most part, having been overdesigned. As for the blackberries – they encroached upon this area because they like it. We'll probably yet find the remains of someone that had fallen over with blackberries the day of the event. Probably some security guard, considering the time." In his back pocket he had a pair of handheld pruning shears.

We directed ourselves toward the original walk, through which Father had previously cut a path, and now pruned back. Still, we'd have to grabble our way to the front steps because of the severity of the overgrowth. I noted an odd weed with leaves like a succulent and some grass in between some steps. At the front door, Daddy had put a chain on the swinging doors, and now he pulled out a small bottle of oil from another pocket and a key from a keychain. "I didn't want to use this lock. I was afraid it would corrode." He fumbled with it, then held steady, letting the oil soak in. He laughed, pulling out a small hacksaw from yet another pocket, saying, "Just in case." But with a few more jiggles the lock came undone.

He had to push at the doors, saying, "I'd swung them back and forth each time I came here. Still, they're stiff." As soon as the doors opened, I breathed a stale dry air that would become familiar.

The extensive main lobby was white, embellished with utilitarian columns and arches. I rushed through in my excitement, finding room after room and cabinet after cabinet of patents. The front of the building was older, and wings and additions were added, just as the underground "wings" were added as much as a century later than the original building. In most areas, the rooms were dry, and the cabinets were in good condition. I found a picture on a wall that showed the original stone building being stilted upon a steel structure creating a new foundation and framework for the rest of the structures surrounding it, and under it. They'd rebuilt the existing structure to construct what might have been the perfect drainage system. I looked in the cabinets full of papers, most of them archival quality, and only stray papers and notebooks for daily activities had yellowed or faded.

Being a natural scholar, I didn't want to go home. I didn't even want to eat. I just wanted to live here and digest all this knowledge. Speaking through the hallways as I spirited about from room to room, I said, "I need a toilet and a broom, some food." When going between wings I yelled out, "Can I get my own room in here?" In one room I saw some caulking in a window, and the caulking cylinder was in a trash pail. A maintenance person wouldn't have done that, or the trash would already be taken out by the end of the day. But years of dust had accumulated on the caulking cylinder.

After a good look around, I met Daddy back at the lobby. I was panting, smiling. "Daddy? When was the first time you were here?"

He looked up at the ceiling, threw his gaze around the room, then said, "Not long after you were born. I had some cars still working. The roads were clearer without wash-outs. We could have moved. Mother said that Adelardus would still fare better with time. There were other considerations, as the farm was there and that would be our mainstay. There was something in the plastics of all those cars that gave out. Fuses failed. Air filters failed. Sparks failed. I'd take parts from others and still couldn't get the damn things to run for long. Gasoline – I had to do the calculations. Unless I botched a decimal, we didn't have enough gas to run generators and vehicles too. Without generators to run freezers I'd have to triple the number of animals, and that would work better in a farming community. That old truck from the village, like a few others, wasn't built like the new ones. It still runs. And there was plenty of gas if we stayed in one place and didn't use it all up traveling back and forth. For years, it was better to be at the village."

"So that's why the need to move and not just visit."

"I – I can't maintain two hundred kilometers of roads. I'm just one man."

"Not if we rebuild the machines?"

"No. There's a lot of clay, limestone, sandstone, loess and soil, but no tar pits. Asphalt was shipped into this area. Any aggregates like it would be packed, settled and useless. Gravel – we could do gravel if we could get – ah – never mind. We really don't have to do it all at once. But could you imagine being apart that much?"

I knew it meant having a store for gasoline or other fuels again at both locations. I knew we couldn't maintain two farms without more people, and that was the fundamental problem, as it took a group to thrive.

We walked back out through the main entrance. I knew he couldn't just leave me here now. But there was food – sweet blackberries (my fingers were already stained), vegetables and apples. I just needed some extra chickens. I hesitated back of him a few steps on the walkway. "Can I stay Daddy?" I found myself saying though I knew better than to think he'd leave me behind, or that I could do it. I was longing for Chloe and my baby and concerned for Mother.

"Yes, but not without the rest of us," he looked back and smiled. "I've come to think I've won you over."

"I'm going to cry at the village. I'm going to cry," I said, fearing the grief I'd have to dump to be able to move.

"You'll see it again – after we move. But it's no place to continue living right now. We're better off here. In time, maybe we rethink it. But I can't fathom rebuilding that whole village. It's not greed – it's necessity."

I understood. "Then we'd better go," I said with ample consternation.

"First we unload what we brought. If we're staying, we'd better go back with as light a load as we can."

I went to the garden to collect a couple of days' worth of vegetables. I pulled down a few pinkish apples, and before leaving, went back across to the Patent Office yard to collect a bowl full of blackberries. Again, the drive was slow and difficult.

When we drove back through the overgrown tree-lined main street of Hattonville toward Adelardus village, I noted parched leaves everywhere. It already looked like fall, dry branches fanning a "Pedestrian Crossing" sign. It was raining very lightly, turning the dust on the windshield to little gray dots. Once we stopped at the house, Chloe came out. My heart jumped at the sight of my beautiful girl. She held out her hands and expressed, "It's raining!" It wasn't enough rain to make a difference, as the sky showed such a scattering of clouds that within minutes the hot rays would parch all foliage of the minuscule moisture that made it to the ground.

Chloe's odd greeting came with a great smile, but the words weren't quite what I'd expected, "You stink, woman! I'm going to give you a bath." She took my hand and dragged my weary body up the path to the main house.

But I stumbled in tears. The love for the present houses and property rushed to greet me too.

"What's the matter?" asked Chloe in these simple words.

"We're going to move," I said. "Aren't you upset? Don't you like it here?"

But she was just glad to see me. "It's not my planet. I don't care where we are. Bigger cities aren't that bad. Of course, it would be better if there were millions of people. Now – come – bath – stink!" She fanned her nose.

She was too excited to see me to be thinking about the move. I followed into the property, putting my attention on the warmth and excitement of her hands pulling mine. Her beautiful face – that was enough to motivate me.

My supposition that I would cry heavily once back to the village did come to prevail. I sat in the bathtub like a pouting child.

"So, you don't want to go, huh?" she said.

"No, I do. I didn't want to come back and cry over this place. I wish we had working telephones. I would have called up and said, 'Hey guys – come on over. Don't be late. The party's starting.' I'm going to long for this place." I gave a sad grimace. She knew about my party the night of the event.

Jack came in after his nap, reaching his arms up with a great grin. "Mommy!" he shrieked, acting the part of the child body he occupied.

"Do you want in the bath with me?" I offered.

"No," he said. He reached in to touch the water, saying, "It's cold."

I pulled up and let the cool water drain off. I guess I'd become accustomed to cool baths.

Jack and Chloe both helped me dry off and we all tumbled into the bed to tickle and kiss and to warm up my skin. Chloe set out clothes for me then left to give Jack some time alone with me. He didn't want to let go. I had to put him on my back when putting on pants and put him on my legs when putting on my upper clothing. Once dressed, he was on my back again as I made my way to the kitchen. As I passed through, I noted how small the house was compared to the mansion's east home. The parsonage was always big enough before. Now the stairway was narrow and steep. The kitchen table appeared dark and small. The whole thing was lacking straight lines. The back stone wall with the fireplace had been darkened by years of fires. But it had all been so normal.

The next day Jack and I went to the library. Daddy and I had previously blocked off the parts that had been leaking, but now those boards were warping, and some vivacious vines were reaching through. Books near that section were molding. I went to the little reference room with the desk. I pulled at a drawer I'd kept a favorite dictionary and found the drawer slightly warped, barking loudly as I pulled. The book was still useful, and I simply said, "Thank God."

I took Jack to a children's room and read a few stories. I picked up the books, saying, "I don't think we'll check these back in. Let's take these."

He nodded and smiled.

As we walked back through Adelardus, we passed an old barn used as the maintenance garage. Father was working on one of the old trucks. "I used to run these. I'll get them yet," he foretold. There was a primitive lead-acid battery set aside and an "Instant-Start" car charger next to a generator that had wheels. He motioned to stay back. Gathering the whole image, I recognized the anachronism. After ten minutes or so he waved up his hands. It wasn't going to start now. Jack and I continued to the house.

ELEVEN

The Move to the City

At the dinner table later, we discussed the plans. We had three trucks we could get working. Most of the road had been cleared enough to be passable. But there were significant obstacles in the last stretch of the freeway leading through the downtown of the capital. One potential overpass was cracked up at its abutments to the road. The majority of the on- and off-ramps were washed out, one ruined by a meteorite. To get truckloads up to the house we'd have to cut out a section of guardrail in the freeway or come down the other lanes, which also meant taking out a section of the guard rail or shoveling lots of dirt to make a path through a ditch, which required complete collaboration. We'd first take the most essential things and perhaps once a month make another trip back. But Jack was just a couple years old so that would complicate the trip. Once he was moved, I didn't intend to take him back. With five people, that didn't give many options.

We were all to make a list of items to take. Number one on my list was that little black book with the end-of-the-universe instructions in it. Number two was Jack, though he was really first and didn't need to be written.

First on Chloe's list was me. First on Mother's list was a selection of herb starts and a foot-pumped sewing machine. First on Father's list was *critical tools*, then *all living things*. First on Jack's list, though we wrote it, were some kitchen tools for making his food and a baby bath. He needed diapers for nighttime, but not having lost all of his memory, he handled day-time body functions well. He was quite the little man.

From a dry-cleaning shop we had thin plastic that hadn't degraded and wrapped everything we boxed to reduce the chance of losing property on the road, hoping that this undertaking wasn't beyond the ability of our equipment.

Daddy got the next truck working and used it to teach me how to drive. I knew from the previous life how to drive small cars with slow-shifting automatic transmissions. This one had a clutch and I had to be gentle. With a load, they wouldn't go much more than five or ten kilometers an hour and puttered along, often backfiring. He taught me how to get out of a puddle if the wheel got stuck by rocking back and forth between forward and reverse, and where to expect the wheels so I could dodge rocks and small stumps. He set up a series of lines on the road with old white plaster and made me stop between them and tell him exactly, to the width of my wrist, where the wheels were. He told me, "These old wheels are solid. If you break one. We haven't got any spares. Accuracy is a necessity."

"And if I do break one?" I asked.

"Then we have three spares for the other trucks," he said.

When I was packing and doing chores, Chloe and Mother had their turns for driving lessons. I looked out the window when I heard voices, seeing that Mother was taking Chloe's place in the truck.

In the house were boxes set up for a later trip. Chloe had a number of boxes in our room next to my pile. If we cared to bring more stuff yet, we'd have to box it later. So much was left behind. We didn't need much of the kitchen items except some Dutch ovens and items we'd need on the road. We didn't need many blankets, but I had a favorite with pictures of dolls, similar to a pink one I'd had in my treehouse on the island. We didn't need to take towels, but I packed a few to use during the trip if we got into trouble. I packed extra shoes and boots because I hadn't initially seen any in the mansion that fit. Each room had its set of boxes ready for later. We could only hope that the parsonage didn't burn down from a lightning strike before we returned.

Chloe said, "We should split them."

"What?"

"We should split the boxes between the houses," she offered.

"If one of these houses burns, the other does too. You'd be better off taking them to the library, and it's not exactly weather secure."

"Okay. I'll find a place," she said. "I just don't feel comfortable leaving everything in one pile."

"Heard any voices? Premonitions?" I asked.

"No. I just don't feel comfortable."

She went off and I didn't pay that much attention to her running about until she gave me a location in a brick house on the main street. Even it had cracked windows.

"Are you sure?" I asked.

"It will last a month, won't it?"

"Certainly, if it stays dry and doesn't burn," I said.

Mother had been resting. We all knew she hadn't been feeling too well these last few months. She hadn't said much except that the food wasn't agreeing with her for half her meals. Because of her condition, she'd spent more of her time caring for Jack. She couldn't get out on the grounds for the tougher chores.

Daddy did his final evening checks of the trucks and wagons. They were fully packed except for the pigs and goats. Once he stepped back into the house, he cautioned, "We'll be starting in the morning. After that last road crew fixed things up, we might be able to make it in a day. We start early. Early! We all head off to bed." *Road crew* referred to the trip I'd taken with Daddy.

The sun wasn't even down yet. Chloe and I went back to our room. We'd put Jack down and he'd already gone to sleep. It was bittersweet, how this would be the last night together in a room we'd spent so much time in. I guess we'd worked hard that day. We both fell asleep quickly.

But I heard the night, waking and seeing moonlight filtering in from outside, I stood up and saw an owl in a tree. The three-quarter moon, directly overhead, had the village lit up like street lamps. I pulled the window up to lean out and feel the cool summer night air. I hooted at the owl, but it ignored me. Then the majestic winged creature swooped at the grass at another house and pulled out its prey in a single snatch. Much like the night on the island when I couldn't sleep the morning of the event, I needed to nibble. I wouldn't find summer sausage and crackers to munch on. I would find some fruit, vegetables and a canister of flour ready for a quick breakfast.

In the morning, Father had woken before me, though the sun was still just below the horizon. I heard one of the trucks. Looking out I saw the wagons were loaded with animals. The full reality of moving was unfolding now. Leaving Chloe asleep I got dressed, checked on Jack, and went on down to start some pancakes on an old liquid fuel camp stove, using up all the flour that hadn't been packed, allowing extra food for the road. Vegetables and fruit, including raspberries and blackberries, were in bowls too. A small crock of candied honey was tantalizing, and I swiped some with a small spoon.

Father came in. He said, "Animals are loaded. I'm getting the others up. And when you're done, be sure to wash everything, otherwise it'll attract bugs." He passed on to the hallway, calling toward the upstairs bedrooms, "Rise up. Sunshine."

Mother moaned.

I went upstairs to get Chloe up. Sitting on the edge of the bed, I ran my fingers over her forehead and cheeks. "Time to get up, Love. It's almost time to go." I kissed her, knowing I still had a little honey on my lips.

"I'll go anywhere with you, sweetness," she said, kissing back. "Who's getting Jack up?"

"We let him sleep until breakfast is ready. We've got last chores to do to leave the house safe."

"I know. I'm getting up," she said.

When I went down the stairs again, there was an odd quiet. In my previous life, I had the experience of leaving the college dorm. The air conditioning system had been set to a warmer temperature and the heating long since turned off. The small refrigerator we had in the room had been unplugged, and it was so quiet in there. At this old house, I likewise heard a new level of quiet. The ever-present hum from the outside generator in the shed had ceased. We all gathered back at the kitchen table and ate. The sound of people eating was almost too much.

"It's too quiet," was all I said.

Then I washed dishes as Chloe got Jack ready. Mother got her last things. Then we blocked the outer doors and went to the trucks. Mother was getting in with Jack, Chloe with me, and Daddy by himself, leading the little caravan. Engines started, we clumsily started down the street.

Chloe said, "Fourteen years here. That's how long I've been."

"Twenty for me. Mother – thirty-four."

"Jack – two and a few months," she said for me. "Father – fifty-two."

I watched the beautiful trees and messy street go by. Silent tears fell.

"Are you okay to drive?" asked Chloe. "Father taught me too, you know."

"Yeah," I said. "I'm okay. It's just emotion. I'm used to that – I'm kind of heavy on emotion. You'll get your turn to drive. You can count on it."

"Sure," she said, head bobbing as the truck passed over some sticks and debris that had collected in the road.

But with the need to pay attention, I passed through the major tears. Recalling all the training from Father on the drive to and from the Capitol on our first trip and the further instruction at the village, I was replaying the knowledge, working about each hazard – how to pass the stalled car; how to get through the wash-out that Father had to help Mother with. We'd progressed just twenty kilometers down the road when mother said she was sick. Chloe and Jack switched places. He would ride with me.

After an hour, Mother got into the passenger's seat, Chloe took up driving. Before Mother got in, she leaned over, apparently nauseous.

The next hour of road was worse, having more sideways jolts. Jack was getting tired of it. We needed a break. I tapped at the horn, but it didn't work. I waved out the door, hoping to get Daddy's attention. On a straight section of road not much further up, he held up. We had a chance to run about so I brought out some food to nibble.

"You've been driving well, Chloe." He said. He went to Mother. "Avelynn. Dear – you don't look good."

"I don't feel good. I think I'm pregnant," she revealed.

We girls smiled at each other. But it was short lived.

Daddy had asked, "Is that a good thing?"

"No. I don't think it's viable. I don't think I can keep it."

"Is it going to happen on the road?" he asked her.

"I don't know," she stuttered with a little cry.

We all wanted to drive with Mother, but we couldn't. Chloe would continue as her driver. The rest of us ate and got fresh air. We checked the gas tank gauges, then decided we had no choice but to push on.

The next twenty kilometers were easier, having been a fairly flat stretch of land not far from a river. So, besides the sandy clay caked across the road, trees were scarce. We were making better time than hoped. But the next ten kilometers or so would have some gentle hills and had more obstacles. It would slow us down. Through parts of it we could have walked faster.

We stopped again. The pigs in my wagon were mostly packed in tightly enough to keep each other from bouncing around, but I could see a pig poking his nose through the sideboards of the wagon. Mother and Chloe's wagon had goats.

Father's had a few goats at the front and the rest of the wagon was packed with chicken crates and other goods.

We ate, getting Mother to nibble. She'd been lying over Chloe's lap. Chloe said, "You might have to take over with Mother. My leg is half asleep from Mother's shoulder lying over in my lap. She's – she's..."

Mother pulled up, slid out of the seat, knelt on the ground and threw up.

"Yeah. She's sick," I said. "If the gods, the voices, had gotten busy up there, maybe we wouldn't have to be going through all this."

Chloe returned, "Take care of Mother, please. I'm done. I'll take Jack unless you want Father to take him."

I had squatted to stretch my back. I looked up at her. "Jack's been really good. But I think I still want you driving in the middle."

"Okay," She said.

We walked up to sit with Father and Jack at the first truck. He'd set out chicken crates to make some semblance of a table and benches. Father voraciously ate up bread and leftover pancakes. Mother hadn't come to the table. Jack nibbled berries, getting red and purple splotches all over his mouth, and I couldn't help but think he was acting the role of a child more than necessary.

I took a pancake and filled it with berries, stuck together with a little of the sticky honey that flowed over the candied portion, and to fill the quiet, just said, "I'm glad we didn't spill the honey."

"Get some goat's milk for Jack, would you," said Father, handing me a glass. I got up to handle a goat through the sides of the middle wagon.

"You want some fresh milk, Mother?" I asked. I didn't hear anything from her. "Mother?" I dashed to the other side of the wagon.

She was bent over on all fours. In a soft crying voice, she lamented, "I'm losing it. I'm losing it now."

She didn't mean her mind. She meant the pregnancy. She'd already removed her panties which were in her hand. I grabbed those old towels from the cab of my truck to put under her elbows. When I tried to extend it under her knees, she protested.

"It'd get filthy. Just let it drop out. I'm done. I'm done with pregnancies. I'm done with trying." She grunted and pushed. I got some water and washed her up after the tiny fetus was expelled. It would have been another boy.

"Do you want to see it?" I offered stupidly.

She took it as a torment. "No. No. Please no," she pushed her head lower with her arms about them.

I grabbed a shovel and carried the little blob toward Father. He saw me walking at him, saw the shovel, looked into the blade, and cried immediately. "No!" he yelled and rushed past the wagons to Mother. "No. No. I'm so sorry. I'm so sorry my beautiful girl. My beautiful girl."

Crying like a toddler, I buried the tiny baby deep in higher ground off the side of the road, avoiding an outcropping of bedrock. Then I went back to finish getting the glass of goat's milk for Jack. I saw the look on his face. He might have been little and look cute as a cuttlefish when he put his hands to his head, but he understood about Mother.

It was like we'd just lost a member of the family, because in a way we had, even though no soul had joined us. It thwarted the potential of having another.

Jack scanned the area while waiting for us to load up. He'd found a box turtle along a stream a few meters aside the road. Father checked to be sure it wasn't dangerous to him and showed him how the turtle closed up in the shell. "I know turtles," said Jack. "Turtle – it's a turtle," he said a few times to learn the word.

Mother rode along with Father after that. Chloe had to drive alone, and Jack stayed with me, bringing the turtle. We put as much attention on getting down the road as we could. It was dusk as we drove over the last hill to the main road into town.

Daddy stopped the truck and got out, calling back to myself and Chloe. "We can't go through that last stretch in the dark. I don't see any weather to worry about. We're best to stop here."

We ate what we could. I got more goat's milk for Jack and drank some myself. Then we let Mother sleep in the first truck. Chloe slept in the second with Jack on the floor, and I slept in the third. Daddy had a tarp and blanket and rolled up under the first wagon.

The moon made its way across the sky, and I woke enough times to see it in many positions until the sky began to lighten up to reveal a hazy horizon. I went to the first truck and checked on Mother, holding her hands for a minute and giving her kisses. First light mixed with moonlight revealed that beauty again, reminding me of the fire-lit image of her face the night I got born. All she said was, "I'm okay."

I didn't wait until later to get myself a little more goat's milk, refilling the cup. Then I went to pick up little Jack, and showed him the sunrise, offering him some of the milk. The air was completely still so a little chill didn't penetrate the skin. The roosters crowed. I rocked Jack then lifted him to see the full sunrise, seeing the reflection of the colors in his irises. As the sun was up and the sky lost color, he said, "Thanks, Mommy," and laid over my shoulder, falling back to sleep. I put him back to slumber in my truck, saying, "There you go, little prince."

I checked on Chloe, opening the door to her truck. "Sun's up, Princess."

"We should always travel with goats," came her sleepy message as she took the glass of goat's milk from me. After swallowing it all, she leaned up to get a hug, then I pulled her out.

She needed to pee and scurried to squat by the side of the road. I went to Mother to help her do the same.

Despite the crowing of the roosters Father wasn't up. Once Mother was sitting on a seat in the first truck, I ducked under the wagon to check on him – the tarp was moving so he was breathing fine. Perhaps he was covered enough to still see darkness. Chloe and I giggled a little, seeing we were up before him, which was a very rare occurrence.

I heard a knocking noise. Jack was hitting the glass in the third truck. I went to get him, lifting him to my side. I let him down and he settled on a chicken crate we'd set up, reconstructing the table and chairs from the crates like before.

Father heard him speaking about being hungry and rolled out. "Jack, why are you out of the truck? What! The sun's up." He stood up and got his bearings, looking over the hill and down the long highway into the city. Long shadows of trees obscured most of the ground.

"Looks like I'm the milk maid this morning," I said. I pushed a kid aside and filled the glass again from the nearest mother goat. "We're going to run out of milk." With the glass partly refilled, I said, "Here, Daddy."

We set up a few more chicken crates and they clucked happily. Daddy offered, "I'd had half a mind to cook up one of those birds last night. I guess we were all too tired to eat."

"If traveling makes us all that sick, I don't want to travel much," said Chloe.

"You got sick too?" asked Father.

"Sick as a dog until I drove. I was about to barf like Mother."

"Okay. I guess you'd better keep driving then," he returned.

He checked on Mother, pulling her out and getting her to sit on a chicken crate. She nibbled berries and a leftover pancake.

Father checked over the caged flock, finding some eggs. He cracked a couple into the cup with the goat's milk and drank them raw. "Anyone want a fried egg?" he asked as he pulled out that liquid fuel camp stove I'd used yesterday morning. With the griddle in place and fire started, fried eggs came off quickly, then Father added some pans to make oatmeal. Under the table, the chickens clucked. Chloe took an egg and leaned down to the chickens, saying, "Any chickens want a fried egg?" One of them tried to peck her through the crate.

We could see down the main road but couldn't yet see the main buildings of our destination. Years ago, this area had wide open farms between rows of wind-breaking trees. Now it was intermittently forested with young, slow-growing trees. Step by step we finished our food, put the camp stove away, then picked up the chicken crates and all the small items. Daddy got his sleeping gear picked up and onto the truck. We checked the animals and threw them some feed or grass. The goats looked fine. The pigs looked nervous from being penned too tightly. The chickens didn't care until we were moving, when the tumult of the trucks would throw them around.

We loaded up, Mother riding with Father, Chloe again in the middle truck with Jack, and I was alone at the rear unless the turtle counted. We pulled out gently and drove down the long gradual hill to the main straight road into the city. This was the last stretch. Like starting the trucks yesterday made it seem real for leaving, now seeing this highway made it real for arriving. From the road, as the city built up around it with kilometers to go, I'd spied a small family of foxes had taken up residence at a gas station. There was a swinging door that had been set up for a pet. Now the foxes used it for their den. I was reasonably sure I'd seen a deer among some trees, essentially hidden by shadows. And though I hadn't seen the animals, I was sure I'd spotted a squirrel nest a kilometer outside the city. Other than that, there were nearly no indigenous species remaining. I'd never once seen any dogs or cats, though I personally had no fondness for them.

When we arrived between the president's mansion and the Patent Office, Daddy stopped. He looked at the guardrails, which were two opposing pieces, one meant to deflect traffic from either side. He got out and fetched a few hacksaws. "I brought ten," he yelled at us before we'd quite got out of the trucks. "I hope it will be enough. Pace yourselves."

We all took hacksaws except for Jack, who'd become the water boy. We worked for hours cutting through two facing sections of the guardrail. I'd picked a line that had rust near the rivets, having pinholes already cut through it. I thought it would make it easier, but in fact, it probably made it a little harder. I had to change how I held the handle, how I guided it, how I pushed my weight into it to reduce blisters and assure no superfluous effort.

Daddy got one end of a section cut and let it fall. He went to the other end and cut there for a while. Mother and Chloe held the opposite ends of a hacksaw and tried to speed up their cut. My diligent hands hurt with every squeeze of the woody handle.

Breaking for lunch, my overexerted hands wouldn't work right. I had to work around a blister on the inside of my thumb where sweat and food acids stung as if I'd submerged them in vinegar.

I went back to work on the rail, getting to about three quarters down on the section, my left-hand seeping from a couple blisters. The day becoming warmer, we were going to start smelling pretty ripe soon. But we'd still not surpassed the animal odors, which was getting rich too, so I took a break from cutting to scoop out a few dung piles with the shovel, being marginally effective and getting crap on my boots.

Between fetching water Jack played with the squat-bodied turtle, scuttling about on the road, getting dirtier than the rest of us.

Mother and Chloe tried another position, cutting up from underneath. Daddy came to me, saying, "I'd never cut a whole guard rail before. I didn't know the effort. I'll take over." But his hands were blistering too. When he got the section cut through, he told Mother and Chloe to stop, and he and I awkwardly carried the ten-meter rail to bend it away, opening the section between the traffic lanes. Setting it down was harder, as the heavy rail caught Daddy's trousers, nearly ripping away the cloth. We walked through the opening we'd made, sensing the dampness of the ground through the tall, lush, rain-watered grass.

Next, we took gravel laden dirt from the edges of the road and dumped it through the opening, making two primary tracks for the wheels. "Well, the idea looked good on paper," Daddy said. Jack continued playing with the turtle, letting it get some weeds to eat and so he could play in puddles.

My blisters had begun to bleed. Besides the stinging, I still looked forward to getting up to the mansion. I couldn't wait to see Mother's and Chloe's expressions, but I wasn't sure how Jack would take it. He'd come from a more sophisticated society than this one. Perhaps having a building with a flat roof would bring back unpleasant memories. It did for me.

In the afternoon some clouds came across the sky, but any rain appeared to stay toward the coast. I was thankful for the shade because we were getting warm, sweating. And the stink coming off my body, being so close, was getting richer than fresh animal dung, my armpits getting raw. Yet we all worked like slaves or criminals out on work detail. None of us were giving up. We just worked at different paces. Father walked back through, packing in the gravel and soil, and said we needed a little more, so we continued.

Soon enough, though, he declared the activity successful. "I can't say I didn't hope we'd get here late enough last night to get in an hour or so of work and have to continue today. At least it would have broken up the toil."

No one responded beyond a grunt.

Next, we drove through the dirt and gravel. I feared that Daddy's truck would get stuck right away, but we all pushed, rags tied about our hands, to help it through. The truck and the trailer of chickens partly packed the dirt and rocks as it went.

Then Daddy drove the next one through. Again, we ladies pushed. Jack rode with father in the truck, and again, the truck and trailer of bleating goats packed the dirt and soil. It made it through, but as we walked back through, I noted a soft spot. "To get the pigs through, we'll need more soil here," I said. We all looked at our hands, then the shovels. Keen to finish but unenthusiastic, we all worked again to fill in the soft, low spot.

Daddy drove again. Jack and the turtle watched from the second truck on the other side. We ladies walked along and guided it. While jerking about, the pigs hit the rail, pushing at Mother, who fell over. "Shit," I said, tumbling to get her. I saw her hand as the rag came off, noting bright red blood. "No – that's not a trifling blister," I scolded her like a daughter. "You can't risk infection with this. No more helping with the pigs for you."

I told father to hold up and walked my speechless Mother to the second truck.

"Chloe, it's on us," I said.

So, Chloe and I helped push the last trailer across. Again, we left driving to be Father's job. And now the path was better still. The back wheels spun, throwing some loose dirt as the truck was pushing up onto cracked pavement, but once there, the wagon pulled on through.

"Now we got the hill," said Father as he pulled out of the truck. "I hope they have enough power. If not, we'll have to chain two trucks together. There's chain stored in the garage at the big house." But with only a load of chickens and a couple goats, the first truck and trailer slowly made it up the ramp to the street level.

Father walked back down to get the next truck, having Jack come out to me. He first drove backward until he ran out of flat road due to a jagged crack in the pavement and accelerated as well as the truck would go to make a run at it, then brought it skillfully down to first gear, moving slowly toward the top. But it stopped a little short. He locked a parking brake and waved at me to join him, so I followed up the hill with a fast walk, allowing Chloe, Mother and Jack to stroll their way up. As I arrived Father said, "You're the next best driver. We rope these together and help pull up the load. I doubt we need the chains for what's left."

He backed up the first truck and trailer to be in line and roped them to the second truck. I got into the first truck and tugged by letting out the clutch. We were both to stay in the first gear and never go beyond a slow walking pace. When we had it up, I gave him a chance to untie it and pull onto the overpass.

We all cheered despite the pain. There were few times in this lifetime I'd exerted myself so much, and those would match my preparations for the hurricane and getting provisions from the relief vessel. But these were not as challenging as screaming in the middle of the hurricane or dying from a tidal wave.

Daddy went down to get the next truck. He ran it hard again and ran the ramp, running each gear as long as he could, then shifted into the next gear down. This third truck wasn't going to make it either. He stopped and got out, shaking his head. "I wish the newer vehicles worked. It's just too much for these old trucks. I'd never had a load like this."

But I was already backing up the truck and trailer, getting the feel for how to keep the trailer from going sideways.

"Close enough," he said. It wasn't lined up as well as I'd hoped. He was tying the ropes, then I heard his door close. "Give it all you got. Last shot. Last time. Go."

I pushed the accelerator pedal and let out the clutch and a hand brake. There was a jerk. I felt the truck lurch sideways and it was struggling forward and back. The load was moving but just centimeters. The clutch was slipping too much. I put a hand out the window to indicate to stop. Daddy came up to my truck window.

I said, "We'll need the chains. Without the trailer and on level ground we can do it. I can't get it to pull."

"Smell that? We're burning up a clutch. What the – chains! Chock the tires," he said.

We put sticks under the wheels to be sure the vehicles didn't roll away with our animals. Then Father drove the first truck toward the mansion, Mother and Jack inside with Father, with Chloe and me standing on the side steps clinging to the doors and the bed. Mother and Chloe should have looked excited, but this trip had been arduous, and it wasn't over.

In the back yard, Father pulled off the chicken crates and the few goats and closed a gate. There'd been a trough collecting rain water already set up for the goats. They loved it, bleating as if thanking us. I'd helped with the crates. Mother, Jack and Chloe were directed to the garden. Daddy asked Mother to fix a chicken for dinner, but she held up her hands, saying, "I can't cut it."

I looked back at the pear and apple trees, more apples showing color. "Grapes – apples. Eat." I waved them on to follow me. I knew the move was hard on them. Other than moving to the parsonage, Mother had never had to move before. Jack and Chloe – that was another story, having come from far-away planets. Because of a familiar cityscape, I feared Jack would be worse here despite how much better it would be for the whole group.

Daddy got the chains on the first truck, which was now free from the wagon, and we drove back to get the pigs. He backed it up in line with the third truck, and we chained the bumpers. I'd learned a little about slipping clutches the first time, and without the weight of the extra wagon, we pulled it right up.

I switched trucks, leaving the first on the overpass. I pulled the second truck with the majority of the goats. Daddy continued pulling the pigs. Once they were unloaded into the gardens, we called it a day for the hard work.

"We're home," he said.

"We're home," I echoed with mixed emotion.

All this work made me closer to Daddy. I embraced him. "Considering Mother, perhaps soon I should try again?"

"No. Too much work to do here first. Then we try. Consider the seasons. Closer to the coast – winter might be milder, but wetter and harder."

I could see the awkwardness in his expression, though as we walked up to the big house, he looked back at me a few times.

Inside, Chloe, Jack and Mother were in the kitchen. Mother went to the sink to wash her hands, turned the handle and found nothing but some air noise as the pressure adjusted.

Daddy blurted out, "I'll get that. I've got to turn the handle." He disappeared up a large stairway that led to the roof water tower.

I stated what she probably already knew, "There's a water tower on the roof. It'll be rich with iron. You'll want to boil the water first."

Mother got a pan to put into the sink, and as the water began to flow with dirt and rust, she cried with frustration.

"Give it a minute," I said calmly. "It'll clear."

She knew that. It was just the exhaustion. "Have you heard any voices?" she said toward me.

"No. Not in years – not since Jack's birth," I returned.

"I don't know if we are supposed to be here," she shot back.

"Yes, we are. Daddy heard them," I offered but she didn't appear to listen.

Daddy came back down, saying, "I checked for leaks in other rooms. Toilet's flush."

Chloe looked up. "No more outhouses?"

"Not until you clog the drains," he cautioned. "We'll just make that a new rule. If you clog your toilet, you dig your own outhouse."

We'd tended to reserve the toilets for urination for that reason – they could clog and ruin all drains from the house. At the historical reenactment village, we'd resorted to using chamber pots and outhouses. Chloe ran through the halls for her first look.

Jack was just sitting in a chair, eating an apple. "Nice house. Nice apple."

For his strange degree of awareness, I couldn't ascertain he possessed a more sagacious mind. It worried me.

I went to find Chloe, who was lurking through the halls. "Our room is this way," I said, having found her on the second floor. "Probably dusty again. Be ready to kill some spiders."

"Sure," she moaned.

We walked down to the room and I offered a similar fanfare as Father did, pretending the music of horns, and opened the door. She examined the ornate furniture, the huge bed of dark wood and pink marble, and then examined the attached bathroom and a small sitting room.

"Daddy prepared it for us. I didn't get to sleep here yet. We slept in the lounge."

"Together?"

"No," I said as if it were an accusation.

"Not what I mean. You need to have another if Mother can't. I want to, but I'm not old enough yet – I mean I could. I shouldn't."

"Right. You shouldn't. The time may yet come for you dear. For me – well I asked Daddy tonight. Not ready. Not for Daddy. Not for all the work we'll need to do here – exhausting as it is. Then, maybe. Then – we'll try again. As for tonight I want to be with *my* beautiful girl," I said.

I pushed her back into the bed. Dust flew. Spiders retracted up the wall. We laughed. Then we sneezed. We took all the sheets into another room and shook them, adding to the dust already there. We flew them around in the hallways and then back to the bedroom. With painful hands, we got buckets and wiped up the dressers. But the mess was too much. "To the lounge," I said. "Have you seen it?"

"No," she said. "From the toilet to here – that's all I'd seen."

"Well, we need to check on Mother and Jack."

Like weary schoolgirls, we walked back through the big hallways, down the house stairs, and into the kitchen.

Mother had bandaged her hands. Father had just brought in a skinned chicken, throwing it into a roasting pan. He poured a few cups of boiling water over it, then threw it into an oven. "If we don't overuse the oven, it should last twenty years on their reserve gas supply. I checked the amounts. It was probably reason number one for moving here."

"What was two?" asked Chloe.

"The water tower on the roof," he said.

"Three?" I asked.

"The industrial quality generator. And the fuel reserve for it too."

"Four?" asked Mother wearily.

"You," he said. "You, Avelynn."

The appearance of his face exuded concern and love mixed up into one. He didn't say anything else. He looked at her. She looked at him. I think we all felt closer to him as a result of all the interaction lately, adding to the unity of the family. It was a good thing to work together, to plan, to run into bigger problems and difficulties and resolve them as a team.

Since the bedrooms were still too dusty, Chloe and I moved to the lounge and cleaned up the loveseats and sofas. When done, I'd wrapped my hands in the little first-aid room. I put some antiseptic on them and the popped blisters burned. It had been such a long day, and the sun had set. I lit a taper candle on a small hand-held brass holder with a finger loop. I moved to the lounge as the others had done. Jack had been asleep awhile. Chloe had just fallen asleep. Mother and Father were also laid out on the sofas, their breathing patterns indicating their certain slumber.

I was so abnormally tired I feared I'd fall asleep while walking. I was careful with the candle. I got my bearings with the sofa, then blew out the flame. I laid myself down with a light blanket over me. I looked up at the ceiling I couldn't see, hoping that spiders wouldn't come down out of the chandeliers in the night. I must have completely switched off after that.

The next thing I recall was a dream, much like receiving a telephone call, asking how I was doing in the new house. I had an odd sense of awareness in the dream, where I was certain that the body was fully asleep. I could feel it breathing and could otherwise feel that it was okay. But the rest of my attention was in the dream. "Who's calling?" I asked.

"Me, your little girlfriend from beyond the galaxy."

"Oh – that's lovely, 'pedestal girl.' Are you a god?" I found my dream voice saying.

"I'm not really a god. I guess you could call me a spirit, and angel, in a sense. We're just people at a different level."

"Great. Fine," was all I could say. I had the thought of *why do you call?* But she answered it anyway.

"I want you to know I love you. I've been working with many, many souls. You were doing the right thing. Keep your sessions and notebooks as you have. It is your purpose, the reason you live." The ethereal connection suggested this telephone conversation was about over.

"Okay," I said and hung up with the sense of still being connected only in thought, leaving me with an overwhelming sense of love and an afterthought. "There will be another member of the family."

My body was a little stiff, and I jolted it awake. I sat up on the large leather sofa, reorienting myself with the lounge I could barely see in the middle of the night, the moon barely rising. "The girl!" I said out loud. "I got the voice!" I crawled to Chloe and shook her using my elbows to avoid the pain in my hands. "I got the voice. I got the girl's voice."

Her eyes opened but I could only see a glint of light off the wet corneas. "What?"

"I got the voice – the girl. She just spoke to me. It was like a telephone call – she told me we were doing the right things with the writing and to continue, and that – though she didn't say it quite the same, not as loud, that… "

"There would be another," said Chloe. "I heard her. What's a telephone?"

I was confused. I was sure we'd talked about telephones before. "Didn't you see a box with numbers on it?"

"I mean – no. I read this complicated card – it was like a telegraph or switchboard, like in the old mail shop at the village, covered with cables and plugs. The card came out of it."

"Oh," I said. "A call from a telephone – a message from a telegraph – same thing." She referred to a shop in the village we used to play in when she was a child, playing like we could talk to each other on the old telegraph and early telephone system.

I went to Father. I shook him and said I'd heard the voice. He just groaned and said, "We'll talk in the morning."

I went to Mother, but she too was completely out. I touched her wrists, but she didn't respond at all. Her breathing was regular, her heartbeat was fine. I kissed her forehead. She still didn't respond.

Since Jack's birth, I finally had a small connection again. I had confirmation that the girl was working with other souls and our actions were correct, to write the confessions backward along emotionally harmonic chains. It was imperative to keep that going, day by day, even if only a little bit. It had to keep going.

Morning came. I sat up, my body stiff. My hands were in pain. I drank a little water – it had been boiled and tasted strange. My head spun. I was sick. I rushed to the nearby bathroom and I barfed that up, so I sat by the toilet and rested. Chloe came in, did her duty and flushed. "Help me with some milk?" she requested.

"We drained the poor animals yesterday. Let them rest," I suggested. But there were many chores to do. We just threw on boots and walked outside. The morning air was clear, almost smelling like the sea. It didn't have that tainted, rancid odor of dead bodies. We made our way out back to the trees, and in the morning light, I looked for some color in the pears and noted a number of them ready for picking. I was excited to have something to go with the pancakes. Chloe dashed to chase a mother goat. I put the pears in a bowl and rushed to help her with a large mug. With barely half a cup of milk collected, we carefully took our prizes inside, starting on some pancakes. We were trying to learn how to start the stove, a detail we'd missed before. Father came in and said, "I'll get this. You girls get the table ready."

Mother and Jack came in next, overwhelmed and not knowing what to do in the luxurious house. Chloe helped Jack get some fresh water. Mother helped with some of the cooking. She also cut the pears.

I said, "Who else heard the voice last night. It was the little girl. She said they weren't fully gods."

At first, no one answered. Father had a pan of water boiling, then took the remains of the chicken we'd cooked last night outside to a new trash pile. I couldn't remember having eaten any. Maybe I forgot to eat? Part of yesterday felt like a dream. What was real was the phone call in the middle of the night from the little girl spirit *living at a different level*, another echelon of existence.

Once we were seated at the table, I asked again. "Did anyone hear the girl?"

Chloe nodded. "Just like you said. We have to keep the confessions going."

"No," said Father, just meaning he hadn't heard the girl.

"Nothing," said Mother.

We all looked at Jack, seeing if he had an answer.

"I get a sister," said Jack.

On that keynote, we all blurted, "What?"

"A pretty girl told me Mommy has a baby girl," he said.

"Which mommy?" asked Chloe.

Jack pointed to Mother, not to me.

"Interesting," said Father, candidly expounding with theatrical haughtiness. "Perhaps she did talk to us. These confession chains have improved us immensely. Haven't we improved enough? Hell, we're the most ethical and decent people on the planet. We should be getting gold medals and international awards. I feel manliest, right and dandy killing animals, fornicating with my daughters, stealing huge properties, and well, assembling a revolution, treasonously throwing out an old constitution and ratifying a new one, and living like an opulent dictatorial king without any accord to grant me power, taking fascist domination of all lands and seas."

Chloe treated it like a line from a book, adding, "Said the boastful tyrant."

"Not that I can reach them all," he followed up.

I got the sarcasm but frankly wasn't the judge. I kept to the initial train of thought regarding our confessions. "She wasn't bothering us because we *were* doing the confessions. She said she is working with many others. It was only so many words." I turned to Jack. I wanted to preface my next questions with *simple minded mini-man* but didn't. "Jack. Did you hear anything else? What did the girl tell you?"

"She's mine," he said.

"Mine what? Do you get to kiss her like me and Chloe?" I asked.

He nodded affirmatively, holding his bright eyes up assertively.

"Little Jack gets a Little Wife," I acknowledged like a story title, waving one hand across a pretended book. I had the thought *we all become lovers* but kept it to myself. I knew it would upset Father.

Chloe reached over to tickle Jack's neck. "Oh Jack," she giggled.

Father and Mother were not especially pleased. Father shook his head, humphed, and continued with the pancakes. Mother heated up some chopped pears and threw in a little of the honey, making a pear syrup.

Mother only said, "I'll have some proper bread made by this afternoon. I'll try to keep the blisters out of it."

Whether it happened sooner or later, it helped Mother's spirits to think she'd be able to have another child. Indirectly, the "call" I'd gotten was an acknowledgment that we were doing the right thing in moving to the capital. It meant there was indeed future here. This little incident broke Mother's months-long slump and certainly helped her get over that miscarriage from the previous day.

TWELVE

The Patent Office

It was just after breakfast, and Daddy gave me the key to the padlock at the Patent Office. He also gave me a large steel bowl. "Show Chloe the Patent Office. Pick blackberries and bring the first truck to the main garage by lunch." With his hands he proposed a level across the bowl, indicating his expectation of the volume of blackberries. It would be a few pounds.

If I wasn't so much in pain, I would have rushed. But Chloe and I walked slowly, being tender with our travel-worn bodies. As soon as we got on the level roads we held hands. "I love you," I said softly.

"I love you," she said softly, then turned up to me and smiled. That image right there – so pretty, so loving – that could be etched into my mind for years, galactic years, universes. My heart jumped. I squeezed her hand. My eyes teared up a bit. I was so glad to have been hand-delivered a beautiful girl that I could love – my truest dream despite all things, including the event.

"Jack will get a girl," I said. "So cute."

"We don't know when," said Chloe, giving my hand a squeeze. "She didn't say. I'm assuming he'll still be a toddler. I'm not sure but that was the thought – not in words. Just a thought."

"I can neither confirm nor deny that," I said randomly.

"Goofball," she quipped, attempting to skip forward.

I was tempted to skip following Chloe's lead, but pain shot up my legs. "No. Can't skip. Can't but walk. Ouch." So, we slowed down. I'd dropped the bowl and it clanged against the ground. Chloe got it. We walked slowly on. At our pace, the overpass was huge. "We need bicycles. Everything's so far."

"I don't think I could ride one today." I looked down at my leg, irritated by a partial cramp. "We should have planned on two days to begin with.

"It took two days," she said.

"Three, then." I shook my head. I knew we needed to move as much as we could in one trip. I wished the newer vehicles had still been running, rather than the century-old trucks. "There's a lot of view," I said because she was looking around.

"I've been remembering more than just the incidents. I'm seeing things directly sometimes. My planet had a lot of islands. None of the continents were so expansive. High – yes, mountains were abundant. Expansive – no. A lot more of them – yes. Big oceans – no. The ocean currents were better. The rains comparable across all the islands, even the largest. This world is strange to me but now familiar. You are home. The family is home. The planet may never be. But with the events on my planet – it wasn't really home either, not in the aftermath. This place, I don't know how you can see it as home either, without all the people." She cut off.

"Right. The island and Altontown. It lost the sense of home. More like a trash bin to pick from. I could give myself the illusion that they'd all just got on a boat until I ran into the next corpse. I never understood the end. I missed something somewhere. I felt an earthquake, then came a wave. I suppose they are connected – it wiped the entire island. Completely wiped it out. If people had been alive – they would have all died without any chance of survival. Not one. Zero. Zip. Nothing."

"Continental plates shifting can create a wave if they push underwater. The best islands on my planet had rings of islands – not full rings – outer islands were the risky ones to live on. Inner islands were the stable ones. Any island could get hit by a great wave, though the outer ones were lower. In the history books they told of islands that got washed completely over, like you say."

"Yeah. The earthquake knocked me down. I thought I was scared already until I saw the wave that would victimize me. I knew it was over."

"Well, at least yours wasn't just stupid. I should have stayed on the island I was on. Bad navigation. I don't think I was meant to survive. We were meant to be here." She squeezed my hand again.

I pointed out, "We're at least tracked. I heard her voice again,"

"I know silly. We already conferred on it."

We'd reached the briar patch of blackberries. "We've got to start somewhere," I said. We picked blackberries as we could reach them while going up the path to the front doors, bumping a few long-legged spiders to scramble up the vines. I went ahead and unlocked the padlock while Chloe grabbed a few more handfuls. But she ate them before we went in.

Again, as I pushed at the stiff doors, the sterile smell hit me.

"Weird. So dry in a wet land," she said. She gazed about at the high ceiling and huge lobby. Hallways went from end to end and several went back from the main lobby and hallway area. "Where should we begin?"

"First we've got to find our way around. Older stuff is probably better to start learning from. Then we find specific things we need to fix and study our way through it. Should be like eating crab legs."

"What's that?"

"Um – we'll have to look that up too, I guess. A big crustacean with meat down the middle of the legs. If we could get to the sea, we could get..." I felt overwhelmed as if the wave was hitting me. "No. I'm not going toward the sea. You might expect fish from a pond if we can find one." But the thought of the low animal count struck me – perhaps the fish were also depleted in a similar way to the people, considering all the dead things that had washed up on the island during the hurricane.

I showed her the room with the picture of the construction, or reconstruction, of the building. With that, she had a much better orientation of the hallways. "Maybe we could set up beds here. Like we had our own house in the village. We could have our own building?"

"Please! I already asked Daddy. Bicycles are the better idea. Let me show you something else." I took her to the room with the caulking tube left in the trash. "See this? Daddy came here years ago, after I was born, trying to move us then. He'd fixed the windows here and chained the doors. Mother didn't want to go, and the village was in great condition. They stayed. I guess I'm glad they did. But Jack won't really know Adelardus."

"His girl won't know it at all," she said.

"Hey – it will still be our sister."

"As if the old rules matter more than desperation," she recited a line that had become common to us.

I felt clarity in my mind, perhaps from being in a sterile environment with large white walls and plain cabinets. The doors were wood or steel. The air was clear and so were my sinuses. Perhaps it was a reawakening I'd just had because the "telephone call" from the little girl. I began to understand the impetus behind rules – they were codified for survival, not for arbitrary reasons. Rules could change. The ethics behind it was the decision-making process to arrive at the rules, regardless of how volatile or permanent. A rule was just a decision, and decisions could change.

I began to stumble. I laid myself over. All I got out was, "Chloe. They might be – huh," before I laid over softly onto the floor.

Chloe rested herself near me.

My surroundings faded, and I saw images from the girl, being at a utilitarian desk in a simple room. "I understand that better now. I wasn't making good decisions. I'm sorry," the little girl was saying. "Billions of years and I didn't fully understand that. I'd have to say sorry to all my divided selves."

She turned to tears. I felt the grief and the accompanying sense of relief. "I understand better. Sorry, everyone in my universe – my universe shared with many other souls. It may have been a better universe if I hadn't been so dumb."

"Okay," said a male voice but the sound was soft. "Please see the quality department for verification."

She got up from a chair. I felt the touch within her hands. I felt her small lips. I felt the tendrils of her hair along her wet cheek, sticking slightly as a result of the tears. Then the whole scene faded. I had no idea what the process had been. She could have just been studying. She could have been doing her own confession chains, or it could have been something more serious – one that could draw us up into herself with a mad clashing end of *her universe.* I got more confused as I sat up. What was her universe and what was the quality department? Perhaps we needed our own quality department to check that we did finish all the confession chains we started. I wish I had more of their knowledge. She may have felt diminutive in her situation. But for the moment, I felt overpoweringly diminutive in mine.

Getting up from the floor, I felt as disoriented as I had in college last lifetime when I'd taken an elevator to the wrong floor and entered the wrong classroom a few minutes late. "We'd better get more blackberries," I said while trying to sort out my new perception. Chloe's gaze wasn't much different than the students in that classroom. "I heard her again," I said.

"I saw it," Chloe offered. "Some rules *can* be right."

I nodded. But I felt so small relative to the building, the city, the planet, and the whole universe. Quite frankly I felt like an idiot among geniuses. I walked back out to the main lobby and grabbed the bowl.

"Well wait for me," implored Chloe.

I turned back to look at her. There was concern in her beautiful eyes on her beautiful face. I loved looking at her even though I knew it was just flesh, as was my body.

We walked out, and I chained the door again, latching it with the padlock which had been loosening up with each use. Back to the blackberries, we picked until our sore and stinging hands were purple and we had as many scratches as blisters from the previous day. I should have brought the pruning shears. Next time I'd have to.

The walk back was mostly quiet. "That building is so huge. First, I was excited. Now I'm just overwhelmed. I wish everything was different," I said.

"Every day. Except for you," concurred Chloe, attempting a smile.

"I miss home," I said. "This isn't home yet."

"But it's right, isn't it?" she queried.

"Right," I observed, with a little thought on that last cognition from the girl regarding rules and correctness.

When we returned, Father had a book. "There's something I'd like to get running. There's a patent number – a whole series of them – on the book here. See?"

He pointed it out to myself and Chloe. "Your job is to find these patents. I hope you find your way around that place by doing so – at least part of it."

"What?" I said. The picture was of a machine I'd only seen in children's books about vehicles and powered tools.

"Mostly I need the tank and how to deal with the fuel," he said.

"But what is it?" I begged.

"Oh. A forklift."

Chloe filled in, "Okay," as she knew I was emotionally crushed.

"Beautiful hands," he teased. "Good blackberries, though."

Little Jack came running in. "Mommy. I have my own room, and it's next to yours."

"Oh. The nursery," said Daddy. "I guess we were too tired. I hadn't opened it."

Jack wanted me to go with him, but I sat down and picked him up to hold him. I was still sad. Daddy looked at me with concern. I looked upward. "When she cries, I cry," I reminded, lifting my eyes upward.

Daddy nodded but left the forklift instruction book on the table.

Each day, Chloe and I tried to find our way around the huge Patent Office, then walked back to the mansion and cleaned. I'd found a pack of rubber gloves in the first-aid room that hadn't aged to a crisp and wore them in hopes that my blackberry-purpled hands would yet heal. We washed laundry, mopped floors and wiped down whole rooms. We took turns watching Jack while Mother bathed, otherwise she tended to food and cleaning. She too used rubber gloves to clean with. Over the week we were healing from the move.

We studied what we could find at the Patent Office and began to learn the organization of the content, balancing that with the rest of the chores. Apples, pears and vegetables were ripening, and our next job was to can as much as possible all the extra that we couldn't eat. We fed scraps to the pigs and threw in all the wormy apples and pears. We threw grain to the chickens but let them eat whatever they could find in their section of the yard. We were here for the exploitation of the home, the surrounding area as a farm, the city for anything it offered, and the Patent Office for knowledge.

Within a couple weeks of arriving, Father had already made a trip back to the village, leaving in a truck at sunrise. I'm sure Mother knew. Chloe and I didn't know until he was already down the road. Within a couple days, he showed up in the Patent Office, looking filthy and beaten, and asked me to join him towing a trailer back up the highway ramp.

"I still couldn't quite make the run," he said, panting, walking with a limp. Boy did he smell. He was holding his left arm still, having wrapped it in a pair of pants. He didn't offer any further comment.

I walked to get the other old backfiring truck. Each time I cranked it I'd had to prime the cylinders since it started repeatedly with several pops, backfires and a stall. I'd hoped Father could hear the shotgun-loud pipes as they were aimed in his direction. An hour had passed by the time I drove up. He was resting, waiting at the completely overloaded truck and wagon. I backed up to his front bumper. Together we got the chain tied up and pulled the load up to level ground. He was yelling in pain occasionally as he had to use that wrapped-up arm. So, I didn't stop pulling the truck at the top of the hill. I waved him on and took him to the drive at the back of the house.

"It'll be a little harder to get out," he said when we got out.

"It's okay. I'll consider it a challenge." I turned to note the boxes on the trailer. Several were full of flour we'd ground before. We'd need it to get through the winter. As for him, I couldn't tell the difference between the sweat and the tears.

He justified, "I'm in pain but I'm alive. I'll be okay. As for the village, it's good. It's all good. I think it's gotten a little rain. At least it hadn't all burned down."

"How're the roads?" I asked.

"About the same," he asserted as he winced, picking up a box, putting the corner at the elbow of the wrapped arm.

I nodded toward the arm, "You're not going to tell me?"

"Does this have to be a confession chain now?"

"No. But it could be if you want," I appealed.

"No. We'll get it later. Now the damn thing just hurts." But as he twisted away from the truck, he blurted more expletives and tumbled to the ground with the load. "Owe!" he cried. He rolled over to level himself on his back.

I feared it was about that arm. But he was reaching to his back with the good arm. I waited for the expletives to yield to some explanation, but nothing useful was immediately forthcoming. He just rolled side to side in an effort to find a position to pull himself up. I reached to him and pulled at his right arm, but he told me to wait. "Get the wheelchair from the first-aid room," he barked through his disappointment.

I was frustrated with his eagerness to work so hard. I did as told, wheeling the awkward contraption down an overgrown walkway. I pulled him up by the good arm and he struggled painfully into the chair. At this point, he said, "My back snapped out. Shit!"

Settling into the chair and nearly crying, he requested, "I've got this wheel. You help with the left."

Once on the smoother walkway, I rolled him up to the back door. "There's a fold-out walker in there too," I offered.

"I'm going to need it," he growled. "Oh, I'm so stupid. But I got the load. Your Mother wanted the flour. Too much stuff in too little time. I should have waited. God – I knew that back was getting weak. But I went to get more."

"Crutches too?"

"Better than a walker. Yeah. I don't think I can hold the walker."

I rolled the chair past the first-aid room and fetched the crutches. Pushing further, I proudly said, "Chloe and I found the patents you wanted. The forklift, including the tank assembly. Maybe you just do some reading and study for the next few weeks while that arm heals and back gets into place."

"A hot bath would be nice," he hinted.

"You'll have to ask Mother for that one. Looks like someone else is going to be feeding the pigs, at least for a few more days." I rolled the wheelchair to the kitchen table and set the crutches by him.

"They've got enough to root through for a while yet. But if needed, there's another garden beyond what I'd shown you. A very good area to grow things – melons and squash took well to the area. Throw a few to the pigs each day and they'll have all they need."

"Daddy!" I said, already aware of the squash garden. We'd already been keeping up with the pigs since he left. "The pigs are good." I set some fresh cool water out for him. But I'd wanted to spend more time in the Patent Office.

"Look. A few hours at the Patent Office a day. More than that and you'll get weak – Patent Office, chores, help your Mother, feed the animals, clean the house, do the laundry, fix the meals. Do you think it's really turning out to be too big?"

"No. We don't need to clear all the gardens. The goats are doing well on the first. We don't need to clean the whole house, I couldn't begin to count the rooms. We'll feed as many animals as we need, and we do need to keep them breeding to catch up after the drought. And you were going to get a freezer going."

"Oh. I was. I guess I got busy and we had plenty of apples, and the garden.... Just flip that switch over there."

"What?" I said bluntly. I hadn't recognized the freezer since it was built into the wall like the cabinets, all covered with plain stainless-steel sheeting.

"Just flip that little switch by that upright freezer unit right there. The generator's running, right?" he pointed.

"We had some lights last night if that's what you mean."

"So. Flip the switch. It'll cool down in a few hours."

I opened the door and recognized the temperature gauge. "Daddy!" I shook my head. "You need a bath."

"I know," he laughed. "I really need that hot bath," he begged.

I went to the door into a main hallway to yell in the direction where Mother had been cleaning. "Mother! Father's back," I roared.

In the next weeks, our cleaning extended further from our intended living area in the east house, which was hardly the main area of the mansion. The kitchen here was more than adequate but not the primary kitchen where the chefs would have prepared state dinners. I scouted the building in search of better pans and utensils, as well as jars for canning. I'd found a jackpot of jars in a cabinet – there was nothing but jars and lids for three cabinets in a row, likely more than we could ruin in a lifetime without ever scavenging through other houses. I could see why Father had intended to come here first. I wasn't sure why they waited except that the village had been providing well enough.

In the house there were no installed carpets, but there were large rugs. We'd had to slide rugs out with bodies still stuck to them. We pulled out furniture with bodies glued against them. We cleaned up the whole wing of the "palace" though it wasn't one, and as we did, the accompanying smells ceased to pervade it. We didn't immediately bother to remove bodies from the guard station in the back as we didn't need it. But we did pull a little equipment except for flashlights and handheld walkie-talkie radios that needed batteries since there were no small working batteries anywhere. I wondered if we could find a way to make batteries too.

We did venture to nearby housing, additional mansions and estates, to scavenge from and collect many useful items. We found gas bottles. We found intact camp stoves. There were freezers and we'd hoped to find backup fuel and generators. In one "palatial estate," we found canisters of dry plaster and glue powder intended to strengthen the plaster. From the looks of it, someone was just getting started on a project to place tile. Beside it was a detailed drawing for a fresco intended for the center of the wall. That plaster substance mixed up with water and the glue powder made an acceptable paint. Daddy had said, "It'll be stronger than the paint. Kind of expensive, if we had to pay for it. Just the same, we should use it sparingly." We had to seal up some windows, using more glue powder than plaster as an acceptable formula.

We needed to turn our attention on how to build things. There was an engineering design firm nearby with a modest machine shop. Daddy's next interest was to get some of the machines running but they required more power than the small portable generators could deliver. Hoping to find better solutions, we all took turns taking trips with Daddy to the surrounding areas, even finding a good map we could mark the places we'd been. Daddy kept a notebook with the addresses with a list of usable items in each, plotting correlating numbers on the map.

We found whole-house "portable" generators as we made more trips, collecting all the fuel we could into nearby utility structures, not putting all our eggs in one basket. Daddy could get them to run but couldn't get them to deliver electricity throughout the shop. We had bad circuits or ground loops or something. He nearly gave up, but then we took an educational slant and learned about math and electricity from books in the library that would help us connect them. Within several weeks we had power for the machines in the shop, Daddy could start making parts for the things that had broken. Our first were common items we had replacements for anyway, such as a blender that didn't work – we found the patent from the number on the machine, found the diagrams, and found the specifications from that. A new part – a restored machine. A freezer didn't work, and we found a part for the bearing and tried to make them. But despite our diligence, bearings were particularly difficult things to make. Though we tried, the motor burned up on us. Then we went on to find additional freezers from homes, lining up the working units in a utility building near the mansion.

We had daily meetings while getting the home set up with generators, tools and other supplies. Daddy had found a flip chart and wrote out two things as he spoke. "The first big thing we need to figure out is how to make methane gas to keep powering that big backup generator. And I figure there's enough gas in the existing tanks to power us for a while, but once the pressure drops, no matter how much total volume of gas is in the lines, we get nothing useful. We had a small biogas generator in the village, a very old style and it hadn't been productive while I worked there, but I took down some sketches of it and put it into my truck, now in my boxes – I'll have to dig that out. Certainly we can find an example of such a contraption in the patents. Biogas generators are not usable in an urban area, so you won't likely find any just sitting about. They've got to have compost, and now that we're turning the president's grounds into a farm, we've got the needed biomass."

"Biomass?" I had to ask.

"Shit. Chicken poop. Cuttings from the garden. All the waste from the kitchen. If we get a mower running, grass, hay. We can use chaff from the wheat and oats. Anything organic we can drag on a sled or pull in a wagon."

"And that gives us natural gas?"

"Something really close. Just like pig farts, but I'm not hooking tubes up to all the pigs' back ends," he jested.

I laughed with cockeyed eyebrows. "You big brat," I said.

"But there's a second thing – water. We've got plenty of water in the roof tank above the mansion, and we've got huge stores of water in the other water towers, but leaks claimed a lot of it. My first trips here I looked for main valves and closed what I could. Some of the towers had stuck valves and are drained. Of the seven nearest towers I got four closed for certain. Two I wasn't sure of. One didn't close at all. At least for the four, we can get water ported with the trucks. Generators and pumps would get it into the roof tank. Safe water needs flow – has to be combined with air. But the best would be a well. These are new buildings on very old property. There's got to be a well around here somewhere. When you girls are scouting about, look for water sources. If we can't find one, we dig. We're not much above sea level, the water table can't be far down."

I noted that a pump would be easier than porting with the old trucks, which had an unknown lifespan.

Mother chimed in, "Ever witch for water?"

The rest of us shook our heads.

She went on, "We've got fruit trees. You need a live, green Y branch. I can use it to find the underground water flow. That should lead us to any old wells."

"Do it if it works," he said.

Chloe raised her eyebrows, having more zeal for the subject than Father. "I want to know how that works!"

"We'll try as soon as we can," Mother offered.

For days, perhaps weeks, the activities cycled between all the essentials like tending the animals and gardens, scavenging for essential provisions, and working on our two primary targets of gas and water.

Within a month, the rooms in our chosen family wing of the president's mansion were clean and livable. We'd found a bicycle and a small wagon and Daddy made a bracket to hook them together. We found more bicycles and did similar things with them.

The goats, pigs and chickens multiplied, and the freezer got the meat of several animals all wrapped up in paper and plastic wrapping. We had set up a backup freezer in case the big one in the kitchen went bad on us at any given time. We found better clothes in acceptable condition and Mother altered them as needed. And Mother got pregnant again.

With a baby bump, Mother regularly requested more help. I was helping with pots of water for boiling a soup. Mother was nervous, but we knew the premonition that Jack offered, one that Chloe and I also heard parts of. He was particularly interested in the baby. His language was improving rapidly despite otherwise appearing to be a typical toddler, despite my previous worry. I think he caught onto the patterns of the language, and suddenly burst forth with a rapidly expanding vocabulary.

Jack looked up from the table in the kitchen. "Grandma. I want my wife. When are you going to make her?" he badgered. Those were words that would have been dangerous in a normal society, but then the situation was not comparable to normal in any respect.

"I'm working on it, Jack," she said. "No one can make a baby in a day. It's inside. It takes time like the other animals. They don't hatch like eggs."

"Oh, I know that," he said. "I'm just teasing you. I am going to marry her. The girl voice said so."

"I know, Jack. I know," said Mother, appeasing him.

"She will be like the rest of us. We all love each other," he said.

A different phrasing from a child? Was this supposed to be the correct phrasing? Had we misinterpreted it? No. I knew what I'd heard. Father stated the same independently.

Mother's pregnancy would induce her to slow down and spend more time reading with Jack, who loved cuddling up with any of us if we were kind enough to help him learn the language, which thankfully we had not diverted into our own contrived parlance, instead staying with the definitions in the dictionaries. With the pregnancy going reasonably well it gave us hope, and the hope gave us energy. It spawned us to can vegetables specifically for the baby, so we'd have that surplus.

We cleaned thoroughly through the east house and continued to the main mansion. It needed it once in a while, but it would have taken a staff weeks to clean through the entire structure. With the wing cleaned up, Chloe and I sometimes changed sleeping rooms for the fun of it. Jack would come with us and climb in.

One specific morning we were on the west side of the main structure and the room remained dim even with the early sun. Chloe and I got ready to spend time at the Patent Office to study (still chasing patents for biogas generators while Daddy made new pipes and fittings for a water heater), wearing extra clothing for a cool spring day. Jack remained asleep and we tried to sneak out. While we'd gone to the kitchen to prepare some oatmeal, Jack woke and found himself alone. He came down through the hallways, yelling, "Grandma! Chloe and Mother left me alone again!" But when he came into the kitchen, all of his four-year-old body standing firmly, his index finger shaking, he saw us instead.

"Why would it be wrong for us to leave you asleep?" I charged.

"Because I don't like it. I don't like being alone!" he fumed.

"Oh. So you'd rather we get you up and take you with us in the cold?" Chloe asked.

"Yes. I can read now, you know," he said, folding his arms. "I didn't come here to be left alone, asleep, in a dark bedroom. I can help you."

"Okay," I acquiesced, flopping a quick shrug.

Chloe filled in, "You can go with us. Just know it's cold – chilly – there." She pointed toward the Patent Office.

"Okay," he said, his eyes up and ready to go.

"You'll eat first," I said. I filled up a small pan with oats and poured in boiling water, cooking it to a mush. Chloe took him to get overdressed for the few hours we'd spend in the cool building. Being creative, we wore tights and leggings under pants, with shirts under our dresses; for him we did the same. We got some snacks ready, including some bread, and loaded up everything, including Jack and a children's dictionary, into the wagons behind the bicycles. The trip was easy despite a brisk morning wind, and we took the bikes and wagons right on through the doors into the lobby, as we normally did.

We moved on to a study, Jack holding my hand, anticipating the work. I put him up to a small desk, raising an adjustable chair to its limit, giving him a patent document for a very old stool with adjustable height. I asked him to read it and copy all the words he didn't know onto a sheet of paper, so we could look them up. I did much the same with a different document, then went to the pile of dictionaries to look up all the terms.

Jack looked over the words, starting out with many on the paper. Within half an hour he appeared bored. In another twenty minutes he was tearing up his notepaper, a blanket getting thrown aside in his moment of crisis. Perhaps he thought we were just instigating his decision to remain at the mansion with Mother.

When I'd studied in the previous lifetime as Miranda, I oriented my knowledge around the purpose of writing. Words were important. I instantly reacted from that point of view. "No!" I said. "We can help you learn the words! Don't ever give up. You'll just leave the confusion behind and build on it. It's how to be stupid."

"There's too many. And when I look them up, I hit another one that's spelled funny and I don't know how they sound," he argued.

"We start with the first, silly little man. I didn't bring you here to watch you give up in a day."

"Oh," he conceded. "First one, then," he pleaded.

So, you could say my occupation changed that day, from a self-proclaimed student of the Patent Office to primary educator for my son. His ability to learn outpaced anything I'd ever seen for anyone, let alone a toddler of four years. And I had to go over the simple words, like *as* and *to*, like I'd never gone over them before. I had to peruse grammar books for the structure of the language just to be able to get simple definitions conveyed to Jack. I considered rewriting the dictionaries. What if you had a dictionary that you could learn the words in order, such that the words you needed in the definition of the next word were always covered in the previous words? I must say that he prompted me to consider the order by the way he asked his questions.

Language became simple, such that you needed a subject and the action or a simple statement of what it was like. After that, the majority of grammar was tense, modes and modifiers and the order used to state things clearly. Symbols were much like words, each having a clear definition and how to use them. Jack was going to have a better teacher than any I'd ever had. I took all the words from the patent and lined them up on cards, including all the small words. I put them in the best order I could and rearranged them as we studied. Day after day we just studied the words, making up little stories to use them. I showed other drawings and gadgets we had on hand to show what the items were, as part of the word definitions. We had reached a point where we'd covered every word in the short patent, big or small. Once we'd gone through all the words, we stopped for the day, and I told him, "Tomorrow, you go back to the patent and make a new list for any words that don't make complete sense to you. We'll try them all again."

"Yeah, I know," he said, certain we'd have more words to study.

The following cold rainy day stood out in my memory. Because of the rain, we'd tried to leave Jack with Mother but he wouldn't have it. We covered him completely, a tarp covering the wagon, while we rode the bicycles across to the Patent Office. Chloe and I had the appearance of demons, covered with black tarps that had been custom fit like a baby's jumper, complete with a hood, and legs long enough to drape to the shoes. They were Mother's handiwork. There was no need to hurry but some degree of motion was needed for body heat. Sometimes Chloe and I raced, but today we rolled slowly through moderate rain. Inside the "cloak" I was getting warm. I hoped Jack's experience was good, so I called to him, "Jack? Are you okay under there?"

"I'm fine. Keep going. I don't like it under here," he said because it was slow.

"We're going. We can't go fast," I said, hoping it would keep him talking.

"You're taking too long," he complained.

"It's raining!" I called back.

We pulled the bikes up the steps together, so we'd have the strength to pull Jack. We uncovered from the rain gear and went back to our work areas, leaving everything, including our bikes and boots, to dry in the lobby. Jack settled up to the desk with the patent on it. At first skeptical, he read it over again, ready to make a list of words so we could start over after weeks of study. Instead, he mouthed the words and shook his head. He didn't write. He read another sentence, twiddling the pencil in his hand.

"Jack, you're just four years old. I don't think you have to understand that all at once," said Chloe. "Go ahead and write the words you still need to study. It's okay."

Chloe's appearance of amazement is what grabbed my attention. Jack had a different look on his face, one of comprehension rather than confusion. Instead of writing out words, he wrote out the illustration from the patent as a new drawing on the paper. We both quietly got up to watch him draw, making a wonderful replica of the adjustable stool, which used a large screw as a post. He didn't draw dimensions and numbers, but he did illustrate a workable view of the stool from the side, then added another view from the bottom. He wrote "metal" and "wood" by the seat, base and other minor components.

He didn't stop yet. He added arrows with words, indicating the name of everything. His concentration was so intense he didn't realize that Chloe and I were moving up behind him until he was about done and heard our breathing.

"If you turn it this way, it goes up and down. And if you don't latch it, and you sit on it, you spin up or down. If you latch it, it stays, right?" he turned back to me and entreated with his handsome little eyes.

Breathless, I mouthed, "Wow," I was overcome, seeing that the word list worked like magic. I instantly reached out and grabbed him for a hug. He started pushing back because his interest was on the drawing. But as I giggled and pulled him close, he got the idea to accept the acknowledgment and smiled.

My primary regret was that millions of people were not present to share this delightful moment. "Jack, that is so wonderful. The study was a success!" I said cheerfully. I roughed his hair and embraced him.

In the next days, Jack replicated the drawing better yet, and Chloe and I helped with dimension. We'd given the work to Daddy, and he would attempt to make a physical replica as soon as he could find the materials.

Chloe found several old patents related to biomass gas generators, and a few modern designs for large scale farms and remote site usage to power natural gas generators, just like we needed. There wasn't a chance of finding such a unit in this metropolis, but we'd be able to build something.

In the afternoons, after tending the animals, Mother and Chloe took an apple branch for a dowsing rod and witched for water, mapping an underground stream across the back gardens of the presidential property, which led them to an old well head. It had been cemented closed, and we feared it would have been filled. It became Daddy's job to bust up the cement, which he did for about half an hour a day, considering the effort balance with other chores, and that we had plenty of water for the time being.

I was out tending chickens, gathering chicken droppings for compost and Daddy went out to the well head with a pull wagon loaded with a small gas-powered pump. "If I get it open, I want to be ready," he said. Noting a microscope was also loaded into the wagon, I supposed that meant he was close.

Because of my curiosity, I continued working in the back gardens. I heard the gas pump start, run hard a few minutes, and quit. I was up on a wooden ladder grabbing apples, sorting them for table use or for the pigs, when Daddy came running across the field. He had a jug with him, holding it up. "We have water!"

He was as happy as a little girl, as the expression went. I'd have to admit that my childhood wasn't as happy because the more confession chains we'd done, the less morbid, and less introverted I'd become. I stepped down carefully and walked to the edge of the inner garden, waiting for him to come across a gate. "It's water. Fast and clear. The pump couldn't pull it dry.

Full force and I got a steady stream. We've got all the water we need."

I looked at the water, seeing it was clear, and said, "I know all the risks – shouldn't we test it?"

"Already did," he said. He pulled some microscope slides out of his pocket. "Evidence on these. Nothing microbial, anyway."

I took a drink of the ground-temperature water. It was crisp, had plenty of calcium, and certainly fresh. I couldn't think of anything to say, so I just smiled and drank more. Then the proper thought came to me, "Best water since the village."

In the next days, we set up some tubing to the house and tapped into the main water system through several outside spigots, expecting it to backflow through the system. Another hose went to the roof tank. We'd get better piping instead of garden hoses later, but for now, after flushing the system, we had much fresher water. It was the first time we could run water from the tap and drink it directly.

Back at the Patent Office, Chloe and I worked on a new design for a biogas generator. One of the old patents had the use of a huge tree trunk, partly hollowed out, and it could be filled with various compost. The primary part of what I laughingly saw as this patent explained the means of covering and sealing the stump and collecting the gas. The drawing was so trite, showing a huge stump near a cabin, the contraption on the stump and a tube going into the side of the cottage for use with a small woodstove converted with a gas burner. The design had one inherent problem: the trunk itself would get consumed in the process and soon succumb to leaking.

Some patents were too simple, with no reservoirs, not giving a high enough grade of gas, or too complex for our present ability. We had to combine ideas. Some generators needed some heat to keep them going. Our concept had converted a commercial water heater we'd found in a factory and integrated it to a composter, adding additional tanks to clarify the gas. Its working life would give us five to ten years at least, and to be sure it was warm enough to produce gas, it could use some of its own gas to warm it, using a restricted burner.

Convening the following morning in one of the studies we'd converted to the "control room" we presented the plans to Daddy.

"Oh. These are the units from the factory?" he queried.

"Yes, Daddy," smiled Chloe. She was quite proud of the drawings. "All the conversions are stated. There are enough parts in the factory to make as many as we'll ever need."

"Unless we end up repopulating the planet and become legends. I'll get to work on it and see if it's viable. I'll let you know if there are other parts we need to draft as I'm integrating it."

Jack was there curled up in my lap. He turned to lie on his back, awkward in the chair, but his smile warmed me. He understood the impact of the invention. The compost biogas generators were our largest project up to this point though the requirements were simple – a safe means to produce methane gas to run generators and stoves. I knew that the house itself had a reservoir of natural gas for the stoves that would last for years. I did, however, feel we had more control over our lives if we had the means to produce gas.

This biogas generator project, much like the water project, took up all our time. I pondered on the wasted time in the previous lifetime listening to radio, television, and music. I longed for a world with more communication – communication that was useful. How much of that had been a waste? How much noise can people make that is useless? How much entertainment do people need? We had been noise junkies. We'd become used to wasting our time finding out what other people were doing without doing anything ourselves. All the noise of radio and television advertising, useless television shows, endless commentary on radios, finally ceased when they all died. I'd experienced a cessation of vocal salesmen and disliked songs, a welcome deliverance from a cluttered world, allowing a calmer and clearer mind this lifetime than the previous. Was all this noise necessary? How did that help the society? Or did it just define it? And most of all, why did we buy it? Because we'd been told? Because someone wanted to be heard? Into which part of survival did all this activity fit?

Chloe and I spent time at the machine shop with Father, measuring each component for accuracy. These manually adjustable lathes were difficult, but Daddy was mastering them. To be compatible, every piece had to be custom made. And we couldn't neglect the other items on our chore list – fueling and restarting the water pump daily, handling the animals, gardens and food.

Through the winter, Mother turned her attention to concentrate upon horticulture, repurposing a study for her own library in the main house. As spring approached, she searched for useful plants in the area and found places for them in the gardens and pergolas. She cataloged her own experiments and successes. The back atrium became her laboratory, even setting up her own microscope to examine the health of the plants. She'd keep a working notebook on each type of plant, keeping the whole history on a shelf in her study. She'd collected important herbal formulas into a binder placed with cookbooks in the kitchen; it included teas and tinctures with antiviral, antibiotic, anti-inflammatory, immune-enhancing and many other properties, augmenting the handful of formulae she learned while at Adelardus.

We collected all the biomass we could, already setting aside barrels for experimentation. A few were avidly producing streams of marginally flammable gas. Daddy and Chloe completed the sequential assembly of a first prototype for the filtering and cleaning process. After the integration with the composter, we all helped scoop the "shit" from containers to the enclosure in the main unit, into which we'd put a filling chute with a tight cover. We stood back as Daddy connected a small camp stove, waiting for the pressure to build up and boil through limewater to clean the carbon dioxide. While waiting, we examined all the fittings, then Daddy had us all step back while he used a long rod with oilcloth at the end of it to put a flame next to the pipes. Nothing blew up, but he kept on checking, saying, "I want to check for any first flames not wait until it would blow off the roof."

Then, he set the valve open for the old camp stove and lit it from afar with that long rod, and it lit as expected, first showing yellow, clarifying to blue.

"We need more of these," said Father, flashing a prominent smile.

This unit was large enough that we were compelled to drain and separate the parts to transport to the water pump behind the mansion property. We took two old trucks to get the tanks moved, having lifted them by rolling the tanks back and forth across two palette stacks to the level necessary. "I wish I had that forklift running today. Be less likely to be the bungler," said Father.

Mother watched from the back of the property, with Jack on her shoulders as we hooked up the new biomass generator twenty meters from the well. Why so far from the wellhead? If the unit failed, we didn't want to blow up the wellhead or the house. Once hooked up, we were all quite pleased with the new system. We'd have to inspect it every day, reviewing anything in the design that didn't function as expected, checking the quality of the flame. Over the ensuing weeks, we built a wire fence to encompass the unit and later added a shed to help moderate the temperature, ensuring a steady flow of methane. More biogas generators were built to handle our increasing demand and tracking sheets were affixed to the refrigerator and freezer for convenience in scheduling the replacement of the limewater and metal shavings.

The new units being operational encouraged our production for animal dung, overproduction in the luscious gardens and restoring lawnmowers for collecting additional biomass, machining in the shop to get metal shavings, and proper warehousing of a store of calcium hydroxide we'd need for the limewater. It was great that Daddy found the calcium hydroxide in a warehouse because I wasn't quite ready to take on a limekiln project.

THIRTEEN

Another Meteor Shower

I found myself longing for the old home because this one reminded me of the hotel I'd died in, and even with large fireplaces, it never got as warm and cozy as the parsonage, despite the fact that the winters were milder than the village. The summers wouldn't be quite as hot as the island, so that wasn't that much of an issue, considering we were a couple parallels north of the equator. The northerly climate was balanced by the presence of the sea.

Though the year-round temperature was less variable, occasionally there were exceedingly vicious storms that battered the coast. That frightened me more than anything, playing on my final poignant experiences as Miranda. It prompted me to continue the sessions no matter what, partly because I didn't know if we could continue such spiritual endeavors as disembodied souls. We needed knowledge from the Patent Office just for physical survival, but we also gained knowledge when we ran through these confession chains.

Daddy had been taking excursions, often announced only by a note on the kitchen table, to the surrounding areas in search of a place to catch fish and for supplies. After venturing about for several days, he came in to check on us all where we'd gathered at the Patent Office. Mother was pregnant and hated the idea of being left alone. As a backup, we'd set up the first-aid room in the Patent Office as a birthing room and were moving a blanket and a bucket. Our sun-browned Daddy came in through the front door, bellowing, "I'm back! Did anyone miss me?"

I saw the familiar man, who had the appearance of a crazy woodsman having escaped marshy thickets full of venomous snakes. "Of course, Daddy," I said and dropped the bucket and rushed toward him, followed by everyone else.

"Hugs, everyone," he tempted.

Jack was quickly behind me, having rushed to Father's legs, about to grab them, but the smell and muck set him revolting. "Yuck! You're disgusting!" he barked and tumbled back to sit against the wall.

"I wasn't expecting obedience," laughed Father. "Good to see you, son," he added.

"Um – good to see you, not to smell you," offered little Jack.

"Avelynn, you look pregnant," Daddy asserted as if he'd just recognized it.

"And it's my Daddy's baby," she shot back.

"Well, then. It's a good thing the overly litigious prosecutors all died," he stated. "Or we'd be in trouble." They giggled and kissed.

"The law changes in a desperate world," whispered Chloe, reflecting from her previous lifetime. She also rushed up to him, giving him a loose hug. "You stink. You need a bath. Did you find any fish?"

"No. Just little tiny fish – I caught them to use as bait – but nothing. I stand baffled. Just nothing, like there are no pets and only a few birds."

"Like the owl I'd seen at the house before we left," I noted.

Chloe reached over to me, "You saw an owl?"

"I woke in the middle of the night before we left the village. A beautiful owl swooped down to get a mouse."

"I saw an owl behind the mansion a few weeks ago. I came in to mention – you must have been giving Jack his bath," she said.

Mother and Father nodded.

It was dim in the night when I'd seen it, but I recalled the faint image. "Yes – perhaps it followed us."

"Anyway – I didn't find any fish. Nothing we could eat," Daddy said. "It's the anniversary of the meteor strike. I thought it best to be home."

Mother had backed up because of the smell, but stiffly turned, gasping, "Today? You were still out today?"

He corrected, "Um – this week. Any day. Not safe anywhere. Perhaps we split up – some here in the office, some there in the mansion."

It left us with a serious confusion. How best to split up the group?

He then added, "Everyone decide on your own, which house you'd rather be in for the next week and I'd suggest to mostly stay there. To our best degree, be separated. That big hole out there by the bay – it is a bay by itself. If one struck right here, both structures would probably be gone. But it's all we got."

"Maybe you should still be out gathering fish," chided Chloe.

"No," he said sadly and walked up to her to kiss her hair. "I want to be near my family. If it's time for us to go, we go. But we separate to stretch the odds." To lighten it up, he jabbed Chloe and added, "And dear, you need to get into a bath yourself."

She gave him a light smack across the arms. "I don't need one nearly as bad as you. You'd almost smell better if you wallowed with the pigs. At least I'm used to that."

Mother and Jack went back to the house, Chloe and I did our time in the Patent Office then split up, sometimes I'd be at the mansion and sometimes she would go for the chores and to make meals. We'd use the bicycles and wagons to move food.

About the third morning, I'd slept in the first-aid room at the Patent Office. Chloe had stayed in the mansion and I thought she was late in arriving with food. I scrambled out to get on the bicycle, hoping to keep my food run short, pedaling as hard as I could without tumbling the wagon over. The morning air was salty and crisp, a breeze blowing from the direction of the new bay. I ran in, begged for food from Mother, Jack and Father, who were there in the kitchen, finishing up breakfast. Father was just taking his last bite, rising from the table. Chloe wasn't there.

I was confused. "Where's Chloe. I thought she'd bring food?"

Vacant eyes rose to greet my mounting panic. "She's over there somewhere," offered Father, nonchalantly, "Certainly safe."

"Grab some food anyway and take it back. Maybe she's hiding. Check the lower level," suggested Mother.

I gave Jack a hug, and he climbed up on my back while I got food together. "You have to stay with grandma," I said to him, pulling him aside to stand him on a chair, but he wouldn't let go.

"I call her Avelynn now, Mommy," he refuted. He held back, staring at me. He began entreating, "I want to go with you."

"No," cried Mother. "We are going under. Today *is* the anniversary of the meteor shower. We haven't seen much in the last few years so this is just a precaution, but I won't change my mind."

Jack's arms relaxed away from me as a result of her stern voice. He gave an acquiescent grimace and a long look, like when Sandy had played with me on the last day of college, but this was serious. What if we never saw each other again?

"Jack. Now. We're going under. To the basement," demanded Mother.

"Dahilana! Get your things and go take shelter," dictated Father.

He rarely used my name with such intent, so it pulled at my heart, as if I could feel the command even if he would never have opened his mouth. So, I hurried to get some food and put it into a big pot, and put the pot into the wagon, cycled across the overpass, tugging along like a sitting duck in an arcade game, and rushed on to the Patent Office.

I had a thought of where Chloe might have been. In the diagram of the Patent Office, there was a strong room roughly central to the whole structure that would make a fair bunker, and we'd dubbed it the "legal vault." I'd checked it before, having mostly historical content about the Patent Office itself, including thousands of court documents on patent cases. I'm sure it had been interesting to those involved, but it wasn't of much use to us now.

I climbed up the steps and through the main doors (we'd not been locking them unless there was a specific threat of a storm) and clomped to the interior staircase that would lead me to the legal vault, and there in the vestibule before the stairwell was her bicycle, thus I hadn't seen it on my way out. I led myself down the stairwell to the lower level, pacing slowly through the dim hallway, lit by a handful of skylight inlets on the outer walls. Though there was a mechanical code box on the door, the door pushed in easily. A book cover fell out from between the door and the frame.

"Don't let the door close," Chloe said quickly.

I couldn't see her at all in the dark room. I kept my body between the door and the frame. "Why?"

"We could get locked in," she informed and stepped near to get the book cover placed against the doorjamb again.

I dragged in the large pot of food items from the hallway. She put the door to, the book cover securely in place. The light of a single oil lamp only illuminated a small group of cabinets. The darkness hurt my eyes; I didn't move until my eyes adjusted. In this large building with large windows, this room was the darkest thing since a foggy and rainy night in the old homesteads at the village.

In the dark, I sat against a cabinet. Chloe sat next to me for a while, then straddled me, kissing me quietly. I could see her face with the dim yellow light. I recalled the night I'd been born, seeing Mother's young face in the firelight. It reminded me of that moment, seeing Chloe's bright eyes with a strange color. She was roughly the same age as Mother when I was born. The love between us was so strong.

"Why does it all seem so much more serious this year," she said.

I wiggled my chin and offered, "Ah – the uneasiness is because Mother is pregnant. I hadn't heard any premonitions. No one said they did. We're just getting nervous – Daddy says they are worse every dozen years or so."

"I thought there was a five-year pattern. Back and forth – a dozen times? I hope they are just overreacting," she offered.

So, we stayed, talked, cuddled, kissed and just sat about and nibbled for hours. At some point, I put a cabinet into the door to hold it open to add more light, but Chloe didn't feel as secure. "Chloe! I got a premonition during the last big meteor shower that we'd have enough years here to accomplish what is needed. We wouldn't inherit the Earth if it wasn't, would we? Besides, it has been years since the bay got ripped up," I said but shouldn't have mentioned it. Her gaze back at me said it all.

Instead, I went to the building's maintenance shop and got some screwdrivers and then came back to take the door latch apart. I lectured, "I don't think you feel secure without a door, but I don't feel secure with it able to lock us in forever. How long would it take Daddy to find us? Hopefully not more than a day, but then if we were passed out, if the big souls up there started a session…." I didn't offer that a meteor could hit the mansion and not the Patent Office. Once I got the door so it wouldn't get stuck closed, I went back to offer my arms to Chloe.

"Dahilana," she said. "I love you."

I thought she'd be upset with me, but she clung to me like a scared toddler, the kind of child we'd seen before the event occurred. The clarification is necessary because Chloe, Jack and myself had been anything but normal, being one-hundred percent precocious.

In midafternoon, we noted flashes of light reflecting down the hallways and into the vault. I scooted to the door to look down the hallway. The bright flashes strobed through the skylights. Chloe cried. "No – come back."

I'd noted no booms yet.

I went toward Chloe, who slinked back further into the vault, away from the door. I held her hands, and I could feel her fear in her actively-clawing grip.

"To the day," I whispered. Our faces were together. She nodded, and I could feel her wet cheeks collect a little of my long hair. I pulled the hair back and kissed her. It turned to expressed passion.

But much like my extended vision of the moon during the first rampaging meteor shower, I was thunderstruck by my sudden extended perception above the roof of the Patent Office, superimposed upon my expressions of love for my girl. Having a point of view between the sparse clumpy clouds, I could see the meteors burning up the sky, leaving trails of flame and smoke. Far in the distance, one of them exploded during its entry, creating a bright flash and fireball turning upward into a mushroom cloud. Deep within my heart, I was concerned with our potential destruction and transferred that to my desperate kisses. I feared yet that I'd lose my life, and worse yet, lose Chloe.

"I see the sky," I whispered. In expressing that, I found I could turn to look in the direction the meteors arrived, watching the flourishing balls of fire rain down, hearing the earsplitting sonic booms and sonorous echoes from the ground. Many of the trails ended before they made it to solid earth. Many wisped though the high atmosphere, leaving only tiny streaks of light, never making it any further.

A monstrous scorching ball of fire headed directly at me, deviating neither left nor right, up nor down. But my viewpoint attained a higher level, yet above the clouds – I watched the burning meteoroid whiz past and head to the sea at a very shallow angle. As it struck, water boiled into smoke and spray from the force of impact. I feared for worse and examined about the sky. Fortunately, the number and scale of meteors arriving had begun to abate. One oddball meteor came in at a different angle, tumbling nearby, slamming into an old pile of ash from a coal-fired iron plant (I supposed). I could see the direct impact and the ash flying all about, leaving a smoldering pit in the ash pile which now resembled a volcanic cone.

Hundreds of tiny meteors continued to pelt the upper atmosphere, but the main show was over. Still seeing from above, I felt Chloe's soft shape under me, and I dripped my tears of thankfulness upon her.

My extended vision beyond my body faded, becoming nebulous as I was drawn back down, as if hands were on my sides, guiding my viewpoint back to the body I'd felt all along, and I again saw only the heavily shadowed cabinets and floors of the vault room. "It was like I was out there. I saw it all. Last time I saw a meteor crash into the moon like I was there. It wasn't a premonition. I think it was to show I was going to be okay. Did you see it?"

Chloe's wet eyes and warmly lit face nodded. "Yeah. I saw it – not as clear as you. I saw streaks and stuff as if it were coming across the ceiling." Glad to be alive, we kissed yet again. As we stood up, she never let go of my hand, her body right up against mine. We walked up the stairs and through the hallways, no faster than the box turtle, and out the front door. A few last straggling meteors burned up tiny trails, partly hidden by the clouds.

Across the way, I could see Mother, Father and Jack coming out on the front porch of the mansion. We all cheered jubilantly, and though I hoped we hadn't been cheering too soon, the evidence and history suggested this shower was complete. Grit fell from the sky, raining down like volcanic ash to the sidewalks and roads.

After waiting out the ash "rain," Chloe and I grabbed the bicycles and pedaled to the mansion. Once there, we screamed and hugged, expressing how glad we were to have blood circulate in our veins. Mother was just a month from being due for the next baby, and Father offered his assurance, "Little one, you'll have a chance to be born yet!" He kissed at Mother's belly.

We all acted crazy enough that had we behaved like this before the primary event, the "little men with white coats" would have come to strap us up for a fictional malady. We didn't have to worry about those bastards now. What were they anyway, as such people were often against religion of any kind? They eschewed any notion that there was a spirit as the primary constituent of the human being. They called people crazy when caught in moral dilemma, and rather than helping people understand right from wrong, they openly claimed that right and wrong and any concept of God didn't exist, proffering it was therapeutic and freed the mind of ethical conundrums. While I'd never seen any direct evidence of a single unique God, I certainly had plenty of evidence of spiritual existence and capability, and something on the order of God, if not one single God.

As would often happen when I had some "opening" of my mind for whatever reason, new musings would fall out. My concept today was: "They were like gatekeepers. The psychiatrist 'intellectuals' with their secular humanism were those that helped keep us down into the universe, 'helping' us remain oblivious of our spiritual nature. We didn't have any such gatekeepers and their doctrine here because we didn't need them. We were on our way out, and God, as a concept, was the first clue."

If I'd ever believed any brain theory and pseudo-psychoanalysis, or biology's claim that the origin of life was exclusively cellular, I certainly couldn't vouch for it now. I could hope for one thing – if I could just become adept at having such spiritual revelations without being terrorized by meteors.

FOURTEEN

Molly!

Preparation for the birth would dominate the next weeks. Mother got more relaxation time while the rest of us got things ready for the baby, including the final setup of a crib and baby changing table we'd found in the mansion. They had everything stored somewhere in the building because guests would have brought children or pets. We had a baby bath and children's toilet seat covers. Items were scattered among the various kitchens, a small stockpile of bottles, little silver plates and spoons in the main kitchen and personalized items in the private family kitchens in the wings, like the area we'd chosen for our primary living quarters.

Now that we had plenty of towels and containers, we had sterilized a stack of towels and washcloths, having them packed up and ready. Another container had a bundle of diapers.

With reduced hours at the Patent Office, Chloe and I struggled to understand how a unique motor controller worked, as it was highly magnetic in its circuitry, rather than being purely electrical. It was part of a machine from the shop, and Daddy hoped to rebuild the unit because it could fabricate larger parts. But the more I studied the words, the more I just folded up. I hated that machine, wishing I had a smelter to throw it into. My mind collapsed in on itself. I wanted to give up and just be with Mother to help handle the birth.

We had hooked up solenoid control wires between the house and the Patent Office, and we could remotely ring a bell in either. If Mother went into labor, someone was supposed to ring the bell five times then repeat. Yet on the day Mother went into labor, I'd given up my study and already headed back to the house. Assuming the birth was days away, I again washed the baby's blankets and hung them to dry. Mother had been resting, so she wasn't aware I'd arrived. I heard five-year-old Jack stomping loudly through the hallway. He stopped at the bell switch, theatrically counting off five. I ran toward the front doorway where the switch was located, seeing him nod while counting. Then he waited, then confidently pushed the button five times again.

"Jack – I'm here," I said to him.

"Did you get a premonition?" He'd cocked his head.

"No. I got frustrated."

"Avelynn said to call you," he rose his eyebrows, flashing huge eyes.

I looked out the front door. Chloe was just taking a seat on her bicycle at the Patent Office, heading our way. "Good. Chloe's coming. The bell worked."

Jack smiled, clutching my legs.

I squatted to give him a hug. "Did *you* get a premonition?"

"No – yes. Just a little one." Jack shrugged.

"What's that?"

"First she dies. Then she gets born." His eyes gazed into me.

I wasn't sure he knew what the premonition meant. I acted tentatively, much like Mother, "What do you mean, Jack," I asked.

He shrugged.

"Does Mother die?" I asked.

"No. Not Avelynn. Just Molly."

Half pleased, half surprised, I threw my hands aside. "You already know her name? Where does she come from?"

He stepped to the open front door and looked up, holding out his hands as I had. "I don't know. I don't see the stars," he said like a little prince.

"You can show me tonight, okay?" I offered, not having any idea when Mother would be in final labor or whether the planet would be pointing to his desired constellation.

"Okay. If they show up at night," he paced in and out of the door, acting disoriented.

"We've got to check on Mother – did she say what is happening?" I took his hand to run through the hallways and arrive at her room.

"No. Just to call you," he blurted while we ran.

"Mother?" I called as I entered, seeing her half pulled away from a wet area in the bed

"Oh, dear Dahilana! I've got such a mess," said Mother. Her water had broken.

"Where's Daddy?" I asked.

She complained, "He's at the machine shop – took a dental chair like we'd used for Jacks' birth. I said a seat part wasn't placed right and made me sit a little off. He insisted on fixing it."

"Shit!" I affirmed. "Will it be done by the time…?" I rolled my eyes, recognizing the need to intervene. "Alternate. I need an alternate." This place had everything except a birthing bed. I thought of a large black leather reclining chair in another wing. If we moved the birthing area from the kitchen right next door to the dining room, we'd have enough room for it.

Chloe stepped in, face up and curious, winded from her bicycle ride.

"Chloe – you tend to Mother. Daddy took the chair to work on it. I've got to set up a birthing bed."

"I could have the baby right here, you know," suggested Mother, huffing through a contraction.

"How far apart?" I asked.

"A while. Go do your thing," Mother said as Chloe stepped in and took over.

With zeal I fetched a furniture mover from a utility closet and towed it with its attached rope along the floors. There was a wheelchair ramp in the central structure I could take the chair through, once I found it, searching a dozen rooms before I said, "There you are!" to the inanimate object. I fumbled the chair onto the flat frame with wheels and rushed back, taking it down the ramp and back toward our favored wing. I took the extensions out of the large dining room table (a room we rarely used) and put it all off to the side, and placed the collapsed table, the big recliner and a baby-changing table into the room. I moved a bassinet and baby warmer Daddy had taken from a small hospital during one of his excursions, making certain the warmer was in reach of one of the few live receptacles. The recliner could potentially fold up if you tripped over the lever that set it back. It was the best I had for now. I mopped up and disinfected the whole room, taking some things out to put them into another guest room we weren't using. I was proud of my instant conversion.

Then I heard a clanging, banging noise, the sound of a small generator, and a hesitant electric whine. I went to the large front door and opened it. Here was Father on a forklift, rocking up the elongated steps, not with the old dental chair, but with a proper birthing bed standing on end. His hair was wet with sweat from the heat of the summer day.

"Daddy!" I reprimanded. "Mother is upset with you, you oversized brat."

"I'm sure she is. How's she doing?" he asked, hands on the controls.

"Water broke," I said as I opened both sides of the large double doors.

"And you wouldn't badger me?" he questioned with big eyes.

"No! I'm not feigning," I thundered.

"Oh shit. Just in time, I guess." He drove the forklift, the large battery replaced with not one but two small generators, right into the house. I put the recliner back onto the furniture mover, pulling it out of the dining room, and directed him in.

"I thought I'd have to rearrange all this – better than what we started with!" he yelled in placing the bed.

I grabbed a bucket of hot water to wipe down the new unit, a manually adjustable bed. "Where the hell did you get this thing?" I called back to him while he was driving the forklift back to the main entry.

"A hospital," he only said.

He must have been working on that plan for a while. It was a very old bed with no electrical workings and had been fully restored with new paint on the frame, and the springs, partly pitted from rusting, were cleaned up to gray metal. Where did he get some paint? I rushed through the hallways to gather clean sheets for the single-sized bed.

Chloe came down the hallway, pushing Mother in the wheelchair.

Father dashed back in, asking, "How much time have we got?"

"Hours," I suggested, looking up at Mother for confirmation.

Mother nodded. Father rushed off, saying he was getting a bath. "Just boil more water. We've got to get all of this stuff washed," he said, referring to the all the birth-related items.

I did so, grabbing a large pot that I'd used for so many things. Now it would have Molly's birth as a memory. While the water was heating, I got a small piece of cardboard and put "Molly" on it and placed it on the changing table. The back side was plain – if we changed the name I could write it on the other side.

Mother was nibbling on ice, Jack and Chloe attending to her. This should be the easiest birth, I'd hoped, and I was glad that it was Mother. I didn't know the future yet, but I did not wish to go through that kind of pain again. I placed the towels from a closet to the new birthing room that had been the dining room just hours before. I continued to clean the room, wiping the walls, the baby warmer, the changing table – everything. I heard Mother complaining about the contractions. Chloe took Mother off to a bathroom to let her spend a little time in a warm bath. A little later, Chloe came rushing through to get some water. "She's already getting diarrhea."

"Not unexpected. Contractions are?" I asked.

"Um. What?" Chloe asked.

Mother called out from the bathroom, "Fifteen minutes."

"Chloe, time them," I ordered. I realized we'd been spending too much time on patents and should have changed our study to midwifing. From a drawer near a pile of watches we'd kept running for years, I pulled out an old journalist's notebook and threw it at her, a pen stuck through the top spiral.

"Okay," she said.

Jack also attended Mother, his interest being the girl that would be born more than the birth itself. During a quiet moment I pulled him aside and asked him, "Did you get any premonitions? Anything more?"

"She's my lover," he said softly to me.

"You're not just saying that because we teased you before?" I inquired.

"No," he asserted sternly, his eyes firm, then he cast them aside. "I love you, Mommy. But I'm going to love her too." I could see he expected me to disapprove or be hostile.

"Oh. I'm not going to be jealous about it. I know she's yours, Jack. It's okay. I have Chloe the same way."

He smiled shyly, dropping his face, nearly turning to tears. He was such a big soul in that little body. He looked up again, his smile returning as if vindicated from a crime. He didn't say anything; the smile was enough.

"Great," I acknowledged.

Chloe came in, saying, "Do I have to pull the afterbirth again?"

Daddy had just returned, saying, "Probably not. Only when the body has trouble with the placenta detaching do we try to help. But you can have the job of taking the afterbirth out in a bucket like before."

"I'd rather not," Chloe rejected.

"I'll do it," offered Jack.

I appealed to him, "No, son. You'll want to be with the baby. Molly is your baby, say the voices."

"I know," said the little man.

To Daddy I pointed out the sign I'd made for the changing table, saying, "Molly."

"Ah. Okay. Molly it is then," he said. He got some food prepared for the group. He snickered, "This baby doctor doesn't have many babies to deliver tonight. Might as well double as chef."

As the hours went by and Mother's contractions came up to five minutes, I took over as midwife. I checked inside Mother, proclaiming three fingers dilation. Jack took a position up by Mother to wipe her with a washcloth on this warm summer evening. Chloe coached the contractions. I adjusted the bed to the final position and got her legs strapped up. Prompted by dimming late afternoon light, Daddy brought in an electric flood lamp. I kept on checking and washing my hands in a successive series of pots of sterilized water. I put a small silver tray and a pair of scissors into the current pot of boiling water, allowing them to steam dry before settling them onto a cart. I pulled the cart into the makeshift birthing room.

"Do you want me to take over," asked Father.

"Not yet," I said. "I've got it so far."

Jack smiled at me, then plopped down to get a fresh washcloth.

With the proper birthing bed, we had a better way to catch the messes that came forth. We washed up Mother and I checked her again. Hours had passed, and she was getting into the final stage. Inside, I could feel the head.

Daddy got some gloves to verify. "She's a full hand," he said. "This baby's coming with fervor. And head first is always a good idea."

Thump!

I felt like I'd been hit in the head. Jack had been returning with a clean washcloth. I watched his face distort, and he tumbled to the floor. Pain racked through my skull, as if it echoed side to side a thousand times in a fraction of a second, a ringing in my ears at first so fierce I heard nothing else. I grabbed at my ears, even with messy rubber gloves.

Jack also placed his hands to his ears, deafened by the internal noise. He got up and rushed to me. I crouched down to sit on the floor. He grabbed me, "She just died," he cried. "Molly died."

"Okay," I said to him, mostly withdrawn from the haunting debacle in my head. My voice sounded as if coming from another room when I said, "Where is she? Reach as a spirit."

More about what happened, and her location, was answered by another transcendent vision that encompassed myself and Jack. An angry man was yelling; I didn't know his words, but the concept was conveyed, "There's little else we can do with her. She's sick – sick in the head. A disgusting perverted criminal!" I saw an image from the point of view of the young woman, her arms scarred, bruised and hands tied, wrists painful, scuffed by coarse rope. She smelled unwashed, of old sweat, body oils and urine. Her waist and feet were bound behind her to a post, and farm-attired men and women alike were leering at her with immense hate. I could feel from within – her heart racing, her mouth dry, her jerking motions difficult to control, her stomach fully empty. Amidst the clamor, a man rose a rifle and I saw the muzzle flash and experienced the knock of the bullet going through her forehead, commensurate with the blast noise that cut off, leaving the ringing. Her legs failed like those of the first goat I'd seen Daddy kill. In her head, there was complete disorientation. She had a problem of location, finding she was not within the confines of her flesh. I pulled at her soul, extracting her, though I recognized other spirit hands grabbed to claim her. Much as I'd been guided to pull at Chloe's soul, Jack was helping to pull Molly.

Jack got up and ran to Mother, "I have her!" he said. He climbed up on the bed over Mother and straddled her belly, pushing his hands toward her groin. In any other birth, in another other time, you'd be whipping a child for such a peculiarity. But not now. He was placing the soul, probably with a little help from the voices above.

Mother arched her back and let out a gruff cry, intensifying the need to push with a contraction. Jack rolled himself aside and landed feet first on the floor. The birth went into full play. Father stood by me, offering to switch, but there was little time. He instead brought up the bassinet and sat on a small stool, one he had replicated from the patent that Jack had studied. The head crowned in record time, and we saw it emerge, showing us the shortest little blonde hair on the wet scalp. Daddy suctioned the mouth and nostrils and turned the shoulders this time, and the baby slipped into my hands. I braced her perfect little body on my knees. Daddy and Jack helped wipe her up with warm washcloths and we patted her dry, putting her on Mother's belly. We cut the cord and even had the proper clamp for the umbilical cord. A bucket was ready for the afterbirth. Chloe held onto Mother and helped hold the baby with Jack assisting from the opposite side of the birthing bed.

I had the baby warmer on and ready, so despite the warmth of the evening, we placed Molly into the warmer, Jack diligently watching without interruption.

To my surprise, Father handled the afterbirth just fine on his own. "Thanks, Daddy," I said. I looked over the baby, not finding any missing fingers or deformed bones. I didn't find a hermaphrodite. I didn't find any oddities at all. I found a perfect little girl. "What are the odds? That we all come from one Father as such and we all end up nearly perfect!" I said to the baby. That thought I had with Chloe's birth came back to mind: *It's not odds. It's a plan.*

Jack was talking softly to baby Molly who looked severely confused and frightened. "You are a baby girl now. You're going to be okay. I guess those people didn't like you for who you are. I think you are on a different planet. Those people can't follow you here. And your name is Molly." The little girl cried. If she hadn't lost her memory as was promised, our language was different. I don't think she understood. Nor did I have any certainty that her death had immediately preceded the birth. It could have been hours, days or years prior.

When the baby slept, and Chloe took watch, I took Jack to the front porch. "What did you find, young man – in the vision?" I squatted to the steps.

"She got killed, just like I said," he looked at me with melancholy eyes.

"But now she's here. Why did she get killed?"

"Because she's like us," he observed.

"Yes. She's like us. Disgusting," I snarled, looking down at my scuffing feet.

"Bad. She's a bad girl," he agreed, slumping to the porch surface.

"Horrible. So bad the demigods offered her to us," I blurted with tears, acting like my old, typical crybaby self.

"No," he assured. "Because we can help her, and she can help us." Jack got up from the porch, walking out along the wide walkway, scanning the sky.

He sounded so smart I pushed further, "How?"

But Jack shrugged. "I don't see her stars – they said you know how."

"I do. I do know if I can handle something that traumatic with confessions and studying words."

"Yeah. I was bad. I was bad too," he said, pursing his lips.

"Bad where?"

"My planet – well it wasn't *my* planet. I wasn't the president. I was bad. Everyone died, and they left me. I was bad. I feel bad. I still feel bad even though it was another planet."

"I can help you, Jack. I'm not just your Mother. I'm very smart now."

"I'm really smart," he claimed. "I'm just learning your language." He picked out a constellation with a double triangle, pointing at it. "There. It was that, I think."

"Okay. Your planet – what did you do there? What was your work?"

"I ran a machine shop like the one Daddy is putting together."

Dumbfounded, I said, "Jack? Is that you? You didn't swap souls with someone just now, did you?"

"No," he giggled.

"Little man! Why didn't you tell me?"

"It wasn't all clear at first. I didn't want you to blow a gasket. People don't normally remember through birth," he said.

"But we all did. I did – as the first, I didn't tell Mother until I was three – of course she knew something was different. Chloe remembered. You did and now Molly, we hope, will. She might not want to right away. But she will."

"Well if she does, she'll cry about it," he theorized. "I didn't know your words. I probably told you already. You just didn't learn *my* language." He giggled.

"Yeah, I know. Molly won't understand us either. We'll have to be here to help her. She'll be as frustrated as you. Probably more," I offered a hug with my words.

Molly exhibited more crying and frustration than we could have imagined. We had to take turns holding her in a baby carrier, and she was best if she was strapped in where she didn't see the person, but the action instead. Her little arms would always push at you if she were facing your body and reach out to objects if she were facing forward. As if she had an internal timer she'd take to crying and we'd exchange baby duty more than any other chore. Everything else but essentials was on hold for the first several months. Sometimes we referred to her as "Little Miss President," as we were in the president's mansion and we were all following orders as if her slaves.

For Jack, we made a short cart for him to push Molly about. For months she adapted to him best, and while she was still a baby he could kiss all over her and get her to smile. As for the rest of us, she'd last about a half hour then throw a fit. Even Mother had a hard time with her. While Jack was doing so well with Molly, Chloe and I returned to the Patent Office to study and redraw parts for some household items for a couple hours each day. I had failed to figure out that odd motor controller.

Several months after the birth Daddy checked on us girls at the Patent Office and arbitrarily said, "Why don't you do confessions on machines? If you want to know something, maybe confess off something and let it lead you to very specific knowledge. Things you might already know." He didn't say anything else, he just turned to leave, and I heard the big doors bump the frame.

I pondered all day on that idea. I kept looking at words I didn't know and couldn't absorb; something must have been at the core of my mental exclusion of concepts behind these troublesome vocables. What if I had heard those words before and didn't remember? What if I'd seen those things before, in other lives, perhaps having been an inventor or manufacturer of something we could use? I tumbled in my sleep in the large mahogany and marble bed, Chloe by my side. I pulled up, seeing how pretty the teenage girl was becoming, rolled over her, kissing her on the way, and I went to take some notes. I conceived, "Will harmonic concept chains work on words?" I thought we could maximize the knowledge gained and the confession thing at the same time. Freeing up knowledge did seem important, especially if that knowledge had already been latent within us.

The next day I asked Chloe to help me with an experiment. So, after breakfast, instead of going directly to the

Patent Office, we went to a small white vanity room we'd converted to a private session room. I requested she ask me if I'd seen the term "reluctance" in a past lifetime. It was an engineering term found in that motor controller patent.

Her reply was simple. "Are you serious?"

"Ask me if I did anything wrong with it. I want to see what comes up," I said.

"So, have you done anything wrong regarding 'reluctance'?" She asked.

I got a vague idea, "Certainly a past life. It had to do with a coil of wire or could be put together in various kinds of circuits. I'd put a schematic on a counter then refilled a cup of coffee at some office without paying the fee. I don't get anything else about it."

She asked me again and I found something related. "Um, further back in time, there were these big coils of wire that were set up for power transfer. Once the main circuit from a major power station was closed, it would first go through these coils for 'reluctance' to slow the action and then fuse together, welding the giant circuit closed. There were white-hot arcs when the giant switch moved." I blinked, believing I'd seen some of the flash. "I'm not sure it was really so wrong – I just felt we could have come up with a better design and not burn up so much metal."

"Okay. You know the process – give me something earlier," she insisted.

I thought of another one. "I'd been doing a science project for a school. I was a nerdy boy and had a crush on this girl. She was wearing a dress and had long brunette hair. She had soft hazel eyes. I was supposed to be demonstrating my electrical circuits but saw her and got mesmerized. I'd gotten a little bit aroused, so it was really embarrassing while the other students became actively pejorative and laughed. I'd not expected a physical reaction to ruin my day. That display had concentric coils next to a magnet and had a word that meant reluctance, and it measured how much magnetism reached past the coils." Something was still confusing. I couldn't get to the base idea yet.

Chloe asked me for an earlier situation. I found another incident, "It was a science model of some planet, and it had something to do with the magnetic coil within the planet itself, and there was a really fine meter. The magnetic field would interact with some electricity going through a magnetic coil fed by a battery. If you turned the contraption, it would show different current, since the magnetic field of the earth affected the flow of electricity. The 'bad' part was that I did a really poor job painting it. I wasn't going to get the art award that day anyway." I knew for certain we were talking about magnetism but, yet I felt confused.

"Are we done?" she asked.

"No. I don't feel good – I feel blocked. I have data, but I don't have the bottom of a chain."

"Okay. Find another. You know what to do," she said.

I found another one – much earlier. "I was an engineer with a firm making trains which were levitated by magnetism, and we had to be concerned about the 'reluctance' of the materials that were about it. Oh, I get it. Reluctance blocks magnetism, whether by a magnetic field within materials or one created by an electric field." Now I had a new perceptive curiosity with the concept. "Thanks, Chloe. I get it. I think I can work with that."

I took that idea back to restudy the patent and could finally explain how the motor controller worked because "reluctance" was the stumbling point. I was simply overwhelmed with the simplicity of what appeared to be just a superficial idea when presented by Father – we had a new way to look at knowledge. We could recover vast data from our own minds, not just from reading the books, waiting on premonitions or haphazardly collecting what showed up in the confession sessions. We might not even necessarily need the books and patents. It was such a revelation we had a party, and even baby Molly was included.

So, the new plan was for everyone to do their confession chains on words or the machine parts we were attempting to fix, deriving the concepts. Sometimes we hit the concept very well on an individual. Other times we had to run it on everyone to unleash the predicted knowledge. But with a little willpower we were all getting so intelligent. We even tried little words and found additional meaning for those. Though we never created our own colloquial dialect, we'd gone from a muted version of the language to an expressive command of words. I certainly could have become a novelist now.

We spent more time in the machine shop, and we'd learned how to clean up metal with a modest amount of corrosion through electrolysis or through the use of chemicals. We also learned how to electroplate metals to prolong their life. We were using know-how we could find in the Patent Office but had to avoid the more highly toxic chemistry. We had a lot of parts to clean up. One of the backup generators at the president's estate had years of wear and tear. With that larger machine running in the shop, we fabricated a few parts and rebuilt some switches and got it running in top shape.

Jack started learning how to do simple electrical circuits, hoping we could fix some power transmission lines and larger generators in the forward years that would help us get yet more powerful machines running in the shop. But again, every day we worked on words through these past-track (past-life) chains. I began to feel like there was nothing we couldn't know. And there was no age limit. How soon could we get Molly to learn the language if we were applying these techniques?

I pondered through my names Miranda and Dahilana and wondered who I was with respect to the "little girl soul" that we'd heard. I knew we had heard the voices, received help and even some premonitions. I didn't understand the premonitions. How could someone know the future? How could we see beyond the events that had occurred? Were these voices really from the current souls or from these same souls but far in the past? Were these, if the little book had been right, the original souls before dividing into the massive population required for a universe? Had they not only created the universe from the start, but created it all the way through, leaving us to play as oblivious pawns? These musings never let up. I gained knowledge but forgot spiritual details over the years as the voices turned silent. I was certain I'd lost contact, and though I never let up hope, I gave up the daily anticipation that the voices would start talking to us regularly again. What if we all died before then? I'd just have to turn my attention on Jack and Molly. From there we'd at least be helping from the lower level, the standard plane of the universe.

How many little children would know to look up a word, and if immediately having some problem understanding it, say, "Mommy, I think I have past life confusion. Would you help me take a word back to see if I can understand it?" Well, that was Jack, who had the disposition to study anything. In the next months he had updated the solenoid-bell system to an intercom using typical desk telephones, repurposing a small power supply to draw a little power off of the generator.

As we used up the large stores of items like salt, we returned to scavenging the surrounding areas, first heading to restaurants, but the old items were far beyond expiration dates. Salt could again be refined by diluting it in water and decanting it off to another pot to boil it dry. We could find usable soaps and detergents, buckets and mops, so cleaning wasn't much of an issue. Food was always an issue. Thus, the size of our gardens grew beyond our ability to weed them.

To our dismay, Molly was becoming an unequivocal, disheartening nightmare. As she was able to walk as a toddler, we'd set food out for her, because if sustenance, or just about anything, was handed to her, she'd more likely smack it from our hands and it would go wherever it would go – flowing over clothing, splatted to the floor, poured at our shoes, strewn upon the wall, scattered across the table.... I could curse the "voices" every day for their dictate that she be sent to accompany us.

A particular day when Molly was about three years old, she came toddling into the kitchen where Father and I were cooking a special meal, making a large hog roast from a piece he'd smoked with apple wood just earlier. The aroma was amazing. Daddy offered her a piece of the delectable meat, holding it out on a long culinary-sized fork. His arm was held straight out, his expression pleasant. "Try some meat. You're not a bad girl. Try some meat. Take a bit there."

But Molly fell perfunctorily backward, cried with the timbre of a siren, then scooted away to hide, crawling into a cupboard.

"I don't know what I'd done. What had I done?" supplicated Father.

"Molly! What's going on in there? What's the matter little one?" I was leaning down, pulling the strings on my bonnet that Mother just made for me.

When I opened the door to the cupboard, Molly's face turned to terror. She hissed, put up her hands past her face as if to shield danger. I saw the light from behind me glinting off of her eyes, which were racing to examine my face. In terror she screamed and kicked her legs so hard she was bruising herself, even roughing the skin, against the edges of the door frame.

I reached in to grab her and pull her out. She slapped at me, then leaned up and bit my right forearm. I had to pull her hair to get her to let go. I was so mad I grabbed her and threw her out, and she slid along the floor, my blood on her lips. I screamed, "No!"

Molly remained on the floor, petrified by her terror.

My hand became numb, my forearm throbbed, swelling.

Mother had just walked in from the garden, getting lettuce for the meal. "What the hell?"

Little Molly pulled up, dashing from the room, quietly finding respite from our certain wrath.

"Molly!" I yelled at the vitriolic child, tempted to call her *Melee* instead. I turned to Mother, "Molly bit me. She was in the cabinet." Blood dripped with an even cadence.

"She should apologize. You'd have been better to have left her there. Never reach for that child. Never." She walked on through, still holding the lettuce. "Molly! Molly? Molly!" She yelled repeatedly through the hallways. Finally, she gave up and yelled, "Come back when you're hungry. I'll have some food set out for you."

I didn't like Molly being about the mansion on her own, but I had to acquiesce. I couldn't keep my attention off of her, but I had to wash up the bite, wondering if the name Molly was given to her on purpose by the gods as derived from the prefix "malé-" from "malevolent" or "malefactor." After twenty minutes, I heard an echo of a calamitous crash that even I couldn't ignore. I rushed down the hallway, up some steps, and down a long corridor from the family wing to the main wing. Molly had somehow pulled down a heavy marble pedestal with a bronze bust upon it, despite the fact that it was in a semicircular alcove. It was likely some previous governor or president, the nose blunted. A piece of the stone flooring was cracked, and fractured marble fragments littered the floor. Molly wasn't there. I knew that chasing her would not be effective, but I couldn't find any reason to perpetrate a crime against all this old stuff, despite the fact that it was mostly useless to anyone.

I heard a sneeze. I traced some little footprints further up the hallway to a small study, originally intended for a guest dignitary. Again, I heard another little sneeze. I circled about and saw her under a secretary. I didn't reach this time. My arm was bleeding through the makeshift bandage. I threw off my bonnet and sat back against the wall. Softly I said, "Molly. We want to love you. Why do you treat us so badly?"

"I don't belong here," she sounded apologetic. Despite her general intractability, her language ability was coming in fast.

"I don't understand. We told you. The spirit voices brought you here. You do belong to us," I tried.

"You hate me!" she hissed.

"There has to be a reason you came here. There has to be a reason. Make me want to love you," I advised. "Let me help!"

"No!" she snapped. She pulled out from under the secretary and smacked at my chin on her way to the hallway, spewing disparagement, to another hiding place.

My mistake had been sitting so I could be attendant to her but couldn't get out of the room in time to see which turn she made in the larger part of the mansion. It could take hours to scout her out of that section of the massive estate. She could take a nap and leave me searching indefinitely, only to wake and sneak from place to place. She could get hungry or need a bathroom and come out early. I'd have no idea, but I had no choice but to go from room to room, searching everything, hoping that the dust would give her path away.

I'd already been through all these rooms, knowing what was in them. I searched under beds. I searched under desks. I searched in dry bathrooms. Each time I passed a window I noted the changing angle of the sun.

It had been too long. I was hungry and in need of a working bathroom. I called out as loud as I could. "Molly! I have to go back. Come back when you are ready!" I walked slowly up the main hallway, headed to the connecting vestibule back to the family wing.

"No," said a little wet, pouty voice.

I turned back, seeing a little figure just inside a room I'd searched. "How?" I asked rhetorically. I walked up to her, again reaching instinctively.

"No!" she said again.

I pulled my arms back across my breast. "I'll walk ahead, and you can follow me. Is that okay?"

She gave a cute, slight nod, her shifty little eyes conceding. It was so adorable I wanted to melt and give her kisses. But I held my ground, softly saying, "Okay," again.

I walked forward, and each time I looked back, she stopped. But I needed certainty that she would follow. The child in tow by her need, I gently guided her back to the kitchen. Mother said nothing, but set up a fresh plate for her, placing it on the table in front of a high chair. She climbed up on her own and sat down, picked up utensils and ate properly. She wiped her face with a napkin.

Mother suggested, "Would you like to take a nap?"

She shook her head, softly saying, "No," once again.

Frankly, I think she was frustrated with herself, having too much memory for a small body. Nevertheless, she got down from the table, walked to the lounge, and settled herself into an oversized playpen we'd found at another estate. It had a little hut with a mock chimney, and the fold-out floor had areas that looked like grass and a garden. Inside the hut was a toddler-scaled bed, complete with a quality mattress. I could look into a flap at the roof peak – she was in there sound asleep. My god, she was precious!

I had hoped that was the breakthrough we needed. But my hopes were misplaced, except that she did tolerate me a little bit more. The others saw no real change, and Mother often complained to me specifically, when Molly was clearly asleep, or we were out of her presence. It was the same story – if she came to us – was sent to us by the spirit voices – why was she so opposed to being here?

But it was Jack that was the most upset, turning to tears when she wouldn't let him get close. He had been "little Daddy" to her much like I'd been "little Mommy" to Chloe, but one day she just shut him out. No matter what he did, she'd smack, cry, hiss, fight, and if he persisted, she'd scream until she was hoarse. We were all looking for the source of her confusion.

With passing months, she'd allow me to hand her a plate with dinner if I asked her what she wanted and if it was okay if I sat it down. If I didn't ask there was a near certain probability it would fly across the table and spin off the other side. It happened often enough that I got trained, and when the others mimicked me, she still threw the plate. I couldn't throw tears as often as I use to. I didn't feel as morbid as I had on the island when my name was Miranda. Yet sometimes she still brought me to tears when the hard work of fixing a meal went to waste.

It was midwinter, the outside temperature just above freezing. The production of the gardens through the summer had been supreme, but I guess my pattern was to be very careful with food during the winter months. I'd prepared some thick soup – and it was, per my taste buds, excellent. I'm not sure how my mind lapsed – I asked Jack to set the soup on the table for Molly, but she was already in her seat, so I should have done it myself. Little Molly flung the bowl of soup right back at him. It splashed into his chest. I could see her touching her fingers – she'd burned herself a tad in the process. But Jack backed up, holding his shirt out to minimize the burning. I could see his gears turning – his eyes turned to hate. He was about to strike.

I could feel the adrenaline shoot through my veins. "Jack!" I cried out. "Don't you touch her!" I had been filling another bowl, dropping it with some spillage and flopped the ladle back into the pot as I rushed to Jack.

Molly's eyes contained fear and hate, hoping to thwart his expected reaction, her little arms crossed before her face, ready to block any incoming punches.

The look in his eyes, a mix of sadness and rejection, tore at my heart. He huffed but failed to make words, snorting as his expression mutated from hate to anguish to stiffly contained anger. He held his arms frantically to his side, making fists so hard his fingernails clawed into his palms. He screamed and stormed outside into the cold, stomping all about the yard, then entered the atrium to escape the wind.

I said to Molly, "Molly you should feel ashamed for that. I understand I should have given you the soup. My mistake. But Jack feels pain too when you hurt him. And I feel pain when you hurt him. Because I love Jack too."

Molly bit her lip, showing little remorse. Someday we'd get through. It wouldn't be today.

"May I please get you a bowl of soup?" I tried again.

Her head down, she nodded.

"Okay," I said to her. Once I had the bowl, I asked her, "Where do you want me to put it?"

She pointed to the table just in front of her.

"Okay – it's hot, honey," and I set the bowl there.

She said, "No."

"No, what?" I asked cautiously.

"No honey," she said.

"No honey what?"

"I'm not Honey. I'm Molly. Don't call me Honey."

"Oh. Honey is not a name, it's a word to say when you like someone."

I saw her little eyes raise up to look at me, checking my sincerity, and to my credit, I had the most sincere look I could naturally give.

I believe she said, "Oh," but I could barely hear it. Being finicky with her spoon touching into the liquid, she slurped up some broth, keeping her eyes low.

I went to check on Jack, as he'd been outside too long at that temperature. I found him sitting, curled up over his knees on a table in the atrium, in an area that had spice plants on it just months before. He wiped his eyes when he saw me fumbling with the door latch. I let myself in and walked his way, then sat opposite him against another table. "Jack?" I prompted.

He raised his red eyes above his wetted knees, hands pulling at the moisture.

"Jack?" I attempted again.

"I'm sorry," he said like a child.

"I know you're more than a boy in there, Jack. You have to control that kind of temper. I thought we'd have a broken bone, or worse." I hesitated. "Jack – you scared me. You genuinely frightened me."

"She needs to know I hate it when she does that – that's the fifth time I've worn burning hot soup!" he noted.

"In the old world, I wasn't close to my Mother on the island, but she had an expression. Some people are like a player piano, some people are the piano player. A player piano can be given a paper tape and it'll play beautiful music right off of it, but won't play it the same without that crutch, losing the ability or forgetting it completely. Some people are like that. They do things easy. They forget them just as easy. Others are like a piano player, having to learn the art for years before being able to accomplish the same thing, but then if you ask them tomorrow, they can still play the entire piece without referring to the paper. We thought Molly would come a little more programmed and ready to play. But I don't think it happened like it did for myself, Chloe, or for you. We were gifted with full memory. Maybe Molly doesn't have the same degree of memory, or has it mixed up with something dangerous."

"You mean she thinks we are bad people, or that we'll disappear?"

"You said she died then got born. We saw the flash – it was brutal – we know they shot her, but we don't really know why. She's – she's got something mixed up that makes her think we are the bad guys."

He still looked grumpy. "Oh. So, you'll give her the soup?" he pleaded.

"Yeah. I'll give her the soup from now on," I smiled at him, hoping he was understanding the full concept. "But there's no guarantee she won't throw soup."

I could handle Molly if I was delicate enough. Everything we did for her as a group, to help her feel included, backfired over and over like one of the old trucks. Daddy said, "Her little thinking cylinders are missing a few strokes. Her mind's engine isn't turning like the rest of us." Several years went by with Molly displaying the same impossible character.

We had tried to give her a birthday party for her seventh. Mother baked a cake with extra eggs and honey in it, and it would have been delicious. We were declaring she'd made it seven years, but she misunderstood the program. She took it as "made it seven years without us taking her out." I don't remember the multitude of cacophemisms she spewed at us, many expletives from her previous language and even a few from the current. I don't remember her accusations and rants, resorting to dysphemistic phrases we never knew. I don't remember how many plates got broken. I do remember feeling deflated. Father told her she had to clean up the mess she made. She threw the remainder of the cake and with both arms held out, slid everything else off the table and counters, including a blender Jack helped restore. We all left the room to wash ourselves up from the splattered cake and icing, and the homemade goat's milk ice cream sweetened with pulverized fruit.

The next morning, everyone got up but Molly. "Molly! Breakfast – chores," called Mother. I was headed toward Molly's room since I was her most accepted adversary.

Half muffled from blankets and pillows, she belted, "Leave me alone. There's no reason we have to follow the ways of all the dead people. Let's declare this 'don't act like dead people day!'"

Father had followed up to act as reinforcement. He went in and threw off her covers, expecting her to be in nightclothes, but found her stark naked, curled up on her side. He firmly said, "You came here. You got born into this family. You do your fair share of the work. It helps us all. It helps you. It's about survival. No breakfast if you don't at least get your own eggs."

She turned to lie flat on her back, arms and legs spread out like an archetypal girl. "Fine – you rotten potatoes! You pig farts! You rancid guts," she snarled each harmless dysphemism and pulled up out of bed, not putting on a stitch, and rushed out to get her own eggs. In a few minutes she came back into the kitchen. Mother was just pulling her fried eggs aside, the frying pan still hot. Molly pulled up a stepping stool and took over the skillet, cracked her eggs and tossed them together.

"No goat's milk?" asked Father, acting affable.

"No. Leave me alone. I hate all your food," she chastised. There was a small pop from the oil in the pan and a hot drop hit her chest. She jerked and winced.

"Shirt would have helped," offered Father. I could see Father's lips shape restrained words for euphemisms or worse.

Molly bit her lip. Some laundry was in a next room, so I grabbed a dirty t-shirt for her to don. I threw it at her feet, where it folded over the step-stool. She put it on but gave me a stare that indicated she didn't appreciate the help. The shirt reached down to her knees.

"Can you work with her today?" Daddy's eyes begged, pleaded. He tilted his head, so I'd have to add *demanded*.

"Yes. I'll give it another try," I consented, or rather, complained.

Then Daddy added something out of the blue, "Have her *bring to now* whatever is stuck back in her mind, so she can examine it, evaluate it, and resolve it. I know from working the confession chains that we have to see it like it's happening now. It was in the book. Time in the mind is always referenced *from now*."

I turned to the melodramatic urchin, "Molly, as soon as you've eaten, meet me in the white session room upstairs."

The naturally combative child articulated exhaustive expletives in at least two languages, verbalizing so quickly I couldn't absorb any of it.

"I mean it," I said and walked to the doorway. I added, "Everybody's done with you. They're just done." I grabbed a better set of day clothes in her size, and then stepped upstairs to get out a notebook I'd tried to keep for her. There were several pages of aborted sessions, where despite my prudence I'd been unable to get through anything that would resolve. Chloe had entered a page where she'd tried to run a session too, ending with "she hit me and ran out" and a big question mark. I turned to start a new page, put the date, and a little background on the scornful events of the birthday party.

A little to my surprise, Molly walked in but threw off the long shirt. "I'm too hot. I hate clothes."

"Molly, please. I'm trying to help," I exhorted with civility. I offered a maroon tank shirt and a pair of white cotton panties and pink shorts.

She at least put on the panties and the tank. "We tried this. All I get is this big blank and it always hurts. I don't know why you keep trying," she raved. To be defiant, she flung the shorts at me. Despite the fact that her studies were going slow, she acted more like a belligerent teenager than a seven-year-old girl.

I spoke automatically. "Molly! You were a special delivery to us. Your soul somehow matches up or they wouldn't have sent you."

"No and no. I don't match up and there is no *they* that sent me to you."

On the edge of losing my fortitude, "I'll remind you again...," I blurted.

"You all remind but the 'remind me' always hurts. Stop reminding me!" she reproached. "There it goes again," she rolled her eyes, holding her head. "It really hurts!" Molly cried, slumping to the floor, folding her arms over her head. "I don't want it."

Well, *remind me* was clearly evocative of pain. "I wholeheartedly agree you don't," I assured. "But I don't have a better process. I'll give the question again. Please, please, please tell me something you could confess." I pondered on Daddy's phrase "bring to now" and how to integrate it into the commands.

"I smacked Jack until he got bruises on his face for trying to ask the same thing," she said, testing me, apparently being confrontational.

But I was going to take this as the confession and not a threat. "Okay. When did that occur?"

"You know. You were there," she said.

"That one – okay, got it. Give me an earlier time you did something like that? Bring that moment to *now*." I felt I was on the precipice of a blast of demoralizing as she would run out, and I'd have another note on the page for a failed session.

"No," she said bluntly.

"Please, Molly," I pleaded and waited with full attention on her.

"I – I put smelly dirt into Jack's bed and when he asked me if I did it, I said no. And later, just to make him wrong for asking, I got into an argument about who would get the eggs. It ended up in an egg fight. We didn't have pancakes that day. Not until the chickens laid more. And he looked funny with egg yolk all over his cheek." She nodded in reflection.

"Good. Please bring to now an earlier time you did something like that?" I articulated, having found a way to get the phrase into the question.

"Um," she said. Her arms were less tight about her head, perhaps indicating that we were skirting the pain reaction she'd get. "I was, um, four. Jack got me oatmeal. I didn't like seeing him. I threw the bowl at him. It was hot and burned his chest. He shouldn't have done it. Food was your job." Amazingly she sighed, "I didn't mean to burn him." She let a tear loose, but the defiance remained in her eyes. "That doesn't mean I have to like him."

She hadn't decided to demoralize me yet. I continued, "Good. Bring to now another one, earlier like that, whatever you find, please."

Molly thought introspectively, perhaps surprised by her own mind's picture. "I get an image – it's not painful – but bright. Um – oh – Jack was changing my diaper. I didn't want him there – no reason. I threw my arms and legs all over the place. He was frustrated because I was making a mess. It smelled like – ugh – poop. He pulled up a leg and pinned my feet, then his hand grabbed my hands. I felt so tied. His head! Bright light!" she yawned. She blinked a few times, her eyes practically crossing. "He was in front of and away from the light. Bright – oh no – that hurts. The light hurts my head. The light did it," she cried out, then emitted a long wail, her arms folding to her head. "I don't know what's wrong with the light. It's – It's…."

"Is there something there?" I asked because I couldn't delineate the images in her head, knowing I couldn't bypass it. Sometimes running a session was like a being a blind person and having someone describe a scene for you.

"The light overhead. Framed – a lamp shape, like – like – the dining room. I think that was it."

"Yes. We put the dining room together as the birthing room and left it that way for, um, about two years. Were you on a changing table?"

"No. I think it was the bigger bed. It was lower. There was a changing table – a cart? Jack moved me to the bed to change me, but it was messy – poopy. He got upset because I fought him. I couldn't figure out what he was saying. He threw his hands at me, again and again, maybe mad, maybe trying to make me laugh." She shrugged, "It didn't work."

I'd become aware that reaching for her was dangerous, a likely remnant of the incident we were after. "Okay. Anything else on that one?"

After a moment she replied, "No. Just blank after that."

"Okay. Bring to now an earlier time you did something like that?" I asked.

"Like obstinate? Oh, I got obstinate. I got plenty of obstinate. Um. What's…?" She was quiet, folded down, still sitting on the floor in her panties.

For a moment I thought I'd lost her attention and interest. "Go on," I feared she'd hit that pain and balk on the whole session. I couldn't botch this one. I couldn't let some unexpected mental landmine detonate my last chance. Everyone had been getting so frustrated with her, and she knew it. Maybe that's why she tried.

Through a wet voice she stammered, "I got obstinate – with some kids. Brothers? Sisters? Kids – an orphanage? A rough place. After a lot of people died – my – my old planet – they – many were left, hundreds or thousands. They made towns and acted like families – did lots of the things you're doing here. They restored stuff – set up machine shops. Then… ouch!" she said. She tightened her grip over her head again, and the grief rolled off like a screaming banshee. "No!" she cried. She turned to look at me like she finally wanted to communicate but couldn't.

After minutes of sobbing, spittle and tears, she looked at me with a sense of recognition, and pulled up, hurtling at me. I was so used to her hitting I started to block, but she instead grabbed about my neck and shoulders with a tight embrace. She put her head on my shoulder, sobbing and snorting. "It wasn't here. The flash of the gun – the light – got smashed together. It wasn't here." She kept grabbling at me as if groping to find me in the dark. Her legs were pulling up to straddle my body. Her little form shook with heaving sobs.

I cried wholeheartedly with her as I realized the significance of the moment. In the aftermath of one or more ascension events on her planet, her dystopian society had turned to martial law and exiled her with a bullet. I kissed her hair, thankful that this was the first time I could kiss her and have her accept it without her being asleep. Then with a smile emerging between her tears, she pulled back, looked at me kindly, and smacked me heartily across the face.

I was shocked in the middle of my pleasant moment, somewhat confused by this physical reproach. I'm sure she noted my surprise.

"That might be the last time I smack you," she said. Then she pushed her face up to mine and gave me a strong kiss. Pulling back, her beautiful saturated eyes gazed into mine. "I love you Dahilana. I'm sorry." Her lips bent tightly with that "oops I was wrong" expression only a beautiful child could make and get away with. And in that moment, that vision of her face that I'd associated with so much anguish, hate, difficulty and defiance, could suddenly be associated with a real lovable person.

I fell into tears again. I wanted to say, "A great breakthrough," but I could barely say it. My frustration-turned-resolution poured out in sobs. Now it was my body shaking and heaving.

When I could, I looked up again, nearly embarrassed for my effusive outpouring of grief. "That was good for both of us," I said, referring to the cathartic nature of the session.

For her, that was enough, and she pushed up as quickly as if she'd fallen into a nest of ground hornets. She rushed out, yelling, "Jack!"

I followed her as she made her way out the back door. To Mother she said, "Where the crap is Jack," which only mimicked her previous, expected tone of voice.

"Tending the rain buckets," Mother droned with her expected tone for responding to Molly's normally defiant nature.

Molly ran back through the house, through hallways to the main mansion's service stairs as if she were running from the same ground hornets or a swarm of bees. She slapped her bare feet up the steps, declaring "ouch" as she stumbled at a landing. I followed her up. Out the roof door she cried, "Jack, where are you?"

He was hesitant to answer, huffing, "Over here." He'd been collecting rainwater on the roof and replacing regular buckets with some he'd attached tubes to, to collect the rain into a larger set of barrels at ground level. I leapt up the last steps, following her to the exposed surface. She skipped over the buckets and tubes on the way, her confrontation instant. She punched him right in the chest, then smacked several times across his face. His feet were near buckets and tubes, so he adhered to his balancing act. She vociferated, "Why didn't you tell me? Why didn't you tell me, you fool? You idiot. I didn't know!"

"Know what?" he begged, throwing arms out to block her punches without attempting to hit back.

"That you didn't kill me!" she shouted harshly, loud enough to get Mother's attention. She called up from the side of the mansion where she'd been tending to a garden, a barely audible, "Is everything alright up there?"

Jack was still in self-defense mode. "You should have known. I thought you remembered everything. None of us forgot through birth."

"Everything but my – the bullet!" she bounced on her feet, crying excitedly. "I'm sorry." She embraced him. He wasn't sure what subterfuge she yet held in store, and hesitated to put his arms around her, but her persistent holding gradually convinced him.

Mother came huffing up the steps to the roof. Holding hands, Mother and I stepped over the tubes and around the buckets. I whispered to Mother, "We had a breakthrough. She had a deep-set idea that we were her killers."

Mother giggled but kept mostly quiet, throwing her hand to her mouth. Her warm face already showing age, and she'd lost a front tooth. Her hair appeared a little dry and scraggly, her skin a little rough, and her hands were dirty from the garden work. But we embraced. She whispered, "Thank you, my dear. What persistence! What you've accomplished!"

Molly still held to Jack, crying softly.

"I helped you get born," said Jack. "The voice guided me – the girl up there – she gave you to us. She gave you to me." He knelt down, adjusting foam pads he had on his knees for the work, and held her tightly.

She kissed him. "Sorry I hit you, but you made me mad."

Jack looked up at me, and Molly turned to see Mother and myself approaching. "How long have you been there?" Molly asked with surprise, displaying a teary-faced smile, wiping her hand on her face and wiping the tears on Jack's shirt. Defiantly, she turned to kiss him again. "Dahilana, Avelynn, I think I just married Jack," she concluded and held to him, pulling up one foot while kissing him again.

Jack had put up with so much foul treatment from Molly that he'd all but given up hope that this little girl would ever snap out of her vile, violent, hateful treatment of him. The resolved confusion came off as tears, and the restored hope presented smiles.

We agreed to withhold the breakthrough from Father and Chloe, who had been at the machine shop, working yet again on a newer vehicle, hoping to get all the electrical parts working enough to start its engine. Molly would just start acting her new self, and we'd see how they reacted.

She rehearsed an idea, instructing, "I'll walk in and not look at anyone, throw my clothes on the table, and demand something else for dinner, using old words from my language or make up replacements. Daddy will get mad. I'll run out...."

"No, that would bungle it," I said. "That's the same as the old behavior."

"Okay. Then I'll already be seated and have my food, then suddenly ask for the salt, all politely, then demand that Father give it to me."

"Oh, he'd be confused about that," said Mother.

"Then I throw salt on him," she suggested with a laugh, "and rush in to lick it off."

"No throwing. You can't surprise him by bad behavior," I cautioned.

"Yeah," agreed Jack. "I'm sure he'd be surprised by the licking. But the best surprise would be no bad behavior. Just act like a normal kid, like me, then watch him."

Molly shook her head and laughed, "Okay, but I don't know how to act normal." I found that statement oddly profound. She'd only had us, her resident family to draw from – we were *not* examples of normal.

Not knowing what time they'd give up and return, we scuttled about, watching the windows while we worked on a meal to be ready for the surprise. We were not quite done with dinner as Daddy and Chloe rode bicycles back up a trail from the machine shop. They rode around to the back door, and we let Molly get up to the table in her high chair, though Daddy had trimmed the legs shorter as she'd grown.

I wasn't quite done making the soup, throwing in a few extra quick-cooking vegetables.

Chloe stepped in ahead of Daddy. "So, you didn't make it to the Patent Office today, huh?"

Completely quiet, I shaped my lips, "No."

Daddy stumbled about with a frustrated gait, looking in the refrigerator and freezer, apparently checking on the stock, as he'd followed up by poking about in the pantry.

Chloe came up for a kiss. "Tough day?" she asked, bobbing her head slightly into Molly's direction.

"You could say that," I conferred, nodding.

Molly put her head down since she was already cracking a smile.

Jack said to Molly, "Molly – don't throw anything tonight. Just don't throw anything, please?"

She wasn't sure how to answer. Her hand moved across the table. I was sure she'd smack at him out of habit.

Father cut in, "Don't prompt her, Jack. You know she'll do it if you tell her no." Quietly he added, "God! Another evening of madness."

Again, Molly kept her head down, containing her laughter. "Yeah, Jack," she mocked.

Chloe took off an overcoat and hung it up in a back foyer, then returned to wash her hands.

"Car's not running yet, I take it?" I suggested to Chloe.

"No. Not yet," she cautioned, again making a little tilt with her head, this time toward Daddy.

While Daddy was cutting bread for everyone, he explained too much. "First the distributor and then the battery clamps – got to using a generator tied to the alternator but I don't think the rectifier is working and that's a piece I'll have to find. These cars – twelve attempts and none of them have worked yet. Whether you have a diagnostic book or not, those junk materials just didn't stand up to dry rot. They made so much cheap junk, so you'd have to buy parts and call tow trucks. Everyone bought parts for – hell, nearly new cars were already breaking. A racket! Just a racket. I worked in a shop you know. Couldn't have rebuilt a whole car. Just worked in a shop. I wish I'd known more." He put bread on a plate and pushed it to Jack, then put slices on other plates and pushed it to other seats except for Molly's, which he held back, saying, "I've got Molly's if you'll give it to her, Dahilana."

"I'll get it," I said.

Molly decided it would be fine to start now. She simply said, "Daddy, may I please have my bread." The salt shaker was in her fist.

He tilted his head back while pushing the plate forward, wondering if she was baiting him, ready to launch the salt at his exposed forehead. He kept the reach a bit short, so it would be out of her instant grasp. So, she pulled up from her seat and got the bread, saying, "Thank you."

Daddy's eyes shifted to Chloe and Jack, seeing if they already noted something out of line with Molly.

I poured thick soup into bowls, counting them out. Mother had taken time to alter a shirt for Molly, bringing it into the room. "Molly? Do you like your new shirt?"

"Yes, ma'am," said Molly. "But I'll wear it later, thanks."

Father looked up, half expecting that salt shaker to take flight at Mother.

"Molly, knock it off," snapped Jack.

"I might anyway," warned Molly.

I put the bowls of soup onto the table, hoping this would go as expected. Too much habit directed my thoughts. I pushed each bowl to each person's setting. I'd put two bowls into my spot as usual, then said to Chloe, "Won't you push that one to Molly."

"No, dear," Chloe declined, appearing offended. "You forgot to push that bowl to Molly. I'm not getting drenched with hot soup. And it smells good. I don't want it wasted."

Molly begged, "Please, sister Chloe. I'm hungry. Won't you please push the soup to me?" I'd have to admit that Molly's attitude could be taken as covert hostility rather than politeness.

"No. I'm not that stupid," refuted Chloe as politely as she could muster.

"Would you let Chloe push the soup to you, dear?" I requested of Molly.

She started with a long "No," then followed with, "Yeah. I'm hungry. Please pass me the soup."

Chloe pushed it with her fingertips, getting it just within reach of Molly, who gathered it to slurp right away.

"Please wait, Molly. Politeness is a virtue," I said as I collected some white goat butter into little cups for us to spread on the bread.

"Okay," she said and held up her slurping.

Daddy recognized something was amiss. "Molly. Are you being polite?" he asked, knowing how severely it could backfire.

"Yes, sir. I am being polite."

Chloe threw up her hands, expressing exasperation.

"Don't – I wouldn't do that," cautioned Jack.

"Why are you being polite my little dear?" Daddy continued.

"Because I realized that Jack didn't kill me. It wasn't here – the people that killed me – and it wasn't you. Dahilana helped me."

And Jack admitted, "Yeah. I was just teasing."

"Oh – so that's it, then!" Father declared, half choked off with emotion.

"Yup. That's it!" Molly cracked a big smile, now free to act congenial.

"You finally – and no salt in my face?" he dared.

"Yeah – and nope," she said, happily rolling her head about.

"No soup on the floor?" he gasped.

"Nope," she affirmed.

We were all breaking out into smiles.

"Is there something else you want to tell me?" Daddy begged, smiles and tears already breaking out on his face.

"I'm marrying Jack – I kind of married him today. On the roof," she added with face beaming. She cocked her head.

"Not sure I expected that. Is there anything else anyone wants to tell me?" he said, unable to contain his own smile.

I came back to the table, sat down, and asked Molly, "Is there anything else you want to say?"

"I'm sorry," she shrugged. "I don't hate you. I hated the people – the ones that killed me – where I came from. What I mean is – I love you." Those were words we'd never heard from that little voice.

Chloe let loose tears. Daddy was definitely surprised and finally convinced.

Molly held out her arms, desiring a hug from Daddy. It broke him into tears and he rushed about the table. She reached up as he approached, turning to follow him. He picked her up and she wrapped her arms around him, sobbing convulsively again.

"You did it," concluded Chloe, shaking her head in awe. "Oh my God you did it." She got up from her chair and stepped carefully toward Molly, who reached back from Daddy and accepted Chloe's offer to hold her.

"I – I don't know what to say," said Daddy. "I told you to fix her and...." He threw his hands to present Molly's changed attitude. "I have to congratulate you!"

"She fixed herself," I said. "She just needed the right prompting."

"Molly?" started Mother, "Do you want to try that seventh birthday meal again? I have enough ingredients for another cake thanks to a good year of sugar beets and some happy goats and hens."

"No," she said first. She pushed down from Chloe and rushed to Jack, scooting his chair out enough for her to climb up and embrace him, fully straddling him. As a full-blown example of her precociousness, she kissed him. Still looking into his eyes as she pulled up, she requested, "I want a wedding cake."

Jack looked up at us. Was he embarrassed?

Daddy snorted. Mother gasped. Chloe waited for the responses from the rest of us. I was betwixt the old mores and new circumstances. None of us children had lost our memories – we were not really children – but young bodies and new languages had been quite a challenge. Would the old rules have been different if this were the norm prior to the event? I concluded quickly that they would. But I wasn't sure I was ready for that, though Chloe and I had a young relationship that continued. She was just teenage now. I had no baseline of my own decency to impose upon them.

While I was cogitating, I heard Father say, "I think they are still a little young yet? Don't you, Dahilana?"

I shook my head out of my concentration, hoping my answer wouldn't be too contentious. "Young bodies – not youth. No." Was I overreacting from my elation for what I'd just achieved?

"What?" snapped a few present voices.

I clarified my expressed thought. "They have child bodies, but they are *not* children. But I'd like this first party to be for today's breakthrough, not for the birthday and not for a wedding. Let's celebrate what's most important – our souls."

"Aye," said Father, using an old word they'd used in Adelardus Village. "Maybe we should finish our soup. I'd hate to let a good meal spoil for any reason. But this would be the best reason I'd ever had to stop and stuff myself on cake."

Molly scooted her shortened highchair toward Jack's chair. We all got back into our seats. Jack and Molly held hands. It was so quiet except for the slurping of soup that we broke out into laughter again.

I had a thought in the back of my mind. In this large house, there were many leftover items from guests including tuxedos and fancy dresses. While they were not much use to us for a utilitarian day, I suspected a beautiful little gown would fit Molly, and a small suit would fit Jack. I'd recalled that the first encounters with various places in this home were traumatic and I'd not returned to certain rooms nor the west home. I'd just have to search through them again. I knew of other gowns, some quite extravagant, that the rest of us could wear, even if we had to alter them. We could have a beautiful wedding.

Molly's pretty eyes rose up, looked at Jack and said to him personally, "I'm still married to you, Jack."

"I know. A voice told me when I helped you get born – you married me the day you came here."

She gazed at him, letting the little cylinders fire in her mind. "Yeah. I did," she confirmed.

But tonight, Mother got up to bake a cake.

"You don't have to make the cake tonight, Avelynn," Molly said to her mother.

Mother kindly retorted, "Yes I do little girl. I missed out on cake last night, and I had my heart set on having cake. If I start now, I'll have a cake ready before it gets dark. Won't you please help me?"

She smiled and shrugged. "Yeah."

Out of habit, the family was unnecessarily vigilant against Molly's potential aberrant wrath, and it would take months yet before we could let down our guard, and sometimes she'd just act "the old Molly" to tease us, but the real fights were over. She'd always been interested in studying, but no longer did she assume every correction was an admonition, so once she was willing to cooperate, she was on a fast track for parity with Jack, as he was teaching her everything he knew. Watching her suck in knowledge like a whale sucks in krill, seeing her partake willingly of the chores, and overall realizing the gravity of the change, I had to classify it as a miracle.

FIFTEEN

Identity and Vows

The concept of the wedding being my inspiration, I'd sneaked out of the Patent Office after having understood how to rebuild a spring scale, and took the low path to the East House, down the on-ramp and back up the off-ramp on the other side. I slid through to the main door and sneaked up past the east family home into the main. I scuffed my feet through the hallways in a little-used primary area of the mansion, searching from room to room for the outfits I'd recalled seeing. Mother had us clean up at least one room each month, just to keep the mold and dust to a modest level, but I could still skate on the light dust across the smooth stone floors. Dashing through the suites, I'd found a dark brown suit that would fit Father with alterations, and a pretty cream dress that would most certainly fit Chloe. I'd set them aside on a bed in a suite along the main hallway but needed something better.

There was a far wing I'd rarely been in, the West House, and headed that way while I held a stick in front of me to catch spider webs. A long, angled hallway adjoined this family wing on the opposite side. Molly and I could have used it much like we had inhabited a separate house in the village, treating it much like a summer home. It had a great kitchen scaled for need, several bedrooms, a very comfortable living room, and several studies, a play room, a small library still containing books, and it had been occupied by a large family at the time of the event. That meant that most of the beds had been soiled from the corpses. We had cleaned out the bodies not long after our arrival but some of the old stench remained, as we'd never fully cleaned the beds and blankets.

It was a windy day, one of the first cool days portending an early fall. Loose windows bumped in their frames. Little noises and changes of odor haunted me. I followed into a bedroom that had been occupied by two young girls. The sheets of each bed still thrown aside, I could see the darkened shapes where their little bodies had rotted. It brought the thoughts of the event back – I wish I could have been here to embalm these girls. I'd still hope to use them as dolls if I had. With all those things in mind, I didn't like disturbing this area.

I opened a closet. Hanging were dusty clothing, all the best and most expensive at the time. Pure white blouses with peter pan and middy (sailor) collars were speckled with spider droppings. Also speckled by the arachnids was a beautiful high-necked pink dress with at least three layers of thin white lace overlay and a matching pink belt. I could hope to clean it up. It had a second collar that merged with a double-breasted look with beautiful irregular pearl buttons. I wished from the bottom of my heart that I could have worn this dress.

It looked a bit large for Molly. I looked inside it for sizing information. It had been custom made for one of the girls, having a tag "For: Gretchen, 8 years." Seeing the name brought me back to the midst of my panic just as I was discovering everyone dead. "Gretchen," though it was the name I had given her, had been one of the children I'd embalmed and had been with me at the hotel. By now I had suspected that none of those souls were lost and these bodies, from which they'd ascended, had become useless for them, so I couldn't otherwise explain why I took the dress down, held it against my chest, and cried. And I sneezed, so I took the dress toward a window and attempted to open it. All my might couldn't open the window, so I followed outside and shook it into the wind, which curled about and brought the dust back to me. I couldn't hold my breath long enough. I was losing my wits and nearly beat the dress apart. I could not explain my breakdown, being overwhelmed by some of the original torments, the confusions, the sense of being forsaken and alone, all striking back at me after years of such resolution in many other areas of buried emotion.

I concluded the source of the emotion wasn't me – it had to be someone else's session having a side effect upon me, either Chloe, or one of the voices at the spirit level above, so I sat and let the grief subside, and it vanquished as if it never happened. I stumbled back through the house in search of more clothing, tossing the pink dress on the kitchen table.

I went into another room, finding beautiful clothes including a dark school girl dress that didn't show the spider spots so much. But I looked it over, seeing it would more likely fit Jack, and though he would probably wear it if asked, it would have to wait for Molly later. It seemed a shame to leave it here, so I put it on the kitchen table too.

Looking through the dresser drawers, and in suitcases that had been in the closets, I found additional panties and socks, some that would fit Molly sooner or later. I didn't need to grab these up just yet.

I ventured into another room, finding another ugly spot on a bed left by bodily effluvia and rot. I checked the drawers, first finding boy's underwear, and it had a size – twelve. Not much different than Jack's age. I turned to a wooden wardrobe and opened the door. A perfect dark pinstriped suit hung on a thick wooden hanger. As I removed the suit, I marveled at the garment as much as the hanger, which was completely wood and heavy – it must have been very strong wood. I'd never seen another like it, as it wasn't plied nor impregnated with anything as far as I could see. I'd have tasted it if it were not so dusty.

I looked over the suit and found the pants to be a tad long, and the jacket looked just a little large. There was a black belt in the drawer, and there were enough holes, but the leather was dry. (I was sure I could fix that, much like we'd once oiled up some leather machine belts to get an old lathe to function.) I checked the rest of the wardrobe and dressers, and found the shirt folded in a drawer, and socks to match.

Shoes? Why wasn't I thinking of shoes? I checked in a side closet – there was a whole stack of boxes, dusty and dry, and almost no spiders had been in there, though I pushed my stick at the boxes in case any troublesome little biters might have been hanging about.

I pulled out a box and put it on the bed, and upon opening, found neatly folded clothing for a younger boy. I got out another box and found a photo album, fully protected by the clothing wrapped around it. I opened it up, finding a family portrait, intentionally faded to almost black and white, including a very well-dressed fellow. He was much larger than Father, so his clothing would be of little use to us. But the woman in the photo wore a beautiful dress completely overlaid with lace. She wore white matching gloves, and her shoes appeared covered in diamonds. About her slender neck, she wore a diamond laden white choker. She was not a large woman, her size might be in line with one of us, though taller.

There were six children pictured, including the two younger girls, shown sitting in front at the right at their mother's feet, at about the ages of three and five. There were two boys to their left in front of their father, one appearing to be about four, and the other I guessed would have been nine. Then by the parents were two others, older still, both girls in stunning outfits. One girl appeared twelve to thirteen in age and wore a dress that was much like the Mother's but with a similar high neck collar like the little pink dress. The other girl appeared fifteen or sixteen and had a V-neck collar that didn't go low enough to display her youthful cleavage. Their eyes shown forward, all perfectly looking at the camera. Based on the "For: Gretchen, 8 years" tag I could only assume the second youngest girl in the picture had been her, making the photo about two years old. And based on the number of stained beds, one of the boys wasn't present or had died before the event.

In the picture, their faces had similar characteristics, a strong nose bridge, slightly narrow forehead, and an angled chin.

Their eyes were a little narrow, and eyebrows thick. I'd say they were good looking people, but not what I would call my ideal image. Only the father was full bodied while the remaining were mostly slender.

I'd been mesmerized looking at the pictures too long. I opened more boxes but found little else of use to us now. I closed up the boxes and put them back into the closet.

I took a look in the next bedroom, finding a dress similar to the high-necked one from the younger teen girl's picture, ornate and gorgeous. The dress would be too large for Chloe. If she wore it long and with a lace sash, perhaps it wasn't too far off.

The next bedroom had clothing that I could wear, likely from the older of the daughters placed by the side of the parents. Here was a dress fit for a real princess – draped with clear plastic, white though not devoid of any spider droppings, covered with the most delicate smocking below the breast to the waist, and all the way to the back. Otherwise, there was lace, pearls and flowers accentuating every practical place they could be put, and hand-embroidered everywhere with gorgeous paisley-ivy designs. I couldn't imagine that a girl this age would have a dress so girlish and so incredibly ornate. Inside a wardrobe was a white hat that could match well enough, having little jewels all about it.

In the closet there were yet more dresses, though a couple were heavily spotted by our little eight-legged friends, but some of the web had protected them from much of the dust. I found typical panties but tucked aside was a very sexy little pair of panties and a garter. It made me stop for a second. I turned back to the closet, overturning some boxes, finding the most beautiful white shoes. I dug through everything else in the room to look for evidence, and when I opened top drawers of her dresser, I found an engagement photo of the girl and her fiancé. I stopped short again. This girl had been planning a wedding.

I didn't cry like usual. I broke down, falling directly to the floor, eating dust, having to spit out an old bug corpse left by a spider.

Chloe and I were implicitly married, but much like my wish to marry Tori in a wedding with all girls, we'd never mocked up a true wedding, never observing a true ceremony. If we were going to mock up a wedding for Jack and Molly, there was no admissible reason that "Chloe and Dahilana" couldn't also have a ceremony. Still heaving sobs, I sat up, pulling spider webbing from my face, my chest heavy with dull pain. I wondered if it had been a mistake to come over here and explore this on my own. I couldn't let myself remain stuck in this grief. I had to cry it through and dump it firmly.

I hadn't fully explored the younger girls' room. I went back, certain it would weight my already heavy heart. I checked through drawers and found usable items including some white tights, partly discolored by age. There was a beautiful pair of lace socks. I found a pair of white shoes and laid one along my hand to compare size and hoped these would fit Molly.

I would have scooted through the room to get back to the closet, but the dust drove me to get up again. I got into the big closet and there lying flat behind boxes of good quality day clothes was a suitcase, the kind you'd expect a clothing magazine to have in an advertisement with a little girl in premium clothing as if she were taking a boat or train by herself. Unrealistic for humans who had lost their memory at birth – it wouldn't have been unrealistic if all humanity were gifted with the ability to recall.

I pulled out the suitcase and flipped the latches, expecting nothing except extra, otherwise unneeded items. Instead, I found another dress. I hadn't seen this dress – I clearly hadn't fully examined this wing of the complex in the nine years we'd been here.

It was perfect and appeared to be very close in size to Molly. This little girl's dress had all the ornate perfection that the pink dress had, except it was white, and it was free of spider droppings or other bugs. I gasped so widely I feared I'd choke myself on the dust. I pulled it up and checked the size closely, seeing it was intended to be a mid-length little girl's style, such that tights or socks would be needed. Under the dress was a special pair of panties and a matching panty-shaped bloomer and a matching slip. In the pocket on the upper suitcase lid, I found a hat matching the one from the other room. Was she to be her flower girl? Why was there only one? Was there only one? I must have been thinking of my dream wedding – having two little girls bringing in flowers.

I dug into the closet further and found a second suitcase back of some random boxes, a few of them empty. I came to expect the same, but when I opened it, there was a much more modest dress, more like a bubble dress, the skirt puffed out, heavily embroidered with shiny thread and flowers. It was stunning but would have fit the younger girl. The shoulders appeared wide enough, but it seemed a few centimeters too short.

I put the suitcases on the kitchen table, then in my excitement, I stripped. I put on the wedding dress, finding her shoes a tad large, but the gloves and hat fit well. I grabbed the suit and the smaller dress and paced back through the hallways. The shoes were slippery against the dusty floors and I had fun slipping along until my feet got away from my balance point, but only my thigh got bruised. "Oh, how did they walk in these – they're trying to make chairs out of shoes!" I complained.

I slowed down and kicked off the crazy shoes as I went through the main area of the big house, then put the suit and dresses in the closet in a nearby study. I had time, so I rushed back to get the accoutrements, using two of the larger suitcases to pack in the shoes, socks, underwear and slips. I took those back to the suite, then I ran back again, fetching my original shoes and a few other items of clothing from the older girls' room which I packed in more suitcases.

Before I went back to the main house, I checked the parents' room. The big bed, now containing only the box springs, still airing out for years, had the worst of the discolorations all over it. And likewise I opened up the closet doors and wardrobe. But as I scanned the room, I noted an onyx jewelry box on the lady's dresser, inset with semiprecious stones, and moved to open it. Inside were various necklaces and bracelets of rubies and emeralds, and the same white choker that she wore in the family photograph. I vainly picked it up and put it to my neck, latching it easily. I looked into the mirror, seeing the glow of the clear diamonds and the gentle blue hue of moonstone. Despite my scruffy hair, I looked stunning. I'd never had anything of value on my neck while I was named Dahilana. In the previous world, it would have been worth a fortune. I also found a hatpin or broach that depicted a little girl in a white dress. I pinned it into a hat to keep it secure.

I turned again to the wardrobe, scanning the clothing. There was a woman's dress suitable for a sociable occasion, not nearly as fancy as the one in the photo, also white, perhaps of silk. Was this the mother's dress for the wedding? When I pulled it out, it did appear to be much longer than my mother's proportions. At least it wasn't too short, but it was a tentative solution. We'd be best to find something that had a nearer fit.

There was a man's suit there, but it was double if not triple the volume of Father's physique. A belt hung near it on a separate hook, and oddly, it didn't seem so dry. The shoes in the bottom of the wardrobe would have Daddy looking like a clown.

I thought about the whole idea of the wedding, the importance of the clothing, even the lack of a wedding photographer. What virtues did it have if you couldn't snap a picture? How long had civilization been enjoying ceremonies before photography took root? Did the exactness of the clothing, the need for rings and a cake, the certain phraseology of vows really matter? Why would an oath, a vow, a promise need artificial reinforcement? Did we need a wedding to seal such a pledge to "join our souls" when, for all current evidence, we might already have been divisions of the same soul or souls? And what of the significance of a partnership defined by artificial rules – consistency was a theme in the black book? How is it consistent if we had inauthentic flesh bodies aside from our true spiritual forms – should we partner just for the sake of having children? Did the larger souls, the élan vital of which we'd been constituted, the impetus of our (wayward) existence, bear children? Did they have a need for sexuality? Did they love in ways I could not imagine? If I was indeed a fragment of such a little girl entity, how could I ever conform to the strict rules of human existence?

I couldn't. With some variation in constitution, I was still her.

And the complexity of these cogitations brought me to an epiphany. I'd been so stupid for not seeing the obvious. Just as we created *good* in the universe, we'd created *bad*. Everything, not just a vow, has a quality. Just as Molly and her new attitude had a positive quality, the obstinate attitude had a quality too. Just as a flower, though fleeting, has a quality of beauty, it can also have a quality of ugly, or a quality of survival as an organism. Every soul exists at some level of quality, despite its unadulterated purpose, from great and good to horrible, nasty and despicable.

As Miranda, I had erringly thought I was a somewhat decent human being, but I was mostly oblivious, afoul with apathy, and hiding that I was on the edge of being pathologically dangerous, contracting more insidious plans and thoughts which I'd hoped to defuse through friendships and writing. I wanted to be good, but the extremity of my obsessive folly could have overruled every decent facet of my being. With the help from above, and from Chloe, I'd made a lot of progress – a truly metaphysical melioration. But at this time, I assessed myself low on the scale, perhaps up to innocuous, upsurging from deplorable. It had been quite an achievement.

I felt so stupid for envisioning a beautiful wedding and pursuing the effort to dig out these clothes. I'd been lost in my excitement. I'd been overcome with an old model that shouldn't be needed.

If we acted as quality people and were true to our statements, there was no need to contrive a pompous and wasteful show. With a notable population, there were indeed other reasons it could be necessary, and that was as communication to others, meaning, "These two are now mates, you'll have to go find another," or as a celebration. Aside from the concept of the enforcing the vow, most of the ceremony was meretricious.

I gathered up the reclaimed clothing and treasures anyway. I didn't wish to imperil Molly's dream. And like Molly, I could be arbitrarily obstinate in view of the truth. Walking through the long hallways, I'd balanced my enthusiasm from my contemplative achievement with a simpler view of our little wedding. It was just a celebration for us; it was just experience, the primary reason we'd entered the universe.

For now, I'd put the clothing into the suite with the other things I'd gathered. I'd keep it a secret from even Mother until I had it cleaned up and I could get Mother to alter them for fit.

"How are we going to get them to try on this clothing if they don't even know they exist?" asked Mother.

We were at the suite where I'd set aside the newly cleaned items, all the dresses and suits for the presumed wedding between Molly and Jack. I'd already conceived a means. "I would make some sack dresses the same size, then have them try them on."

"Well, that's a solution. Obvious," she rolled her eyes. "Sack dresses for the farming and garden work."

Split down the sides with ties, the little "fashionable burlap" gowns were sewn to the same dimensions as the wedding clothes, then as we'd "admit our mistakes" for the fit, we'd fix them. Chloe got hers first, taken from the dimensions of the lace-covered dress I most hoped would fit, but least expected to have ample room at the waist.

At dinner that evening, Chloe came in after a rough time in the garden. "Too many bees. Where'd all the bees come from?" she bickered.

"Ah! Bees!" cried Mother. "We need to find the hive and move it closer."

"Mother! Bees. Bees sting!" Chloe interjected.

Mother said simply, "Bees – honey – food. Bees – pollinators – food. It's getting dry at the end of summer and into fall. Expect the little stingers to get feisty. The best way to keep them happy is to spray some water – they are seeking the water in the gardens and on the roof."

Chloe's confused expression led to her question. "Spray at them or at the gardens?"

"The gardens. The surrounding area. Let the poor creatures have a drink," instructed Mother.

Father had been walking in, hearing part of the conversation. "Let who have a drink?"

"The bees," said Chloe.

Father raised his eyebrows, "Oh – I guess it's getting to that time of year. You've found bees?"

"And I'm the only one that didn't know about bees when it's dry," sassed Chloe.

"And when you go out, I've got you a smock. Let's see if I got the fit. As it cools outside you'll want to have an extra layer and it will protect your clothing. It ties along the side. Simple, huh?"

"Sure, Mother," consented Chloe. "It's not very stylish."

We all laughed a little on that one. Mother tied it up. I was impressed how well it fit, leaving a couple centimeters gap on either side at her waist, considering that it was over her current day dress.

Molly came in after sorting some laundry. "I got the piles sorted. When would you... Oh, I want one of those!" she said as she saw the smock on Chloe.

"Good," said Mother, improvising, "Because I'm going to make one for you too. I hadn't thought of it, but now that bees have been mentioned, I think I'll have it come up on the neck. You can fold it down like a collar if you like. What do you think?"

"Sure. Got any boots? Mine are cracking through."

I checked her boots. "I don't have any more, Mother. We'll have to scavenge for more boots she can work in."

"Hum. That gives me an idea," she said.

I knew what she was up to. We'd find shoes and boots the same size as the dress shoes and have the others try them too. I winked at Mother.

The following day we made Molly's smock and scavenged into a neighborhood in the north, where we'd gone before, but not just looking for boots. We'd taken "Old Number Three" as we now called it since Daddy put numbers on the trucks. We first looked for houses that had evidence of children, and it reminded me of my psychotic breakdown after the event. I knew there were still dried up corpses in these houses. Into face masks with filters we'd add air fresheners or spice extracts to cover any remaining smells. I preferred vanilla, but the bottle was low, so I had to deal with "Island Mango." Not much worse than vanilla because I'd used that to cover the decaying smells of bodies in the hotel many years prior.

"I'm present now. I'm in the present now. This is not Altontown," I repeated like an incantation. I found a house that followed the same pattern where I'd found the molested girl – a swimming pool, lace curtains on an upstairs window. It was likely to have children. "I'll take this one," I said.

Mother got out and came along. I didn't know where Father had found them, but we had lock picks. I set to work on the door, reminding Mother how they worked. She looked on as a good student, though I think she was teaching me more than I taught her.

"Ah yeah. I think I remember," she thanked, her eyes pleased.

"Yeah. Here we go. Masks?"

I pushed into the stale house. The stench wasn't so strong after twenty years since a back window had been broken, twigs left on the carpet having come from the fallen branch that did the damage. Some sprouts were growing up in the carpet but hadn't made it very far. I followed through to the kitchen, looking for anything useful. Everything was unusually organized. Even noodles had been in glass containers. I grabbed a box of trash bags. I found soaps. I found silverware in the drawer, the organizer half full of dead bugs. Bugs were everywhere, but there hadn't been anything set out for them to eat. The counters were dusted. The cabinets above had been rotting from termites.

Mother checked the laundry and garage. I think she was looking for things to help with the gardening. I heard the garage door making noise. I went out. She had been cranking it up.

While cranking, she said, "Thank god they spent the extra for this one. Nice door opener. Potting soil – the good stuff. Fertilizer – still packaged. These people were crazy. Nobody else would package everything they'd opened like that."

I looked up, finding two dozen forty-liter fuel tanks. There were stickers on them that said *Stabilized*. "Hadn't we been here before?" I asked Mother.

"No. Next street south. You've never been to this house. Good choice I might add."

"But – I was sure," I started. "I've seen this house before."

"Maybe. Maybe not. They made them all by the same pattern here. Not my style of housebuilding," she pointed out.

"We'll have to get Daddy here to get the fuel tanks. It might be good."

"Write it down in the notebook. We have to catalog it all for your father's sanity anyway."

"Okay. But first, shoes," I said. I looked all over the garage for extra shoes. I found holiday decorations of various kinds, some I'd never seen with odd depictions of strange spirit creatures, a combination of people and animals, all in flowing gowns and jewels all about them. I found old wooden shipping luggage packed with clothing and textiles. "Mother – material – about a basket's worth."

"Just write it down," she said, looking over something else.

"What are you looking at, Mother?"

"Seeds. There's soil, pots, and to go with it, seeds," she said flatly.

"Old seeds," I said. "Okay. Shoes, again. Shoes...."

I found holiday plates and decorations. I found old artwork and homework from the children's school, all collected and labeled. Finally, I'd found a box with shoes – I found a whole row on a shelf. I found the man's shoes – too big for Daddy, the woman's shoes – too big for any of us, then a large box with children's shoes, mixed with girls and boys items. I found slightly molded leather shoes. I found canvas topped sneakers. I found winter boots. I had a note with me about sizes and matched up a few pairs.

Before I returned inside, I put a few more drops of "Mango Island" on my air filter, then lugged myself and an empty suitcase up the stairs to the bedrooms. I found the girl's room first. Seeing the body still in the bed, the hair visible, I tried to see how long her body was first but didn't want to disturb the covers, lest anything supernatural happen. I looked at her clothing to get the sizes. Mostly about a size eight, or eight-year-old child. There were good clothes here, all the best stuff. All the panties looked new. All the socks were clean. Apparently,

Stephen Michael Ferree

nothing that looked remotely dirty ever got back into the drawers. There was too much accumulation to assume they'd just moved in. The only other possibility was an adoption.

I checked a closet, full of games and girlish things. This was not quite as organized as the areas I'd seen so far. Sheets and blankets up top, board games on the next shelf, then hanging clothing. Several of the outfits suggested a private school. Others were pretty. Molly would love this stuff. It was all good. I couldn't leave it. I packed, repeatedly telling the girl in the bed that I was sorry for taking her things.

Mother was at the door. "What are you doing?"

"They'll fit Molly in a couple years," I said.

"Then we mark the house and we have a couple years to get them. Get some – don't worry about it. Get some. Did you forget your mission?"

"Oh, me and girl's stuff," I mumbled. "Yes," I added as confirmation. I redoubled my effort to look at the shoes below. There were school girl shoes and a hanging organizer that held tights. I grabbed a white pair. I pushed further into the closet, finding some soft rubber boot covers that were not too crusty and dry. "These will help," I called back to Mother, but she was not by the door.

I got up and collected my items into the suitcase. Seeing that the suitcase had room, I grabbed some camisoles from the drawer. With winter coming, she could certainly use that – oh – and why not more tights to help with winter. They were a little large, but they could provide insulating layers.

Packed as if leaving, I followed through the hallway. I turned to the parent's bedroom, finding Mother kneeling on the floor.

"Mother?" I said softly.

I heard little cries. I hadn't heard her cry much since her hands were bleeding after we'd blistered our hands during our arrival.

"What's the matter, Mother?"

She was holding a traditional man and woman cake topper she'd pulled out of a drawer – an item I would have thought would be kept in the garage storage. "I – I didn't have a wedding either. I don't know why it matters. I really just don't understand why it would matter. Why would a wedding matter?"

"When I went to the far wing at the mansion, I found myself thinking about that, and you know, I really don't know why it matters so much. My best answer today is that such an occasion would matter to all of us even at the highest spiritual level. The oath. The vow. Somehow, it's important. For me, I believe it must be an influence of my origin – from her," I looked up.

"It is," Mother agreed, examining the figure. "Put this in your suitcase, please. Protect it – I'm afraid it might be brittle."

She looked through the remainder of the room's items, finding a top-quality fashion sweater and usable belts. I went on to another room.

It was a boy's room, complete with a depiction of a solar system upon the wall from a comic book story, along with a face of an eagle-headed fellow, probably some superhero. A tuft of hair stood out from the stained pillow, but I couldn't see much of the body defined. I turned to open a drawer, finding the boy's socks and underwear. I checked the sizes. The underwear was marked "6 years." This would all be too small.

"Next house, Mother," I said, but I followed through to a small office at the end of the hallway. There was a nice electric typewriter on a desk and a stack of folders. Someone had been writing articles and the top one was some epistle to a newspaper's editor on religious diversity. Bookshelves lined the walls from one side to the other, barring only the main door, a closet door, and one visible window. The other window had a shelf in front of it. I cautiously pulled up the breathing filter, checking the room. A light stench of the bodies had permeated the house; here it was only partly musty with a woody, paper smell. I pushed at the books on the shelf at the window, and one of them crumbled. I noted that they'd been getting eaten by insects. "Damn!" I cried several times.

Mother came up to the door.

"Bug-eaten books," I pointed to the façade of book covers on the shelves. But I opened the drawer to the old metal desk. Inside, despite spider webs and crusty remains of their dinner, I found wrapped in plastic one of the little black cabalistic books. This one had the title gilded on the cover, simply: "Ascension."

"Mother?" I said. "Look."

"Another one?"

"I think. Look – the folder. 'Book review submission, Prophecies magazine.'" I was going to grab up the folder, which itself had resisted the insects, but the typewritten paper inside was burrowed and unreadable. "Damn, again," I cursed.

I opened the plastic bag with the book, finding it was in good shape, though the binding stiff and cracked. The embossed cover was leather and the title likely gold leaf. "It seems to be the same book. No index – no table of contents. Just heavily printed text." I turned to the picture of the confession chain. It too had a star, which had been drawn in. Somebody had thought these important enough to print and bind by hand.

"Well," I said to Mother. "I got another one."

She cocked her head, holding enough bras and undershirts that I felt less concerned about my girl clothing obsession.

I rolled my eyes. "Well, I hope something fits."

We went back to the truck and set our smaller treasures into the cab, then added the soil, fertilizer and hose into the back.

Mother and I took the truck up the street, again looking for signs of children. I saw a modest house with a play set in the back. You could call it a starter home in an upscale neighborhood, with unique architectural details. Dark shingles, old red brick and an elegant door with double-arched construction marked the curb appeal. Squares of cobblestone were laid for the entry. I could see sheer curtains with an image behind them that suggested some contents, though there was still a faded sign indicating, "Foreclosure Sale – Sold!"

Stepping through the overgrowth with pruning shears, and a stick wrapped in previously snagged spider webbing, we approached the upscale bungalow. I found recognition and comfort as it reminded me of an old home near the library in Hattonville that had not been part of the village. The small trees and shrubs had not been able to damage the brick siding. Ivy shrouded the structure, even crossing the window panes and halfway up the roof. I enjoyed the anatomy of this little feudal house. Mother looked it over too, but I noted her reminiscing gaze. "I know," I softly agreed.

I picked the lock and entered. Inside it first smelled woody, not like old body rot. Wooden crates, luggage and trunks were scattered. Only a few furniture items were present. The new occupants had been moving in and never took occupancy of their new home. The movers had a bill on a polished granite slab of a kitchen counter.

"Mother – I like this house. I wish we had this in Adelardus," I dreamed.

"No. Underneath the surface it's probably just junk wood and plaster walls," she refuted.

"Let's see?" I pounded on a wall, hearing plaster chunks falling back of the typical lateral wooden slats of cheap house construction.

Mother laughed. "Looks nice, anyway."

The stone fireplace in the living room was real. The slate floors in the entry and kitchen were real. I wished I could see beyond the finishing touches.

Still, we sorted through the items. A large box of clothing had large blouses and oversized panties and bras. They were not much use to us unless we needed to strip off a piece of elastic or a clasp. Other boxes contained similar clothing. There was a box of shoes, all double wide.

The hallway led to an open stairway of oak wooden slabs and black wrought iron frame and rails. I let myself make tracks in the dust, holding my stick out in front of me to catch spider webs. I found a child's room. There was a small pine bed already in place, and near it was a set of boxes. I opened and sorted them, moving slow to avoid breathing much dust. I found toddler clothing. One of the boxes had a hanging rail across it, and it was full of dress up clothes and other "princess dresses" – beautiful, but mostly useless unless we had another little girl.

In the next room was a young girl's bed, mostly constructed of an enameled metal frame, painted creamy white, and still shiny in most places. Similar boxes stood aside like lost luggage at an airport. I opened the tall one, expecting similar dress-up clothing, and for the most part, I was right. In the middle, however, was an elegant dress wrapped in plastic. Not as wealthy an item as those dresses from the far wing of the mansion, the size appeared closer to Molly's frame.

"Mother!" I called out.

Through the doorway I could hear her exclaim, "A dangerous spider? At least that's what I thought it was from your tone of voice." She emerged from the stairwell, eyes darting about the room.

"You won't believe this!" I held the dress back until she paused. "Jackpot!"

"For all the silk caterpillars in the world I wouldn't have guessed this," she said, holding it up and looking it over, then she dug into the collar and inside seams to find a tag. "It has a little tag with a six. I hope that's a size in years. Molly is still able to wear sixes."

I dug into the other boxes and found no supporting accoutrements except a lace play scarf and a set of gloves. Little brass-framed glass cameos were sewn onto the gloves.

Mother held back to look at the items. "Well, those are nice for a child's costume. Not quite wedding items but perhaps Molly decides. What traditions do we keep?"

"No firm traditions. She can wear them if she wants. You know Molly. She'd be just as happy nude. But I don't think it unjust to request she wear one of these dresses. Or maybe Jack wears the dress and Molly the suit?"

"You'd be more likely to get Jack in a dress than Molly in any kind of masculine clothing – she is all girl. Well, pack it, anyway," offered Mother.

I leaked a satisfied smile, "Okay – there's one. But who's keeping score."

We searched everything in the room, finding play clothing that was perfect for Molly – thank god we'd fixed her attitude – because now she'd cheerily accept these cute styles. I wished I'd had more access to affluent neighborhoods as a child. Hattonville and Adelardus had little beyond utilitarian items. I noted the influence on myself, my tenacity toward cute things, girlish things – because of the girl at the pedestal (though I'd not seen her at the pedestal recently), so I looked upwards to acknowledge my identity followed her pattern.

We pulled some boxes of clothing with us to the truck, packing it into the bed. The day was warming up, so it was best if we ate now, before our packed lunch basket was filled with spoiled food. Boiled eggs for protein and plenty of late summer vegetables and apples satisfied our appetites. I enjoyed the view of the ivy-mantled home from the curb, pondering the life that had been happening there up to the event.

"Another house?" I asked Mother.

"I don't like these. They've got old-people yard ornaments. Try the next cul-de-sac," she said, pointing back toward another street.

I drove up to the end of the present cul-de-sac and circled about. In doing so, I noted a swing set in a backyard. "I'm going to check this one anyway," I insisted and got out, leaving the truck running. I scurried up the walk and picked the lock of the modest split-level without much frustration. The hinge was stiff and reported its misery as I pushed my way in across a dusty, course entrance rug. The air was like an old musty basement, lightly acrid. As I pushed into the house, I noted nothing that would pertain to children. In the maritime-designed bathroom the floor was spongy and weak, the outside wall mildewed, the paint appearing smoked. I pulled back, passing a cabinet. I checked inside, finding typical items, most too old to be of any use. In a basket there were baby care items. Below, there was a baby bath. I turned to walk through the house, cautiously making my way upstairs. There were a few rooms, one set up as an office, one was the master bedroom, still with lumps in the bed, and one more small room beside an upstairs bathroom. It was a nursery, now with a weird soiled lump in the crib which had once been their baby girl. I'd seen too many remains. I didn't feel a jolt by viewing this.

I went into the parents' room and examined the clothes for sizes, finding that the young Mother's clothing was my size. I looked through the drawers, finding an especially sexy little cream babydoll set. I knew I didn't need it. I greedily picked it up. I forced myself to put it down. Then grabbed it again, wrapping it into a T-shirt with socks and regular underwear. I examined a pair of shoes, and they fit as well, being a style I would have bought and worn on the island.

I looked about at the pictures on the walls. There over the bed was a large image of a sunset at a beach, not much unlike the westward view from my treehouse. In a corner were a few dolls, one almost like a porcelain doll I'd had – I checked the back of the neck, finding numbers but no artist's name. It was oddly like mine. I could see the woman's hair, light in color just as mine had been.

I checked a jewelry box. Earrings with little starfish were right at the top, exactly like the ones Seria had worn. There were no specific markings on them but there had been a shop that crafted these on the island. I opened another drawer, finding the woman's swimsuit, being the same brand, and very close in design as one I'd worn just days before the event.

Like peering into the future, except for the fact that there was a man in the bed, I stood in near shock, seeing what resembled so closely my own life. If the event did not happen, would I have succumbed to societal pressure and found my way as some man's wife despite my propensity to do otherwise? Would I, as Miranda, have had a baby girl and would I have been good with the child, or would it eventually have been taken away from me?

My feet had become glued to the spot on the floor, my eyes examining everything, and the more I viewed, the more I correlated with my own tastes. I released those feet and turned back downstairs through the main living area, finding binders of photographs, grabbing one and spilling it open. These images shocked me further. Not forgetting to grab the clothing I'd selected, I grabbed up a binder and carried it to the truck. Mother had been waiting patiently. I tucked the clothes into a box I'd reserved for my own items and threw the photo album on the seat.

Mother didn't know what I meant to do, so I reached in and showed her several photos and how the woman looked much like I had as Miranda. As I looked further, I'd recognized the background. "They *are* in Altontown," I blurted. I pulled up the binder and looked more closely at the pictures. "Oh my God!" I cried out. For what I'd seen there, it didn't immediately strike as deep as I might have expected. There, in one of the photos, acting as a tour guide, was an image of myself next to the couple. I was young, beautiful, smiling with a semblance of happiness. It was before their baby had been born, perhaps their honeymoon. I'd been working during the summer, having been sixteen years old. It was unbelievable that such a thing could happen. I had physical evidence of my previous lifetime right there in that photograph.

But like the delay between the earthquake and the killer wave, rushing emotion caught up with me. I hadn't stated clearly what I'd seen; Mother could not understand my blubbering and hadn't known me prior to my birth so as not to recognize the girl in the picture as me. I kept my finger pointing at the image of my previous incarnation as Miranda.

I tried again, panting awkwardly, getting control. "That's me, Mother. That's me. There. We look like sisters. She's just like me. We – they – could have been my life."

Mother just watched me, her soft eyes sad, affectionate, and compassionate. It was not beyond her ability to understand.

"Oh, Mother!" I cried, believing myself dumb again for my deepening reaction. "I'm such a crybaby," I slurred with tears.

Cautious and slow, she offered, "That's not crybaby material. Crying over a lost favorite sock, or a fallen crystal vase – that's being a crybaby. Crying over an image of yourself from before you were born – that's mind-blowing." With one hand she pointed all fingers to her brow then spread them outward as she pulled away.

I nodded. "Take note of this place in the log. This one is important to me."

"It's already in the log," she said softly.

I didn't immediately grasp what she'd said. Instead, I turned my attention to the house, seeing I'd left the door open. "I'll get the door." Of all the places we'd scavenged, this house seemed the most like home, even though the framework wasn't much different than most houses at the time. I looked the split-level house over as I locked the door and returned to the truck. Mother's comment on the log caught up with me. "Did you know, Mother? Did you know about this house?"

"Only that we'd found a travel brochure in the living room – Altontown – and plane tickets from their honeymoon," she admitted.

"Oh Mother, you don't have to hide such things. This – yes it brings emotions – strong ones. But I don't cry as much as I used to."

"Well you cry as much – just not as long," she observed.

"I suppose you are right. But if there's already a log entry for this one, you'd better write in Dahilana's house – or better yet, Miranda's house." I pushed in the clutch and set the truck into gear, saying, "Let's go back to the mansion."

"You mean home?" she gently suggested.

"No. Considering all the past lifetimes I'd recalled, including this most recent one, the whole world is home, some places more than others."

Once back at the house, I put the photo album on the kitchen counter and waited for the family to gather for dinner. Mother and I busied ourselves to get dinner started, though my arms were sluggish against my emotive day. Jack returned with Father.

"I think this will work for a while," said Jack, putting a restored blender upon the counter. "It's like the one Molly banged up on her birthday." The metal base was newly brushed to reduce the scratches it had suffered from previous owners.

I checked over the fit of the jar to the base and plugged it in to check the motor and blades. Having filled the jar with plain water, I started it and watched the water whirling. The hum of the motor was harmoniously clean, the swish of the water was firm. "Yes, Jack. I think it will do."

Chloe returned with Molly, who walked by, taking notice of the blender. "Did you fix it?" she asked.

"No. It's another one. I had to fix the cord and use a metal brush to clean up the scratches, that's all," offered Jack.

"Well I'm glad you got another blender working," Molly added. "Gosh, it smells good in here. What's for dinner?"

"Dumplings, but we need these salad vegetables prepared," I stated.

Molly looked up at me. "I'll get them." She moved to the sink to wash her hands.

Father noted the water. "I've checked the pump and fuel generators. All looks good for today." As always, he watched over everyone to enforce our least-waste policy, unless that waste could be used to feed the pigs or stuff the biogas generators.

The typical bustle of the kitchen activities brought us to gather around the table. Before I sat down, I appealed, "Before anyone makes a mess eating, let me show you what I'd found." The photo album was nearby, and I carried it to the table, opening it up. "Altontown. It's where I lived – my name was Miranda."

I flipped through the book, showing picture after picture despite that most of the pages were filled with the couple on their supposed honeymoon, but it included the cove, beaches and the hotel. "Now – look at this!" I turned the page to present the critical image. "This girl – that was me." A mild wave of emotion passed through me. I wiped a couple tears.

Father's eyebrows rose up. Mother nodded. Jack's eyes bugged out. Chloe got up and came around the table for a better view. Molly came about and climbed up on Jack's lap, obscuring his view, then settled back against his chest. I pulled away from the table, letting them see, as I started pouring bowls of dumplings.

As they all examined the image of my beautiful self as Miranda, Mother stated something I'd not known. "I understood when Dahilana found this today. Though I never found a picture of myself from my previous lifetime, I'd lived in Adelardus before – really it was young Hattonville. The village name was given later when they decided to preserve that section of town, naming it after one of the first settlers."

"Mother?" I complained, tasting a dumpling. "Why have you not mentioned it?" I fixed a bowl for myself and Molly, placing Molly's bowl out of habit.

"Don't know. Just thought we'd never leave the town if you all thought I was that attached to it. I knew the town was dying. But at any rate – Dahilana and I found some shoes that might fit Jack and Molly. I'll fetch them after dinner."

The amazement settled, but Molly threw in, "Gosh Dahilana, you were so beautiful. I'd miss me if I were you."

"I do miss me," I said. "But if I still had that body, I'd be twenty years older." I knew there wasn't much sense in dreaming about it. Instead, I focused on serving the dumplings.

Mother and I spent some secret time each morning, after her horticulture work, my patent study and before lunch. After lunch, Chloe and I would tutor Molly and Jack on regular studies, and if Mother could, she'd sneak in a little extra sewing time. Within a few weeks we all wore "garden smocks" of burlap, and all fit perfectly. And the suits and dresses were in the last stages of alteration.

Chloe challenged my short-lived daily study at the Patent Office, complaining that the weather could turn cool within the month, and more progress now meant easier efforts through the winter. I had exited the Patent Office alone for too many days, pursuant to these important but extraneous activities.

Since the breakthrough, Molly restarted her studies of the language, inclined to cooperate with little reserve, cognitively grasping the concepts at an unprecedented rate. Using ordered lists of words I'd used when Jack was four years old, we studied children's books, advancing ten times the rate I'd ever expected. Molly would so easily cuddle into my lap, her back against my breast, and absorb with a lightening pace. If there was one thing I'd learned about education, there was nothing cerebral or genetic about the absorption of knowledge. It was the soul building upon concepts. Her curiosity was inexhaustible, and her primary complaint was when we were out of time, having to turn to more laborious chores and preparation for dinner.

With hope, we could unveil the secret within a few days. Father, with Jack's help, had been constructing replacement biogas units and restoring general household appliances. Jack and Molly together handled the basic animal feeding, and depending on the weather, the household cleaning, though that was usually a group activity anyway. Hilarious it was when Father broke out into song, mimicking a track on the old Victrola, cranked up to high speed. Once he stepped into a bucket of bleach water, acting as if consumed by the chemical composition of the substance contained within. Other times we just sang, reading off of sheet music we'd found in abundance. It was at this time that Molly decided she'd "make some attempt to relearn keyboard percussionist instrumentation" so she called it.

My curiosity bested me. "Molly? You've played an instrument like this before?"

"Yes, my dear sister," she said, examining an impressive baby grand piano. "I'll dust it. I fear, Honey, that it will need tuning, a feat that will require some study."

Having listened to the extensive collection of common music that permeated the radios of my days on the island, I'd known music, but little that was worthy of an instrument such as this. I poked at the keys, surprised at the dynamics, though many strikes discorded with detuned strings. Overall, however, the instrument could be played. "It's not grossly off, but it will need to be tuned, Honey," I agreed. She gazed at me warmly, her visage commensurate with our growing love for each other, her appreciation stronger every day we studied. I added, "I can only teach you what little I know – a handful of chords. The rest will have to come from books and the old vinyl disks."

"So be it," she said, reflecting on a story we'd read recently. Her mind had flourished like a budding spring since we'd handled that incident that had condemned her. In the chains we did on her confused words, we'd opened up even more of the incident. Knowledge on running an "after event society" poured out, though we'd already invented a large percentage of it, what she knew was scaled for a group of thousands of survivors. There was neither such luxury of effort nor burden of the group in our family structure.

It wasn't for two weeks when the dresses were complete. Mother and I staged a newscast for an upcoming fashion event. Meeting everyone after a nutritious dinner of chicken and pumpkin squash, we rolled a covered baggage cart into the kitchen.

Having pushed all the chairs so they were mostly to one side of the table, we began our outrageous performances.

"This just in," I roared as if speaking into a stage microphone, using a milk bottle to create some reverberation. "New styles for everyone's fit, with a specific event in mind."

Mother said, "Tailored to everyone's fit and needs. We now present to you, after weeks of construction and alterations, your new...."

I echoed, "Your new!"

"Special event clothing for... "

I echoed again, "beautiful and tailored special event clothing for...."

"A wedding!" cried Mother as she pulled Molly's small dress from the back of the covered cart.

I lost my own breath as I saw the perfect little dress, now with a matching lace train attached.

Mother paced about with Molly's dainty, laced, and stunning gown. "Molly first because she's the first bride." I don't think the others knew what 'first' meant yet.

Molly shook her head, blushing and crying. "It's so beautiful!" she blubbered and rushed up to compare the size. Mother and I nodded, seeing how well we'd done on the alterations. Molly stood with the dress and smiled, looking all about.

"See, Honey. We didn't forget you," I said to her.

"I see, Honey," she said back, a glowing visage extracting the most from her beauty.

Mother went on with the so-called newscast. "Now before I expound on the current dress, let's include our next member – the groom for this little girl!" She pulled a dark elegant suit we hoped would perfectly fit Jack.

Jack jumped up so quickly he banged his knees on the table, then stumbled over to compare his size to the suit. As he did so, he repeatedly turned to Molly to see her dress.

"What's the matter, Jack? Did you want a dress too?" chided Chloe.

"Well – I'd wear one if you made one. You know there's no one who'd care," he offered.

I wouldn't have expected anything spiritual at that moment, but one of those *thumps* slammed in my chest. I saw how Jack hesitated. Molly stopped for a second. Even Mother. It was as if time had experienced a glitch.

"No! I feel..." I blurted out. I tumbled to the floor. The image had me caught in a time and space dispersion, a groundswell of past images hectically passing up through the floor and through myself. I heard the girl's voice, though I believed she was in a chair not at some pedestal, revealing a specific epiphany, "I'd convinced myself that in all my characters, throughout all these conquests, I could play both male and female roles. I'm not that good at being men. Maybe I was dumb to try. I'm just a silly girl." The helper's voice came through as well, "So you're getting a little grief off that one, huh?" She went on, "Yeah. I'd like to be able to play all the characters in all these worlds and kingdoms. It shouldn't be some evasive, cosmic thing for me to do. I should be able to act as anyone from God to Devil – at some point with the degeneration of a universe I have to be all human variations due to genetic bodies – but I'm best to stick with girls that prefer girlfriends. My souls are more plausible that way."

The engulfing scene faded from view. I found the floor at my face, apparently with no sense of up or down. As I felt the weight of the body, I also felt for damage that may have been inflicted, finding only a sore knee.

"Dahilana! Dahilana!" repeated Molly. She pulled me to my back, straddling my chest, bending over, her nose just a thumb-width from mine.

"I'm fine," I said, but I grabbed at her concerned face and kissed her. She didn't hedge. I sat up and carried her up with me. "I'm fine," I repeated. She bit her lip. I could feel her love while I panted to regain my breath.

Father was dumbfounded, not offering a thread of analytical explanation.

Chloe cocked her head. "You two are becoming lovers," she said softly.

"Just let me explain what I saw," I requested.

Mother said, "Please, Dahilana, go on."

"She," I pointed up, "is a girl – all girl, only girl, likes girlfriends. I saw Jack jump too with the *thump* that hit me in the chest. Molly too. Maybe we all did. But I definitely saw Jack. Jack? Did you see anything?"

Perhaps we'd been ignoring him too much, as he had set himself on the floor against the counter. "Jack?" I asked again.

He appeared defeated, sulking. "In all the kingdoms that have ever existed, I don't make the best men, she said – the girl."

Father looked side to side, making an attempt to understand. Pointing to me, he said, "Jack – if Jack's also a part of you, as may be Chloe, then that might explain why little Molly has gained such an affection for you, too. She likes him – she likes you." But his hand was on his chest as if his heart had skipped a beat.

"Chloe? Did you see or hear?" I requested of her.

"Everything you said, though it didn't knock me to the floor," she presented.

Mother waved a hand at Molly, asking, "Molly dear? Did you hear the voice?"

Molly nodded. I could see the impulses in her hands and legs. I thought she might attempt to escape, much like she did as a toddler.

I quickly asked her, "Molly? Please?"

She gasped, "That I'd be better with a girlfriend. That's what I heard. And…"

"And what?" begged Father. "Out with it. We're all … friends and family."

"No – we're all lovers. And – she's right," said Molly.

I thought perhaps she was just hesitating for effect. If not, she was hedging a crisis. "Molly?" I requested again.

"Well, the girl god sent me here to marry Jack. And I'll marry him. But it's true we all want to marry girls. Jack doesn't have to wear the suit…."

Jack put his hands to his head, but no one took up the reason yet.

Father looked to Mother, "Avelynn?"

Mother told him, "You know me well enough now. And I know you – deeply. I know you put on a façade of masculinity just as well as any of us could."

"Oh, whatever – I've got a good façade going. Jack?" Father pressured him to make a response. "We'd like your opinion. And what did Molly mean about the suit?"

Tears welled up in Jacks sunken eyes. "I'll wear the suit, but…"

"It's okay Jack," said Molly softly, moving to him, kissing him on the forehead. "It's okay to say it."

"They won't love me – not like they do now. I don't fit – and after this, I really don't feel like I fit as…"

"As what, Jack?" begged Father again, followed quickly by Chloe with the same question.

"I don't fit as a boy. I never did. I didn't last lifetime either. But not – today – it's like I suddenly have the feeling of being in the wrong body – not just having a mismatched body – but like being in the wrong thing – like suddenly finding myself in a goat."

Molly spilled the detail that he thought would condemn him. "I like it when he sleeps in the clothes you've put back for me – girl's nightgowns and panties."

"Did you have to say that!" barked Jack. "It would have come out in any confessions I did with them anyway. It's not like I couldn't have admitted it."

With soft eyes she replied, "Sorry. But I love you – and if you don't like the suit, you can wear a dress too."

"I didn't want to wear a dress because none was made for me. I liked well enough being cared for. I liked being loved. How can they love me now?"

Father chimed in, "I'll wear whatever you want me to wear for their little wedding, Avelynn. But now I'll admit I heard the voice, and I don't feel so comfortable in my own skin either. Jack, I think we all understand more than you could ever have expected."

The thought crawled through my consciousness. How many other souls in the universe just had the same revelation, the same rotation of identity from fixed male-female gender roles to something alternate, more suited to the eternal gods above? I found myself quite pleased with my body, only wishing I was about the size of Molly, able to wear that child's beautiful wedding dress Mother had crafted.

"Whew!" I said. "Mother? Just continue. The rest will settle out over a few days. Revelations from above sometimes sort themselves out – uniquely."

Mother redirected us back on track. "Well enough. I have more to reveal if anyone is interested, or has this spiritual vision just blown us all away?"

"I'm in," said Chloe.

"Ah – aye – continue," said Father.

Molly nodded. Jack threw up his embarrassed hands.

I said, "Okay, Mother. Please continue."

"Okay. For – I guess I can't reveal this all too slowly but Dahilana and I already know. Chloe? We have a dress for you, but it might not be quite the bridesmaid dress you were expecting."

"Well, that's okay. We'll have a wedding for the youngsters with the best we can do," she appealed.

"No. More like this," said Mother, unhooking the heavy dress and revealing the high-collared lace dress from the west house, to which she'd added a modest train. She hooked it on the outside of the rack. "You won't fully understand this until I show you Dahilana's." So, Mother unhooked the next dress and pulled it forward. "These are your wedding dresses too."

It took a second for Chloe to absorb the thought. "You don't just mean Jack and Molly's wedding, do you." She rose up, already dripping tears.

Mother and I shook our heads. Mother took my gorgeous dress and hooked it on the other end of the rack.

Chloe got up and paced herself slowly toward me, tears dripping at their fastest. When she reached me, she pulled at my arms to extract my embrace. Her legs weakened from her astonishment, she began kissing down my body.

"Well I'll be damned," said Father, more curious than ever.

Mother went on, "And now mine, Josephus." She pulled out one more dress, another stunning wedding dress made from the best of the finds. Puffed sleeves would reach to the elbow. A train would lead only past the back of the dress, and it was adorned with a sash of satin roses that flowed down and back as part of the skirt.

Father recognized what it was – her wedding dress. He cried, hands half-covering his face. Then he rose, half dumping back the chair, and stumbled to Mother, embracing her, crying like a girl on her shoulder.

I picked up Chloe, and she gave me a hundred little kisses.

She laughed through her surprise, "I should have known. I should have known you two were up to something. I – I thought maybe you were pregnant again."

I explained, "Once we had the idea for Jack and Molly's wedding, there came this overwhelming need to complete what we hadn't completed – to observe a wedding for the sake of the vow."

Jack, still acting shunned by his forced confession, applauded. "Mother, you are a genius."

"It's okay Jack. If you'd like a dress for the ceremony we've got one that may fit?" I offered.

"No. I'll wear the suit. But don't get rid of the dress," he finally chuckled.

I blurted my prevailing postulate out into the open, "Could we all be the unwitting divisions of the same soul, or at least girls?"

Father had kept with the conversation, replying, "Perhaps after today, we shouldn't be so unwitting about it."

SIXTEEN

The Weddings

With extra food thrown to the pig pens, the goats moved to a new meadow, and automated feeders filled for the chickens, we prepared ahead for a wedding dinner. Thanks to having freezers, I got Mother to recall the idea of partly baked bread, ready to finish browning after thawing. We had apple pie and salads in the refrigerator, and Father had brought in a special batch of brandy, three small bottles, to share for the occasion.

"I take it our souls up there don't have the propensity to imbibe. We just never have had a problem with liquor," he said. "Not that I haven't used a bit medicinally here and there."

I responded, "Not this lifetime for me. We just never made it a habit beyond being, as you say, medicinal." We were both dressed up like the mansion's kitchen staff, donning the double-breasted jackets, apron and toque. I was breaking up and chopping nuts for a fruit salad. He was handling a sizable pork roast, getting it ready to marinade.

"Marinating only?" I queried.

"No – this is a quick dip to clean it – then I'll smoke it whole. You didn't see the smoker?"

"Oh – I do. I missed the obvious again," I said peering out the back window to see the lofting smoke.

"Yeah. I hate to fix this large of a roast at once. We've more than trebled the stock this year, but I think we're getting the wind knocked out of us in keeping up."

"We're doing fine, Daddy. Bigger gardens also mean extra for the animals," I said as I took a taste of some walnuts.

"Give me some of those," he said. I didn't let him take them, I fed him from my fingers, so he wouldn't get raw pork in his mouth. "Why don't you shell more of those – like the bushel?"

"Not economical. We've got too much else to do. I'll shell what we need for the wedding salads – and what I can eat."

"And I can pilfer," he added.

Chloe rolled a cart through the hallway with an old wind-up Victrola, claiming she'd found the perfect wedding music both for the ceremony and for dancing afterward. Molly followed with two more flat recording disks, adding them to the dance pile. "We've worked on this for days," said the newly pleasant little girl in common clothing.

Jack came through with a few more disks, claiming he had his favorite for a dance with Molly. His clothing caught my eye – he wore boy's jeans and boots acceptable for chores, but he wore a yellow camisole and a pink jacket, being open in front. I just noted it. He looked back at me without comment, then went on out into the yard, running like any child. At the backside of the covered breezeway that led between the mansion and the east house was a veranda we'd used little, being circular not unlike a gazebo. Jack said he was going to clean it up for use with the wedding. It would be a great spot for any little wedding, being surrounded by shrubs that he'd severely cut back over the last few years, perhaps premeditating this series of events.

The fall air portended a cool, dry week, consistent with the previous years, though an occasional fall sea storm could befall the area. So, we had an alternate location, using the grand staircase of the main entry, which we'd adorned with ribbons. It would at least serve as a staging area for the setup. In the open area under the great dusty chandelier, we placed a number of garden chairs, all white wooden frames, and placed into each a piece of clothing to resemble the friends and relatives that couldn't be there, each having an affixed name tag. I'd placed dresses for my past-life friends and acquaintances, Tori, Seria, and Debbie, as well as Sandy, her little sister Charlotte, my mother, and even our housekeeper Xiu Mei Lum, for all the right things she did as my nanny. I placed more dresses for my little embalmed girls and some for those people I'd only partially known. I placed one for the young mother from the house I'd claimed, where I'd found the photograph of myself from my previous lifetime, and put a suit for her husband, and a beautiful satin and lace dress for their baby. I placed suits out for Father, Vincent, Charles, Jeffrey, Chow and a number of others, even the dead boy I'd smacked during my breakdown after the event. I found a profound moment with the suit I called my past-life father, embracing the suit, telling him that I missed him, hoping that I'd discover the soul of his origin when I'd attain my own spiritual authenticity with the child-soul I could most accurately refer to as "the little girl at the pedestal."

Below and between the double staircases, the granite floor made the optimal location for a podium of sorts – I made a decision to place three white marble pedestals, taken from busts that rested quietly in the mansion's regularly spaced semicircular alcoves. At this triangle, we could ceremonially rotate through the vows, written independently by each of us, based on a rough template, stating only what a vow should – who we were and the vow itself. For an additional effect, we requested each vow to be written on some kind of paper that would be related to our identity and tied with something that denoted our commitment. I hoped to articulate my purest intent.

Mother potted plants that could survive the cooler weather despite our claims of indifference toward any kind of flora. Molly was known to like sunflowers, and I generally preferred roses, if only for consistency with the lost bustling world. The sunflowers were still in bloom. Roses were not going to be so easy. Mother had been nursing them in the atrium, but I ascertained that she'd have more luck training violets.

We each staked a claim on a suite to suit up, though it was clear that we would need help with zippers on dresses. I barely recalled anything about makeup – it was never a need nor expectation – perhaps just a little blush? I tried some aged silver-white sparkly nail polish, too gelled to get a clean coat, and it reflected with the likeness of electroplated metal. I couldn't accept it and removed it with acetone. I pondered whether we should have spent a little time finding out how to restore some nail polish while I set up my suite. I hung my dress on a baggage cart and set the accoutrements upon a dresser, including better fitting shoes. I had the sexy panties and garter that had accompanied the dress, and the pretty babydoll set from the house I'd said to mark "Miranda." Lastly, upon the dresser, I laid out the diamond and moonstone choker. The choker itself was simpler than one might design for a wedding, but these were first-water diamonds and collector quality moonstones, with the most admirable sheen. I pondered the vanity of such an item, and in essence, it didn't have a value any greater than all the busts we'd cast aside to bring in the needed pedestals.

As for the nail polish, I'd concluded that such an adornment would be a distraction and not flatter anyone. The choker was already a stretch for our post-civilization reality, and too many reminders could be distressing. To the myriad of wedding magazines we'd left in houses, and even to the few we returned to collect, our baseline attitude was "fluff and unnecessary." Some hours of our wedding day required chores for the sake of survival. Again, much like the cacophony of advertising, music, and entertainment, most pageantry and wealth was for naught.

So came the day we'd say our carefully worded vows. A strong southwesterly wind brought cool clouds over the decaying city, which alleviated the need to move the staged wedding items to the veranda. Having completed the necessary chores, including setting up extension cords to hotplates to heat water for our baths, we gathered in the lounge about noon, with no specific time assigned to the affair, drafting ourselves away from the normal day.

"Are we all ready?" asked Mother, poised at the back of a brown leather sofa, wearing a fall work dress that resembled a quilt.

I sat comfortably in an overused dress, layered from two original dresses for warmth. It had various stains, but the soft mellow flow of the banana-pineapple and country style had its utility. I piped up, "Sure – I am. I'd like to get into that dress you helped me with."

Chloe's eyes rose up, "Wouldn't we all – like to see you in that dress that Mother helped you with." She raised her eyebrows at me.

Molly sat cutely in one of the loveseats, her legs crossed. Jack was pensive nearby, sitting on the arm of the nearest sofa.

It was cooler weather – we didn't smell that bad, did we? I sniffed my armpits, not reeling from any disgusting odors.

"Well that's it then," said Father. "We'll go get cleaned up and dressed." He was in dark work clothing, so his coloration wouldn't significantly change, but he'd look professional for the first time. None of us were heavy – the last person I'd known that was heavy was Debbie. Oh, how I missed her now. She could have been a bridesmaid if our society would have allowed my past-life dream of marrying Tori.

I watched the group slowly disperse, each set of eyes carefully examining the rest as we walked out, ambling quietly through the east house, then on to the spacious hallways of the main mansion. I gave one last lip-biting smile to Chloe, and stepping up a stone staircase, I lost sight of her.

Into my chosen suite, I stepped across the threshold, recognizing each step as significant. Without the pressure of a crowd – the aunts and uncles, cousins, friends, acquaintances, organists and pianists, ministers, an audience and photographer – there was little pressure from the earthly realm. The pressure upon me regarded the souls above, the girl, her helper, the others at that level, at whatever altitude they existed. Was this ceremony a conduit of our deliverance or was this a divergence from the final goal of good?

I stripped off the comfortable dress and everything else. Using a full-scale bathtub that dwarfed any we had in the village,

I sponged myself down much like a sink bath, pulling water from the first of two overheated pots. I soaped up my hair and brushed it while it was slick with the freshening shampoo, and conveniently used the suds to wash more of my slippery skin. Then I poured the rapidly cooling pot of water through my hair, liking the warmth and sliding awkwardly on my tailbone about the smooth porcelain. I double-checked the pits and crevasses for perfect cleanliness, and rinsed again, the steaming water from the second pot inflicting a little pain. I toweled up, still smelling effeminate like the soap and shampoo, and started with the towels, drying my hair as well as I could, strand by strand.

The impetus for the wedding had started with Jack and Molly. But that wasn't my primary focus. I was stuck on Chloe, and all the variations of mates I could have had if the old world hadn't vanished. There was nothing in our present partnerships that would have been acceptable – Mother was yet Father's first daughter. Chloe and I were both girls and technically sisters, and Jack and Molly were severely underage, despite their obvious relation. The world would not have understood their reprieve from birth-related memory loss accompanying the transmigration of their souls. Except for those growing number of religious zealots, the entire world regarded reincarnation with incredulity, holding it at arm's length much as I had anything spiritual a few decades prior, when my home was still where the island gods left the impression of superficial advertising rather than longstanding knowledge.

Quite frankly, the rationalization for ideal genetic offspring was outmoded. This ceremony was about souls, not flesh. However, the end goal of marrying a young woman was too tantalizing to scrap. The thesis was that I could swear an oath to the girl I loved. The antithesis was that I would immorally break the rules, entrapments of not only our previous society, but possibly that of the beings that transcended this human existence. All the clues suggested Chloe and I were the same soul. Thus, the speculative synthesis was simply to love myself by loving Chloe.

The white bridal panties and garter rested on a dresser with my few accoutrements. I considered the reverse order of undressing, so I started by putting on the choker, then the panties, garter and a slip and thigh-high thick embroidered stockings, which I folded above the knee. To my awareness, I had the best of everything, though I knew that Mother had slinked aside with at least Jack or Molly on independent trips to smuggle distinctive elements for the occasion.

The vow – the utterance of willful statements of compatibility, accord, consensus, a pledge. Of what import had this to the girl at the pedestal? I looked over my silver notebook containing the words I'd fabricated to impart my deepest dreams and wishes. It was surprisingly few.

To get help with the dress I poked my head out the door. "Molly!" I called.

"I'll be a few minutes, Dahilana. Then you can help braid my hair!" she called back from another suite.

The stunning gown hung heavily upon the hook, so I came up under it, unhooking the hanger as I rose within. The weight settled upon my shoulders, having slid freely over the slip. The cool dress tried to warm up from my body heat. I looked into an old mirror, seeing the speckles of detached metal, which was imperfectly sputtered upon the hand-poured glass. We hadn't mastered chemical photography, so I could not capture this image representing a hand-colored Daguerreotype, as if the glass covering had been painted.

Molly, wearing just a slip, came quickly behind me. She climbed a chair to view much the same impression, gasping. "I'd marry you myself – if I could."

"Oh Molly, your hair looks terrible," was the first unreserved observation I had for her. I stepped back out of the weighty dress and let the hanger support it, stepping quickly to grasp brushes, clips and combs. I sat upon an armless giltwood chair and let her sit between my thighs. Leaning back, I pulled as gently as I could at her wet, dreadful, not quite dreadlocked hair. Starting from the bottom of the locks I wasted no time clarifying the strands, building up to a double Dutch braid. This was not the easiest, but her clear face would benefit most from the lower light-blonde braids flowing down to the sides of her childish neck. The precious child turned to the mirror, then turned to present her satisfied countenance. Telepathically, I clearly felt this soul's intent – to present me with a kiss. I grabbed her up and knelt before her, and the kiss, similar to what happened on the kitchen floor weeks before, didn't stop with a quick smack. She wiggled in my arms like a morning stretch while clutching at me. She finished off with a little bite to my lip. I speculated she did it to remind me of her love throughout the day, even through the evening, as I formally married my already-claimed wife, Chloe. I did not voice *we all become lovers*, but it was loudly present.

As I cogitated, I had not released her, her delicate ribs rising with gentle breath. "I'd marry you too," I offered.

"But I do love Jack. I came to marry him," she whispered with dropped eyes, then raised them with a smile.

I rubbed my nose against hers and we reached into another little kiss. "We'd all marry each other – perhaps our vows should say that."

Molly perfunctorily grabbed a brush and sat on the edge of the chair, having me squat to my knees and sit upon my feet. My hair wasn't tangled, and in moments she requested I lie back across the chair to let my hair dangle. I enjoyed her occasional kisses to my nose, eyes, forehead and even ears as she worked my hair into a configuration she didn't reveal. "I braided dummy heads – the kind they used to teach hairdressers. I ruined two wigs."

"I hope you can do it today," I mumbled up to the ornate tin ceiling.

"Okay. Sit up but lean back," she wanted.

I did so, my skin cool, desiring the dress for its warmth. Her little hands continued working the braids, then said, "Oops. Forgot something – be back." She handed me the end of the braid to hold it, then flittered out like a scared bird, but dashed back in just as quickly, concealing a small object in her hands.

"Hand it back – just a moment – there. Please now examine this work of art," she pleaded.

I stood, once again viewing my image in the old mirror. I hadn't realized she'd put in bejeweled French combs at the base of my hair braids, near the neck, and a small comb placed with clips at the bottom of the final braid. Did she know about the jeweled hat? All of it worked with the choker, and ultimately with the dress.

"Now the dress?" she asked me.

"Do you need more help from me?" I asked.

"No – Mother has another surprise," Molly smiled.

"Okay – my dress, then." I turned to get the dress, crawling up under it as I'd done earlier. To be silly, Molly crawled up under it with me.

"It's so big under here," she said, acting like the child she couldn't factually emulate, the child she appeared to be. I pulled up through the slender waist and fitted my arms. Molly dashed out from under to handle the zipper, and I moved to the chair once again for her to complete zipping my back.

I looked once again in the mirror – I looked as good as the west mansion family's older daughter as she had in her family photo or engagement photo. And despite being in my early thirties, my skin was smooth, my belly taut, and body fit. We did not endure privations, but hard work exercised us daily.

I watched Molly tear up, her hands to her mouth. "We should always look like princesses," she expressed. "I don't want to grow up." She hesitated, then asked, "Is there anything else you need, Dahilana?"

"No, my dearest little Molly."

She gaily flittered out as before. I only needed to step into my shoes. Nonetheless, for a special touch, I dabbed a little blush on my cheeks, and a smidgen of lipstick to add the slightest bit of color to my lips. Needless to say, the greasiness felt strange. The only addition that could have allowed my image to surpass that of the wealthy family's photograph from the west wing would have been to wear earrings. I would not be inclined to pierce my ears with a needle for that.

Standing again before the mirror, I prayed for approval from the heavens, whatever those beings were based on all those clues we'd collected. It couldn't have just been myself and Chloe that were somehow related. It had to relate to the whole family. This would be an important day for us all. I slipped on the shoes and traversed the cavernous hallways as if floating, gathering myself at the top of the west grand staircase. I was early. "Hello?" I called out. No human voices answered, nor those from above.

Others had followed my example with the suits and dresses, even shoes and hats, among the garden chairs, and at the back of the room, standing quiet guard were a few dozen busts on additional pedestals, also standing in for the audience, in total numbering some two hundred. Amused, I laughed at the semblance of these men and woman at the back as ushers. Upon the pedestals below were two small boxes on either side of two small scrolls of paper. I hadn't known about the boxes. I stepped carefully back to a settee in an adjacent hallway. I'd have to wait.

I'd heard "Ah!" echo down the hallway. It was Molly's voice. Mother was working with her now. Turning the other way, I saw an impression of my father, profoundly different than any image I'd seen in any day I'd gathered memories as Dahilana. I had that notion that I might be expanding beyond my skin – not dissimilar to experiences during moments of enlightenment from above, or during the meteor showers. Where was my nose? It was right there where it was supposed to be, slightly ahead of my presence. I wasn't in the sky yet. But to Father, noting the evenly trimmed hair and beard, I said, "You look beautiful."

"I thought you once wanted to be a writer – I believe the word is *handsome*," he suggested while patting an impressive tuxedo.

"Where did you get that?" I blurted, seeing he had upgraded our original design.

"Dress shop – wedding shop downtown. It was one of the last buildings not wiped out by the meteor that struck the bay. They were a little dusty." His eyes were fixed upon me.

"I would have wanted to see that, Daddy," I reprimanded.

"No, Dahilana," he caught his breath as his eyes looked me over, unable to look away if he'd tried. "If there was something there better for you, we'd have brought it back too. But there are more surprises."

I shook my head. I thought I'd been the master here. They'd taken control and surpassed my creativity.

"Here comes your love now," he said.

Faint swishing noises accompanied the clicking of dainty shoes. Flowing gracefully was a shapely angel coming to greet me – Chloe. Her hair was in rows of braids about her head. Her teenage body wore a dress I'd not been familiar with. As soon as she'd come within range of speech, she explained, "Mother and Father found this. I loved the work you and Mother did, but Mother allowed me to choose. The train and bustle were reduced to match more closely with your own gown. What do you think?"

I couldn't think. I wasn't sure if I could recall my vows. A crying noise found its way into the echoing grand entrance, reflecting back as if someone in the audience. That sound had come from me, but a displaced giggle followed up my throat. "For all the times you'd wanted to act the boy of the couple, I thought you'd wear a suit. For all the palaces in the world I could not have imagined you'd...." I couldn't get the words to form, having to take a few deep breaths. There was a prevalent idea of a hand on my neck to the right, and I knew no one was there. Someone was looking through my eyes, perhaps like a lucid dream – the little girl. With that recognition, I completed the sentence, "look so beautiful," as if she were saying it, barely recognizing the movement of my own flesh. I voiced, "You look so beautiful. I could desire to be you."

Chloe cocked her head, viewing me with amazement. "Did you see – you – you didn't look like you?"

"It was her, I believe," I belabored to say, unlike the ease of the previous syllables. "Look for her – use your eyes for her. She'll see through your eyes."

Chloe appeared stupefied, "Oh my God – you do look beautiful. Everything looks beautiful – oh. Oh! Thank you. I mean 'thank you' – said the girl."

Father looked on with amazement. "Uh – I saw – something. Must be the excitement of the day. But I almost forgot. I have a small matter to attend to. The platform – we chose against being blown with the winds – I need to bring the platform in for the youngsters." Daddy stepped up one of the hallways that led toward the veranda.

"What else is on the pedestals?" I asked of Chloe.

She smiled, shaking her head, her braid shifting along her back. "No," she only said. "Well, the vows we each wrapped. But no. You don't get to know the rest."

I rolled my eyes. She came to sit with me on the settee, and we held hands and waited.

Within a few more minutes, Jack came clicking upon the mezzanine above the entrance. Chloe and I snickered as children. Jack turned. It was within my memory that a child dressed in like manner would be a ring bearer or an usher. "Are you going to lead us to our seats, young man?" I said with a fake affluent accent.

"How does it look?" he asked, unknowing of my reference, which didn't appear to compute for him. "Dahilana," he said resiliently, "How do I look, ma'am?"

I supposed he'd caught on a little. "You look fine, sir," I replied. Again, Mother had supplanted our previous plan with an elegant tuxedo.

His shoes glistened like black onyx, and he spun on his heal. "I do recall weddings – only went to a few, with parents, back on my earth."

"Your earth?" I nodded as I caught the phrase. "Didn't your planet have a name?"

"I contemplated the variation in planet names and their meaning. Eventually, I realized that it is simply a translation of a good place to live and grow under the sun – much the same as Earth anyway. I could use the old name – doesn't matter as long as I have my memory of it," he confidently placed his hands across his chest and relaxed to hold them loosely crossed.

"Have you got your vows written?" Chloe asked him.

"Of course – down there on the scroll," he shook his head in the direction of the entry.

"Anything to relate about them?" asked Chloe.

"No," he shook his head, his eyes looking a tad sly. He looked quite comfortable in the small tuxedo.

I heard more swishing with short steps. I hoped to see Molly, and in moments, the delicate child walked sheepishly into view. If Chloe had been an angel, Molly was a little goddess. It was as if the girl at the pedestal had entered the room, dressed for a ball in the whitest dress, perhaps ready to marry us all. Her beautiful hair was now adorned with ribbons and individual pearls, though probably on a hidden strand or clipped in with bobby pins. The dress was a combination of the elegant dress we'd found, having the high neck, shoulders and narrowly puffed sleeves, but the skirting was doubled while it kept the lace overlay. A highly puffed bustle laid out in a train that graced the floor.

Jack's face blushed, turned red, and his arms rose to his tear-covered face. "I tried to cry it out before we got here." Was it that he wanted to wear a dress after all, even though he'd agreed to wear something masculine?

"Perhaps I should have worn the suit," said Chloe to balance the thoughts. "We should have worn what we wanted to."

"You didn't want the dress?" I turned to her, half surprised.

Chloe grabbed my arm to quiet me, using her eyes to refer to the crying boy.

I whispered to her, "We have no world to distaste a boy in a dress. I have a beautifully fashioned dress set aside if it comes to that."

"Oh – I do too," she whispered back. She worriedly cocked her head, adding, "We'll see."

But in another moment, Jack bowed to his little lady. It was so precious, the little man appearing to ask a girl to dance at a formal ball, mimicking a veritable training session for the young of a court.

"Oh – Father's getting a platform. He'd dressed. We're just waiting for Mother," Chloe thoughtfully threw out to the youngsters, lest they become completely mesmerized. "Um – I'll start a recording." She rose awkwardly to her feet, then skated across the floor with finesse. The little couple drew from the hallway to a grand meeting room just back of the mezzanine and practiced their dancing, eyes gazing fiercely into each other.

I realized that I was almost behaving like the old Dahilana – on the edge of crying every moment. I feared I'd cry through the whole ceremony. Was a wedding reminiscent of a loss – perhaps some loss in previous lifetimes? I attempted to get my thoughts off of it lest I get embroiled into images of such things, likely to be eidetic enough to displace the present, and even then, looking at these children, I saw vestiges redolent of past horrors, like the past life events I ran through when I was pregnant with Jack. There were still confessions from many past existences I could still take responsibility for.

I stood, having heard noises from below. Approaching the thick brass-lined banister, I looked over the edge to see Mother pulling in potted rose plants. "I didn't know the winds would sustain. I had these in another atrium. Blooming well considering they thought it was still summer." Father was with her, rolling a modest rectangular platform in front of Jack and Molly's pedestal. He put the furniture mover aside, and said, "Frankly I've got to pee again. Is everyone about ready?"

"I believe so. The audience certainly is," she said, referring to the suits and dresses with name tags.

Father disappeared for a moment, and I examined Mother's hair, having a waterfall braid of smaller loose braids interlaced with ribbon and lace. Molly had done this one – she was quite the expert.

Music entered the room, a flowing piano piece replaying with tinny overtones. Chloe had chosen well. I was compelled to take my place at the mezzanine, moving aside only a handful of steps. Mother and Father walked formally up each of the east and west stairways, pausing near the top.

"Jack, Molly," I called gently, allowing them to arrive top and center on the mezzanine.

I heard something sliding below. Chloe was positioning a few potted sunflowers as Molly had requested. "Is everything else ready?" she called up.

"Yes," said Mother. "Come into position."

"Okay," she said, then changed out the recording to play a tune I could only have described as a fully orchestrated soft baroque march.

The oddity occurred to me that the last six people known to us on the planet were staging a triple wedding. What were the odds? Again, "not odds, a plan" struck me from within.

Moments after Chloe positioned herself opposite me near the top of the stairway, Mother and Father paced their steps to promenade toward the entrance doors and come forward between the chairs. As they approached the front of the group, Chloe and I did the same long walk, stopping about the middle of the row, wishing to watch Jack and Molly splitting to separate sides, revivifying the concept of soul division, and then meeting up the aisle, signifying the roads we'd taken through the galaxies and planets, to the front of the room, where stood the pedestals, which represented our potential recombination. The children followed through, and we all took our places at our pedestals. In a minute, the music had completed, and the record-player machine placed itself into a suspended state.

Pensive, I paused and held Chloe's hand, partly for love, partly for stability. I had to remember to breathe. She squeezed my hand, pulling at her lips, her expression mixed with joy and sadness.

Mother reached for the small linen scroll ahead of her. Untying the multiple strands of vines and lace that kept it coiled, she said, "The linen is for the clothing, and thus the protection and fabric of life I provide, the lace and vines represent the elements of life that sustain me – one lace for each of you, and vines for my contribution to the gardens." She unrolled it and kept her composure with her clear utterances:

"By cosmic election, I have been brought to stand with a man I once thought only to be my loving father. But in a transformed world, this man has clearly demonstrated devotion, ensconced us into the best home available, performed the necessary actions of life with the voracity of an entrepreneur, and loved endlessly. He's been the perfect match to my imperfect heart, the best complement of industriousness, and an unrelenting champion of our enlightenment. Clearly, those above have planned for our pairing, a fate I cannot dismiss. It is he that I had chosen to be with – had been chosen to be with – even having a succinct premonition as a younger child, when I myself was proportioned as the known child spirit above us. I stand at this pedestal as a representation of my own forbearing desire to remain with him, with this family, until we ascend to those above us. I, Avelynn, vow my eternity with you, Josephus."

Tears trickled down every cheek as she finished. Father carefully undid the ribbon, a blue bookmark, about his goatskin scroll. He picked it up, cleared his husky voice, and first informed, "The goatskin – I suppose in a sense I'm a herder, raising the animals, and the ribbon is from a *Machinery's Handbook, 19th Edition*, because I keep everything else working, including keeping the lot of you studying." He slid off the ribbon and unrolled the smoothed skin, and getting serious, formed a few foul consonants, but having induced control of his vocal cords, expressed the words he'd carefully written:

"I was neither an eloquent nor educated man, a weary failure except for the desire for hard work. I was the ultimate in oxymorons – resilient but nefarious; warm but capricious; devoted but devious. I found a loving wife who was not meant to remain with me. And in the essence of being delivered into a horrifying world, found truth and love with the girl I'd previously birthed. I heard the voices instilling the necessity to enjoin with my precious girl, and – and was told with audible and distinct words – I shall marry this girl for her spirit, for her soul. They know – they are here, watching from above if not in this room, my vow I'd already deeply instilled within my heart, to you, Avelynn to remain with you to the end of time."

They kissed, but the little boxes remained on the pedestal. They held hands and nodded toward Chloe and me. I had thought the vow I had written was stunning. I wasn't sure whether I'd been outdone with these acutely designed words.

Though I had reached for the pedestal, Chloe also reached, and nodded, asserting that she wanted to read first. She undid a little tag of burlap and rolled her little scroll of roughed watercolor paper open. "I'd drawn a little picture on watercolor paper reused from previous hands, just as I thrive on reusing and rebuilding our world, and the burlap is to show my commitment to simplicity and pragmatism, taking what is before us and reusing or restoring it." Then, turning toward me so I could not read it from her hands, she read beautifully written words from her little scroll:

"I have never in the expanse of the universe been so loved, so cherished and adored. I was shunned in many existences, not often finding a place in the hearts nor souls of the societies I'd lived with. A stray dog, a shameful villain, a detestable friend, a hedonistic degenerate – these were the roles I'd been condemned to act. But I vow to the best of my ability from these demigod's point of view, to assail my heinous intentions for the benefit of all, at every plateau in every corner of this universe. Having been granted by their intention a lift from the echelons of hell, I vow myself, a soul with a greater purpose, to love and cherish Dahilana by that or any other name, and pursue the dream for enlightenment for eternity, even beyond it to the absence of time and space alike, beyond this universe and to others." She'd memorized most of it, holding it for the formality.

My eyes glazed with additional tears as she had read. I'd felt her words beyond the speech. Her love reached right into me, as if her hands were not on the paper, but were in my chest, beating my very heart. I was certain I would only babel had I tried to speak.

If I had entered a contest with my vow, I feared at that point I had just been bested. I was blown away. Pure and direct to beyond the end of time. My arms barely functioned. I grabbed forward to steady myself against her, my partner in love and enlightenment, my support in everyday actions. I needed a tad bit of help lest I teetered over. I wanted to see the faces of the others but couldn't break my gaze from the stunning beauty before me. Was I worthy of this? Would the universe allow this to continue? Would I be condemned to serve some penance for this aesthetic, which was too high, too voluminous, and would it balance back and knock me down in whatever manner? Overcome, I considered withdrawing from the pedestal and crying apologetically, begging for forgiveness from the very souls that had created us, when I again experienced the touch of a hand on my shoulder, by my neck. As if someone was stroking my back, I regained my composure and reached ahead for my vow, bound with a grapevine. I stumbled through my explanation of the elegant stationery with my best calligraphy. "The common stationery represents the way I bring together everyone and truth, even finding the *Ascension* books, and though I can only take partial credit for understanding the contents, pushing for the gains in knowledge, hopefully toward the ultimate. It's because the actions are ordinary to me and are so much a part of me. The grape vine is my intertwining commitment to life itself, despite … everything." I took a few deep breaths as grief shuddered my lungs. Chloe held my elbow to add confidence and control. I blinked, then wiped my spilling tears, then read slowly:

"I followed a wretched sea of obsession and secret malevolent acts, only turning course as the souls above revivified their existence, initiating the revivification of my own. Guided by grace, I gratefully accepted membership into the family as the first child, and inherently knew the next child would become mine. Despite the interference of the deities above, I stand willful, impelled by my deepest impulses and most salient of dreams, before the one I love. Having diverged from the girl at the pedestal, I vow myself as your partner, to toil to the end of the universe to reverse the parturition that was our genesis and follow that compass until the ultimate expression of love can be manifested, to be *one*, whether that includes only us, extends to the family, or thousands more, to the closure of the comprised firmament. I, formerly known under many names, then as Miranda and now Dahilana and perhaps later by another assignment, extend my vow of love from the current to the highest horizon, to you Chloe, and to all the family."

Chloe nodded, her gaze fixed within mine. We embraced, again as much for stability as for love, holding for minutes without being rushed.

"Molly?" requested Mother, barely more than a whisper.

Oddly, I felt a pat on my back, but Chloe's arms had been about my waist.

Molly's little hand reached forward to the pedestal, which, having been up on the platform, wasn't any higher to her than ours had been. She picked up her little scroll, written on a crisp sheet of parchment, wrapped with a strap of cracked old leather, which had been glued against a piece of delicate antique lace. "The paper is the best of things – I am suddenly a 'best of' and that is my new identity. The old flaking leather and lace is my need to be rough, but I couldn't be more perfect being a girl, expressing my desire for the qualities of existence." She undid the little scroll and poised to read:

"I, Molly, came from another world affected by a series of ascension events, and like so many lifetimes before that, I wasn't a good person. I'd taken my roles of the living play as handed down by the universe souls that existed before we'd lost full awareness and later could not change our roles. I now know, with all of your knowledge and Jack's persistent help, this was not the first time I'd taken a bullet for my obstinacy and deviance, hate and backstabbing." She stopped to smile, giving me a pleasant look, hopping on her toes and mouthing *thank you*. She turned back to the parchment and continued, "I therefore again dedicate my existence to those of you, as I'd been given a final chance at living by the favor of those greater souls. And I dedicate and vow myself, of any name, in any body, and any gender, to Jack, by any name, in any body, in any gender, from here until ascension takes us up, independent of how many days, years, decades, lifetimes, planets that may be."

I watched Jack's head nodding gently as she read easily. It was evidence beyond any doubt that this was a fully educable and aware soul, not just a precocious seven-year-old child. *There were no children here* – not myself, not Chloe, not Jack nor Molly. We were ageless souls in growing, changing, aging bodies.

Jack's turn was slowed by his tearful response to her vow. He turned to kiss her on the forehead before turning to his little scroll. He unwrapped a twine that held a warped and scorched feather against the little roll of machinists drafting paper. "I'm a machinist, so, the drafting paper, and the feather for our spiritual flight, assisted with the real elements of life that twine us all together." He stalled a moment as he untied the twine, then held up his words to read. He turned to face Molly, and much like Father, stumbled on his speech.

An unexpected breeze crossed my face. I squeezed Chloe's hand again, and she squeezed back. I turned to her for a momentary kiss, then put my eyes and attention on Jack. We patiently permitted him to gather his momentum, and he spoke:

"I am the phoenix from the ashes of my previous home, and this family has been the crucible for my resurrection. All was lost there as the universe closes to our final destination, a course through which I'd only wish to be with Molly and this family. By the determination of those souls of our origin, we play out our final acts as demanded, but it is well within my volition to follow this course, taking this stage and acting out their wishes for us. I, to you known as Jack, take the course of my premonitions as ordered by the gods, to vow myself and everything in my essence or body, to the girl who was brought here to me, the one I'd most want to be, the source of my frustrations as much as my fulfillment. Molly, I vow myself to be yours forever, to have you as my wife, to devote myself to our conjoined spirit."

Molly nodded, then reached up. Jack knelt and embraced her as her tears turned to sobs.

Mother and Father nodded. New tears trickled down Mother's light cheeks. Father appeared bright in a new way, as if glowing.

Chloe tugged at me, "Time for the boxes." She put a small box in my hand, nodding to have me open it.

I took the small wooden box and opened it at its hinge. A box by this likeness would have held a small specialized tool. But what I found inside was a traditional wedding ring. I couldn't have been more amazed to find a modest diamond surrounded by an infinity symbol and engraved on either side with "Dahilana" and "Chloe."

"I thought present life names were best," she said. She took the ring and fitted it to my ring finger.

"Perfect," I whispered.

She took the next box and opened it, handing me a similar ring, sized perfectly to her finger, which I'd discovered as I placed it on her hand.

Mother and Father did likewise, then kissed the rings, then each other.

Molly and Jack followed suit, but in their boxes were multiple rings, allowing for their growth. "Take the smallest one," suggested Jack. He must have known – perhaps he'd engraved the rings. I watched them kiss the rings and each other.

With that, Chloe and I also kissed the rings and each other again, and with smiles, we all had a few more kisses. As I pulled my head back from Chloe, my presence remained forward. I saw her skin and eyes with greater detail than I'd ever seen before. So stunning, I thought that the lighting had changed, perhaps the sun's angle had allowed yellow rays to bring the room awash with airy light.

It had become sunny, though the wind continued to blow outside. A second breeze passed me as the colors elsewhere in the room glowed as if lit from within. I looked at Chloe's hands. They too were glowing. The area between all the pedestals unleashed a prevalent fog. I couldn't imagine where this fog would come from, but instead of dispersing, the fog coalesced into an image, though quite faint at first expression, it waxed into a recognizable and definable holograph. The *girl* stood between the three pedestals.

I blinked in disbelief.

Chloe tugged at me, letting out a breath.

Molly gasped with wide mouth.

Jack stooped forward.

Father wiped his eyes.

Mother's head tilted as she gazed into the apparition as the girl walked up to her, took her hands, and kissed them. The girl reached up further, requesting Mother to lean down. It was apparently a kiss. Then to Father she did the same, providing the kiss and leaving him wide-eyed. She flowed across the floor, never specifically giving any indication that she touched it, toward Chloe and myself. I'd felt a tug in my heart – a *thump* much like the rest, with a need to drop closer to the floor. The girl, long blonde tendrils flowing over a white dress, came toward me. She paused, motioning to the dress as if requesting an acknowledgment that her clothing was appropriate. I was compelled to nod. She flowed directly to me, took my hand in a manner I could feel. I attempted to place her temperature but couldn't ascertain whether it was very hot or very cold. I noted her face, so stunning a permanent beauty, raising up toward me, and much like Molly just a while ago, I felt within me her desire to kiss. The apparition pushed forward, providing an image of a kiss that barely had any substance, but in the process it solidified like any other kiss, bending my lips with careful and gentle pressure. I'd even felt a tad aroused, not by her appearance, but by the way her intention reached completely into my body from head to toe. She put into me a thought that I was closer to perfection than I realized, often shutting myself down from my capability, and that we were not that far from the goal – years away – but within reach.

Chloe had knelt, awestruck while holding the little paper containing her vow. The girl took it and rolled it back up, putting it firmly into Chloe's hands and folding them. She didn't directly speak to her either, but an effusive approval crossed into my mind. She reached to Chloe in the same manner, wishing for a kiss. Chloe leaned into it, savoring the heavenly moment.

The girl flowed from Chloe toward Jack and Molly, floating above the stone to the level of the platform.

"Kneel, Jack," I hinted. "She's not quite as tall as you."

Jack dropped to one knee. The ethereal, eternal child went to him, smiled and nodded, looking at the dress Molly wore and looking back to him. "I see," he affirmed. I didn't catch that personal thought. But Molly also smiled, so I guessed she had. The girl touched Jack's cheek and pulled him into a gentle kiss.

Then Molly was specifically graced with her presence. Even Molly was taller than this spirit girl by a centimeter. The girl reached to her face. There was a kiss, and it was longer than I'd expected. As the beautiful impression of the smaller girl withdrew, Molly licked at her lip, having gotten a little bite much like Molly had given me earlier. I licked my lip in the spot I'd been nipped and verified the little defect. Molly then put her hand to her mouth, smiling through her surprise.

This beautiful apparition, this child from some highest echelon of the universe, centered herself in the room, speaking that familiar little girl voice, "I also vow to all of you, that your vows will not decay like the materials of galaxies, and will have my full intention to remain in force for the duration of this universe, at least until you all recombine with me, when we are one."

On the word *one* she looked at me, acknowledging the word had significance to her. But she also looked on around to Chloe, Mother, Father, Jack and Molly, who remained mesmerized by her beauty and spirituality.

"We're *all* one," whispered Jack.

"Oh my God!" blurted Molly.

"What? Behold that!" stumbled Father. He looked down and steadied himself against the pedestal. It was a good thing these were real stone and not cheap stage props. He brought his amazed countenance up again, not wanting to miss the heavenly view.

Mother simply nodded, tears suddenly running. Head down slightly, she looked back and forth at us all.

The girl said one more sentence, "Continue your work." Then the most beautiful apparition spun to view us all and faded back into a fog, which dispersed into the air like smoke from a quenched fire.

I was elated but had never expected this spiritual progenitor of mine and Chloe's to also admit to being the genesis of us all. I wish someone had means to capture a photograph to catch my overblown amazement.

Father enthusiastically said, "That image – that reach she had into me. It's intimate – it's just part of her energy. It's not icky and immoral. It's – it's outside of my words to describe it. It's just a presence of her vibration – a truth about her."

"I felt it too," I offered. "And she smelled like vanilla – one of my favorite scents."

Chloe said, "She was like being encompassed by roses – and yet they didn't smell like I'd expect roses. Flowery, maybe, but still much like vanilla as you say. She simply said she was glad she brought me here – it's important to be together."

Mother had her hands to her chest. "Is that real? You are all talking about her – that confirms she's real. Vanilla. Yes – vanilla and wow – how she reached into my – everything. The sense of love for us all, and as a Mother, consumed me completely as if I were the child. I would have to agree with intimacy – a longing to be like us as much as we have a longing to be like her."

Jack bit his lip. Everyone had turned to him, containing a statement he wasn't so quick to say. But he knew we would ask, so he dumped it. "I – can be anyone – as a – not sure the words – a person, soul, *identity* she'd created – I am more like her than the body I *wear*. I can wear whatever I like."

We all smiled, letting Jack resolve himself.

"Molly? Anything?" asked Father, turning his attention to her.

"She would marry me if she could? But she did by also being Jack." Then expressively lifting to her toes, she threw out, "And like vanilla. I so love vanilla."

"Dahilana – you mentioned feeling – concept?" asked Father.

My message was more scholarly. "I think it's important – that we are closer to the goal than we might think. We're years away – not eons," I said cautiously. "I'm not really certain the correlation of her years to ours. Anyway, I think that's the best way to convey the thought."

Gathered at the pedestals having virtually lost our mental functions, we gazed at each other and giggled and made further expressions of the wondrous images, still correlating our perception and comprehension for confirmation of the reality we'd had numerous glimpses of, but never so blatant. While containing this serum of joy, I pulled myself from my position, putting my body in between the pedestals, with the hope I could feel residual sensation of her presence, perhaps a clue to finding her again. My arms and legs moving about, I felt nothing but the same air I'd felt in any other position in the room. Yet I danced about in childlike steps, considering the possibilities. Mother came up to dance with me. Chloe stepped away to start another song on the Victrola. Daddy came into the mix. Jack and Molly stepped back off the platform to join us, and we opened up the space to let them have the center. Glee and smiles, I don't think we'd ever had so elated a moment. It was beyond silly, well into flamboyance, flippancy and improvisation, because no one had ever made it mandatory to have to learn to dance.

Until I was about exhausted from the frivolity, finding the need to replenish my body's fuel, I danced with everyone in the family. I danced with Molly while she was at the edge of the platform for a slow dance, also provided by the musical selections. I had kissed about Jack and offered to change his name to something girlish. His response, "I've had stranger names as a girl in previous incarnations. The name doesn't matter."

"How about Phoebe, which is generic, or even Phoenix?" I had asked.

"Um – I'll have to think about those. They do ring better than Jack," he said, settling his head on my shoulder. In the warmth, he added a poignant statement, "With these vows, with her presence, I think everyone just married everyone."

"I'd have to agree. Here's our kiss." I planted a kiss worthy of any wedding right on his lips. It didn't feel as awkward as a normal world would have deemed. It didn't feel awkward in the least. Molly and Chloe were dancing on the other side of the platform. Chloe saw me and mimicked my actions with Molly.

Then we switched partners. Molly came to me. "Dahilana," she said. "I'm marrying you too." Her eyes stated the rest, and the sensation of her intention bled through the air into my heart. Love. The purest love, equipoised with that of Chloe, as strong as what I'd flourished upon from the apparition that came presently today. I brought her near me, grabbling at her much as she had when she got her big realization that we hadn't been the group that shot and killed her. She giggled, understanding my reference to that wonderful moment. I kissed at this beautiful child, the closest to the likeness of the spiritual girl since my body had aged to be incongruous, experiencing a depth of emotion I could only describe as transcendent beyond the sensation of love that a universe could contain.

Then when Chloe came over to me, I noted the same equipoised or unweighted sense of love beyond the physical confines of any cosmos.

I spun above my head, exhilarated by the love I had for these girls, but also Jack, Mother and Father. To believe we were all the same soul was already a far-fetched concept, but to have found out succinctly plotted a new future – this meant that once she solved the problem of soul division, we would all be consumed into her – and no one would be left behind.

On the thought "no one would be left behind" I cried in a strange way. It wasn't my body crying. I was crushed with grief while perceiving from over my head. This grief was too strong for the body, but I could handle it while I expanded beyond it. It cried, that was for sure, and Chloe held me, and she also looked about, sensing for something ethereal. "I swore I saw it cloud up – but it's still sunny, and windy," she pondered aloud. I nodded my head upon her shoulder.

The song had ended, but Chloe kept ahold of me. Mother and Father stood aside, perhaps feeling the breadth of emotion through the air. Father was saying, "I feel like we'd been washed over by her wave." Mother elbowed him, holding a concerned expression in my direction.

There's one little problem when you go up in emotion – sometimes the emotional storms that were bigger than you, to the scale that they could not have been handled before, snap into view when least expected, and make every attempt to slam you back to a false semblance of normal, but normal can be at a state far above what one has become accustomed to. I stepped up that day, finding a new echelon of existence for myself, having handled a hellish piece of me, the larger part of the loss of the first ascension event that left us as stranded souls on a planet of corpses. Like having legs too short to reach the surface, I floated above my head and my body slipped to the floor at least twice by having been out of synch with it. I knew resynchronization would come again with practice, as with any physical endeavor.

Mother and Father went on to handle the meal, a large pot of slow-cooking pork probably ready in the east house's kitchen.

For a group of people so stricken with the loss of a world's population, surviving on our own, we behaved as if oblivious to the decay about us. Chloe and I dashed to our room to change into normal clothing, though the yellow spring dress I picked for the dinner could also have been described as fit for a princess, it was much lighter with only a single layer of fabric, so I wore two long slips underneath to keep warm. I put on a white cashmere cardigan sweater to complete the look and to add to the warmth.

With my help Chloe undressed and donned an affluent dress suitable for a father-daughter dance, but simple across the front, having a white belt with embroidered vines and flowers. She would have looked pretty in a burlap sack dress. She was my angel in the light lime green dress that accentuated her slender form. She kept the white stockings she'd worn with the wedding dress and pretty things she kept hidden from me under her slip. For the most part, I believe we were too elated to speak. All she said was, "I feel girly today," with the brightest and most extroverted smile I'd ever seen from her outside of a breakthrough in session.

Once back in the kitchen we each had our priority. I helped set out my expected portions of the dinner. Father worked the meat, Mother warming the ready-made pies and two small loaves of bread, Jack serving an apple and berry salad, I tossed up a garden salad and late vegetables, and finally, Chloe served up fresh apple and pear juice, the milk and the white butter.

Molly said she had a surprise, but we couldn't have it until after dinner. "I had to study and practice a lot. I hope you like it."

We assembled the wedding dinner on the table, serving on the finest china we could find throughout the mansion. As we found our chairs, I threw in, "I was impressed with everyone's choice of scrolls and ties. And the vows – I'd thought I had you all, not that there were any prizes. I felt bested – especially by you, Chloe." Clinking of silver against fine porcelain filled the area.

"No – I felt I was upstaged by yours," Chloe said.

Looking at all of them I complimented, "Well I was impressed to the core of my being with all your words."

"That's right – we're not just children, are we?" said Molly.

"We are," said Father, shifting his shoulder to refer to Mother. "Our bodies just don't match. We're all little girls – every one of us."

Of course, we laughed – we laughed to tears, but haughtily returned to avid consumption. I was certainly the glutton as if I'd been deprived of sustenance for days, savoring every bite.

Jack, wearing a soft girlish peach sweater but boy slacks and black shoes, said, "Okay. I'm just going to do this." Being flippant, he got up and left. I heard the clomping shoes through the hallways, then a door banged. With charades, we attempted to express what he was after. I think it was Father that moved his hands in the shape of a dress' bodice and skirt first. We all followed. We waited quietly, even holding up the meal.

In a few minutes, there was a soft knock at the doorway.

"Come in," I instinctively said, taking words rarely used this lifetime.

Pretty pink gloves edged around the door frame, and then stepping in soft pink flats, a girlish image with Jacks face came through the door. He wore pretty pink stockings that came up to the calf, and a pink long-sleeved dress suitable for early spring or this moderate fall. In his hair he'd stuffed in two French combs, each with a row of pearls, to pull it to either side. He looked down slightly but presented himself boldly. He pushed his true personality forward. I gasped as I saw the patent image – beyond the boy body – I saw the true girl soul in front of it. Quite frankly, it didn't appear much different than the girl that visited today, adding green flecks to his eyes. We were all divided from the girl, but we were not identical – we had been given unique characteristics.

"Oh!" said Father. "I saw – I saw it – I saw the girl. I really did."

"Wow!" said Chloe in her characteristic terse style.

Molly piped up. "I picked the dress out for him – for her. I've known Jack's true form – we've known this from our sessions. But that – just now – that was really clear, Jack. I saw the real you."

Without further presentation, Jack stepped lightly toward his seat, the pink flats tapping lightly against the floor. He picked up a linen napkin and tucked it over the breast of the dress.

"Quite flattering, Jack," noted Mother.

"Did you wear the bra I picked out?" asked Molly.

"No. I couldn't get it on that fast. I wore the slip. I doubt the little girl up there needs a bra either," he phrased shyly.

"I like it when you wear the bra," Molly confessed.

Giggles went 'round the table. I couldn't hold myself back. I got up and went to Jack at his chair. I raised his glass to first give him a drink. "Phoebe – Phoenix – Jack, I love you to the end of the universe." I gave him a strong kiss.

Chloe followed lockstep behind me, and Mother got into the train. Even Father gave him a kiss like a girl, saying, "It looks like kisses are the fad today." Molly lingered with her kiss the longest, pulling up to straddle him. Her pretty pink dress flowed with his, making them appear as conjoined twins.

Extending beyond Jack, a shadow, a pall, spun into the room. But in his elation, he saw what it was. Like my recognition of my grief earlier, he had a comparable experience. His face rose up, eyes toward the ceiling, expressing, "Oh my god – I see everything." The thick air drenched my head with past life experience – not mine but his. I saw the buildings burning. I saw the world he lived in – there had been a series of ascension events as had Molly's planet. The great mystery wasn't ever solved for him, as he had jumped off the building while it was consumed with fire. It wasn't the suicide he was releasing the grief for, but the loss of society.

My skin chilled, my heart fluttered. I didn't strictly see the room. I saw his images. I believe everyone did for at least several seconds.

I gently filled in, "That's what happened to me – I got bigger than the loss. I got able enough to handle the grief."

Jack nodded, catching his breath. "Oh – that was – that was big. We'd hit some tough ones – that was big!" Panting, he looked around at everyone, then looked himself over. Molly remained bent over his chest. She too heaved with sobs.

"Be bigger than it, baby," I said to her. "Handle all the grief."

Her hands clasped at Jack's shoulders, her head rose up. Her own images flashed about through our minds – the first wave of deaths on her planet threw everyone into a great confusion, crime and order swapping ranks. Quickly declaring martial law, people were put to work handling the bodies. Accusations flew, and governments went to war with the remaining populace. Molly flaunted all the new and the old rules, manipulating people with anything she could, including sex. Another wave of bodies dropped, and the cities were evacuated. With each wave evidencing more predestination for the chosen, those left behind had determined they would not be salvaged. Transferred by the last of the military to a rural town, she found herself unable to reform. Then came the bullet.

Years prior, I had pondered the grief at funerals for the ones who most loved the deceased, and I had pondered the grief of the deceased, having lost all their friends and family. But that was with the supposition that the general population remained alive. My own death as Miranda happened after the event. My deepest loss had been when the population died – not when I died. It was likewise for Molly and the apparent extinctions that took her society.

I could see that Molly's emotions, with a little willpower of her own, found a level state. She left Jack with a quick kiss and tumbled aside, then rushed up the hallway, her dainty shoes clicking, the sound turning to echoes.

Chloe turned to me and smiled. "Big day! Anyone else?"

A sound came up the hallway, like wheels, one of them wiggling. "Damn wheel!" said Molly as she rounded the corner. A stainless-steel chef's cart with poles on the corners and a sheet over it came through the door. Her cheeks still pink from grief, her face beamed, "It may have been my wedding in the first place and someone else should have – but I made the cake." She pulled the cart adjacent to her chair, and standing upon the chair, she pulled off the light sheet, revealing a modest three-tiered wedding cake, delicately placed on the most ornate silver platter designed for such a thing. It had crystals dangling all about. It had strings of pearls laced about the edges. Crowded on the top layer were two standard cake toppers and one that had been adapted to have two girls for myself and Chloe.

"Oh!" said five vociferous voices, and we all clapped.

Chloe slapped her forehead, "Look at us! And cake!" she laughed, pointing toward the cake toppers.

Molly was so proud of her creation. "The bottom cake is just for show – it's just a hat box. The middle one we can eat. The top we save in the freezer. I read up on traditions." She glowed, bouncing on her feet. "And don't eat the icing off the hat box – it was made with really old sugar."

I pretended to snap a picture. I believe she knew what it meant. As for colors, it was off white, and the frosting was thin, barely enough to cover the cake. But if you hadn't seen a wedding cake in thirty years, you'd be just as bowled over with joy as we had been with this tantalizing display.

"Let's serve it up," said Chloe.

"Traditions have the bride and groom – or in your case, Chloe and Dahilana, the brides, share a first piece. Jack, or Phoebe, get that pretty pink dress over here!" Molly ordered.

Jack flowed girlishly in that direction, and the kids shared their first piece, kissing with icing all over their faces.

"Please, Mother and Father, Josephus and Avelynn, please share your cake," I prompted.

"I guess we go," he looked to his beautiful bride, my beautiful mother. They stepped to the cake as Jack returned to his seat, but Molly instructed them on the method to serve a slice of cake. Father took the instructions, and according to another tradition, guided Mother into linking arms to serve each other a piece of cake. Laughing and messy, they returned to their seats. "Dahilana – Chloe," beckoned Father.

"Come here my beautiful sisters," said Molly. Again, she instructed how to cut the cake and serve the pieces, and Chloe instinctively came at me to smash it into my face. "Oh my! Cake!" I shouted. But I really didn't want to waste any of it, though about half the cake found its way down my chest. I moved to the table to catch it, dumping it into my plate. "Whew!" I said but Chloe came at me again. "No – I'm not wasting Molly's efforts. Please don't attack me with cake."

It didn't help. And a small hand found its way to my plate, and the small feet associated with that hand found their way into my chair, and a small piece of cake found its way to my mouth. I pulled at Molly and put my mouth right to hers, letting her share the cake too. I put my arms around her small body and tugged her feet up from the chair, and all the while, pushed my face across hers, smearing the icing and cake across her face. Then I licked it from her. I didn't let go. I didn't want to let go, much like not letting go of the girl's hand after a play when I was just a young Miranda. I wanted Molly as much as I wanted the rest of them. But her giggles helped bring me back from my obsession, and the rest of the grand emotions of the day helped disperse any desire. Nonetheless, as I pulled back and our eyes caught, we gazed into each other, seeing beyond the flesh, seeing the undiluted truth of ourselves, just as we'd seen a girl image overlaying Jack, we saw such images now. "You are so beautiful," I gasped. "The true you is breathtaking."

"So true for you," she said, gazing at me as if focusing beyond me.

"I see you too," said Chloe, and instead of displacing Molly, she crowded up to embrace us both.

I looked at Father and Mother, expecting to see similar images, but I saw them as they were, dressed up with cake all over them. I laughed, losing control.

"Mama," said Jack, using a word I'd heard rarely. "I saw you – the real you." He gazed at me dreamily.

Softly, I requested, "What did you see?"

"You look like her – just like her," he said.

"Except for your eyebrows and chin," offered Molly.

Jack shrugged, "Yeah," cocking his head a tad to show it was an imperfect statement, but good enough.

Father was enjoying a little more cake, complimenting Molly on her accomplishment. "We don't have many occasions for cake, and from the looks of it, that won't change much. I am enjoying the cake. I haven't had cake like this since I married Michaela."

I blinked and looked about as if suddenly discovering a missing puzzle piece, though I hadn't even attempted a puzzle in years. "Daddy?"

Mother leaned her head to his shoulder. "That was my mother," she imparted.

"But neither of you have said it before! Why now?" I demanded. "Daddy?"

"We – this morning – had our own wedding-related breakdowns. This wedding has been the most cathartic thing we'd done. We've been joyously floating off our skin the rest of the day! And then we saw *her*. Why I'm just – overwhelmed. But I can finally say it."

We all paused to see what else he'd say in the silence.

"I'd not been able to remember her name. Even when Avelynn would try to remind me, I'd fall into a blank in my mind because it was all part of that loss – society. And my wife,

Avelynn's mother, your grandmother, was buried beneath the core of it. I couldn't get around that big hole in my head no matter what else we ran into on those confession chains. Nothing would break through to that area. Today – I broke through to that core. I could even remember my first wedding. I'm getting to be an old man, but today I feel like a child."

We continued watching for more comment, but he ended with, "Well – I'm still going to have to go to bed on time."

"Aww, little one. I'll be sure you get to bed on time, little boy," chimed in Mother, looking around to note how dim the room had become.

"No – I'm a little girl like the rest of you," he noted.

I went to the sink to wash sweet icing from my face, then returned with oil lamps for the table.

"You can turn on more lights." suggested Father.

I shook my head, "No. I'd like the flame light." I sat back down to stuff myself with more pork. I thought to myself that I didn't want the day to end. I hated to put a dividing line between this day and another, even though the spin of the Earth, position of the moon, and the hours of the clock would force that separation anyway. My belly stretched full, certain I shouldn't bend forward lest I rupture something, I walked about. I went to the front door of the east house and gazed outside, watching the horizon, tinged yellow by the falling nuclear fireball. I wanted to know more about energy and matter. I pondered the physics of the girl and the apparition. Was she an image in our minds or was this physical – was it real and was there a difference? Molly felt her lip get nipped. I felt the kiss, though the sense of temperature of her wasn't fully sensory. I wanted her – I wanted to be her – I wanted to know. I resolved that I could study books on physics, with a hope I'd better understand energy and matter.

I returned to the kitchen, my psyche overwhelmed, and body ragged but well fed, and offered to help clean up. An industrious group perforce our situation, the family quickly assisted. Molly ensured that the top of the cake was wrapped for the freezer. Father still handled the pork, partitioning it into individual portions for lunches the following day. I gathered up salad and vegetables, covering bowls with plastic wrap, which we had enough of to last centuries. In pulling the wrap, I felt that static electric feeling. "It was a little like this – when she touched me," I said into the room. "I've felt this before."

"Static electricity," offered Jack as he cleaned up some plates from the table.

"Be careful with that," Molly told him as he'd tried to pick up a cream pitcher on a plate, snapping porcelain against porcelain. I wasn't too concerned about her behavior today, but it was just weeks since she'd been a pugnacious brat. She glanced at me, followed by a coy smile. She mouthed *I love you* to me.

I mouthed *I love you* to her.

In short order we all went to our rooms. Though I had changed from my wedding dress, I still had on pretty underthings. But frankly, the physical had lost against the spiritual today, and I changed quickly. As Chloe arrived at the suite a few minutes later, I was pulling under the covers. She was quick to lose her dress and throw herself on top of me, the covers protecting me against skin pulls and bruises. She crawled up and kissed me, biting a little at my lip. "You!" I cried out. "Molly did that to me – and *she* did that to Molly. What's with biting today?"

With a cocked head and cute smile, she said, "You know? We're her. We do like her." She pulled at the covers bit by bit, revealing the babydoll outfit. She gasped deeply. "Oh, so pretty. I want one like that."

"You have one like that right under you," I presented myself.

She quivered and bit her own lip.

"Dim the lights and go to candles," I said.

She pulled back with her gaze transfixed on me, then turned to light several unmatched and scuffed candles we'd scavenged from various homes. I reached up to help, but she said, "No. You stay put. I'm the man tonight."

"You can't be the man." I bit my lip too, "I never wanted one. We weren't designed for this world as it was – we're misfits. If I'd made my own planet, they'd all look…"

"Like girls!" she finished for me. "Look, I have a vanilla one – smells like her." She lit the candle and set it on the bedside stand, filling the nearer air with the delicate aroma. As for the lovemaking, let's just say it wasn't as weird as my evening with the girls in my treehouse, nor did it last nearly as long, but it was spiritual, refreshing and we felt mutually appreciated. I'm sure the rest of the house had similar experiences.

Holding Chloe just before falling asleep, I had a less metaphysical and more pragmatic thought: For having been people who were not surviving well in the worlds we'd come from, we were surviving exceptionally high on the scale today.

In my dreams I was aloft of the flesh, and the images about me became lucid. Being a princess with five other little princesses, I was the owner of a section of the universe beyond our grand castle of highly crystalline stones, platinum and gold. Though we had some unique features, each girl was replete with the utmost beauty, as if sculpted by an artist deciding she had completed the work because there would be nothing that could be done to improve it. I effortlessly flowed from a wide hall onto a terrace, looking out upon a wide-open space, feeling comfortable in my dress fully adorned with faceted yellow sapphires. "There," said an unknown voice, "is your space." I knew it had been the voice of the one in white, the mystical combination of us, and the purest of all.

"No," I said. "It is my destiny, my future. I aspire to create immediately. I shall fashion my attainments from my desires. I shall populate my captive attendants from myself as template. I shall flippantly divine amusements, both honorably and capriciously, among these self-perpetuated denizens. I shall take praise and criticism; I shall embrace curiosity and stupidity alike;

I shall flourish and embrace privations. I shall play through, and beyond the circumference allotted. Because I am here, I shall push my dictates cursorily. In which games shall I partake? I shall delight in them all. At the end of this universe, I shall vainly inform myself, and I shall, for the lack of having anything else redeeming, be beautiful. Only then shall I return to my incorporeal oneness."

I came aware of the bedroom, seeing the outlines of the doorway and the bed, the glints from the windows from a dim, waning moon. Curiously I observed my position a couple meters above my comfortably breathing and sleeping body. *I am beautiful.* I could see my own outline. Fearless, I observed the gentle rise and fall of my chest. So beautiful in fact that I wished to kiss myself, so I approached my own lips, and when I touched, I felt a static electric sense of recombining with the nervous system's circuitry of the body.

Then I opened my eyes and peered up to the ceiling, then to the window, viewing a similar image. The glints, if I rose up to sit, reflected in the same places. I wanted to awaken Chloe to convey my experience and amusement, but my vocal machinery wasn't fully working – a few more breaths and I could finally speak. Given the few seconds and seeing that the dream would not be so fleeting, I chose to note it down rather than interrupt my partner of many things. I swooped to a drawer for a notebook and pencil, and wrote in the dark, allowing the reflection of the pencil markings to show me where to make the lines, though I didn't require viewing to scribble legibly. Having the eidetic images captured in words, punctuated with "We weren't fallen angels, we jumped," I set the notebook on a chair. Again, I rose to put my head near my soul's position just moments before, and I could again view the same details – except that they lacked the degree of clarity – the eyes were imperfect to the same degree as natural sight versus a photograph.

I was much too awake and aware to desire to lie in the bed again. I sat instead in the chair, and though closing my eyes, attempted to see the room directly. The images did not come as I'd hoped. I'd hoped for the ability of extra vision to be stable.

I put my attention on the beautiful little girl we'd seen today, the angelic apparition which eluded all descriptions from physics. Words from *Ascension* stated the universe was a place for souls to play and there were guards against the end from extending forever. Was this a revelation from our own past? Was the unseen girl in the mannerisms of our dreams, and this same apparition we observed today, the combination of us all? Was today's imagery, like many of the voices we'd heard, originating not from those souls currently working on salvation, but from our original souls at the *beginning* of the universe, a message that it is time to wake up? Because I was unusually awake.

SEVENTEEN

Physics and Philosophy

Never having enough day to accomplish everything, even coining the phrase, "Not enough days in the hour!" I cogitated upon time itself and "free time," a thought often voiced in the old society, where I'd heard statements like, "Use your free time wisely," or "Do that in your free time." But with respect to the efforts of living, we'd found no such thing as "free time," since all actions culminated into the efforts and results of living. Free time was not a commodity since the first ascension event, whether scavenging for basic wares, raising animals and managing gardens, housekeeping, preparation of meals and clothing, machining and fixing needed items including the electrical and biogas generators, and of course, learning in general. Atop that was maintaining the properties and the old trucks.

Over the next few years, I spent a fair proportion of my time studying mathematics and physics. I supposed it was just one of my dispositions. Jack and Father, with help from Chloe and Molly, found the means to start some compression-ignition engines, otherwise known as diesels, in some military delivery trucks. These vehicles had been constructed with the durability that the passenger car automotive sector had not been held accountable for, and we had available to us a long-term fuel storage facility, obviously designed to help the world surpass cataclysmic events.

Before I knew about the level of their success, Father hinted one spring morning. "Hey – would you all like to take a ride?"

"How many trucks have we got working?" I asked, only aware that one old truck had been running.

"Just two," said small-statured Jack, now about fourteen years old, wearing woman's fatigues as work clothing. He had a long ponytail with a pink ribbon tying it back.

Molly rushed through in tattered play pants and flannel shirt, obviously headed to feed the chickens. "I'm late. Bad girl! Poor birds would peck my fingernails off," she upbraided herself while she scurried toward the back door.

"Molly – when you get that chore done, please return. We're going to take a ride," said Father.

Molly stopped short, her cute bum twitching. Then she turned. "I need you to be more specific," said the little ten-year-old beauty, her eyes shifting.

"Sorry – uh – how did they use that phrase on your planet?"

"It meant you could disappear – to be killed," she said flatly.

"Well you know we're not going to do that to our loving and beautiful Molly! And yes – I could have been more careful – they've used that phrase here," he said, acting hurt, spreading his hands to refer to the society that came up missing. "Please – I'm trying to make a surprise. You won't be so displeased."

"Well enough. Chickens," she said cutely, tipping on her toes. "As long as I'm not being laminated to a sheet of fiberglass, made part of a boat and let loose in the sea – or any such fates."

"Or embalmed and left about like a doll," I whispered in my own space, a fate I wished on her prior to her breakthrough after her seventh birthday.

I knew I had time, so I went on to a study in the mansion to review my notebooks. Somehow, harmonics of energy was the key to just about everything. I knew it was one of the most important concepts with respect to chaining back confessions and meanings of words, even to remove false meanings. Each earlier memory was entangled by similarities or harmonics of the energies – the feelings, the emotions, the ideas – to the later memory.

Matter also appeared to be harmonic in nature. If a photon matched up in energy to the electrons circling an atom, it would have an effect and create a reaction or fluorescence, otherwise it just reflected. Such was the reason for the blue color in the sky. It wasn't reflection, it was the way the light combined inside the oxygen atoms.

Since the society had achieved nuclear capability, some basic textbooks were available, but I doubted that the empirical observations were properly explained. They had some illusion that motion could not surpass the speed of light. But yet I had recalls from many events in the universe, and even a few beyond it, that suggested this was a hoax, an illusion.

I'd gotten a recall, working on an ordinary chain of confessions that Chloe had helped me with, one of those chains that appeared to have little usefulness, going on for hundreds of items, and it led to a concept that with space travel, you wouldn't need to create artificial gravity – you'd just have to accelerate at roughly "one gravity," that is to say, about the same rate as to mimic gravitational force upon a body, and within a year you'd be near the speed of light.

Of course, I did the calculations based on the present planet's gravity and year and found it was very close, just a little over. The textbooks talked about "frame of reference" but failed to make a distinction between "true frame of reference" and "how you'd see it with light." I believed that was the fundamental flaw, though I didn't have any experimental apparatus for empirical demonstration, and even if this city had been the home of a particle accelerator, we would not likely install enough biogas and electrical generators to have sufficient power to revive it let alone turn on a few lights. I had the textbook but as an extension, I had another way of viewing – through my own recollection from millions and billions of years ago, no matter how fragmented and sparse the recollections had been, I had real clues.

I perused our session notebooks just as much for the same kind of data. In one, the light from a quasar had become visible as a result of relative motion away from it. A considerable speed would be imperative for such a conversion. In another session, I found an interesting hint of an alternate form of matter – an inverse form (antimatter). The hint related to how you'd use it for a spaceship engine. You didn't have to control the flow of the antimatter. You'd only have to contain it magnetically. However, you could gauge the flow of matter into it and allow it to entangle and release the energy at a sustained rate to create that one gravity's worth of acceleration, or perhaps you'd push these energy engines harder, and surpass any modest planet's gravity force. The sticking point for me was that matter literally disintegrated and became energy. In another recalled incident, the spaceship wouldn't be populated with flesh bodies, but with people who had permanent spiritual bodies, but these too were very solid, and in transferring life to planets, they carried onboard only simple cell forms, using them to seed life which would, in billions of years, create fair approximations of identifiable creatures as long as the planet sustained life at all. With these spacecraft, they were not using flesh bodies, so the acceleration rates could far surpass "one gravity," and the duration of the interplanetary travels could take centuries if necessary.

"Dahilana! Are you coming? I don't mean to impede your study, but it's time to go," yelled Chloe, clomping up through the mansion's hallways, appearing in the doorway of the study. The filtered light made her appear dusty. I looked over her figure, one leg crossing the other, accentuating her hips. Her image resembled a pilot in an early flight suit, perhaps my mind too much on physics and space. "Dahilana?" she said again as I was half mesmerized by her attractive appearance.

I wrote a quick note, "Is all matter just energy – is all energy just motion?" and closed the notebook, aware that my phrasing was weak. I'd meant to correlate energy to matter but motion, meaning wavelengths, was clearly involved. I pulled myself around the desk, being careful not to bang my hip into the corner of it. "Are they already gone?"

"In the old truck – but we'll just take the bicycles anyway. I hope you weren't sitting so long you can't move your bottom," she smiled while waving me to hurry.

"I'm coming," I appealed, wiggling my hips to loosen my butt.

She giggled, and we dashed like crazies exiting an asylum, arms waving and making wild noises just for the fun of it, half skipping and touching off walls to appear frantic. Once outside we dashed like a wolf chasing her meal toward the bicycles which waited on the back patio. Riding away from the east house, we looked ahead for the others, but they'd probably already arrived at the machine shop. Because we had the bicycles we could use the ramps on the old highway to act like daredevils, playing like little boys, using the bicycles to ramp over small streams that had cut along the edge of the road, so we could cross and meet up at the other side.

We didn't have the power to keep pace on the up-ramp. We walked and panted to the next overpass, then climbed back on and turned left, south a few blocks to the machine shop. The old truck was parked outside near a sunken loading dock, so we parked near it, putting the bicycles against the building. Through the loading dock doors, we peered in and climbed up a ladder, and announced our presence. "Daddy!" I called. "Jack!" Chloe skipped ahead of me.

The aged industrial setting had a cool temperature, so as I walked in, now out of the sunlight, I warmed my arms against each other. At the center of the floor was this large, blockish military truck, sporting very wide wheels and an oversized smoke stack. The cab looked stunted to keep it short, the back like a box truck but a little low with curved rather than sharp edges. Jack turned his head out the window, "Hey – it's going to work!"

Father said, "Be patient – now got to warm this up. There – that's why I tried to get here early enough."

As I came around the truck, I saw Molly, Chloe and Mother standing back.

"Okay – hit the red button, Jack," yelled Father.

An electric motor whined.

"Ignition," yelled Father. There were just a couple thumps from the engine, having deep exhaust resonance. I felt it in my chest, partly concerned whether the spirits above were working on some process and whether we were all about to fall over.

"Try it again, Jack," said Father, pulling his head back from the engine compartment. The engine compartment was opened up, splitting aside from center, allowing clicking noises to rake the air. I looked about, seeing a steel table where an electric motor had been disassembled. It looked like one of them had been installing a new winding, but for the moment the work was left incomplete.

Jack scooted in the cab, then the electric motor whined again, followed by a few thumps, then the engine accelerated to a regular pace. I heard a curious white-noise and whine. I dashed to be with Mother, Chloe and Molly. We cheered and clapped, but the noise was dwarfed by the whoosh and din of the engine. Father explained something, but it was too loud to hear, the meaning of the utterance lost between the noise and excitement. He closed and clasped the hood parts together.

Forward of the truck was a regular garage door, not elevated or recessed like the loading dock. "All get in," yelled Father and he pulled chains to get the door open. The resonant diesel sounds echoed heavily in the machine shop. I'd put my fingers in my ears as it was quite loud, especially compared to the quiet study where I'd been acting like a genius just before.

Molly and I climbed into the back jump seats, and the others fit across the large bench seat. "It's tougher gears, but drivable," said Father, climbing in. "For an afternoon, we're emancipated. Where would you like to go?"

"The new bay?" suggested Molly. "I want to see the new meteorite damage."

"Just through town?" suggested Mother. "Toward the bay I suppose."

"Not far from there was a plant with big ash piles. One of the meteors landed in there. I'd like to find it," I suggested.

"Anything," said Jack. "I'd just like to see this thing run."

"Well I don't recommend going too far, but this thing will go right over a guard rail, through a ditch – like a tank. She's not very fast, but fast enough for these damaged roads."

He put it into a gear and jerked forward. We were all propelled awkwardly with the vehicle. The old trucks didn't have nearly this much power. Because of that first demonstration, I asked, "How solid is this thing, Daddy? What all did you have to rebuild?"

"All of it – the whole drivetrain, anyway. Engine – transmission – u-joints – brakes. I must say I'm proud of myself!" he quipped.

Jack punched him with a fist. "Thanks for the acknowledgment, old man."

"Ouch – don't you remember? I'm just a little girl like you," he said, setting up the next gear as we pulled into the road away from the machine shop.

They laughed. Chloe turned back to look at me. I leaned up to give her a kiss.

My feet and Molly's were intertwined. Instead of expecting her to stay on her side, I reached my arms to request holding her. She came to sit in my lap. I nuzzled against her shaking body as the truck rumbled on. Daddy steered it down an on-ramp to get to the old highway, leading us toward the bay.

My exterior experiences of the meteor shower gave me "astral views" of the area, but never had we all gone to see the bay. We trusted that Father knew his way. A few times he'd steered from one side of the highway to the other, in one case crushing the guard rail after knocking it down with the bumper.

"Good," said Father during the action, "I'm glad it turned curved side up, edges down."

The speedometer rose and dropped according to the terrain. Rarely did we reach forty-five, whatever the numbers meant. While rocking back and forth through the median again, Molly's head hit my teeth. "Love you honey, but I'm going back over there," she said as soon as the truck was again on level ground. While sitting there, she touched her head while I had been feeling my teeth. "You okay?" she asked, buckling herself back into the jump seat.

"Yeah. I guess. If they don't fall out later," I groaned.

"Shit – I'm bleeding. You bit me," she said, showing me a slight red mark on her finger, taken from the new indentation on her head.

Chloe turned back and smiled, even winking, probably referring to a few times we got a little rough with each other, especially since I had a tendency to push the limits.

"What was that?" demanded Molly. But we didn't have any intention to divulge such private details now if they'd all be shared during our ascension anyway.

This was a new perspective on the city, still appearing asleep since the moments of the event, decaying modestly except for the brute force meteors and various unquenched fires. One structure, fully twenty-five floors high was gutted with the same kind of blackness as the corpses.

The shaking, the smells, the lack of noises besides the truck – this brought back horrific scenes from Altontown. Blockish building after blockish building brought back the Altontown hotel, especially after the hurricane. I reached forward across the seat to feel Mother and Chloe. They too were silent. Each of them reached up a hand to hold each of mine.

Father stopped the truck. "This was a beautiful place once," he said as we climbed out of the big cab. We were at a plaza, one part containing shelters for open-air markets, and another part set up as a park. In between stood several sculptures honoring work and play. The first was set up like an old gas station with a car and two people, one the attendant and one the customer. The customer was handing over a few dollar coins, and the attendant reaching for it while replacing the gas dispenser. Another major work was some boys and girls alike playing a game akin to basketball, one attempting to shoot the ball into the suspended basket. All of this was bronze, signed illegibly by each sculptor, showing the awesome green patina among the cluttered space. I would have loved to transport all this back to the mansion, but the way it was all anchored it would take a dozen men with a dozen high-powered tools a dozen days. It would have taken too much time to justify.

Daddy gave us time to look about, seeing that the grasses hadn't been as invasive as we would have thought – few trees sprung up in this commons. Like the mansion and Patent Office, the grounds had been shallow, and the soil balanced to limit what could grow. Above, an eleventh floor opened up through a building to the sky. I danced about the plaza, looking at the structural damage. Certainly evident were scorches from meteors.

"Come – load up. I'll show you the next point of interest," he said aloud to us all. To Mother he turned and said, "I'm back to being a docent today."

"You made a very good docent. I remember hearing you talk when I was little," said Mother. She wiped a few tears.

In minutes we were driving toward a large sports venue, a great stadium, surrounded by a massive colonnade. Daddy took us in between two columns, driving under the structure. Pushing a little clutter out of the way, we drove out onto the field, trampling briars and small trees between a marsh and a sandy hill. The area near the center contained a shallow pond, and the vehicle splashed right on through it to a dry knoll. I pushed at the others to get out, but instead of dropping to the dirty ground, I climbed up on top of the cab. I recalled a visit to a game when at college, having been surrounded by girls from the dorm, as we'd gone as a group. Sandy was among them, though we pretended we barely knew each other. The only acknowledgment I got that day was when we were in the bathroom and she grabbed at my bottom. She washed several sinks away and never looked back.

Jack kicked about near the pond, eyeing minnows in the water. Molly walked around the pond, gazing up at the repetitive structure, designed for an audience that hadn't returned for nearly thirty-five years. I climbed down from the cab and stepped carefully to Chloe, who leaned against the truck, observing the awesome structure.

"So many people would have been here," she stated.

Daddy looked at me, concerned.

I shook my head. "Let's go, Daddy."

He nodded and pulled up into the truck. We all followed. He put the truck into gear and plowed through to the other side of the stadium, exiting into a street closer to the original bay. Just a few blocks up, the structures were damaged by the shock of the meteor, windows broken and shattered all over the street. Daddy was careful to drive past the larger piles, moving at a walker's pace. Just a little further up, the buildings had been busted up and having been structurally weakened, many collapsed. Just a few blocks further, there were no standing buildings and the newly carved bay.

One structure had little glass by it, where Daddy stopped the truck. "We might get dizzy in the process, but we can climb that one. You'll be able to see the whole bay," said Daddy as he led our procession to a structure. It had more floors than I could count before going through a doorway that had lost its glass. A directory by the elevator indicated 52 floors.

"Uh – Daddy? How many do you think we can walk up?" Chloe barked.

"All of them? No – as far as you need to see?" he returned, guiding us to a stairwell, which was soiled by years of water streaming down it. We climbed, gasped, waited, paced, and before we got very high at all I was sure that my knees would be sore. I used my arms more, but at floor twenty-five, Daddy checked the door. He couldn't get it open. We went up one more floor, and again he tried but failed to open the door. Jack went on up to check doors, banging and clanging as we waited. I tried to count the attempts but failed.

"Got one!" echoed his voice.

"What floor?" asked Father, turning his head up.

"Thirty-eight," came the echo. The sound, despite just being a high voice for distant clarity, had a smoothness to it.

I sang a little song about rainbows I'd recalled from my previous childhood. It was supposed to be a happy song, but with the echo and loss of civilization mixed in, it was sorely bittersweet. I cut off the song as tears welled up. I stepped, lifted, stepped, lifted. My heart was fluttering as we walked into the hallway and stepped toward broken windows. The breeze at this level was stiff, though at the ground it was barely enough to move a dress. I picked a path where plenty of the outer glass still reached from floor to ceiling. Jack moved right to the broken area, open to the air.

A funnel-shaped bay opened up between the shattered structures, having eradicated eight, then ten, then twelve blocks of cityscape, completely obliterating it and what may have been tens of thousands of corpses left in their beds in high rise apartments. Certainly an example of power from the sky, this had been the monstrous rock I'd seen pass by during the first major meteor shower. Of course, I was glad I hadn't been in this area during the meteor shower. I was certainly glad this didn't hit the mansion or anywhere near it, nor Adelardus.

Jack piped up. "My city – not as aged – looked like this. Devastated. Decaying. The life was gone. And then the fire," He bit his lip and cried while Molly comforted him.

Mother watched, leaning on Father's shoulders.

Recuperating from the climb, none of us offered to move out. The rays of the sun changed slowly, still far from noon, but shedding more light into the valley created by the seismic impact, where ground bulged on either side of the new bay. I revivified my experience – the meteor moving so quickly, seeing the pulsating shockwave off the front of it, hearing the massive boom just from the motion against the atmosphere. How big was it? I pried into the recall and tried to see the specifics my mind had recorded, but instead ran into another series of past-life events. I zoned into one of them, a previous museum experience, looking at a diagram of recovered meteors and the craters they'd created. Apparently, I'd been a girl, holding the hand of a girl, looking over the chart because I recalled one of the meteorites from a yet previous lifetime. I told the girl, "There – that one. I remember that. Landed in the center of the city. I was killed in a hot blast." She'd told me, "No you weren't!" and wiggled her fingers to release so I let go of her hand. Assuming I was lying, she pushed at me, telling me I was delusional while I cried. I'd been upset and confused since she would neither converse nor hold my hand. But with this recall, I got the idea of the scale of the rock – it would have been about thirty meters across. I rose my head up and spoke my supposition.

"I guess we're not digging that one out of the sea," said Father.

Bit by bit, we sorted back to the stairwell, carefully moving down, taking breaks, chatting about building structures and how much longer we thought each edifice would support itself until it crashed in. Would the steel be usable? Would the cement become powder, and would it work again if put through a limekiln?

Dizzy, knees hurting, we returned to the street level. I felt an invincible sadness, a weakness in my heart. I wanted to wail like I'd done during the hurricane, or many times when dumping heavy grief in sessions. I tried to ignore it and keep walking, but the pain in my legs demanded I concede. I dropped to the pavement, sitting, then letting myself fall backward, looking away from the planet, my view upwards through several structures, some with names like "Edwards Financial,"

"BioChems Industries," "G.N.R.L. Law." A faded sign read "Underlad Bird Sanctuary" with an arrow pointing forward to the new brackish reservoir that replaced it. From the ground level I could see the natural levee created by the meteorite's strike, dots moving above it, likely some gulls enjoying the breezes. I wanted to reverse time, my head spinning and compressed, and grinding dirt and grit into my hair and scalp. I turned, getting up to my knees and wretched the food from my stomach. I was certain that part of it was the travel, part of it was thirty-eight flights of double-turns on the stairwells, and perhaps the little girl up there was working on something else today. Molly and Chloe both came to lift me, wipe me up, and get me back into the truck, leaving me with rags and a bag to wretch into again.

But on the way back, Daddy took a small detour along a drivable alley, leading to an industrial drive, which in turn took us to the plant, near my observed meteor strike. Interested, I was able to get my attention off my dizziness, and guided Father to the approximate location, finding a large gate into a huge metal foundry. Piles of coal, coke and piles of ash were dumped for at least a square kilometer, and in between was a humongous structure for the foundry. I did my best to recall the scene as I had from the sky, an interesting correlation if it were correct. I got out, feeling the need to drop to my knees and puke, I pushed up and hung on Mother, gasping, to observe the scene about me. Molly soon took over for Mother, guiding me through the expansive area. Walking was frivolous, so we returned to the truck, guiding Father through train tracks between the piles. Just past a veritable railroad yard, I recognized a large pile with a smaller pile next to it. The top of the large pile was plainly stunted. "There – that one!" I said. I was overwhelmed with the desire to see it, I nearly forgot about being sick. With rags about my hands and feet, I trudged up the side of the pile, intentionally kicking heavy ash back down. Thank god it struck the ash pile because a hot meteor might have ignited the other piles. Jack climbed up with me, getting as dirty as I had been. My body protested the actions of climbing – especially my knees. I pulled ash away from the crater, creating a chute for the crud to exit down the cone. I requested something to dig with and soon had a small foldable shovel taken from the truck – Father, always circumspect and overly prepared, had put camping gear into the back of the truck and snacks that could have fed us for a few days in case we'd had to walk back.

I formed another chute on the opposite side while Jack worked my original chute with a spade, also taken from the truck, and material flew from both sides of the cone. I had to remember how to hold a shovel firmly so as not to get blisters. I guess I didn't know how big an operation this would become. Feeling dry, I knew I'd need water soon. The warm day could dehydrate me from the sweat and work.

I poked down again with the shovel and finally, clunk, it hit something solid, perhaps metallic. Expecting to pluck a small rock right away, I pulled more ash aside, and as I did, it tried to go lower, so I was careful to dig it up, supporting the heavy object on the shovel surface. "I got it," I said to Jack. The others waited below. Jack continued by cutting a chute for it, and I was scooting one genuine meteorite into the chute, and then tumbled it down the cone to the packed ground. I dumped myself over, putting my feet to the shovel, and skated down the ash, finding myself tumbling into the hard ground at the bottom. I rolled over to pick myself up and rushed at the space rock. "You were the one – you were the one I saw go into that pile. I saw you." I turned to my family, "I saw this – I saw this from the sky when we were in the legal vault!" In pain, still dizzy and weak, I pulled up and jumped for joy, but my feet didn't even leave the ground. It was proof that the vision had not been just an illusion.

I moved a few more steps then sat myself down upon the packed gravel that only partly showed any plant growth above it. "It was real – what I saw from the sky. I'd seen this – it was all true and real." The others were worn out and emotionally weak from the other excursions. I'm certain they found it intriguing to be here, but this excitement of mine didn't obtrude to them, making me feel a little greedy.

Daddy said, "There is a low storage compartment at the back of the truck. We'd have to work together to get that space chunk into it." We set about making a plan, our first step to roll it onto a board atop of a metal ladder, and then we used the ladder to distribute the total weight of the meteorite. Then we loaded the ladder back into its slot and moved the rock up to the next level, just several centimeters above the ladder, and closed the door to the compartment. That modest space rock had been extraordinarily heavy, at least a hundred kilograms, but luckily it wasn't fully iron.

I wanted to take one of the bronze busts off a pedestal and put this oblong rock there instead. The meteorite was a much better piece for our museum home than any bust of some president whom we'd recalled little. Our memories of such presidents and the associated history had faded; we'd never bothered to make it a priority when there were so many aspects of survival that took precedence.

Chloe and Molly piled into the jump seats. Father and Mother flanked me to assist my steps, and together we traveled with the same slow and jerking motions back to the mansion. We'd have to get the bicycles from the machine shop later since I wouldn't be able to ride, my legs unable to handle the exertion. Pulling up through the drive at the east house, Father said, "Well – essential chores, anyway. Do what you all can. Don't strain yourselves. We're going to sleep good tonight if we're not too haunted by the experience."

Soon I was pushing laundry about in carts while using the wheelchair, exchanging menial sorting tasks for those needing more thought and strength. I'd have to ponder the rock and physics later. I ate heavy on eggs to get the protein. Perhaps that would help the circumstance of my overexertion.

I woke in pain the next morning, my knees so stiff at first, I had to gently flex them. Chloe moved slowly, pulling her painful legs from the bed. "Thirty-eight floors – what the hell were we thinking!"

I commented on our stupidity. "We were thinking we were fit enough to do it. We keep up on chores; we ride the bicycles; we garden; we climb steps here. I thought I could do it until I tried." I went on to our toilet, sitting slowly and painfully, having to pull a small shelf and cabinet to either side of the toilet to lean on. As I thought through the previous day, I realized we'd picked up the meteorite. "Oh shit. The meteor." I tried getting up, but the pain scorched my knees and I dropped back to the hard toilet seat. "Shit!" I said as I felt my tailbone slap against the seat, fearing I'd knocked it out of line.

"Dahilana?" Chloe cried out. She fast appeared in the door, holding firmly to the door frame. "Are you okay?"

I was amply perturbed by these multiple pains holding me hostage on the toilet. "Nearly broke my tailbone," I said, tears falling from my face. "This is pain, dammit." I pointed at the wet lines on my face. "Get me the walker, please."

She walked in further and felt my knees. "I think they are swollen – a little gnarled. You're going to be on bedrest."

"Then I'll need my notebooks," I agonized. "Shit, Chloe. I can't do anything. And I'm so hungry." I was voracious. My stomach so empty I felt sick.

"I'll get Mother and some breakfast, but I won't be fast about it," she said, pointing to her own legs and bottom.

"Fine," I accepted, allowing that I could have been stuck there until she returned.

Chloe hobbled out. I sat there on the toilet, kneading my puffy knees. I pulled myself up and walked as if on crutches, holding my legs straight, bent against the sink to wash my hands, and continued on to the bed, falling into it.

When Mother came in, I thought I'd heard her say, "Miranda let me take a look at that."

I turned up, looking her square in the face. "Mother – did you call me Miranda?"

"No, Dahilana. Let me see those."

"Of course." I turned up and let her check my painful knees, kneading a little harder than I had.

"Well, you didn't squeal – I doubt there's infection. Just aging old knees."

I thought I had heard the noise of a plate scooting across a table, but Chloe hadn't brought breakfast yet. I put my attention on the thoughts – I thought I'd heard my previous life name and dinner plates, and had painful, puffy knees.

Chloe returned, using a chef's cart to bring in some cooked pork and eggs.

It smelled wonderful, yet I smelled sausage. "Chloe – I'm seeing things. I heard my old name, I thought I smelled sausage – like at my parents' in Altontown. I – I remember an accident – not long after my dad built my treehouse – I fell down the steps and bruised my knees. They said I'd almost broken a leg."

"What do you see in the incident?" she requested.

I was glad she'd taken my hint to dig into it. "I saw my Mother's prized china cabinet, full of antique mismatched glassware – stoneware. Daddy wasn't there, and I wanted him. My nanny tried to help but she wasn't so smart. She said we'd have to call the doctor. I said to call to Daddy. She kept saying, 'Your Daddy is at a funeral. We take care.' I watched as the color came into my knees. She didn't cool them – she didn't warm them. She tried to call for a doctor, who came an hour later. I … I." I shook my head since I couldn't see beyond that but bit my lip with an impinging prior moment.

"What happened that led up to that?" Chloe asked wisely.

"I was afraid you'd ask," I said sheepishly. "I was a naughty girl. I looked from my deck and watched girls in bikinis. Ah – there was this young couple – oh she looked good. I pleasured myself as I watched her skittling about her partner, some young guy. But the nanny – Xiu Mei – called me to lunch. I hurried down, being awkward and fearing she might have seen me. I tripped when turning at the landing and tumbled, hitting both knees before going through a somersault that slapped me into the sand. Then I felt the pain." With my attention on the pain, my knees throbbed.

"Anything else about that?" she asked while collecting a session notebook from a drawer.

I ran my mind through the timeline fragment. "Um – I was looking out on the beach, first seeing it as a vacation place – a place I wanted to be – like I had some sentience that I wanted – even chose – *to be here* – to be on the island before I was born. I must have followed my pregnant mother around." I pondered the thought and added, "I was their ghost."

"Okay," she said, taking a few notes. I'd hesitated so she asked, "Is there something earlier?"

I looked, "There's something. Not sure I'm getting it."

"Okay – bring it to now, take a look," she ordered, employing the terminology Father had given me when working with Molly.

It was the horrific event of my second previous death, when I'd tried to act like a little whore and was picked up by seriously deranged hoodlums. I began to emote. "My life before being Miranda. I was a teenager, and a guy had just forced me to act sexually while I was on my knees, my hands tied to a pole behind me. I bit his hand as he tried to wipe my face. Instead of smacking me, he lifted me by my armpits and slammed me back onto my knees. I hadn't expected that, and the shock of the pain jolted through my body. I puked instantly. My back felt strained," I said and cried out a spot of grief, pondering why I'd seen around this incident but never got this detail about the knees. I thought I'd had this incident completely cleaned up.

"More?" she said.

"My throat was cut just a bit after that, but we've got that part before. I just hadn't seen the pain with the knees."

"Okay. Is there an earlier harmonic situation?"

"I'm sure there is," I said, at first expecting something near in time, but it wasn't strictly so, though it puzzled me heavily – having a temporal duality – yet related to knees. "I was a soldier in some kind of game – I was in a theater – I was acting out a time – oh this is ridiculous. I'm so confused." I couldn't get clarity on the principle timeline.

"Well – start at the beginning," she coaxed.

As I resigned to let the details coalesce, I stumbled my words slowly. "Well, there's a beginning – beginning – time – first – there's a theater." Patience allowed a thicker image to evoke. "I guess I'll take up the theater. I was walking in with friends, lovers – we were all girls." I yawned away some thick confusion. "We lined up about a circular pit – not a normal theater – big images of the universe all about it. Galaxies up on the ceiling and walls, huge charts of timescales above the seating, the images extending into the space of the room like pictures hanging from the ceiling or on layers of glass. We'd decided on some adventure, and we'd each play a character." I suddenly realized what that temporal duality was – we were in the theater to create future events for fun, even when the future adventure included horrific death and dismemberment in tough military situations. "I get it," I said, having understood the entanglement. "We were creating future adventures from the convenience of armchairs in a studio, a theater. We all created, not in the current time, but millions of years in the future. We'd experienced a hundred years of future activity within an afternoon."

"And?" Chloe added while writing.

"We – I was a soldier in the future event, and we all played war – I should say love and war – games. A girlfriend had become one of the future nurses, and I – myself really a girl soul – played a male pilot – got regretfully downed by gunfire, busted up my knees, got ported for hours, then transported to the hospital and we fell in love, got married – oh!" I felt a sharp snap through my knees, the false energies falling off and reclaiming the ability to be "good knees" again.

"Oh?" she queried.

"Oh – the knee thing – that was conducive of the positive turns of events in the story – the future we'd been composing. It led me to her!" In the present, I sat and watched the swelling in my knees magically recede, though my musculature was still protesting from having been overtaxed. Her ministration had worked better than expected. "Chloe? Did you see that? My knees! My knees are becoming beautiful again."

Chloe wrote out a few sentences to catch up with my verbiage and then looked up. "Dahilana?" she said and dumped over toward me, losing the notebook and pen. "Your knees. Oh my God." She squeezed my knees. "That's amazing!" she said smiling. "You're going to have to go back to chores!"

"I can't say I expected that dramatic a change – but thank you Chloe for taking it up. It could have been a three-day chain."

"Yeah," she said, half stunned and half regretful. "I could have used three days to heal."

"Do you want a session too?" I offered.

"No. I'm good. But that's good. That's really good," she said and put my notebook back into the drawer before stepping out.

I turned to pull my legs off the bed, and though the swelling had dropped dramatically, I still felt discomfort in the muscles, as well as my feet, back, hands and more. I'd be able to do a few chores, but for the morning I'd finish breakfast and look through the notebooks for more clues on energy and motion. Chloe ran down the hallways to fetch Mother, converse on the session, and come back to examine "the case," i.e. my knees. Were they prized melons from the garden? They used a tape measure to prove they were normal.

I wondered what a professional bicyclist would have felt the day after a long race. My body protested but now in my post-session euphoria, I desired to hit the paperwork right away. I skipped down the hallway – no – just in my mind, my body dragging like a rat a cat brought in – and headed to my study.

When I looked at my notes, recalling I hadn't transcribed my thought perfectly, I read again – *is all energy just motion?* Could I have been right in the mistake? I had a thought: What if I considered astronomically fast items, like the high-energy physics experiments in the books, such that energy was the same as motion? I took the equations that showed "a particle with such mass, add energy, and it approaches a new speed." If you took into account that mass multiplied twice by the speed of light gives energy, which is just a unit conversion, and energy is thus just motion, I viewed this as "take a particle, composed of mass (equals energy, equals motion) add energy (equals motion) and find the new total energy (motion) derived from the kinetic and physical *motions*." What if you? .... Motion? Mass? My mind was moving too fast – the images of items moving faster than light speed – the interdependence of matter and energy – the calculations of acceleration – the viewpoint of looking with light – the potential viewpoint of seeing what is really happening. Internal to my mind, everything congealed.

"Aha!" I said as my perceived image of the room warped. Everything whited out, then I saw the body from outside of it, leaning over on the desk, pen in hand as if to write. Space images and equations danced about as if being in some three-dimensional classroom. With a young girlish form, I put my imagined fingers above me, looking at simple physics notations spelling out one specific equation, saying, in answer to a teacher, "Well, the energy, being just finite motion, combined with the particle, which itself is a folded-up combination of finite motions, have a greater total motion, which we can call energy or matter either one." The teacher had returned, "So, why can a particle, when viewed, not exceed the speed of light?" I had returned, "Because light cannot show the viewer an image faster than itself. The fact is, if it is approaching any practical limit, it is going much faster than light. If an object appears to be going the speed of light, it is theoretically approaching an infinite limit. Looking through light always shows a wrong answer at high speed." The teacher returned, "So how do you see the actual motion of a particle?" I had stated, "Well you have to look directly, as a soul, not as a viewer through light energy. Or you back-calculate the actual speed from the apparent." "One more thing," started the teacher, "What is important about who is looking?" I must have smiled with my certainty on the response: "The soul is looking. This speed of light is always relative to who is looking, and that is the soul. Two people, moving differently, see a slightly different answer." The teacher's voice faded while saying, "Very good. I do believe you are at the top of the class...."

I spun back into the body and felt the stark pain of my back and legs return to my senses. I pulled up and wrote, pen ready, that conversation verbatim. Then I wrote, "The particle isn't solid first, then moving – it's folded up energy, which is just motion, which isn't something moving. It's just distinct, defined, finite motion."

With this revelation, I had some idea of how a soul could create an image. It wasn't a big solid thing we were creating in the first place. It was just motion. Any images in the mind were likewise energy, even if a tiny fraction, as shown by the incidents we cleared up that had a pathological effect on my knees. But when the girl was at the pedestal and was asked to create something, I'd seen visible fragments of that creation. A soul could create something from nothing in the first place, because it was just motion, and all the measurements of energy and mass were likewise just measures of the quantity and frequency of that motion. There was no proffered dichotomy between waves and particles. Regardless of scale, matter was energy was motion.

So, I played with equations, going through a notebook of a hundred pages, redoing each practical examining particles near the speed of light, and translating it to the actual speed, which was over the speed of light, sometimes by a little, sometimes by a lot. All the equations still worked out from the true view, not just the "warped" view of viewing with light.

I was a genius. Had the rest of the world been alive, I'd have been getting a prize. But chances were, they wouldn't even believe it. I'd decided I'd had enough intelligence for a day, my mind overtaxed, incapacitated by the awe of my new viewpoint. I ambled painfully through the home, deciding first I needed to get outside for fresh air.

I moved out the back door, viewing the peculiar meteorite upon a pedestal, sitting like an oblong sundial. It was washed clean, so I examined the mottled surface. The speed of entry was far from light speed, but certainly supersonic. I thought it odd that it took very little damage during entry and landing. Clearly, the others had to team up to get this rock here, for which I'd have to thank them later. I supposed they considered it mine and left it until getting further orders.

I grabbed some pruning shears from Mother's atrium then trimmed the grape vines on the arbor. While trimming vines, I heard a fluttering of wings. I turned back toward the gardens, seeing a shape swoop sideways toward the ground, latch onto something at ground level, and loft itself out of view. I was sure it was that owl, the same one I'd seen at the village, and for some reason it felt obliged to follow us.

About eight weeks later, after stuffing the biogas generators to their maximum as a result of summer clippings, we'd decided on a late evening meal as the days were long and exceptionally hot. Father had set up a few campfires to throw a little smoke to thwart the bugs, and one to roast two chickens on a spit. I'd tried to explain some of the physics to Jack, and though he was interested, complained he'd need more background through reading the same textbooks to get it. He put it off by saying, "If I don't understand it today, Dahilana, I'll understand it after the ascension."

"Yes, you may. But you could understand it now," I offered.

"No, my love. I'll have time to study up on that math, so I can follow. I could agree that the more of us understand now, the better we'll retain it when we get up there, but I'm sure our girl of origin knows." He looked up into the sky.

"Well, I'm sure she does. I just don't want to feel stupid when I get there," I premised. The thought had occurred to me that I could be that refresher course she wanted on the subject – by my learning, she was learning.

Jack continued, saying, "Well I have to consider my priorities. Father needs me at the machine shop. We all need to help with the gardens. Molly needs help with the sessions...."

Molly came to me from the side, holding a plate of assorted vegetables and some chicken that Father had begun serving up. She tilted her head, letting me know to get served. Daddy came up with a plate for me, "Dahilana – I know how you like it. Here's a plate."

"Thank you, Daddy," I said taking the assortment of food, settling into a repaired lounge chair, and eating sloppily, more concerned about all my thinking than the noise or mess as I first mauled recently plucked vegetation. "So, if the particles are just energy, Jack, and the energy is just motion, then everything is just an image made of motions – and that can be made from space and nothing, just by a soul intending it."

Jack hesitated, and his face started several expressions before asking, "So what of these motions? Are they frequencies? Are they jiggles? How can you have something moving if it isn't something?"

"Well because it's an illusion. The motions are wavelengths I guess," I said.

Molly chimed in with, "They are many unique wavelengths. The whole motion of the particle is made up of – partitions of the wavelengths – fragments,"

I recalled the time that Chloe explained the sunset colors after the first major meteor shower. I didn't want to let this pass. "Molly?"

She looked about through the sky as she thought, then threw out, "That's the way they saw it on my planet – in words I've got – hum – fragments do work. Building – interacting – like gravity interacts, electricity attracts."

"Harmonics?" I suggested, not quite sure her connotation. "How energies match up?"

"Well, how they combine from the fragments – they build in the same direction or – they make nothing from being opposite, and partially if in between."

I couldn't put it all together, I asked her, "So what's that to do with fragments?"

Molly went on like a professor. "Well, we were taught, not that this was my best subject – that all matter and energy came from some, ah – fundamental set of fragment motions, not a ripple but a partial ripple. Just like the periodic table of the elements is a set, these motions were a set, and how they combined identified the subatomic particle just as well as the combination of those atomic particles define the atoms. Just like atoms combine into chemicals."

"Damn – what do you know about motion and the speed of light?"

"Well not much, I guess. Things go as fast as you want them, you just can't see it beyond light – I remember that much. I couldn't do that kind of math now. All your books look so much different. But I think they were trying to say the same things. I know you were thinking we just did farming, and I didn't turn out to be one of the smartest kids, but they taught us all, hoping to find we'd have the aptitude to keep the power stations running. Sun power, they called it."

"I didn't realize you were a star child – just from another planet," I said.

"I am from another planet," she confirmed. "I wasn't from the stars."

I wanted more confirmation. "So, no one on your planet ever said no one could go faster than the speed of light?"

"No. We'd consider the thought juvenile, cartoonish, backward. Of course, things can go faster than the speed of light," jabbed the little savant.

"Okay," I nodded. "So, you'd already be aware that all matter is energy and all energy is just motion."

"I didn't say the energies were 'just motion' but I guess they could be. Like I say, I was in a desperate technological society, but I wasn't the best student of it."

Flabbergasted I spoke freely. "Not the best what? You turd! You ugly rotten turnip! You stinking poop! Why didn't I ask you before?" I questioned, set my plate aside, grabbing about her. She put her plate on a nearby chair and turned into me, then I pulled her back onto the lounge. She faced me, and our heartbeats jiggled each other. "I love you, star child."

"I said I wasn't a star child," she pleaded, still giggling from my superfluous upbraiding.

Jack, still near, had heard the conversation, simply saying, "Wow – I think I finally understand something she'd said in session. Wow. Just wow." He set his plate aside too, walking about, saying, "Everything – everything is just an image – a *solid image*."

"Dahilana?" asked Father, who'd been standing quietly behind me. "Can you write all that down and correlate it to the content in the Ascension book. It mentioned energy and images. I'd like to understand that better. And no, I'm not trying to play with atomic power."

"Sure. Daddy. I will," I said.

He further acknowledged. "Okay. It's important to me. It might explain something I got in my sessions with your Mother."

I just nodded, verifying the sincerity in his eyes.

We'd relaxed, and I felt so good with Molly along my body that we both fell asleep. Chloe came to stroke my cheek, saying I'd better get up before the bugs would bite. I felt Molly pull up and I reached up, let Chloe take my hand and guide me toward the house. Father was dousing the fires, the shadowy angles of a rising moon slowing my careful steps. Molly was already walking sleepily ahead of us. I shook my head, wondering why I hadn't asked her before for any of her planet's knowledge on these subjects. Fractions of motion, harmonics and interference – I could put that together into some theory, I was sure.

Chloe and I tumbled into the sheets with most of the blankets kicked off the end of the bed. We had been sleeping soundly when I'd been dreaming of something related to space travel when I was jolted awake by a loud bang. The windows shook, and floors jiggled like a one-shot earthquake or a sonic boom. Chloe leaned up. "What the hell." She didn't wait to get answers. She put on pants and ran out.

"Oh my God!" yelled Jack from across the hallway.

My attention out for secondary visions or blasts, I scurried to put on pants and follow. I looked out the window and noted lightning flashing about the city, most of it distant. I rushed toward Jack and Molly's room, and they were at their window, a glowing light behind them. There was a fire in the shed for the biogas generator near the water pump.

"Jack?" I said, expecting him to tell me anything he knew.

"Uh – no. Just sleeping and heard the noise. Lightning probably struck it."

I hurried into the hallway to our parent's room, finding Daddy on the way out. I informed him quickly, "Fire in the number one biogas shed."

"Oh. Shit. Go – go, go," he said.

We ran out, catching up with Chloe, heading to the biogas generator but leaving a healthy distance. We could smell the fried cesspool of animal dung and incubating grass. Jack followed behind us, having donned old pants and a bright t-shirt.

"Ah shit," said Father, seeing the mess. "I thought we had it proofed against the elements – but not lightning." The burning structure was torn apart, some boards having been thrown aside smoking into the moonlight that faded behind the approaching storm. This mess had been the gas source for the well pump. Just behind us, a lightning bolt struck trees, announcing a hellacious crack. I turned just in time to see an instant flame scorch the treetops and vanish, while the boom echoed off the structures in succession as the sound traveled into the distance where goats bleated, and chickens flapped their wings.

I turned again to watch Father survey the damage. "We'll have to build another one or transport the one from the shop. We've got the parts. Probably too dangerous to move the other one – it'd take longer to empty and refill it anyway. We'll need to hand pump the water until it's in place and generating gas. Or if I can get that electric pump running – probably that and draw off the generator but that would overtax the gas supply from unit two."

"Hey Papa," said Jack. "Doesn't that newer truck have power-take-off?"

"Sure it does," said Father.

"Can we match up the turn rate to a working pump rate?"

"Yes – I suppose. I haven't tried it to verify, but that's the way most of those work – there's a gearing for it. Might work if we can get the gas motor unmated from the pump or find another pump."

"Pumps – I'm sure are logged in the books when we search houses," I offered.

Daddy nodded and looked at Jack.

Jack nodded. "Okay – we can try it. We'll get a pump and get the truck and power it when we need."

Daddy replied, "We'll just fill up the roof tank a little higher – probably needs flushed."

"We can do all that – pump it full with the truck. At least the toilets would have water all the time. Then only pump fresh for food and drinking. Anyway, Father and I got this. The rest of you can sleep," said Jack.

"Sure," said Father. "We'll call you up if we need you. There's no need for everyone to get electrocuted. Though it would be easier tomorrow if we all smelled the same. Maybe some rain will dilute that crap."

I turned to the back of the house, seeing Molly and Mother by the back door. I walked up with Chloe and let the men tend to the fire. Otherwise, there was a light mist, and as I walked toward the house, it turned to drizzle. More flashes filled the sky, one within a second of its thunder crack. I skipped but didn't jump off my feet. "I never did like lightning," I said to Chloe. "Never did like storms."

We hugged and kissed with Mother and Molly and went back to bed. I laid in next to Chloe as before, returning to my space travel dream as if I'd just returned to a movie theater after taking a break, missing part of the show.

At first light, Molly's *fractional physics* having piqued my determination, I directed myself back to my study and toyed with the idea of these fractional parts of motion, the provision that each particle is composed and identified by the characteristics of its fragments. To get more from her would mean years of study for the child. I could go back to everyone's notebooks and look for more clues, and though I had clues, probably not enough to explain everything, I'd try to explain as much as I could with what I'd had.

I could contemplate that harmonics, the similarity of frequencies, helped create interactions, but fractional wave interferences could add and subtract. These pluses and minuses of energy could be used to alter the characteristics of a particle. Imagine a proton and neutron – there was a difference in charge, thus a "charge fragment" could have been added to a proton – or – two aligned charge fragments could have been added to a proton, and two opposite charge fragments could have been added to a neutron, canceling the charge. I was sure that the fragments could be far more complex, but the supposition sounded plausible. I'd have to try to get past-life recollections – actually much further back than past life – if I really wanted to understand this.

I spent hours playing with the equations I had, but I doubted I'd ever hit upon something other than purely theoretical scratching, as it probably needed advanced notation to go with the advanced ideas. I wanted an empirical way to see this. I supposed, once we ascended, we'd know – or perhaps with direct ability, we didn't really even have to understand everything about it. If you could create a space and create something in it, did it matter how?

The more I thought about it, the more I deduced the answer yes. But I could say one thing clearly – that the essence of a particle was its motion, its motion was in turn created by a soul with the ability to do so. At these lower levels of the universe, with little knowledge and ability, we couldn't alter the direction of a photon. As souls, we had no power at all – and there it was in plain sight: *power* was nothing more than the ability to modify a motion, whether that power was a transference from another energy source (motion source), or whether that came from the soul itself.

I'd taken my notes and stumbled up from my desk, realizing more time had passed than I'd expected since my bottom indicated strongly that I'd failed to move it. I was hungry, and the day would be getting too warm to want to stay indoors. It was time to do chores before it got too hot.

I carried buckets of water. I moved feed for animals. I cracked grains that had already come off one of the fields. I tended goats, opting to shear one that should have been handled earlier, and had too many briars and weeds in the mohair, so I left it thick, taking only the top ragged layer, putting the cuttings into an overflow bag – the leftovers that we never dug into.

As I looked over the animals, the converted structures we used for them, and the surrounding fields back of the mansion, which was showing a little age, I pondered the idea that everything was just motion, just an image. And too, the soul could ascend to greater ability and power to the point of making and removing motion, energy and matter. How was it we could ever lose that much power and find ourselves trapped? How could we lose the essence of ourselves and even pretend we were just having fun like going to a theater and watching a movie as grand as the efforts in the whole universe? Was the universe itself, and all the artifacts of galaxies, nebulae, solar systems and living planets a byproduct of our adventures here, the cosmos an artifact we'd naturally deployed through billions of years of adventure?

Returning through the backyard to the east house I again came across the pedestal containing the meteorite. I'd had a little time to study up on meteors and now understood that this rock was very old, chondrite structures indicating it was from the formation of the solar system, more than likely dragged along by the younger meteors in the group of planetoid fragments. There was indeed evidence contained in every deformity of its structure that time was vast. It would be degenerate to think otherwise.

There was the event of my recollection when Chloe helped me with my knee pain, the one of creating future timespans from an earlier point in the universe – perhaps it was itself a lower harmonic of action compared to, perhaps, a higher grade of creating futures of whole universes, including all ramifications down to completely comatose souls, unaware of anything except suffering emotional pain, acting out their daily lives completely oblivious to anything, as I had been as Miranda, until the "ethereal layer" impinged. But it wasn't the ethereal layer – it was likely more solid and real, dealing with formidable power and energy. It was the soul – my soul – that had become, in the lower ranges, the ethereal item, practically unable to touch anything but the amplification circuitry in the brain and nervous system to allow complex ambulation of the body.

The universe was real, but even that was just an image. Because in the descent of a soul into a universe, one has altered and descended through states of being, whether willingly or guided by souls at some other echelon. The souls were true. The matter, energy, space and even time were contrived. You'd create your way into a universe with great ability, adventure and hubris, then with the accumulation of all sorts of stuck considerations and mental masses, you'd have to cry your way back out though it was rapturous and wonderful.

I had condensed everything I knew to one simple idea: The universe itself was inherently inauthentic. Only the soul is the true essence. I pondered an extension, that perhaps we were creating *universes* to find out how to get out of them, extrapolating knowledge, perhaps in vain, toward a higher echelon of freedom, an ultimate power, the ultimate concept of God.

I looked up into the sky, seeing the blue dimming, yellow from a sunset casting its way across the sky. I couldn't reach across the universe. I couldn't move a mountain. I couldn't even move a cell on a microscope slide. But I had seen the girl when she visited at the wedding. I had communications with her otherwise. I found the meteorite I'd seen with an exterior vision while closed up in a vault. I better understood physics by reeling in vignettes of data from billions of years ago. The spiritual side was real.

And I felt pretty, despite my aging body. I knew inside I was destined to come to my true self, my authentic identity. I hadn't heard much from above, from the girl, for a few years – the last strongest communications being around the time of the wedding, however infrequent since. I so hoped to see images like my first – seeing beyond the curtain of the physical to the next level, but the dusky sky would remain quiet tonight. I didn't see anything but stars.

"I hope you are helping the others, because I haven't heard from you in a while," I voiced into the sky. "But I'm you, and you are me. We will meet again." I didn't hear anything in return. I had to hope she'd be successful on her current mission.

I pulled back into the house and followed to my study, pulled about my desk and lit some lanterns. I had some work to do for Daddy, pulling the second copy of the little black leather *Ascension* book out from the top drawer, hoping to be more practical than literary. There was so much mystic knowledge that translated into practical life – where would I begin?

EIGHTEEN

The Processes Continued

It was years later, and very little except sporadic "back of the neck eerie feelings" had come from the little girl above. Jack was eighteen years old. Molly was about fourteen and the cutest of all. My own body had seen enough difficulty, yet considering the world we were living in, I'd never even broken a bone. I had been studying but became tired and laid my head on a large counter in the Patent Office. Like when I'd been a child, I more or less passed out, resigning myself to perceived images of space again. There was an exasperating conflict of great souls over some galaxies regarding who owned them, why they were spinning as they were, the density of the black holes – they were not to order after billions of years of construction. "This is the construction period of the universe. Don't you think these galaxies should be created per the manifest? There's insufficient mass for the anchors. This is going to be our home for the next three billion years at least! Go in there and correct the discrepancies – these anchors, and in the composition of the star clusters we intended to live within. This wasn't supposed to be a generalized job. We have very specific intentions for life in these areas. Sure, there will be life in random areas based on the common formulae. But flatten the blueprint and fix your confusions then clear up these messes. Not all life is the same composition – these are practicable formulations. We've got cities to build there and we can't even get microbial life started on those planets!" There was some discipline I'd had to take for screwing up, having to oversee the reconstruction of muddled solar systems according to the alternate composition requested. I recalled having said "Sorry" several thousand times. But in the end, we got the solar systems even better than specification, with two livable planets per viable solar system. In one system, there were at least three planets capable of handling life. It had been a larger sun and thus the inner planets could still orbit within a livable range. The outer planets, like most, were gas giants. They were there for some reason, perhaps a balancing act for all the planets, so that the inner planets didn't get so far out of whack with respect to their orbits.

I woke and put some drawings in pencil directly on the big white counter, then I got some paper to copy them. I better understood some math that related to orbits that I'd seen before during one of my self-edifying excursions into scientific knowledge. I worked through some calculations and was pleased to see that I got some formulas aligned well, if not perfect. I could now predict the orbit of our current planet.

I must say I got excited and when we'd returned to the mansion, I went to Mother. I explained how the orbits worked and that the whole thing came from this vision, and I explained how the planets moved due to gravity – they move out, have less pull, make a wider arc, slow down, fall in, have more pull, move faster, and it all balanced out. And the moon and planet combinations worked together as if a single body. The outer planets added equilibrium to the system, though I wasn't entirely sure how to calculate that, but it could probably be shown in the equations and (too many) calculations.

Chloe came in and I explained it all to her. She looked at me kind of funny. "I got that vision. Just now."

"And I suppose you should have if it came from her," I looked up. "It may mean they've restarted one of those bigger processes."

"Yeah," said Chloe. "Maybe she's gotten her other soul divisions in line."

"Okay," said Mother, "I felt shaky, but I didn't pass out. I think it's clear that these visions tend to come in groups. Prepare to wake up on the floor, over the table, in the backyard, in the pig pen, wherever. Just be careful what you all do. I'll do the same."

"Or maybe she just decided to kill them off, so they'd quit acting like idiots. Or their planets crashed," Chloe continued from her previous thought.

I cautioned, "Those idiots are divisions of us, too. Whatever happened to them happened to us."

Chloe had her comment. "That's pretty rough. But I can see how we – as her spiritual offspring – are just a bunch of idiots."

"Divided off of a supreme being," offered Molly, having heard the conversation as she brought in a basket of laundry.

"Supreme at what level?" I retorted. "Until we recombine none of us are supreme. And at her level, she may be far from supreme."

"Well I don't think it's much to worry about," said Molly.

I shook my head. "But – we've run into this before. We'd seen similar visions. We'd all passed out at the same time – before you were born – before Jack was born – once at the village. We knew from the wedding when she appeared – we are all created from her. If she works on the real processes – we are affected and have to be careful."

"Careful – and yes we are all one, just not recombined, if there's a need for a reminder," said Chloe. "It's why we love each other. And when you resolve a long-time-ago past-life confusion I sometimes feel it too. Do you feel mine?"

"I'm usually helping you but yes, if it goes back far enough. I couldn't say when that demarcation occurs, when we would have separated," I said.

"How far back do we have to go before we see it as *us* or *I* instead of just you and me?" Chloe asked. "Well that image we just got was before we were separated – it's *I* – meaning all of us."

I offered, "I don't have a way to put an exact date on it. Maybe we should always look for things that are so far back. That way we help each other, and maybe we'll close in on a timeframe." Many images of previous sessions pummeled my thoughts, resolving into a possibility. "Those times we recalled situations before this universe – those usually had us all elated and feeling wonderful, whether it was noted or not. Even the first of them – I'm remembering now. We could scan the notebooks and come up with a rough date, but I'd already guess trillions of years ago."

Mother held up the book with the pages showing the recombination of souls. She cut in, "We are all divisions of the same soul. It's this one soul and our parts of it – us – that are left. They, other souls, that is to say other people, are trying to help *her*, right? She's having a rough time. We try to help here too, but we feel there is only so much we can do – we are doing everything in our power to be good to help her, and by doing so, we help each other."

"The girl at the pedestal? The girl that showed up at the weddings?" I fumbled for certainty since Mother appeared to be coming from some other train of thought.

"Yes. That little girl," she acknowledged.

Mother went on, "And it was important. Don't you recall before the weddings? When we brought out the dresses and suits?"

"Well, of course I do. We all learned we are girls – and from the weddings we learned we are all from her." I complained loudly. "There must be something in the way we were created that intended for us to forget. Some of the details have gotten pushed to the back of my mind. But I knew they were working on resolving any divisions of these souls to us. We've never got the exact time – and certainly not the incident that separated us. If we could...."

Mother continued, "If they could, they already would have. They were working on their higher-level processes, whatever they are. They take a break – we didn't hear anything. They worked on confessions when it didn't work well. They may be starting work again on the big processes. I'd say they were working on one of the big processes today. And we don't see the whole chains of confessions or complexity of their algorithms that they are running. We see the significant event, the bottom of the chain of events. What do you think?"

I pondered, "My data would only correlate and there is nothing to refute. But I guess I knew all this. My confusion is why couldn't we find the incident of our separation? Why can't we be the cause or catalyst of our own recombination?"

"I – I doubt that as pieces of her any one of us would be able to resolve it for all of us," said Mother. "So again, there might be more big events coming. Be careful what you do, Dahilana. You used to pass out all the time. It was you that was always more sensitive – or more receptive – to the events that had been happening."

"Yes…. I passed out this morning. Well not really – at least I was aware through it," I claimed.

"Try not to be alone – never when it's potentially dangerous," beckoned Mother. "I trust they'll continue in the direction that is best."

Days later, again at the Patent Office, because I had a pocket watch that needed a replacement winding gear, I'd looked up the patent, and it was titled "A Mechanical Escapement Mechanism for a Pocket-scaled Temporal Computation Device." There was nothing daunting about the verbosity or the esoteric nature of the language. It was odd that we'd all become so damn intelligent. When the gardens were planted, and animals well fed, we probably spent as much as twenty hours a week on learning and finding past-track knowledge.

Life had become routine but not without purpose, whether studying, laboring, sleeping or loving. Labor involved rebuilding tools and machines and producing things efficiently with them, and of course, farming. Father was the quintessential workaholic. Everyone was crazy productive. If the rest of the world could have been studying and learning by the same techniques, it would have revolutionized every field. The state of the world would have been significantly more advanced when they all died, or more properly, recombined with their greater souls. I had to ponder how many souls there were. By the vision I just got, there might have been some planets with just a few original souls, all divided into a whole society. On others, there might have been hundreds or thousands of souls, divided into millions or even billions of people. Perhaps this planet had just a couple – mostly one since the majority of the people dropped at the same hour, probably the same second. "I" must have been scattered about the universe. I could only think that it was because I'd been so much of a degenerate, a weirdo. First, I didn't divide so much because I must have been weaker. Second, I must have dispersed so that I didn't create much of a critical mass for my disgusting activities. An entire planet of souls derived from myself wouldn't survive without a significant alteration in genetic patterns.

I was likely a horrible, disgusting, weak little pervert that tagged along in this universe and wasn't wanted. The thought brought me to tears. The big white Patent Office room echoed with my cries. I had to wonder if the tears I was feeling was really grief being dumped by that girl spirit, working a much higher process. "Chloe?" I called out.

Chloe slowly came in. She too was crying. Tears falling down her face, she said, "But I don't know why."

I pointed up, "It's the little girl soul again. She's working on something."

She walked up to embrace. We looked at each other, aware that we might drop the bodies and resume our existence at a higher echelon as part of that other spirit. We looked very hard, seeing our wet eyes. We both reached to kiss at the same time. I said to her, "If we go, we probably all go. It won't be a bad thing."

"I know," she nodded, wiping her tears on my shoulder.

We went out of the room, down some hallways, and out toward the president's mansion. We went on to our room and without much hesitation, we simply made love. Afterward, we held hands, looking at each other. We cried for our impending loss. We giggled for our arbitrary silliness.

Chloe broke the silence, "If we are the same soul, we'll never not know each other, right?"

I nodded, tasting my tears on my lips. "We will always love each other."

"I love you so much I could be you," she said.

"Maybe that's the definition of love. Willing to be someone else, and to a great degree," I suggested.

"That's a perfect definition," she said, her pretty eyes smiling.

But we rested, closing our eyes, still holding hands. I saw a few more "space scenes" about early universe violence. Then I actually heard a male voice say, "That's it for today. Go verify the quality of today's session. Off to quality you go. And just a reminder that we'll have a delay." The little girl voice said, "Yes. It was a good session. I feel much clearer."

Chloe and I both waited. I was guessing she heard the same conversation. Then we sat up. We watched each other, remaining on the bed in the room. Then she said, "Well I got to get more chores done. The kids will be needing dinner. It could be years before her next session – if that's what you heard because that's what I heard."

I couldn't concur how long the next session would be delayed. I simply didn't know. Yet I nodded, feeling good for the gains in the session, but a little sad that it may take much more time. I'd kind of hoped we'd all be ready to recombine, and I could finally know what was really going on beyond the thinning veil of our present existence. What was the best course of action? For now, we followed each other like lost dogs to the kitchen.

Feeling half deflated, I pondered whether the fact that we made love was also some indicator that we were not ready to transcend to our incorporeal level of existence. Working on food, I explained my disappointment. "I thought that might be our mutual calling up, our great ascension, our recombining with our greater spiritual identity. I, however, find that I'm peeling beets again in a world with just a few people on it. And they are likely all me. So, in a way, I'm very alone here. And I'm sure that there are other souls, also like us, a division from the greater spiritual identity we could be calling *ourself* or *I* and yet you, as one of us, are also doing menial tasks." I shrugged, using my sleeve to wipe my tears.

I looked at Chloe. She too was wiping silent tears, and she softly said, "I think she's back in session." Her eyes briefly flashed upward.

"Okay. I guess *delay* meant a break," I giggled through my crying. "That's a good thing." I checked my stance in case I passed out. I wanted to be in a stable position, so I'd slide down instead of falling over on my back. I didn't want to hurt my head like I had when I was a child.

Within moments my stability was already challenged, so I slumped to the floor. I saw new images – great expanses of space – cumulating into a sense of being contiguous and complete, viewing the universe from the outside, much the same as I'd seen my own body from outside while still alive. "I see it," said the girl voice. "The entrance to the universe. I can't go there today. I know. But at least I see it." Another voice said, "That's very good. You are ready for the next process."

Chloe had braced herself against the sink, half leaning into it. We were slow to rise up. Neither of us spoke. We went on to fix dinner for the rest, going back and forth between tears and apathy regarding the mundaneness of existence.

The biological plane of living had become a bore. I'd been so distracted by that whole sequence, and the metaphysics, of not just being "out of body" but being "out of universe!" We went through the motions because survival demanded it. I was chronically bored with the gardens, cooking, eating, washing my face and taking baths. I'd become bored with all the patents. I grew bored with generators and freezers and all sorts of appliances that had been so much fun to get working. I just wanted to "go up" and be with my greater spiritual self and reign from a high level of being, fully transcendent of this material existence. But sometimes I wondered if that would be more of a penance than what we had. Despite her success today, was she in trouble? Was she in some kind of "universe jail?" And if I became a direct part of her again, would I find myself in some distasteful situation? Likely – probably – and almost definitely.

Maybe it wasn't so awful to be human for now. But I couldn't eschew wanting to be more, to be a great spirit, to ascend beyond the earthly bounds of existence like so many others had done.

On the bright side, at least I knew what was going on. I could have remained completely unknowing of anything happening up there. Then one day without warning all of existence would change. Would that be beautiful? Would it be terrifying? Would it be Armageddon, the final destruction of the universe? What would be the actuality of Armageddon, the point when the souls that created it left and let it simply cease to exist? Why had so many of the living proposed horrific myths about it?

So, the next weeks were arduous and there was little in terms of higher revelation except a few tears here and there. I had been walking through the hallway of the president's mansion, feeling half recovered when I was again overwhelmed with grief as a new session intervened with my life again. I stumbled against the walls, feeling the floors and fancy wallpaper. I was practically screaming. The grief was sharp and bitter. As it passed, I went on into the lounge area that we'd often convene in for the day's "action meeting." They were there, all of them, with tears.

Father, who had a lot more gray hair, said, "You've always seen it greater than the rest of us. What did you see?"

"I didn't. Just grief – overwhelming, even painful," I said, still barely able to babble out much at all. I collapsed slowly, heavy tears falling down my face. I heard a voice and started to speak as the words came to me: "I didn't have to create such horrible people."

I hated the idea that we were *so horrible,* and I clawed at the furniture I'd fallen by. I hit at it, attempting to pummel the leather and stuffing. The grief was so acute I thought my ears were going to bleed.

As her voice further explained I echoed more, babbling like a crazy person begging not to be returned to an asylum. "I didn't have to create such horrible people. But I did. I created so many of them. I thought it was a balancing act for the universe. I thought it was what was wanted."

Flashes of undefined white and blue struck across the screen of my mind, sorting into what appeared to the foaming surge of an ocean, then into sky and clouds. Wind crossed my face, I felt all about the area. I felt the building, *her* building, feeling the solidity of the stone all about her. I felt my human body as it was in the lounge, feeling very light and rubbery – fleshy.

"I love my body – no," I cried. "Don't take it away. We want to be with you – but we're not ready today." I wasn't even sure why I'd been protesting the one single event I'd desired.

I realized that my entire family was bent over as if praying, actively crying. I could hear Father sobbing. Mother had covered her head, stuffing her face into the back of a sofa, curled up like a disciplined child. Chloe was leaning back in a big chair, crying, her eyes closed. Then she crawled to me, had me lift up, and guided me to another sofa. "I love you, big sister," she said. "I love you, lover," she added. "You can go if it's time."

I about said, "No – we'll all go," but a new calm diffused the disruptive emotions as if I'd been lifted up a thousand meters, but I was right there with my body. I felt about it – like I could see in various directions, even right through the back of my head. I heard the girl voice speaking directly to me, "Thank you. You've been a big help. You can continue helping with your sessions."

"Yes, yes, yes. I'll help you," I said to the girl voice, also speaking into the room. It meant she wasn't taking us up today.

I felt Chloe stroking my hair, pulling it back from my forehead.

Everyone else was calming down from the razor-sharp grief, the release of which would prove advantageous.

"So, we go back to work," said my pragmatic son. "No ascension yet."

I was still weeping, settling to some form of normal. Despite my protests, I felt disappointed that I hadn't been called up to *be one* with my greater spirit. And likely we all would have gone at the same time – but now we just went back to work. As I walked around the area toward the kitchen, I saw clear spots about me beyond my direct field of vision. I felt the walls behind me. I could *touch* the molding above me on the ceiling. Part of the time I'd see the color. I even closed my eyes, and yet I could walk down the hallway with some outlined perception of my surroundings. If I put my attention on something close, like some flowers out one of the windows, I could see it in full color. The perception grew, the colors brighter, the viewpoint more complete. It continued to flourish until I saw a full spherical view from a position in front of my body, and I was watching my own face lit up with wonder. I couldn't explain how I was tethered to the body; I felt my face just the same. Moving toward my face and looking out the window, I felt so alive and warm. I giggled as I walked the body down the hallway, almost like a dog on a leash.

Out of duty, I went back to patents I'd been attempting to study, and images popped up very quickly. I wrote notes so quickly my hands were in pain and I could barely keep up. I better understood refrigeration and how to derive the refrigerant. I pulled out a couple more patents that had always been an enigma to me. One was on a photo-electric effect measuring device. I finally began to understand it, getting the idea that the light itself had very specific energy levels, adding to my understanding that these were levels or quantities of interfering motion, easily tying it into my general knowledge on frequencies and interferences of motion. My new adroitness blew me away. I grabbed from a drawer another patent about motors that I was able to handle mechanically, but never really understood. I studied those papers and put my attention on past life situations. I found more words and ran quick "past-life" harmonic chains on those, then finally understood the mechanism of the motor. So, I went on to the generator – it wasn't just magnets and windings, it was electromotive function. It came clear quickly – but *quickly* was still taking time – I'd been in there for hours. I'd gotten hungry and dashed on a bicycle back to the east house of the mansion.

Eating voraciously and promising to help with the dishes because I didn't help much with the meal, I explained how some of the other things worked. "All that stuff that happened today. That just opened me up. My mind is rapidly flashing images and these things that never made sense before suddenly make sense. It's more like I already understood everything, it has just been lost in confusion picked up along a million lifetimes. All those things I'd figured out on physics now connect better than ever before."

They calmly congratulated me regarding my new perspicacious skill, and they all said that they felt "at least a little better," which I was sure was an understatement, but I didn't know how to measure being perspicacious.

Later, I heard Mother singing and I joyously sang along. I loved to sing, and as a family, we did spend time singing and playing games each week when we got together. But we also went over progress and goals. We went over new words we'd learned. We studied textbooks on nearly every subject and shared newly gained knowledge.

Despite all the spiritual changes, I still enjoyed being with Chloe that night, nestling in skin to skin. We softly and gently made love. I told her, "Even when we all recombine I'd still be making love to you."

She giggled, and we kissed. Then we held hands and she said, "If this isn't the night we pull up into the heavens, I'll see you in the morning."

"I'll see you either way," I said.

We kissed again, and I felt her relaxing breaths against my face. Being in bodies in a universe was such a beautiful thing if you didn't feel so trapped. I would probably miss this level of existence. But I was certainly intrigued about the higher one.

I slept. In the midst of the night, I woke, and Chloe wasn't in bed. Reactively feeling intimidated, I wondered if reality had done a wild substitution on me. "Chloe?" I cried out. "At the toilet," she said back. Well, if she needed a toilet we were still at the human body level. I got up to go pee as well.

We cuddled back into the bed, she in front of me. "I love you, Chloe, you other me."

"I know. I love you too. You other me," she said.

I was sure that she could feel my breathing against her neck. I was sure it was comforting. I had a concept strike me at that instant – it was about intimacy. Intimacy was important to the girl at the pedestal.

As I slept, I heard the little girl voice again, saying, "I want them all to know."

"Yes. You've come to the end of your confessions and preparatory processes. That's excellent," said that masculine voice.

I was propelled into the scene from her viewpoint. They were about to engage a new process. There was a large post or pedestal nearby. "Please walk up to that pedestal," He said. I felt her point of view walking toward the pedestal.

He gave a new command. "Please describe that pedestal. It's location. It's color. Any attribute you'd take note of including its position relative to other things."

"Okay. It's kind of greenish. It's solid, stone or like stone. It's really hard. It's a number of steps from the other pedestal but not too far to walk. Never too far in any universe."

I noted my awareness despite that my body was sleeping. I put attention on it and woke the body, then shook Chloe's arm. "Do you feel it?"

"I see something," she said. She sat up. I moved so that we were mostly facing each other. We embraced.

"What do you think the others are doing?" Chloe asked.

"They're probably hugging each other. I'm sure we all know," I said.

The male voice was then acknowledging and said, "Please mock up a new universe space above that pedestal."

"I shall," said the girl spirit. "Done."

The man's voice said, "Good. Please create something that would identify you in that space. To prove it is yours, animate it with your characteristics."

I wanted to help produce that image. I felt her creating an image of a little girl – so beautiful. It was just like her. She had such a delicate face, a perfect visage. I was awed by her beauty. "Wow!" I said. Chloe nodded her head. It was so beautiful it made us cry a little because if that was our true identity, it was amazing. I wanted to be that!

The mocked-up image danced a little, though for now, her temporarily created image was a little faint to me. I asked Chloe if she was seeing the same. "It's a pretty dance. Very simple," she said.

I nodded and softly whispered, "Okay."

"Good," I faintly heard the male voice. "Now take down all the mockups, that is to say, clear the space you've created."

"Okay," she said. She hesitated. I think that all her broken identities, which included my entire family, wanted to see that image. But slowly, blipping in and out, it faded to nothing.

"Now take down the space itself," said the male voice. I got a faint image of him from the girl spirit's point of view. The fellow looked like a young adult male human but in spirit form. It was somehow familiar, but I couldn't place it.

Her attention turned to the space. "The others want to see it. All the other divisions of myself. They don't want me to take it down," she said.

"Continue," he said.

I could almost hear her think, "Please help me."

Chloe and I nodded, doing our part to consider a *nothing* where the space was. But that meant allowing the only space to exist to be the previous space, that of their current high-level universe, which was yet an enigma to me.

"Good," said the male voice. "Please now, walk over to that other pedestal."

I felt a little spinning and turning but didn't directly see the images. "Do you think she did it?" I asked Chloe in a whisper.

"Yeah," she whispered back. "A dozen steps or so."

The male voice continued, "Now, please examine this pedestal and any characteristics you could note about it. Describe its color, nature, position in space, solidity, anything you'd like to point out."

The girl voice said, "Well. It appears reddish, but that is just an illusion of color. On its own, it emits some kind of gray, but the reflectivity is strong in the red color band. It's very solid, made of some kind of stone, and I mostly recognize it, though I don't know its name – just some kind of hard marble. It's probably a little harder than the green pedestal, though I'm not sure and I'm not going to hit it with a hammer to find out. It's pretty. I'd like to have one like it, though I do like the green one too."

"Okay. Good and great. Now above that pedestal, mock up a space of your own," said that male voice.

I got the idea she did that very easily, as everyone else aware of the session wanted it. "I did," she said.

"That is very good. Mock up an image or a figure of an identifying aspect of yourself. Make it as solid as you care."

"I still want me," she said. A girl image came up into the space. It was like a doll version of herself. The sapphire blue eyes were kind of big, placed a little wide. Her hair was white-blonde. The mouth was rather small. The body was a child's body, her hands and feet quite dainty. It was certainly like a girl in the groin, but no nipples and no belly button. She mocked up a dress over it, and the dress had partly puffed sleeves and a lot of applied cloth flowers all over it. It had layers of lace in the skirt, and the bodice was a satin-like material. It had a rather large bow on the back.

"Now move it to prove your ownership," he said.

She made the image bow. Then she had it put up her hands as if she didn't know what to do next.

"Great," said the male voice. "Please take down the mockup you've made and leave only the space to remain."

"Gosh," said the girl voice again. "I'm having a harder time taking this one down. They want it still. All my soul parts want it." She struggled, even lost a few tears.

Chloe looked up at me, showing tears. "I want it too," she whispered so softly I could barely hear her.

I nodded. But I hoped to consider an empty space for her rather than evading the command. I thought that perhaps I too was ready to obey these commands.

It took a few minutes, but then the girl voice said, "I think I got it. It's just space. Clear of anything."

Again, the male voice spoke, "Okay. Excellent. Please now remove the space you'd mocked up. Make it nothing."

It took a couple minutes, and she said, "Yes – they really don't want me to take this down. Like taking down the space would take them down too. They don't want to *not-exist*."

"Understand," he said. "Have you got it?"

"Almost," she said, and we could feel her tears again. I slipped off the bed to get a handkerchief. I blew my nose. Chloe was going to use it too, but it was wet enough she got up to fetch her own. Again, we climbed back in, positioned by each other, facing toward each other on the bed.

The little girl spirit said, "I can't let them all get in the way." After that, the images were dim, and we'd lost contact. We laid over on the bed, faces toward each other's knees, and even slept awhile. When we woke, it wasn't yet light out. I went to the bathroom, then drank a little water, and laid back into bed with Chloe, cuddling up with heads on pillows in the normal positions.

A couple hours later I woke again, and it was light out. Chloe wasn't there. "Chloe?" I called out.

"Here," she said, having been in the bathroom yet again.

"Oh God!" I said.

"I know. Good to hear your voice," she returned. "What do you think they are doing up there?"

"I think they are still walking between the pedestals," I voiced my opinion. "Anything could happen. We still have work to do. We don't know how long it will last or what the outcome will be. So, I'm going to work, and not do anything dangerous, of course. I'm always the first one that falls down. Besides, I'm hungry."

Having acquiesced the likelihood of dropping into some vision, I went out along the hallway, holding the rails that were available through the hallways and staircases. I felt a *thump* in my chest as if a piece of old junk was removed. I crouched down in the hallway, and for the next set of steps, I sat on them and scooted down, just in case I fell down again. But I made it to the bottom step. I wished I'd had the wheelchair. I carefully walked through a servant's hallway to the big kitchen. I went in and, bracing myself, started working on some food. I leaned heavily on the counters or sat in the chairs, ready to fall over at any time.

While moving between a counter and the table, a spinning turned my head. I rushed to the table and laid over it. I tried to put my attention on what the girl might have been seeing. I could only get some big image of universe stuff – a galaxy but the attention was on so many people being in it. She had a *prime galaxy* where she was mostly broken up into people. I couldn't be sure whether it was our own galaxy. I felt sick; I felt ugly. My body, as pretty as I had been, was nothing compared to the images she was mocking up of herself. I might have blanked out for a few minutes.

Chloe came in the room saying, "How long was I out? I was in the hallway. You didn't see me?"

"No. I was out too, I guess. How long was I out?"

"I don't know that either."

The others were very slowly gathering into the kitchen. We were all hungry and attempting to eat. We chose against cooking meat in frying pans. It was too risky. We ate day-old bread and vegetables. We filled bowls and soon collected into the lounge. Father, lacking boldness and looking older yet, and Mother, appearing apprehensive, held hands on one sofa. Chloe, still quite beautiful, and I settled on a large loveseat and looked at each other. We were stroking hair and holding hands.

Jack and Molly cuddled up on another loveseat. She was young yet and cuddled close with her head against his chest. She looked up, and they each said they loved each other, then she put her head back on his chest. Their hands were locked together.

I felt another *thump* and turned my head, wanting to see Chloe in case this was "the big event." But it was like a sudden outgassing of putrid smells.

Molly said, "Did somebody fart?"

As the false odor dispersed, we had some soft conversation about what we'd experienced in the night and through the morning. Molly described, "I saw her – stronger than the wedding. She's more beautiful than any of us with piercing blue eyes and so-blonde hair. So beautiful. I want to be her."

Jack said, "I think you are her. Oddly, so am I."

"It's not 'oddly' at all. We all are her," said Father. "I never entirely liked being male. If the universe is just a theater, and we the actors, I guess I do a pretty good job of it."

"Mother?" I asked. "What have you experienced?"

"Emotions. An endless profusion of emotions. One moment I'm crying. One moment I'm seeing flowers and I'm happy. Next moment, it's like roses for a funeral and I can't stop crying again. Space and planets. Invisible souls at a grand scale. That's all."

I told what Chloe and I experienced, that they were running some kind of spiritual session, walking back and forth between green and red stone pedestals, mocking up images and taking them down. It seemed too simple.

Molly acknowledged that she'd seen the images. She came over and cuddled up with me and Chloe. Jack held up his hands and said, "What am I going to do?" There wasn't much room left on the love seat. I got them all to go to a larger couch, and the leather was a little bit slippery because it was newer. "I'm glad I cleaned in here last month," said Mother. It was a little dusty. The place was too big to keep up with the cleaning.

I felt a sharp pain shooting through my spine. Jack reached back to his neck. Mother arched her back. Father gasped and held still. Chloe reached forward to me and cried gently. I let out a few tears. Molly bent over further into my body. We started rubbing each other's backs.

"Whew! That was sharp," Father said.

"That was like childbirth!" gasped Mother.

"So be it," said Father. We all giggled a little despite the pain. Then the pain doubled, tripled, quadrupled. We were just a mess of crying. I got the idea that our little girl representative up in the higher universe was having some real trouble.

I heard the male voice, "Please get up and continue to that pedestal."

I heard her cries. "Universes have pain! Why do universes have so much pain?" she yelled at him.

"I got that. Please get up and continue to that pedestal," he said again.

We were stunned, and I perceived that many others across various galaxies were crying. Some additional souls were becoming aware of the situation as if an entourage of ghostly beings were crying into my head, and I had no idea which planets they were on, just that they were mostly in one galaxy, and scattered beyond that.

Molly said, "There's more. More of us."

A huge grief charge was blowing off of our host and all throughout the rest of us, and on through the affected galaxies. Mother sobbed, begging it to stop. The rest of us bowed our heads into each other. This was probably the sharpest grief I'd ever felt. If I didn't know better, I would have wanted to kill myself to avoid it. We all held together. Even Mother pulled off the sofa and crawled to us. Father got to the floor and scooted behind Mother, and soon they were all piled about me. What was so special about me?

Time passed – an hour or forty-five minutes? The heavy grief turned to a mild sense of relief. We were getting hungry again. Our youngest sister Molly stumbled to the kitchen and retrieved some food. It wasn't much, so the rest of us all got up together and pushed into the kitchen, all preparing a light lunch for ourselves. We spoke softly, things like, "This session could go on a long time." "We are so affected!" "I'd never felt something like that. It's a good thing I wasn't on top of a building, I would have jumped," said Jack (who had jumped off during his previous life on his planet). I smiled at him. "I'm like her," I said. "I'm the most like her – that's why you all like me."

Chloe said, "I love you because you're you." Then she added for effect, "*And* because you are like her."

Molly came to me and embraced me. I looked into her beautiful eyes. "Kiss me," she said softly. "We may not get another chance."

I leaned in to kiss her, and it was long and much like girlfriends or lovers. "I will cherish that kiss forever," I said.

None of us wanted to part, so as I was finishing my food preparation, the others lined up for the door and waited. I noted that a generator was still running, and a freezer was still operating. "Shouldn't we shut a few things down first?"

"It won't matter, will it?" said Father.

"No. I suppose not," I replied and returned to the group. We all went back to the lounge.

We collectively stumbled as pain impinged upon our heads. Depending on our place in the hallway or the doorway to the lounge, some fell further than others. I tumbled down, being in the back, out in open hallway. I spilled some fruit and vegetables, crying as I was trying to pick them up. We all cried out in varying degrees.

I said, "She's trying to get up again. She's in pain."

"We know that!" cried out Father, his voice gruff like a shoe scuffing into gravel. He stayed low, using an arm to walk himself along the furniture to the sofa again. He broke into tears.

I heard the girl's voice, now trying to let us know what was happening. But to the fellow, she was yelling, "I can't!" repeatedly.

He was pointing out the red pedestal. "Please continue walking over to the other pedestal now," he told her clearly.

Still, on the floor, I felt another flash of pain. It was so quick it felt like my spine split and the wind got beat out of me, and like my teeth were all just pulled out of my mouth at once. I felt sweat dripping down my face as I crawled to the sofa in the lounge.

Molly was rolling in agony on the floor.

My son was buried in one of the sofas, yelling, "What did she do?"

I cried well enough, but corrected, "It's what we all did. We all were her before we spun off – willingly. We are all part of this. That's why we feel it."

"Oh, fuck that!" he said, his hands slapping the floor about him.

Father was panting in his attempt to handle the pain. Mother was leaning over, vomiting. I was the least affected by the pain, but I felt I'd vomit or get diarrhea, feeling gurgling in my guts. I got up and blundered my way to a cabinet in the kitchen, finding an old pack of large diapers left behind from Molly's early years. I pulled down my pants and panties and put one in. I also grabbed a couple of pans despite the pain in my head and body, stumbling like a bad drunk. On my way back, I took the package of diapers with me.

In stumbling back through the hallway, I saw stars. I saw space and it was hard to find the walls. It was like someone was yelling in open space, trying to find me. "Oh – you! Hey!"

I slid down along the wall, allowing the things I carried to bang to the floor. Then while still trying to listen, I pushed the things on into the lounge. I desperately edged my way in. "Everyone still there?" I begged loudly.

I heard a few *yeah's* and continued pushing pans and crawling, feeling my way to my sofa. I grew very tired and put the diaper package under my head for a pillow. I was glad I'd gotten a diaper into my panties because I was sure my body was leaking now, but I couldn't wake up. It was like I was being forced into a hypnotic trance with the command, "Go to sleep. Penetrate the universe. Be one inside, with, and action thereof and therefrom. Be active with others. There's no need to be aware of anything at this level. Go forth and be yourselves (as fragmentary identities)."

I heard the male voice saying, "There, there. That's the big one we usually encounter. This will take some time to get through."

"Will they live if they get knocked out?" the girl asked him.

"I don't know," he said. "What happens, happens. Either way, we are on our way to recovery now."

I knew she was crying, "It hurts so badly!"

I considered we could have been on the final precipice of our own ascension event. Would I wake up even one more time in my body? Did it matter now? Would it be better if I just left it? I faded, unable to answer my own question.

I woke hours later. The sun was in a late afternoon position. Everyone else was still knocked out. Emotionally I felt almost normal, but I likened my body to crawling out of a casket during a wake, dizzy and weak. I crawled over to check on Mother. She'd leaked urine into her clothing. I checked Father. He had a little urine soaking his pants, but not much. Crawling and sliding along the furniture, I went to Jack. He was lying over on the floor. He needed to be moved, as the pressure against the floor created red and white points on his skin, his elbow had turned blue-white. He began to wake, feeling the pain of those points, crying out accordingly.

My younger sister Chloe, who looked pretty and still looked sexy to me, was also on the floor, evenly placed on her back. I slowly pulled her up to the sofa. "Relax, Honey. Are you waking too?" She was, and much like a child picked up by an adult in the middle of the night, she threw her arms around me and clung onto my shoulders, then kissed my cheek.

I pushed her back against the sofa, where she remained still, and her color was weak. I checked her heartbeat, which was shallow, and gently moved her arms, then she panted to replenish the oxygen. Her mouth was sticky, and she coughed. She only cried for a moment, then she looked about, also realizing she was somewhat normal despite her slow body. "I need a drink," she pleaded, barely audible.

From the permeated thoughts leftover from the session, our spirit girl was working with some quality check and said all was good. I had heard, "Okay. We're done for today. You'll be welcome back tomorrow. Please don't be late."

"I won't," she had said. To us she thought, "That's it for today's adventure. That was a lot of adventure."

I wondered if their day coincided with ours. I wasn't yet able to pinpoint when the next session would start.

I stumbled and limped to get some cups of water for everyone. My body still slow and weak, I drank several cups myself. Having collected a couple dozen cups, I had too much to carry, so I used a waiter's cart to take them all to the lounge, then went back for some additional food. Mother and Father were just now waking. I had them take a light drink. Having been still for so long, they both cried out in pain, Mother more than Father. We had to have her lay over face down and massage her back.

I grabbed the pack of diapers and when taking my turn at the bathroom put dry diapers back into my panties, mystified at the weight of the dirty one. My body was still quite painful, the joints not loosening up. I wondered how just several hours could cause that much pain and dehydration. I felt weak from not having enough food, and though we had eaten light, I wouldn't have thought I would be so enervated. We had a collection of old watches, each with the date on it, which we compared to a calendar. We usually took turns winding all the watches and updating the date – I saw that we'd missed a day.

We hadn't been out for a few hours, we'd been out for a day plus a few hours. "I know why it hurts so much!" I cried from the kitchen, my throat raspy. I took a watch and calendar with me. Once I was in the lounge, I said, "We'd been out for more than a day. Look." I showed them that the watch was a day ahead of our marks on the calendar.

Father was coughing up thick phlegm. Mother had used the restroom but was crawling back to the sofa, still complaining of the back pain. Luckily, I hadn't been in too awkward a position when we all passed out.

"If it goes any longer than that we could die. If any one of us had a heart attack or aneurysm we'd never have a chance," said Father as he walked to the bathroom, then from there he walked slowly toward the bedrooms to get some clean clothes, mumbling, "We wouldn't have a chance with catastrophe anyway."

As we recovered, we all checked the critical items, feeding the goats and pigs and checking the working generator and freezer. We dealt with the garden and fetched just enough food to get us by before darkness, still cutting vegetables by candlelight. But none of us were particularly tired. It was a different kind of exhaustion, but mentally I felt brighter than I had in a long time. I still had this ability where I could see and feel the walls from a distance. When I was out in the hallway, rushing through, I'd touched the wall as if it were solid, but it never connected with my body. So now I tried an experiment as I went through the hallway toward mine and Chloe's room. I put my attention on everyone and said, "Can any of you hear me?"

There was a faint answer from my son Jack, "Maybe."

"Can any of you hear me loudly?" I thought with greater effort.

Chloe came running up through the hallway. "We're all shaken. What do you need? And stop yelling about it!"

I whispered very softly but put a lot of attention on my thought, saying, "I didn't yell. I wanted to see if you heard me."

She stopped in her tracks, which were hidden by the shadow of the candle holder she was carrying. I saw her mouth move very subtly, saying, "Oh that's amazing." But her mind sent me the something more like, "Oh damn! That's so amazing."

I repeated what she said with her soft voice, "Oh that's amazing," then what she thought, "Oh damn! That's so amazing," sending both thoughts to her.

I heard, "What?" but she hadn't moved her mouth.

I said, "Yeah. You can hear me. Like the little book said – again." I hoped it would remind her of the telepathy in the barn at the village years before.

"I can hear you – again," she said mentally, still not opening her mouth as an image of the afternoon in the barn developed in the space between us.

"Kiss me like that day," I thought to her.

So, we started kissing right there in the hallway as she put the candle onto a console table. The kisses were so soft and beautiful. Then she picked up the candle and carried it with us as we walked silently to the bedroom, which greeted us with a little bit of human smell, as we never had time to wash the sheets as often as we would have liked. But we got into the bed and giggled. We exchanged telepathic thoughts for another hour, covering all sorts of topics about living back at the parsonage and now in the president's mansion, and many experiences of our lives in between. When we saw that we could not sleep, we got up and worked in candlelight, sweeping hallways, nibbling on things in the kitchen, and just being silly like kids, and when that ran out, we went back to our confession chains, using a table in the kitchen, taking along a couple notebooks containing our previous work.

I started out, staying verbal and not telepathing, "What is it we are doing that would be so disdainful? What would make us 'such horrible people'?"

She said, "Well we loved, you and I – not to the pattern recommended by our previous societies. Other than that, we've all really been pretty good. What would keep someone in the universe? Why are we trapped here?"

"Well, my impression is that those above are not flesh bodies. They've got their own – a body at a spirit level. And she's a little girl, our *host creator*, and she's the ultimate little beauty. I wonder if that is true. After all, should a spirit have a form?" I recalled the time between lives when I was disembodied, floating with no apparent form but having a consideration of myself as a young woman.

"Do you think we are wrong for having a form, like an identity?" Chloe asked, and by the tone of her voice, was rejecting the idea.

"I don't know that it's wrong to have a form. Perhaps it's wrong to have only one form. I'd think that a spirit could be millions of kinds of people and be able to play any role, any character. Like Daddy – he's a guy. He's not comfortable being a guy. He says it makes him do wrong things. But what if he was a little girl. He'd want the same things, right"

"Like Jack. Like Molly. Like me," said Chloe.

"Well, like me too, obviously. But it's more of a burden on Daddy because it's further from his true form."

"Yeah. Being an aging man is the complete opposite of being a young girl," she said.

"Not quite opposite – being a sea monster with your heart in your head, brains in your tentacles and teeth out your ass would be the opposite."

She cackled instantly – almost too fast. Was I broadcasting my thoughts again? Then I felt her – the little girl soul – in some distant land or strange part of the universe. She put her attention on all of us, the partitions of herself, recognizing our condition. "It was a rough session today. I know I lost some of you. It won't be so bad. I'm sorry for my condition," and I knew she was crying because my eyes were dripping tears too. I had the impression that she was bent over, perhaps sitting on the edge of a bed or a chair. She had sculptured leather-bound books nearby on a desk. Also on the desk was a lamp, likely alabaster with a full relief of a young girl, lace clothing, and a hat. The lamp had a cloth-covered lampshade, having hanging cords or tassels. It was as ornate as any desk lamp we could find in the president's mansion. There were other recognizable things, such as a heavy wooden headboard and footboard for the bed, thick blankets and pillows (the bed was much bigger than she needed). She was thinking about the exchange of work she needed to do to get the session time in return. She thought it was difficult to put in that much effort because she wasn't nearly as strong as many other people. "I'm just a girl – a forever little girl. And nobody ever understands that," she cried. The tears came a little sharper than moments before. I pinched my eyes because of the sting.

I moved back around the table to Chloe. I knelt and embraced her, sobbing on her shoulder. She cried too, dripping tears in my hair.

I tended my next thought to her, "We're being weak. We're all being weak. She's being weak. That must be what we are doing wrong. It must be wrong to be weak in the spirit world above us."

Chloe nodded. "It makes me feel kind of stupid. We'd been spending so much time thinking we were supposed to be smart or shouldn't be lovers, only to find out the problem is being weak," she agreed.

"Ha," I said. "That's kind of funny."

"Not really," she said, but I got a little chuckle out of her too.

Chloe asked, "So when have you acted weak?"

I didn't hesitate to take the queue to start a session. "Well, by the old rules I should be spanking my little sister and our little brother – whatever we're calling him, since we can't figure out what our family structure really is – when they act lazy and rush off to play rather than help. I think they are kissing each other right now and I don't care," I offered.

"Okay. Is there an earlier situation like that when you were weak?" she asked. "Earliest you can get," she reminded.

"Um – back at the village – um – could have done a lot more work one day picking vegetables and then part of it got messed up by a heavy wind storm, but we didn't get any rain, so we ended up with food rotting off the vines. If I'd been more active, I would have had more in the freezer for all of us."

"Okay. I get it," she said. "Is there an – give me an earlier situation like that one? A time when you were weak."

"Well, I was weak when the quake hit the island, when that wave killed me. But no one could have survived that huge wave. It must never have happened before on that island for there to have been life at all."

"Okay. Got it – noted. Give me an earlier situation when you were weak," she said, having rewritten the question as she refined it.

I thought of a few things – like preferring to embalm little girls on the island but failed to do that for any adults. Imagine attempting to give every soul on the island a proper burial. But I said, "I wish I could have embalmed my one special girlfriend instead of all the other little girls. That one girl, Tori. I'd have given up the others, I suppose, if I could have moved her more easily. She was the one I was in love with." I sobbed. "And to get her out I pushed her and the others down the stairs! She flopped, and it broke her neck. The sight was horrific." I cried for a bit, then added, "I loved her – and she died – I couldn't help that. I could get along with my mother if I tried; I loved my father dearly, but I didn't love them like her. I can't say she was the only person in the world that I loved. No one compared – I wanted to marry her, even thinking of wedding decorations and having us both go down an aisle with white wedding dresses on – both of us carrying flowers. We'd have two little girls instead of a boy and girl to walk down ahead of us – two of the girls I embalmed might have become the flower girls." I felt heavy, laden with the grief of my lover. "I wonder who she is upstairs – in the spirit haven or whatever you want to call it." But the grief had pushed on through, and I chuckled a moment later, saying, "That feels incredibly better. So, I guess you know I wanted to marry a girl anyway. So, then I married my sister." I was talking about being with Chloe herself, and our marriage. I found myself smiling brightly, a clear indication that I felt done with my little session.

Chloe pushed her notebook at me, so I took the question and asked her, and opened to a blank page for her answers.

"So, when was I weak," she started mumbling. "I – I felt I should have been stronger when helping my little brother get born, or nephew or whatever – Jack. I should have been stronger when checking inside you for the afterbirth and stuff, but I was young, and it was smelly and gross. Father kept saying I needed to hurry up or it would set up infection. Sure, everything turned out alright. But I felt weak and stupid. I'm pretty. I have a right, I guess."

I scrawled a note – especially about the connection between being pretty and the right to be weak. Our little girl spirit representative could be described as intensely beautiful. Did that make her frail?

I gave the next question, or really, more of a command, "So recall an earlier situation when you were weak."

Chloe pondered, yawned, and then pushed her arms about her face somewhat awkwardly. She yawned again. She said she was cold, then hot, then checked her clothes to see if she was wet. "I feel mashed," she said.

"Okay. Please tell me what you feel," I gently prodded.

"Oh," she said. "I don't know what the situation is. It's dark. It's pressure. It's slimy. She's – I'm – body – Mother – oh!" she said, then threw her arms all about her and slapped them against the table, laying her head over onto it.

"What?" I asked.

"You don't know? You were there," she said.

"Birth?" I suggested softly.

"How did you get in when you were born?" she asked.

But it wasn't my session now. It was hers. "Irrelevant," I said. "Tell me your recollection as it happened."

"Shit. I knew you'd say that," she balked.

I just waited quietly, my eyes on her, my pen ready to take any notes.

"Fuck it," she said. "I was so weak in being born. It was all overwhelming. I was a baby. It's not like I could do much with it. If I had the spirit body and such as our host – she'd be able to walk about here – and she didn't need a human body. I guess needing a body makes me weak. That's my thought. Needing a flesh body defines me as weak."

I took the notes down. She wasn't chuckling and in fact, she wasn't looking well at all. The candle was burning low. Viewing the perimeter of the room, I noted just a little color of the early twilight sky in the windows. I got up to get another salvaged candle, lit it and let the first wax drip into a little plate, and stuck the candle into it. I then got the pen in my hand, ready at the notebook.

"Okay," I said. "Give me an earlier situation where you were weak."

She hesitated, appearing to fade, pulling her hands up to her head.

I waited, giving her a chance to look, but I didn't see any evidence of toxic emotion. "Chloe?" I pushed, "Please give me an incident…"

"I've got it. Damn. I thought I'd be the girl but I – wasn't. I was the dad," and she dumped grief with the same agility as many deceitful performances at my previous parent's funeral home. With the additional morning light seeping through the windows, I could see her hands were wet. "I couldn't not! I'd screwed up so badly that lifetime. She was there – my wife – I guess I had one – was out somewhere – her mother's I suppose. She – my teenage daughter, looking just like my wife that lifetime when I'd met her – she – asked me to come to her bed. She had a subterfuge then begged me to act like a teenage boy again, asking if I found her attractive. Oh, I was so bad. Everything – everything got screwed up. It went from criminal to insane. She must have been a bad soul and I let myself get caught up in it. I think she just hated her mother and used the whole situation to get vengeance. My wife – she caught us – and then we fought tooth and claw – there was broken skin, a few broken bones, and the daughter – she called the police and put us both in jail. God! Why was I so stupid? I don't want to be a Father ever again. I'm glad I'm a girl. With you, I was always the little one, and you had control, your love kept me in line. Maybe I didn't love them. Maybe I'd never loved them. I'd lost control."

She slurred into long subdued cries, but in the quiet, her noise was echoing through the kitchen's own dining area and the kitchen itself. Between cries and sobs, I could even hear the echoes in the main hallways. Across from her at the table, it was just plain loud. I took notes.

She blabbered and gagged, mumbling wet sounds. I caught part of it, and she cleared up as she spoke again, "I'm so evil. I'm the most disgusting human being that ever existed. We – we are disgusting and shunned. That's why we are left behind. We are disgusting representations of a deplorable soul. She's us and she might be a beautiful little girl, but she's disgusting. And we're disgusting. And I'm disgusting." She alternately leaned into her sleeves to wipe tears, snorting and gasping between phrases. "Some people might like to play those kinds of games in a universe but that doesn't mean that we're the ones that always have to do it."

Tears came down my own face. I knew the problem. I was living it. I was disgusting. My son was disgusting. Molly was disgusting. My mother was disgusting. My father – I knew he was disgusting too. But I found it harder to think of Chloe as disgusting. I didn't quite realize that she felt so out of control and had been the one pushing me so much for love and intimacy.

She went on, saying, "We're all going to die. We'll all die and leave these bodies and combine up with this spirit – we don't even know her name – up in some spirit world – and we will still be disgusting." The grief slammed her down like a rapist on that last phrase, her body jerking and arms slapping about the air as if to thwart an assailant.

And I felt that grief saturate me like salt in the ocean. I broke out in my own sobs. I couldn't even write. I put the pen down and folded over on the table as did Chloe, reaching our hands to each other's. We cried like maidens turned old maids that had come to realize why they'd never got married. We continued crying like those bereaved that couldn't come to terms with a death. There was indeed something to this obsession we'd been living. It needed to be resolved but I couldn't seem to escape it – none of us could.

Behind that grief came a resolution, and she was starting to bubble out a little laughter, adding, "I'm just an idiot. We're just idiots acting out our role, given to us by others in this universe." Her giggles turned solemn again, and she said, "We were just actors, our error agreeing to the script. And as a consequence, we descended morally – we fell down hard. We should never have agreed to go that low."

An incorporeal weight had come off my shoulders too, the resolution bearing the thought that we were forcedly disingenuous because we were conditioned to be that way for the purposes of these gods. Faintly, I could see the beautiful little girl from her point of view. She sat at the side of the bed. I could see the beautiful locks of hair curling down to the side of her face. She went to a little desk much like a makeup table with a mirror on it. She wasn't very tall compared to the room and the furniture. She said, "You're right. We're all disgusting." She brushed her hair. Her hands were little on the brush. She looked like a young child and her face was indescribably beautiful, appearing a little older in some respects, and younger in others. She displayed what appeared to be perfect little baby teeth without any gaps. She had such big eyes, somewhat widely spaced. Her nose was so perfect, small and slightly upturning. Her chin delicately female. Her cheeks so smooth and free from any misshapen dips or dimples. Her face could have been right on an eight-year-old girl, but her whole body proportions were more like five or six years of age. But no matter how you could describe her, the word beautiful could not be removed.

In that merging moment, I felt tortured grief dump off. She said, "Sorry," as she knew we were able to communicate.

I tried to ask, "Where are you?" through my thoughts.

"In a church. In a palace. I'm trying to go home – to be done with this universe – as you probably know already. It's being a lot of work. I could say thanks for the help. But I know it is myself that wants it. So, I should thank myself as much. All the sessions we've had so far, no matter who did them or helped, have contributed. So, I guess I will say thanks, even if I realize that it is just another thanks to myself."

"Thanks," I said to her, giving her the thought back as if she'd originated it anyway.

"And my partner – I helped him – he is helping me, but there is more work to do." The connection waned through the statement though I only felt a trace of the ramifications.

Still holding Chloe's hands, I lifted my head. "Hey, love. Did you see that?"

She lifted her head and I could see her pretty face. Blinking aside some tears, she said, "We're beautiful. I thought we saw her clearly enough during the wedding but that – so clear – so incredibly beautiful." Sounding ashamed, she added, "It never ceases to perplex me. I sincerely think she's sexy."

"She is. It's part of our definition," I said softly, bobbing my head in acknowledgment to avoid superfluous thoughts that tried to explain it all away.

Mother, solemnly reserved, came into the room, saying, "What is happening? I feel like I just died and wept at my own funeral."

I said, "Chloe and I thought we'd run some of the confession chains again and thought we'd do it on being weak. It seems to be our issue. Did you sleep?"

"No – not really sleep. Everyone else – we've been crying all night. You mean that was you two in session and not the other?"

We nodded. "I think we woke her up." I pointed up, indicating the girl. "She cried too."

"What?" Mother was stunned.

Chloe interrupted me to get to the answer first. "We ran the session on weakness and though it's not like I have any but Dahilana here said – hey why not take a look there anyway and give me something earlier and it was so rich that we knew that she – whoever, whatever her name is – she merged with us a moment and we could see her in her mirror."

The younger sister, Molly, came in. She was a beautiful girl too, but she said, "I saw her. She's more beautiful than I saw before."

I nodded.

"My god we are beautiful. Sad, but beautiful," Molly dismally added, then turned to find something to eat.

Father had come in, hearing enough to understand. "We need you to break session. We all need to help with the various chores because none of us know how long all this will go on and when the moment we hope for will take place. However morbid it might seem to want it – I'd like to not have to work these animals – but we could all die of starvation or heat or cold or dehydration. If we don't thrive, we may as well be dead."

"Got it," I said and got up, determined not to act weak.

Chloe stood up quickly too. We went to get out some pots and pans and started on bread made with a mixture of grain and vegetable flours. We all scurried about, feeding animals and gathering eggs. I stood guard when cooking, a hand always near the knobs to cut off the flames if I found myself falling again. We all ate as heartily as we could but reminded each other to take small bites in case we all blanked out. Though we nibbled while cooking, we also took plates and trays on carts to the lounge to finish the food and kept ourselves as comfortable as we could.

I put my attention on the situation, wondering if our little spirit girl was back into session. I felt she was back to sleep. We made some attempt to see how that information aligned on the calendar. It was a little more than three days from the point she'd entered one session to the point she'd entered the next. We could plan accordingly. But we didn't know how long the sessions were supposed to last – were they a couple of her hours – or were they intended to be through their working day. Did they need time for eating – I didn't believe so. Did she have a boyfriend or girlfriend up there? I didn't have any evidence of such. She would spend time studying about universe-level things; I was pretty sure of that. So maybe her day was very full, but only part of it would be session time.

We worked on cleaning, catching up on cracking grain for the chickens, feeding pigs and goats. We spent time hoeing weeds out of the garden. We sealed a couple windows. We washed clothing. We were still eating heartily to catch up for the calories lost before. We'd made ourselves big diapers from old blankets with big plastic pants from extra shower curtains. Father had come up with the idea, saying, "I'm not going to shit through all my pants when we blank out again. And if we don't wake up, so be it. There's no one else here to find our bodies, for so much as we know."

We had extra food prepared for when we expected her to start her session. We still didn't have a name. We just referred to this bigger representation of ourselves as "the soul," "she," "her," and "our little girl." Calling her our *author* or *playwright* might have been more accurate.

"Why don't we just give her a name?" Chloe suggested.

I shook my head. "She's already got a name," I surmised.

"Well, ask her the next time you're having a conversation," she said.

I more or less nodded and tilted my head, uncertain that I'd get a clear response if I could ask.

I looked over the food, seeing extra bread, clear water stacked bottle after bottle in a working refrigerator, which despite being old had not been outmoded by newer models. The world we lived in had been decaying or held still for nearly forty years. And despite our expectations that within the next few days or weeks we'd all recombine with our *little girl spirit host* or whatever she was, there was still a chance that we'd all get old and die before that happened. There was a chance that these generators and refrigerators would fail before we died, making daily life much harder.

"So, what about the goats?" asked Jack, "Are we going to just let them starve to death if we all just disappear? And the chickens?"

Father took up the answer, "We can't let them go if we need them. You could tie the fence with something that would decay in a few days, maybe dissolve if it gets wet? But if it rains earlier or later, who knows. It's just a risk we'll take. If we die – I guess they die too."

As the expected session time came, we all had carts with food and drink, and rolled them to the lounge. We'd put on our big diapers that Father had invented, and we all looked like a bunch of clowns wearing baggy clothing. I was wearing a comfortable indigo day dress that had been saved from somebody's house some years before. Underneath I wore a camisole and no bra. I didn't want the binding to pinch if I was out for a while.

Before even sitting on a sofa, I felt a mild *thump* in my chest again. I grabbed at the cart. "Anyone feel that?"

No one answered.

"Maybe it's just me," I said.

My boy said, "Maybe," but shook his head.

Chloe came up and laid with me, and we kissed and cuddled for several minutes.

I felt a spinning feeling and heard a ringing. My body felt alive all the way through as if I could see my heart and distinguish it from my lungs and stomach. I could feel my breasts and inside my thighs. I could feel where the bones were in my chest and legs. I felt expanded, seeing beyond the walls. I could feel the flowers outside. I could feel the life in the grass and the worms underneath.

"I'm afraid I'll fall off," said Chloe, so she pulled off the sofa we shared and crawled to a loveseat, lying back, her shoulders and head over a wide stuffed arm of the rich brown leather chair.

"I feel it now," said Jack. "Wow. I see everything."

I heard little noises from others. Mother made a little high-pitched gasp. Molly, who still cuddled into a sofa with Jack, giggled. I felt elated. My skin tingled with pleasant energy.

I knew that our little girl up there was trying to tell us something. Then I heard via her mind, "Session start," as stated by the male voice. They'd been sitting at a desk, and now they were going toward those pedestals in a big beautiful room, the walls consisting of a base surface of gray granite adorned with a blind arcade, the columns and arches of cream-colored marble. There was a vague recall of the images. I hadn't placed it just yet.

I felt more relaxed, almost like what you would do before going into an operating room, not long before the doctor gives you something to knock you out. I was somewhat guessing, because my only experiences with being operated on were from past-life memories.

"Walk over to a pedestal of your choice," said the girl's partner.

She complied, and I felt her expectation and apprehension.

I was aware enough to feel my body, but I really wanted to see all these images and contribute if I could. I wanted my full attention on the session. I guess I wanted results out of it as much as any other division of her soul would. I guess my biggest reverse consideration was my younger sister was still teenage, not much different in form than I had looked when I died on the island. It seemed such a shame to lose such a young and beautiful body.

I faintly heard the male voice telling our little girl to examine the pedestal as before. I had some expectation on how this session would go – she'd examine it, mock up a space, mock up something that she identified with then animate it, then be asked to take down the identifying image, then take down the space, then go to the other pedestal and the cycle would repeat – for hours. I knew that when we took confession chains back in time that we always got to a bottom item that would release emotion as well as some realization. Apparently, this process would do the same, just a different way. I didn't know what the end result would be – but we all expected we'd get pulled up as part of her soul. What if that wasn't the case? What if we were actually unintended attachments and not proper divisions? Perhaps these doubts were all just additives to keep us separated in the first place. Perhaps it was her session that was drawing up all these old considerations. I felt distracted in thought rather than seeing what they were doing. They'd made it through a whole cycle. The male voice was again saying, "Walk over to the opposite pedestal."

In keeping my attention on it, I tried most of all to see what she was mocking up. My own body would make a nice item. Seeing the images of my family, or of the girls I'd embalmed, or the girl I loved so much when I lived on the island – those were things I could have considered part of my identity. She put up an image that looked much like a naked doll but had a perfect little girl form, completely "spiritually anatomically correct" including a purer revision of what you'd call private parts. She cried upon putting up the image, saying she didn't want to lose that image of herself, concerned that in finding her true self, she'd lose the image of her current body.

She went on through the paces, mocking up that image for several cycles. Then she noted something – there was indeed some "dark and dumb attachment" that was following her, like a shadow, placed almost in synchronization with her spirit body. She started fighting with it, trying to get it to peel away. It clung to her like a cloak soaked with honey. I felt it too, like it was – like it was sticky sexual stuff and energies all over her after being accosted by a hundred men.

She realized it was an event that had happened. She'd been attacked and beaten, used sexually, and left behind completely covered with nasty stuff, being in her hair and rubbed into every spot on the body, including the eyes. She cried out, "I try to be sexy and *they* attack *me*! *They* attack *me*!" Oh, the grief was so heavy – like an opaque ocean wave had tumbled over me, not violently flowing like the wave that killed me, but settling over like the silted water at a river delta, burying everything in a mud tomb.

I could feel the grief flowing, and like the silt in the water, the grief was settling out. I didn't feel encased in muck as much as languishing in a clearing pool. Then my attention came back to present, feeling the outline of my body as it laid on the sofa in the lounge. I heard that male voice saying, "That's excellent. It would be prudent to take a break."

"Thank you for understanding," she said.

I felt my chest breathing. My body felt especially heavy, tingly. My hands were stiff. The partition and seams of the sofa cushions had left a pressure point under my knee. A foot wasn't able to move until I moved a leg to allow more blood flow. I had to pee but hadn't yet wet the big diaper. My back was wet with sweat. The room was warm despite being later in the afternoon toward evening – or was it?

When I could loosen up my arms and legs enough, I went to the others, gently moving limbs. They were not yet waking, so I went on to the bathroom. My bladder had been so full and my mouth so dry; I felt dehydrated. The warmth wasn't from the evening sun on the house – it was from the morning sun. I could see that the sun was just rising. We'd been out nearly twelve hours.

I shuffled back in, checking the others again. "Jack," I said to my son. "Wake! Wake! Everybody wake!"

I moved them all, checking all the shallow heartbeats. Mother had wet her big diaper. I pulled her up to sit. She cried in pain. Father turned to his side, coughing up phlegm again.

I moved so I could keep loosening my joints, still pushing at everyone to loosen theirs. "We've been out for about twelve hours – eleven and a half exactly. Get to the bathroom. Get food. They've taken a break."

I went to Chloe, who was breathing deeply but hadn't gotten up. I kissed her and ran my hands all over her body. "I have got to pee!" she said. But Father was already in the nearest bathroom. She stumbled out to the hallway to run to the next, and on the way she said, "Good thing for the diaper. Shit!"

Molly was moving slowly. I pulled her up, embraced her, wiggling side to side to help loosen her back. She leaned her head back and wanted to kiss, but her breath wasn't fresh. I felt an overwhelming push to cuddle with her. I said, "As soon as you're cleaned up, I've decided that you and I are going to spend some special moments."

She said, "Can we go to your bed? I'm still hungry."

Obviously, she wasn't entirely awake yet. I put some cut apples to her mouth so she could nibble on them. She ate slowly, but it did freshen her breath after several pieces. "Love on me. Aren't you going to love on me?" she asked. I pulled her up to take her to a bathroom and helped her with her clothing. She'd only wet her diaper a little but started peeing before I even got her sat down. "I'm sorry," she said. I got a towel to help dry things up. She peed long and rapid, explaining, "I think it was all the way back to my lungs!" she said.

"Your kidneys were probably full too," I said.

"Yeah. It hurts. My lower back hurts."

We finished up in the bathroom, which took a while, and I guided her to my bedroom. "You really are going to take me to your bedroom?" she said.

"Yeah," I whispered. "Don't tell Chloe," I joked.

Molly said, "No – get Chloe. She can love on me too."

I yelled loudly down the hallway for Chloe. I didn't know whether she'd hear or come along if she did. But I certainly took my little sister into the bedroom, pushed her back over the bed, and we kissed and tickled.

Chloe came in saying, "What the hell are you doing?" Then as she looked, and I made no move to hide anything, she came in and joined us. Giggling echoed down the hallways.

Another one of those *thump's* hit me so we changed clothing as necessary, pushing new rags into our big diapers. We rushed barefoot back to the kitchen, skittling along like schoolgirls, and grabbed up another round of food. We pushed our carts back to the lounge.

"Have a good time?" asked Father.

I stoutly said, "Yes, Father. We did. Did you get everything you need?"

"Yes. But you look like you've expended more energy than you took in. Get more food than that."

He was right since we didn't eat yet. We all got up to do another round, preparing a little more. Father was half bent over and moving slowly from back pain, and he went out to a bathroom, saying, "It's funny that when you don't pee for a long time you have to pee several times." He came back into the kitchen, spun about when startled, and his back went out. He cried in pain and fell to the floor, cursing his old body. It wasn't the first time his back went out, but the timing was inconvenient. "Shit! I'm really going to need that diaper now. This fucking body. I'm so done with it." Positioned on his back he looked up toward the ceiling. "Would you hurry the fuck up, up there?" We knew he meant our little girl spirit, but it felt like a direct accusation – after all, we girls had just frolicked as if nothing else was happening. I'd felt compelled, and perhaps it was even driven from the little girl up there.

Feeling a little shame, I went to help him get pulled up to a cart he could lean over. "I'll get your stuff, papa. You take your body on back to the lounge."

"Somebody feed the chickens. We probably haven't got much time," he barked.

Precious Molly dashed out, saying, "I will," grabbing a bucket on the way.

With ample food and water on the carts, and having the animals fed again, we all retreated to the lounge. Almost as soon as I'd sat down I felt "an awareness call" that was that *thump* feeling I'd been getting, to let us know that the session would restart soon. Was she waiting for someone else to be done with their session? Was she in a hallway or a waiting room?

I ate but kept my mouthfuls small. I drank to keep it going down and not have something caught in my throat. Not quite full, I began to feel the relaxing feelings she'd been sending. "It's starting. She's going into the session room."

"I'm not sure where she's going, but something is happening," said Father.

"I think I see it," said Chloe.

"Ah," was all that Mother said.

"Got it," mumbled Jack, my girlish boy.

Molly was settling onto her own sofa, simply agreeing, "Yeah."

I quickly spat out my next bite I'd taken, not even knowing where it landed.

"I need you all," said the girl voice. "Come – be with me in this session." This command felt as wide as the universe.

From her own point of view, the images were forming. I felt the impressions, almost feeling her hands. Again, she was in a chair across from a desk. The man across from her checking something – I didn't know what – then saying that the session had again started and to return to the area with the pedestals. She was to approach a pedestal and examine it, telling all the details. She was to make the space. She was to put something into it. I tried to communicate, "What is your name?"

So instead of putting up a body image exactly as she'd done before, she first put up an impression or concept of her name. I had the impression it was a false name. The body image followed in that mocked-up space, much as before, with her long golden blonde locks, tendrils falling away from the sides. I saw an image of her face – I felt so drawn to it. She animated the face just a little, showing ownership of the image. When asked to remove it, she did, and when asked to remove the space, it just vanished. Then she went to the other pedestal.

There was a disorienting feeling that hung through many cycles. When mocking up the girl images, she'd concentrate on different parts, but the image's head was oversized, then undersized, then twisted on backward as she mocked up the different images. In another it was fragmented – an arm and hand separated from the rest of the body. Then her head showed up but no body. Then her abdomen was empty. Then there was no groin, but the rest of the body frame was there, much like an electric violin compared to a standard acoustic violin, only the required structure was present. For her body, a skeleton-like form was shown, and it was flesh covered. Then her face showed up, but the back of her head was missing, and the head hollow. Then the eyes were missing. Then the hands were showing up without full flesh content, but just wire-like frameworks. A heart was pumping in the middle. She simply said, "I was learning about flesh forms and what the importance of different aspects of the body were. They were classwork. I guess I kept them – all those images. Design-wise I thought they were terribly interesting."

"Okay," acknowledged the male voice. I still only got a vague impression of his form during this session. He was nearly twice as tall as our little girl. "Go on," he said.

"I guess I could be anything, but this body form matches best with me."

"Okay. Let's continue," said his voice. I wondered if we should take another break. But they didn't call for it. I put some attention on my body. It was okay though I could sense a mild need to pee as yet, as best as I could feel it. I hoped the others were okay.

"Walk over to that pedestal," said the male voice.

I could sense her motions, even feeling a little air flow across her arms. I felt the touch on the pedestal when she examined it, saying the reddish marble details and height and depth. It would have been several centimeters above an average person's belt. The top of the pedestal a little below her chin. She mocked up the space.

"Put some representation of your identity in that space," she was told. It was the same command. But instead of putting her same body in the space, she tried to put her attention on us separate spirits. She picked one, an image of a very pretty girl, not from our group, but likely from another planet. Her face a little narrow, her eyes a little dark, her hair auburn. She appeared 10 years old by her package. But on that planet, she was an adult. "I like this design," she said. "They don't grow up past the ideal image," she added.

"Okay. Move that image and show that it is yours," came the command.

She had the girl image dance about like a cheap cartoon character. She'd realized that the exactness of the motion wasn't as important. This went on for cycle after cycle, different characters from different planets. I'd lost track of the time; I knew my body was leaking urine. I knew it was relaxed perhaps too far, hungry and thus low on blood sugar. I couldn't stop the session; I couldn't wake the body.

Soon I saw the image of my little sister Molly – the girl I'd just cuddled heavily with. Our little girl spirit was saying, "I'd like to love her too, like her sisters." What? She already knew?

The session droned on. I knew my body couldn't take much more. I put attention on the little girl spirit to reach a point to take a break. "I'll try," she directed to me and many other souls.

More cycles. More images. She was analyzing each. Then my body showed up as I had been twenty years back – she was moving it through time rather than through space, so I saw myself playing out the whole lifetime. Playing in the yard, feeding the chickens, working about the house. She was analyzing more than the body – she analyzed my entire life – she knew I hadn't forgotten through being born, and then she was analyzing my teenage life from before – she saw the intimacy with my friends the night of the ascension event. She saw me tumbling my dead friends down the steps. She saw me embalming the little girls and living in the hotel with them.

I felt completely invaded. I cried deeply, knowing that my body was also crying.

She selected others souls for similar examinations, which allowed me to witness ascension events in those worlds, seeing the exact points when fragments, portions or whole populations were sucked up into their master spirits. One of them stood out and elicited one of her memories: a young man laughing in the same room she'd been receiving these sessions in, showing exactly the same stone floor and blind arcade walls. The young man looked like a cross between my daddy (when Miranda) and Vincent, and this propelled into my consciousness the dream I had the morning of the event just prior to discovering the horrific scene of my dead girlfriends.

She looked directly at her helper, matching his present image with the memory. It was him – it was his revelations that created *his* ascension event that took most of the three billion population from my planet, the event I witnessed firsthand that took my father, Tori, everyone on the island, everyone in the world except for my new parents, Avelynn and Josephus. And the little girl had been his helper in the same "pedestal process" up to that major event forty years prior.

It was such a shock that I believe it was I that created a *thump* in everyone.

In the next cycle, she picked a different person from far away. Again, from another planet or galaxy. She said, "Millions without the trillions is still only a small fraction of the population of a universe."

How many were we? Millions? I'd always thought it was in the thousands.

The session droned on. She only leveled out in emotion. The day was coming to an end. The coach, her helper, ended off session for the day.

"Wake up if you can," she said to us, not being very happy, but just being flat, or firm, or level in emotion.

I started waking. My throat hurt. My neck was stiff. I could not feel my hands at all. My feet were numb. My back was painful. My diaper was wet, even leaking slightly. I rolled very gently side to side with increasing motion until I could pull over the side of the sofa. I cried in pain. My hands couldn't yet grab. I pulled at the cart with the base of my palms, bringing it up by the sofa, and pulled up a bottle of water, spilling on the floor as I drank it with both hands. I couldn't talk since my throat had been so dry. I coughed and plenty of gooey phlegm came out. This was the worst I'd felt so far.

I didn't have to analyze the smell to realize the room stunk like urine and feces.

Still unable to use my hands or feet, I crawled on my elbows and knees to Chloe. I shook her. I felt her chest – slow heartbeat. I felt a sense of relief. "That's one," I tried to say but it came out too raspy to be discernable. I just grunted, shaking her body.

"I'm here," she said with no clearer a voice. He eyes were leaking a few tears. I was sure she was in pain too.

I crawled to Molly, where she remained on her separate sofa. I nuzzled her, feeling gentle air through her nose. I felt her chest with the back of my wrist to feel her heartbeat. I was sure I felt it. "Wake slowly, girl. I love you." Vocally discordant she'd tried to say, "Hi."

I went to my son, Jack. His diaper wasn't just wet, it stunk. It would have been too kind to say it was an olfactory intrusion. Oh, that would be a mess, but it was his to handle. I pushed at him to wake. His heartbeat was stronger. His hands felt warmer than mine.

I next crawled to Mother, my hands flopping like duck feet. She had a hard time waking. She cried in pain. "Oh – I can't move yet. It hurts." Her throat was also very raspy.

I looked back and saw the others moving very slowly, getting bottles of water and sipping, even intentionally spilling water to wet eyes and sinuses. Jack tried to get up, but fell over, crashing into his cart, toppling it and the food that was upon the trays.

"Slowly, people," I said, much like a teacher once said to the class in a grade school on the island years ago.

My feet were still numb, so I scooted over to Father. I checked for a heartbeat, not finding anything. I checked for breath – nothing. I moved limbs. He was much like the people after the original event. Other than miscarriages, I hadn't had any experience with freshly dead bodies for about forty years. You can't see many dead people when there aren't people to die.

I lost it. I cried, waving my numb arms about, unable to speak. The others crawled up. Chloe also checked his body, falling to the floor with a strained quiet whimper, looking at each of us as if we could help. I held against him, crying out the tears of a whole lifetime, perhaps augmented by the life review that the girl spirit had done for me. Crying was painful as my whole throat hurt so badly. I pulled away from the sofa and sobbed on the floor, trying to minimize the pain. The body felt better as I was being forced to breathe, improving the overall oxygenation, my hands and feet gaining control.

I knew we'd have a few days before the next session start. That would give us time to bury Father. I put my attention up to the girl spirit. She'd gone through her session examination and now she was just trying to deal with her evening portion of her day. I tried to tell her that my father died. Her reply, "Thousands – thousands of our millions. It was a hard day. But there's no turning back."

I cried back, "These sessions are too long."

I pulled up from the floor as my hands and feet became usable. The others were already heading to bathrooms to wash up. Mother, being distraught over Father, couldn't move at all and needed help. I went back to a First Aid room that had been built into the main mansion. I pulled out a gurney and dragged it through the hallways back to Mother, and had the others help me put her upon it. We took her to a bathroom, guided her onto a toilet, and let her do her thing. We undressed and washed her, and changed her clothing, then put her onto the wheelchair once we had her dry and dressed. We had her sip water through all our care. If the session had run much longer, she wouldn't have made it either.

Seeing how superfluous our efforts for survival, Jack said, "Why don't we all just let it happen? You, myself and Molly – we all had time outside of our bodies. We know we don't just cease to exist. We know what's going to happen anyway. We'll all be dead. There are some medicines back there that would do it." He meant drugs like morphine and sleeping pills.

It piqued my cogitation. "We're meant to survive. That's what we do," I said. "I doubt she would think it permissible. We really don't know the outcome of the sessions she's doing. There might be the recombination and ascension in this current process. It might be later. She might be sent back to do confessions for a while like before. We might all be sent back to do confessions."

Jack threw his hands up. "I guess I'm feeding the chickens."

Plainly that was the answer he'd expected, or my response wouldn't have been taken so quickly. Was I really the leader of the team? My perception of the girl spirit, whose name I still didn't know, was stronger than the others. Besides Father and Chloe first experimenting with the confessions, I was the first to push to have everyone do the confession backward on chains, so that also made me the first to push contribution to the spiritual gains of that little girl. Otherwise, I felt we were equal and none needed to ask me for permission.

I showered. I brushed my hair. I looked over my still attractive middle-aged body. Molly helped Mother now that we had her in the wheelchair. We swapped Daddy's body onto the gurney, so we could easily move him for a little ceremony later. As we each did our outside chores, we found flowers or items that represented him and brought them to the back yard. As we were gathering for our last words over the body, I felt a presence at the back of my head. "It'll be easier this way," said a voice that sounded like Father's, only younger, like he'd talk to me when I was a child. It was Father's soul.

I cried, of course. "Daddy!" I called out. "I love you."

"I love you most," his concept pervaded my head. But I knew it wasn't true. I knew he loved Mother most, no matter what, even though Mother was technically his daughter, and I was his daughter too. But right now, as a soul, he clung to me.

We brought Mother along in the wheelchair. "I wish we could have taken him back to the church at Adelardus," I said. I felt his recall of the church, the houses there, and how the town had been when everyone was alive. If he could go back, he would.

In solemn ceremony, we each stated our recalls of Father's love as was a tradition from our previous society. We each dug into the chosen gravesite on the presidential palace grounds, not to overlap with the food gardens. All the present and past images were jumbling for me. Daddy, as a regretful disembodied soul, was still crying on my shoulder. The hours passed as much as a blur as anything I'd done recently. As much as I should have prepared for anything, I hadn't expected this turn of events. My concern was that within a few sessions we could all be dead. But would that be better?

The more attention I put on the spirit girl, the more grief I felt from others and the multitude of souls that had long since been divided from her. I didn't have any idea what a timescale would be from the origin of a universe, to dividing as souls, to present. Would that be millions, billions of years? No. It would be some vague trillions of years.

We'd been up much of a day. Burying Daddy was just emotionally hard despite all the spiritual gains we'd had. I was exhausted. Even after packing the last of the soil over the grave, I sat back and sobbed. And with the prevalence of emotion, I was sure I wasn't alone in the universe crying over lost family, friends, partners, and lovers. I got the feeling it was weighted heavily toward lovers – as even we'd been told we'd all become lovers.

I scooted, then crawled, then walked loosely to the big house. I was pondering why we didn't just take the sleeping pills and morphine despite my own answer that we shouldn't. I looked into the first aid room as I went in. I looked through the packages and such. There were a few saline IV bags – what if we were to use these to keep hydrated? I looked over the boxes of old bags and bottles. They were very old, but the there was no clouding or clotting. I popped one open and tasted it. It was clear and not spoiled.

I got a garden hoe from the atrium and taped it to my chef's cart. Much like the bottles of embalming fluids I'd set up forty years ago, I hooked up a bottle of saline. I looked at a book for emergency instructions and it only showed slipping a needle into the skin, but not much about how. There were little tiny butterfly needles in a drawer, each having a little release and could be separated without taking the tube out of the vein. I poked myself a time or two and left the bottle connected to see if I could get a flow, or if my arm would puff up. Hints on the bag suggested the required hydration per body weight, and drip rates per milliliter – I selected the slowest, giving myself about sixty drips per minute. I worked in the kitchen to prepare a much-needed chicken dinner while the tube was attached.

I gave the drip rate some time, but within an hour I had a full bladder. I took the cart with me, leaving the thing attached, but reduced the drip rate by half to thirty drops per minute.

Chloe and the others were doing their chores. She was the first to come into the kitchen with the intent to help fix dinner. "What the hell are you doing? Dahilana? Is that morphine?" She glared, fearing I'd been setting myself up for a suicide.

"No, my lovely wife. This here is just hydration. There's enough for all of us," I said. "We can control the drip to be pretty slow, and though we might fill more diapers and wet the sofas, I think it will help us get through these sessions."

Jack had followed Chloe by seconds and heard my reply. "Oh," he said. "Where's mine?"

Chloe said, "Get one for Mother! I'll hook her up." (She was clumsy with the needle when she did. It took a few "stabs" to get it.) I pointed out how to pull the needle back out and leave a small tube in the vein. "I get it. I got it," she said. Within a few hours she'd be up and moving on her own.

I had unhooked my own IV line, leaving the tube in the vein. I went to make myself a new diaper, one that would have more layers and be more absorbent, also made from old blankets. I washed my previous diaper and tarp "plastic pants" and let them hang, opening a window in the bathroom where they hung to dry.

Molly came to me, her eyes soft and loving. We kissed warmly though I was consternated by whether I should have been paired with her instead. I wasn't certain whether we had been divided as specific identities to be paired as natural partners or whether there should have been a natural coupling at all. Or was that a carryover from the necessities of a biological society, not directly coinciding with the rules at the spiritual level? Was I being impertinent to suggest such institutions were unnecessary? I'd want to ask such questions if I could get directly into communication with our little girl spirit host, as I felt mired in a collision of societal rules and unlikely spiritual ideals.

NINETEEN

The Second Event

Our story would be legendary. It was discomforting to realize that no one would remain on the planet to pass this legend to. We understood we needed to double up the chores between her sessions. We no longer bothered with much study, concentrating on the essentials of survival. We checked property, looking over windows and doors, not finding any new cracks. We checked the refrigerator and freezers, making sure that the parts were free of dust and bugs. I checked the biomass for the biogas generators that filled the reservoir for the mansion's original emergency generators, and they had more than enough fuel for days of operation. I went to the power shack and checked on the running generator. It was always loud in there, but we never ran the generator very hard, only having to power a couple freezers and a refrigerator, and some lights including one small light we put up on top of the presidential estate's east mansion, up in a cupola. I added oil into little reservoirs that fed it to the machine bearings. Many of these things had been Daddy's chores. I settled back into a corner of the shack and cried, feeling his presence. I said to him, "I just wish we could have all survived to the end. That's all I wanted."

"The frailty of life is a pitfall. It's okay," he transferred in thought, softened significantly from the coarse manly character he'd become. "It will be easier for me this way. I was plagued with pain. I guess I didn't realize how awful it was. Getting out was more like relief. I didn't feel dying. I didn't sense it at all. You won't likely feel a thing either." If I could have seen him directly, I was certain that the masculinity waned to the point of being androgynous, equipoised between that of the physical body he no longer occupied and the identity from which we'd been derived, the girl, and to which we'd be reclaimed.

I felt that *thump* in my chest again accompanied with overwhelming grief. I knew what it was, our little girl had gotten up in the middle of her night and cried like a baby. She'd left her room and found others, people like her, who'd come out to console her. As the grief charge dissipated, she returned to her room and crawled into her bed. And I returned to the president's mansion, realizing how influential she'd become in our lives, now affecting every action and every moment, and how fleeting our existence, how incipient our ascension.

When I got into the house, Jack said, "We're missing the time. Everybody get ready. I need help," he said, requesting assistance with the butterfly needle to set up his IV line. Chloe and Molly went to help him. They also got their own IV lines connected and their makeshift bottle holders constructed much like mine. Everybody "suited up" with their big diapers. Jack stated the obvious, "It's a reverse birth." We all understood that.

Mother's concerned eyes suggested she wasn't sure she'd survive this one. I cuddled up with her for a bit, even kissing her. I cried with her as she said, "I feel him – your father – my father – doesn't want me to hold onto the body any longer. He says it's quite pleasant without it. Maybe I've been trying too hard."

"I understand, Mama. It happens if it happens," I offered. So, we all took turns hugging her and thanking her for all the love and tolerance, for all the work and help, and for a lifetime of seeing a beautiful woman.

Molly was having a harder time with it. "I'm going to lose a mother – just after losing Father – after coming from another planet to be with you people." It sounded accusative. Then she came up, nuzzled up against my ear and softly said, "I love you most." I never felt I deserved to be loved more than anyone else.

I felt a heavier *thump* as I rose up from Mother, having ensured that she'd eaten and her IV was set and dripping with the correct methodic pace. I nearly fell over, stumbling as if my legs had been temporarily disconnected. Chloe fell into her sofa seat. Molly fell into the nearest loveseat. Jack was already sitting. Daddy was dead and buried, but I was sure that his soul was present. I whispered, "Come on, Daddy. You lie with me."

I stayed low in case I fell again, supporting myself with my arms as I moved past the few pieces of furniture to my sofa. I hooked up my IV and double-checked the slow drip. I hoped it would stay consistent. I felt the bulky diaper as I sat back.

"I love you, Mother," I said. The *I love you's* went around the room. Minutes passed with nothing unusual happening. I closed my eyes, allowing myself to relax. Where was she? Was she late? Was our calculation of the time off by minutes or even hours? I tried to put my attention on her, and gradually that turned into an outline from her point of view. She was walking through a hallway, somewhat pensive, as the images developed. Then she went through to a waiting room. It was an antique office setting, smaller than our lounge, but not much different in terms of being ornate. We had fancy lamps. They had fancy lamps. We had big leather stuffed sofas and loveseats. They had big sofas and chairs. We had ornate wooden tables. They had similar tables, perhaps of marble. A lady spoke to her, saying, "The previous session is going over." Our little girl just nodded and sat into a chair, taking a small notebook and checking some notes. It would translate roughly to, "Additional notes for the minister." She had a note about her crying in the middle of the night. She had notes about us still wanting physical love and affection. Soon the door opened and the young looking fellow said after a quick break he would be ready for our little girl. I almost got a name, was it Penelope? Was it Princess? I wasn't sure but that was the best I had so far.

She waited, sitting quietly.

He came back and said, "Okay. We can go on in now." After the dream connection and the realization he was the product of the ascension of everyone I'd known on Earth, I could feel the familiarity of his personality.

She rose up, emphasizing how short she was compared to the room, the furniture and others. She wasn't but a few centimeters taller than the receptionist counter. She followed him, and he motioned her to a comfortable chair. The door closed, and the soundproofed room was perfectly quiet. As she moved on past the desk, I noted a simple trash can by it. Why would spirit people need trash cans? Were they closer to being human than I thought? I heard the man's voice, realizing at the same time that I'd lost most of my attention on my body. While I had not yet passed out, I checked my IV connection and made sure nothing was pinched. In case anyone in the lounge could hear me, I said, "We're close, guys."

I got another impression from her point of view, sitting in the big chair, opening the notebook with a black cover. "I had some notes. I thought they might be relevant. I had a good cry last night. I must have lost a lot of bodies from the long sessions. I'd like more breaks, even if we don't officially end session, as they are becoming more aware and need to tend to their bodies. And – I still feel very lustful for my body forms. I think I caused them to have sex, and I liked it – and they liked it too. I'm embarrassed."

"Your information has been noted," I heard him say. They negotiated the break times considering someone else's session took a little longer. "I'll try to make those times available to take a quick break."

"Thank you," she said.

I was getting closer to her with every session. How many before I merged in? How long before we all became her? And what condition was she really in? My first imaginings of her being some omnipotent and wonderful heavenly spirit had changed wildly. She was no great angel or ubiquitous demigod. She was a spirit child in trouble, left behind in the remnants of a closing universe.

"Start of session. We'll be picking up where we left off," said the man.

He checked a few things I still didn't understand, and they got up to walk to the pedestals.

"Green, first," she said.

"Okay. Walk over to that pedestal," he said.

I felt her attention upon it. I saw the green. I felt the change in perspective, the pedestal within reach.

"Describe what you see of that pedestal," he asked.

She touched it, told of its texture and color.

"Good. Consider the creation of your own space above that pedestal," he commanded.

"I've got it," she said.

"Good. Now create an identifying element of yourself in that space."

It was a simple girl part – the gender parts – pure and simple like a young girl. It was like a three-dimensional hologram.

"Okay," said the fellow. "Animate it."

She made it move as if being touched with a finger. "I'm sorry if you don't like it," she said.

He flatly said, "Good. Now take down that image."

"Okay," she said sadly.

"Now take down that space," he said.

"Okay," she said, feeling embarrassed. I could sense groveling regret on her part.

"Walk over to that red pedestal," he said.

My perception of the space changed, and a reddish image came into view. He gave the command to examine it, and she did, describing it much like she'd done many times. I wanted to see it. I wanted to examine it and observe it directly. She gave one more look at it, as if it was just for me. I felt closer to her than ever before. I had a sudden thought, though – I didn't want to be the first to absorb with her. I wanted to be the last. Was this some long-standing consideration, not from recent thoughts but from thoughts that went far, far into the past?

She continued the cycles. For many commands, there didn't seem to be anything new. I more or less just passed out, losing awareness of the session. The next thing I heard was, "Time for that break you requested if you are doing well enough. Let's check." They went to the desk. I wasn't sure what they were checking, but soon she was in cool air in the doorway. He went out. She just walked quietly in the waiting area, not choosing to sit down. She put attention on the rest of us to take a break.

She had induced my attention upon my presence in the lounge. I looked up at the IV bottle and noted it had lowered about two centimeters. I checked the clock – a few hours. This was much better. I hurried to the bathroom first. I then went back to check the others, Mother first. She was okay, and I guided her to the bathroom. She didn't want to take the IV line out just in case we knocked out on the way. So, we took her cart and bottle with us. I said, "She only has a break. Ten minutes to her is at least a half an hour to us. Not much in the grand scheme of things."

I checked on Jack to see that he was up and moving. I ensured my sisters got up and they got in line to use the bathroom too. We had a brief time to kiss and hug. But we always did in case it was the last time we got the chance. We chatted reverently about "our little girl's" perceptions of the session. I added, "I think I heard him call her Penelope or Princess."

Chloe said, "I don't think her *name* was Princess. I think they just call her that."

"Ah. Just a kind name or nickname. Maybe she doesn't know," said Jack.

We all ate while collecting back to our favorite sofas. I had to swallow hard to get a piece of apple down. I was momentarily afraid I'd not get the chance to clear my throat because right then I felt that *thump* in my chest again. It hit hard, and my chest hurt, like what can happen when you hiccough and burp at the same time. It was clear that the others felt the thump in that they scrambled to hook up their IVs and laid back right away, and I followed their lead. And within a few minutes, I was sure "our little girl" was back in the chair, but the tone became suggestive of an issue.

I heard the young man's voice. "Time to get restarted. But we have a little matter to attend to."

"Am I being sent back to the ethics department?" she asked.

"Not quite. We'll just clear up a few things," he said.

He started asking if she had any specific issues with people, if anything was missed in the session, or whether she had something she was hiding, etc.

"I was trying to mock up a part of me, but I felt embarrassed – the girl parts. That's as much a part of me as any other part of me. And it's perfect."

"Okay. Did I invalidate that?"

"Um. No – not really. I guess I did. I didn't think you wanted me to do that."

"Okay. Duly noted that the concept got invalidated."

I could feel her smile as if it were my own lips. "Yes. I – I thought I shouldn't have done that. My mistake, I guess."

"Noted well enough. Back to session," he said.

She got up willingly and happily, interested in returning to session.

They returned to the previous process, walking back and forth between the pedestals and – just the thought was arduous, let alone the action. While I was still mildly aware of my body, I again ensured that any pressure points were handled, and that the IV was in a good spot and the hose would not be pinched. Using my hand, I felt where it went into my arm, checking for swelling.

I wondered if I could retain awareness in the lounge and upon my body while still being aware of the session even as her helper started the commands. I fought with that, but did she fight back? She was pushing for her entire presence to be in the room, but I was skeptical it was a requirement. I told her to just do the process she had and not try to solve everything at once. But for me, I'd gotten lost into a state of suspension, an undefined space all about.

I came aware some unknown minutes later, and she was mocking up various body parts that related to female identity. Ears, noses, kinds of hair, lips, crotch parts, nipples and breasts of various types correlated to biological physiology, comparing to her base spirit form. Then there was a little breakthrough. She mocked up the whole body form as a spirit body form and said that all the parts were hers just as they were. With a humbled tone, she said, "I thought I was supposed to be able to be anything – and yet I can – but my true form is still the truth. I shouldn't have this unwitting aberration to be other forms and shapes if they deny who I am."

They took a break. I had hardly realized any time had passed. I pulled up from the sofa, my head stupidly dizzy. The IV bag hadn't gone down much, but a few more hours had passed. I awkwardly rushed to check the others, and they were moving so we marched through the bathroom. I reminded them, "Ten minutes of her time is only half an hour of ours. Hurry."

I rushed through the bathroom. My big diaper was still dry and as odd as it was, I was getting used to it. I checked Mother, finding she was doing better and able to move on her own. I cut up some apples and ate some nuts and dried berries. We all hung out at the table for a few minutes and commented on any perceptions. My comments were simply, "Same process. Something went well at the end. Being able to be her – she's still a spiritual identity. Though she could be every character, every kind of person – she still acknowledges that she should be herself. I'm not sure we know exactly what that self is." I rapidly scrawled notes much like the little girl had, using my own little leather notebook, recognizing that I may never get a chance to read it again.

The clock was nearing the half-hour mark. We handled our last bathroom visits, last bites, and connected our IVs and laid down in the lounge. It was still a few minutes before I felt the *thump* but thank god it was so much lighter than before. Maybe that hard swallow was mostly what caused the pain.

She made us aware that the session actually started. Her helper was already giving commands; she was already describing the pedestal. I felt like shadowing her in my attempt to see the specifics, and surprisingly, she said she felt shadowed. She mocked up additional things – girls she liked, how she liked to love, hobbies – sewing and painting and other design things. She showed a vehicle she'd built. She showed sculptures – all these things were in the mockups. It was all about purpose and help, design and exchange of services with others. All the time I felt a darkness following ever closer – an encompassing concept that suspended like a heavy black fog. With each turn of questions she claimed a heavier burden. "I don't know what this is – fog – heavy. I can't think through this vague darkness. It stinks like moldy leaves."

Back and forth they continued. She acted stoic and suspended, like she almost fell asleep, and stumbled as a result. "I'm so heavy," came her little girl voice. "I'm so heavy. I don't like this. What is so attached to me?"

More cycles. More confusion. More weight. I felt lost. She felt lost. I was sure that the others felt lost in a pit of black pitch – was this an image of having been confined into a black hole? Was this some form of imperative hypnosis we'd been the victim of to remain within the universe itself? And the cycles of the procedure continued dutifully. If this didn't clear up, our very survival could hinge upon the delay of being stuck in session, having physical repercussion to many. Perturbed with the lapse of effort and time, tempting my anger (which was likely a result of the session) I kept asking her to look at it – whatever *it* was. With a general agreement from many other of her broken souls to finally face it, she poised herself for a final breakthrough into the blackness.

I could feel the agreements of a thousand souls align to *look!*

And she did. The specific details of an important event sprang into her mind's view, lighting up a horrifying spectacle.

A violent deluge of grief struck instantly, magnitudes greater than the wave that killed my body named Miranda. It was so hard, so terrible, so immense that I thought it would commensurately kill everyone she'd created. Like being a soldier and seeing everyone about you blown into a red mist, leaving you with one last bullet in your gun, your best answer to put it through your head with a calculated demand to succumb with the least pain. It was as if being a mother and surviving unscathed from a traffic accident that killed your husband and five children, desperately wishing to join them. Had I found myself atop a building and felt that sort of anguish I would have inevitably jumped, wishing only that the ground would come faster. If I had been in a swimming pool I'd have dumped the air from my lungs and struggled to starve myself of oxygen, hoping for oblivion. If I'd been paring vegetables I'd have swiped the knife across my throat or thrust it into my heart, counting the seconds until I dropped.

Savage, piercing, searing, excruciating, scorching, devastating – how could you describe a level of invalidation creating a forlorn dejection to the extent of not wanting to exist, the true intent of the concept *damned*.

Coming into view were the faint images of other spirit-level people, male, female and androgynous alike, laughing and belittling her – it had been a very, very long time ago, back to the beginning of the present universe.

She cried out. She fell. She screamed while rolling on her back. Her little arms were held loosely, bent in front of her chest. Her little fists held hard. "They didn't want me!" she forced out. The grief was too thick. I didn't know what she meant. Neither did her helper. I heard the richest crying I'd gotten so far. "God damn it!" she cried as if damning the whole universe. "God damn them! Send those bastards to the Ethics Department. Dump them in a universe rich in their kind of derogatory shit and let it incubate into gory fire dragons that eat them as they attempt to form into new entities. Take them and rip off their heads as they make new ones and make sure it goes on forever! They were vile and ignorant and should never have been in a good universe. Damn any effort for them to survive!"

As fast as the intense grief came, it washed off into violent laughter. Experiencing a release of extreme emotions, a tempest of *tears of joy* rocked her and everyone she'd created. She looked up – her sapphire blue eyes glowing intensely. With solid assertiveness, she vociferated, "I know who I am now!"

"Good," said the man, smiling down to her as she remained prone.

Her face gleamed. She hesitated for being laden with pockets of grief that still buffeted her. Hysterically she giggled again, emitted tears again and then again, she laughed out loud. She sat up and cried as her thoughts became cogent, "I hate those bastards."

For her helper she described the context of the cognition: "Early in this universe, these dozen or so argumentative guys found me, and I offered to be a little sexy. But they ridiculed me heavily for it. After smacking me around and teasing for galactic-scaled hours, I guess I agreed to be subdued and small and not be the first out of the universe. I was made to believe that I should *never* get out of the universe and remain trapped and subordinate to them, making me dependent. The elitist swine – the pigs – let them stink in their own shit. Let them get lost in their *own* universes. I lost the most important thing. I lost who I was – and this was *our* universe."

Her helper sought clarification for a specific form of realization expected from the pedestal process. "So, who are you?"

She voiced the sincere essence of her discovery: "I'm Purity. My purpose is *to purify.*" It wasn't just her authentic self, it was the truth for every soul she'd spawned, driving every one of us from sharing the excitement to being propelled into exhilaration.

Without opening my body's eyes, I saw every detail within the flesh – every hair and every cell. I saw inside my eyes. I saw the inside of my sinuses and ears. I saw and felt everything. I even viewed from inside the vein where the IV was inserted as if my whole body were a high-grade medical model.

I heard a couple light, happy moans from the others. I felt Father's spirit in the room, exuding satisfaction; he was so bright I knew exactly where he was.

My own essence was expanding greatly outside my body. It wasn't an expanded superimposed semblance of space like previous times, it was direct spiritual vision. As for our little girl at the pedestal – she was laughing and kicking her feet again, having fallen back over on the floor after an attempt to get up.

Her helper said, "This Identity Process is complete." His feet shuffled toward the door and he opened it.

Moments later, I heard a bell. Beyond her laughter I heard, "We have a huge success on the Identity Process! All assemble!"

The other people in that space, what I had originally assumed to be some ethereal projected images at a higher-than-universe area came and picked her up off the floor and lifted her over their heads. They carried her very happily to what appeared to be a chapel, being large enough for a gathering.

"All hands! All posts! We have a success on the Identity Process!" yelled someone. "All but running sessions come to witness!" I could see them better through this view – they were much like young people themselves, most being taller than Purity with a comparable resemblance to preteens and teens. Some were obviously masculine, some effeminate, and a handful of them androgynous. A modest proportion were small like children.

Purity giggled so cutely like a little child being tickled.

In moments she was crying again. Instead of lingering like a spoiled lake, a spot of grief shot off like thunder and the area crackled electric.

"Watch!" said a young fellow – her helper – with great enthusiasm.

Above my actual body, much like participating in a lucid dream, I watched from afar her uncontrollable tears of joy. Another spot of grief shot off like a small bolt of lightning and she returned to cachinnating. Other spirit-bodied people continued to arrive, watching expectantly. Many were touching her, holding her steady, holding her up, and waiting for more to see.

"It's happening!" chortled Purity. I felt a series of sharp thumps again, as if they were echoes of thunder from that lightning of resolving grief. She was giggling as additional emotional charges were "striking" about her. I felt her thoughts referring to souls that began returning to all of us, "… I couldn't be her – so I made her separate. I couldn't be that girl, so I made her separate too. I couldn't be him, so I made him. I made thousands. I made her. I made that one. I made that boy that never had a body. I made all these people. Oh my god, I made millions...."

Cackling energy shot all about me, as violent as the meteor shower, lifting me up from my body, the sofas and the lounge. I felt that the souls of the others in my family were being pulled aloft as well. Language concepts failed me, but the concept of ascension held close.

When the energy of a soul climbs above the altitude required to handle the suppressive energies that have been keeping it down, it sometimes completely handles the problem on the spot, exactly like we handled the deep-set emotion associated with the loss of society on the day of our weddings.

This little girl, in her greatly elated spiritual state, yelled out, "I see it! I'm powerful enough to handle it! *Now!*"

This had been the curtain call of her universe play, the denouement of having the dramatis personae perform for her cosmic novel, and for us, the rapture.

A spiritual explosion flashed across the universe, lighting up the earth and firmament alike. I was sure that my human body's heart stopped with that command. I'd become fully detached as I realized without any doubt, as the little *Ascension* book had stated, the body was clearly a substitute, nothing more than a biological doll. I observed great space and expanse. I saw beyond the mansion, then beyond the city, then beyond the planet. I saw the moons, sun and other planets. I saw the oblique asteroid belts, the source of our irregular meteor showers. I saw the whole solar system drifting aside – or rather, I was traveling through it and beyond it. I realized that small "awareness points" nearby were my family – Father was there, already having changed to a younger, softer girlish image. Chloe was there, her appearance altering to appear younger and prettier as a ghost-like form with escalating brightness. Mother was there, also altering in form to look like a child. Jack was there, his image changing completely from a teenage boy to a younger form, to the image of the girl we'd seen in him before. Molly was there, also gradually looking younger with her eyes turning brighter, bluer. My own form reduced to mimic that of my childhood as Miranda, closer to my true spiritual form.

We all had some name tag we'd held, changing from our given names to something closer to our actual identities, much closer to Purity's form, as assigned from the beginning of the universe when we first divided. Father was "True," a leader and keeper of truth. Mother was "Desire," a handler of forms and designs. Jack, in his simpler girl form, flashed the green eyes, now having the name "Joy," whose unique purpose was to handle the mechanics of things. Chloe was "Love," and her purpose was to restore things, thus her particular interest in the patents and confession chains. Molly was now "Princess," whose purpose was quality, ensuring our consistent push to improve. My true name was "Grace," and my purpose was to connect everything else in its proper way, connecting flows, coordinating action. And yet we were all defined subdivisions of "Purity," and our purposes were all the required actions of *to purify.*

The vast perspective on the galaxy shrunk its significance. We weaved among the stars, as did many other souls that had also been created from Purity, in a grand tour from our planets to the outer rim of the universe. We couldn't explain it yet, but many of these souls came chasing us, sorting to each of us, and combining in with vibrant changes in our emotions and appearance. I could understand the assignation of their individual identities as they merged, and included people as well as many remaining animals, even insects. Their memories remained but the distinction of their initial parturition faded as we traveled. Hundreds of additional souls were drawn to us and combined inside of us, popping away divisive energy, stinging like pinpricks. The laughter of Purity's win had reached us. We effervesced bubbles of pure joy as we journeyed to our ideal state.

Toward the outer rim of the universe was a small spiral galaxy. We were drawn to a specific area along an arm, down to a solar system, descending to a beautiful planet with a thick blue atmosphere and beautiful cities. We were pulled to a huge complex of buildings, many designed like castles and churches with great towers and many with gorgeous flying buttresses, accompanied by adjacent complexes, each with their castle grounds and everything they needed from colonnades to tabernacles. Each was a slightly different style not unlike English, Arabic, Chinese, Greek or Roman, Russian or Prussian. I could imagine a feudal or monarchical organization among them.

Overlooking them all was a larger crenelated castle complex with very thick granite walls and immaculate gold-colored gates, a massive gate at the center to the scale of the ancient complex, magnifying its importance. Along the entrance, up from the oversized gates, was a multicolored stone plaza leading to steps, which in turn led to the main entrance, which had many gold doors under arched doorways.

The group of about three hundred had been taking Purity from the chapel to a courtyard, joining her on and around an isolated circular terrace or dais. Bells continued to ring as hundreds more arrived from other wings of the complex. Purity further cackled with guffaws and cachinnations – I was sure that a human body would have already died from that much laughter. Again, she cried out in a shrill child's voice, "It's happening! I never thought it would work for me."

Thunderous shocks of emotion continued to dump off of her. Completely detached from my body and the previous world, I was thoroughly here. I was watching, seeing and sensing everything. These people were not ghostlike apparitions. They were not ethereal in any sense to the naked eye. They were real, solid, walking, talking people, wearing clothing concomitant for the architecture.

The procession of disembodied souls rushed up to her, some prominently recognizable while some remained ghostly. I continued to recognize souls pushing into me, gradually expanding my own strength and awareness while I felt evermore pulled toward Purity. The assembled group became aware of my family arriving, as our images had become visible, if not completely solid, allowing us to step down to the stone plaza and walk toward them. We had become six of the most stunning and beautiful girls aside from Purity herself. Additional shocks flashed out, like little blips of fire, but she continued to giggle. I kept my family group of six back from her yet as we absorbed thousands of souls per second. I felt this continuing train of entities from all over the universe coming and reaching to us all, as if pushing their hands out – and I understood. They were dissolving and abolishing the energy that had been used to create them as autonomous souls. And as that energy connected back with the original spirits, the shockwaves came away from each of us. Even the owl that followed us from the village was here, rejoining specifically into myself. Put even simpler, the energies involved in the creation of the personalities, if unacknowledged, would allow them to persist. In realizing that we, the six girls, had created a multitude of these identities, we knew we were also responsible for dissolving them. The dissolution of such entities occurred because that energy was now recognized by all of us, entity by entity.

The crowd had become fully aware of us, jaws dropped in awe of our presence and beauty. I felt welcome to a degree I could not have imagined. The group left Purity upon the terrace and backed up to allow us room to act.

In a pattern about her at six points, Father, Mother, Chloe, Jack, Molly and myself, as our newly refreshed identities of True, Desire, Love, Joy, Princess and Grace, closed in upon Purity. Reaching into her space at the same time, there was one final acknowledgement of our existence, eradicating the ancient energy that had been our inception, releasing one final blow – and it created a tumultuous shockwave across the entire castle grounds, extending far into space, even knocking the nearest of the cheering audience on their bums. As a part of Purity, her thoughts invaded mine, "These are my primary divisions. These are the best sub-identities and purposes I'd ever created, a fully divided essence of *Purity*."

Seeing within her point of view, laughing, experiencing the highest level of exhilaration I'd ever felt, we'd become one with her soul. I had what I and millions of souls wanted, being combined with her as the most beautiful little girl in the universe. And I, as the full combination of these millions of souls, giggled happily, loving the sound of my own childish voice. No longer existing was Chloe, Jack, myself, Father, Mother, Molly and a retinue of millions. I could feel and see from everyone's point of view – seeing all the histories. But they were histories, and I could remember them all, even though the specific identities no longer existed.

"I'm no longer broken up all over the universe," I giggled.

I kicked *my* little feet, *my* hands, *my* supple but solid spirit body. I noted the simplistic princess dress I was wearing. I felt my light blond hair dance about me. I reached for others for hugs and little kisses. I felt such great love for everyone. The universe was suddenly a very, very beautiful place.

"Thank you, Michael," I said to my helper. Throwing my hands in the air, I yelled out with my most beautiful child's voice, "*I'm one!*"

TWENTY

Being One

I was in the library doing research on planets that still contained souls attached to body life, aside from the present, which had come to be known simply as *Gate*, shortened from "Ascension's Gate," or "Armageddon's Gate." The name translated a thousand ways in a thousand languages.

Seeing it was break time, I looked up from an antique wooden desk, just as ornate as any as we'd had in the president's mansion. I walked through the picturesque castle complex to find Michael. I noted the warm-toned wooden floors, stone walls and arches, lit by wide clear panel lights, arched to match the curvature of the ceiling, which, in their age, presented patterns akin to looking at galaxies on their edge. As I walked into the Identity Process Wing, and through a hallway lined with historic scuffed and chipped stone pedestals used in sessions over centuries, I was hoping Michael would not work through his break again. Seeing him in his office, the solid wooden door ajar, I pushed into the room that I'd once thought to resemble a dungeon.

"Michael," I started, presenting myself to my best friend and partner as the most beautiful little girl in the present universe, wearing my standard attire, a little white princess dress and mock ballet shoes. "Thank you again for your help," I stated with the purest of intention. After all, my name *is* Purity.

Wearing standard slacks and shirt with subtle medieval flair, Michael, sitting at a simple library desk, covering papers he'd been evaluating for another soul's session, looked up at me, though the direction of his spirit body wasn't required for him to perceive me. "It was my duty, Purity. You'd brought me through the Identity Process before. I feel implored to say 'Thank You' again too. It was riveting to witness a success of that magnitude."

Enthusiastically I bubbled, "I know. I'm still sorting out all my histories. I thought I'd lost you through all those galactic years," I tilted my head. I knew I'd not lost him at all. "I know now that you were most of that last earth. You even look a little like my fathers."

"Yes, Purity, it was a plan – you were my daughter, my crush, my victim, my girlfriend, my girlfriend want-to-be twenty times over, my…."

There was no need for him to start apologizing. I giggled so cutely, knowing my sounds, yet finding them new. "And you'd escaped some particularly raucous meteor showers! Anyway, you were better at being your millions of characters – I'm just a little girl and it always bleeds through."

"That may be now. But with the next scheduled processes, you'll gain in that ability," he pointed at me assuredly.

"I sure hope so," I nodded, throwing in a little grimace, my wavy hair tossing aside and settling against my shoulder.

"You will. There are literally millions of souls out there in this universe that need your help, some planets barely touched by the accomplished ascensions."

"I know," I bit and twisted my little lips, not sure I'd want to commit to several galactic years of work. But I had a thought for an enterprise I hadn't revealed yet.

He looked at me sternly, "Purity – you've stated yourself that you aren't the strongest of us – you need to finish the current processes including Power – but every time we truly help others we gain in strength. There are souls there that are still completely broken up. There are souls that have never had the first clue to their enlightenment. Their plan, unlike ours which set up predestination from the beginning, wasn't vaguely formulated."

"I know now that some of the voices I got – my characters got – were reactionary – from us in the present, and some were premonitions offered from the first times of this universe. Yes – I'm aware I was preparing for my exit at the beginning."

Continuing his apparent entreaty, he enthusiastically blurted, "That puts you at the top of the class. You say you didn't have much power, but you did have the foresight to tell yourself how to turn through the perilous maze. If not, I'm sure your steps through enlightening yourself would have taken much longer. And these last thousands of years have presented a wonderful game with you." He looked at me so warmly. Words were not required to feel the depth of his affection and appreciation. "We've gotten out of the physical captivity of *needing* bodies. We need a bigger game to carry us forward."

I nodded cautiously. "Well – if I pick one planet, that last earth – that seemed like a long time. Forty planet years – my first-tier souls had to brave so much hardship. Aside from myself, I'd concentrated my efforts there, until I had to clean up some others, as you know."

"Yes – that's the same planet I'd referred to. Forty years a long time? But no!" he shook his head boldly. "Some souls would remain stuck for *trillions* of years – perhaps they'd perish completely in this universe if not forced. That's why to some, end-of-universe phenomena are so terrifying. They haven't even considered awakenings and ascension, instead waiting for their rapture as caused by *gods* unknown to them, and they haven't foreseen the need for apologies for their invasion. They are phenomenally stupid fools playing until their pain, despair and unconsciousness comprise the larger part of the dark-soul-matter of the spiritual universe, the anchors and wreckage that keep it intact. Perhaps forever is their ill-formed purpose, but for the rest of us, it makes it hard to exit. I hope we find some higher level of enlightenment that shows we *should* be responsible for them. Otherwise, I can't mitigate my contempt."

"Well – they are stupid, but I don't feel I've got much to brag about. I can't be that contemptuous."

"You're an infinite spirit, Purity. You've ascended to this level. You are nearly at the celestial exit door if you'd choose to take it. No apologizing is needed – you have a lot to at least boast about, and if you help, you'll only get stronger, and with that, maybe the perspective will change. If you want sustained power and ability, there's your next game. One planet – just pick one." There was a little sly smile added to his expression. I believed he was already thinking about it as much as I had been.

I thought about my long track to enlightenment. I'd lost much of my ability except to be able to create an image in front of me and throw thoughts about. Then I'd met an incarnation of Michael, a preplanned event. It was a long valiant game of finding the clues we'd laid ahead of us, even delivering us to a gaudy-looking leather-bound "universe book" containing the processes we'd need. This led to thousands of years of adventurous spiritual improvements against a multitude of adversities, regaining our spirit bodies, the ascensions, and eventually to our current moment.

"I love you, Michael," I said.

"I love you, Purity," he said, dropping the pen and standing. "Come up here," he said, clearing the papers aside.

I used the chair as a boost and skipped atop the desk, then stepped forward into his arms for a great embrace. "Yes – first we created the end, such that we would not be left out of the resurrections. I'm remembering how we started this universe – and then all the tag-a-longs got in. I can hardly fathom the concept of having a universe I wouldn't share with you."

He smiled and pushed his face closer to mine, egging on a kiss, tenderly caressing my back with his fingertips.

"Perhaps," I said to be sassy, "I shouldn't have vowed to follow you through so many universes."

"You vowed a thousand, I think," he said with a genial smile.

"You're trying to let me off easy. You know I take my vows seriously," I asserted.

"That you do. That you do… that you do… even if they get you into really serious trouble!"

I held an *I dare you* position, legs straight, bottom out, chest up. "Oh, shut up," I said cutely, giving him a small smack with my right hand.

We embraced and kissed, then looked into each other's eyes. I revivified images from the start of the universe, not long after creating the space, making plans with great exhilaration for societies, and at the same time, creating this little galaxy as a cosmos-scaled respite against all the mayhem and disaster that comes along with a universe. It would be our ascension workshop, a place from which we'd seed essential knowledge back to ourselves to start the eradication of everything we'd created.

But it was time to get back to work. I knew, regardless of scale, I'd have to help. I'd attempt to find a soul worthy of a little help, perhaps someone a little deranged like me. Or perhaps I should pick someone so much the opposite, a staunchly religious family man, impinging upon every bit of contrived "common-sense" knowledge he'd ever learned. That would be a story – I'd first become a citizen of some space society, then land a flying saucer on "Joe's farm" and bring him unusual knowledge, only to have him find out I'd be some spiritual creature instead. Oh, the entanglements of existence! How to help others without suddenly activating all the painful energies they'd had attached, having them willfully entering mental hospitals for their inability to sort through their shock.

We'd have to start a little more subtly, rather than show up with extraordinary fanfare and superpower. Perhaps just start a library and add one book, like our little hand-bound book, *Ascension*. I realized now that, in our winding descent through the universe, having created characters split off from our own personalities to document and translate, that Michael and I had written it. We had helped ourselves, and now we were to help others – I had an idea of someone else I was looking for, and as the hours had gone by, an image congealed. She was like me.

After the work day, I met Michael on a broad portico. The others here knew us as a team, as a couple. I oddly knew them all, and who had vowed to whom. I knew their purposes, just as I knew Michael's as *excellence* – to provide, present, or even conjure excellence with aesthetics. After all, what was beauty but a summation of aesthetics, as the presentation of my form, a girl, was beautiful as it provided the best summation of the aesthetics that defined me – preciousness, cuteness, playfulness, intensity, curiosity, conciseness, appreciativeness, intimacy, creativity, and many more, and it aligned with my purpose *to purify.*

I would entreat Michael with my own plan. He looked at me suspiciously as I offered a folder. "Another planet – we can go together."

I think he expected it as there were no knee-jerk reactions. "I have to finish my work here," he mildly commented.

"We both do – then we can give it a jump-start. I think it's an odd collection of souls – I doubt it would sum up to one or two. I'm sure it's many."

"That's a large undertaking," he balked slightly.

"No – it's huge." I flashed my pretty eyes.

"So, if you like such huge things, why are you a little girl," he jested.

He essentially knew the answer, but I spoke anyway. "Because I have to be a huge soul to be a little girl and counter all the considerations that come against me. I love countering everyone's considerations if those considerations attempt to make me weak. It's my defiant strength." I grimaced and tilted my head, my eyes drifting off to the side. "But I got weak and succumbed." I bit my lip again. To lighten the atmosphere, I added, "If I put out my truest image, they'd think I was God."

It got a smile from my handsome partner. "They'd *know* I was," he laughed. "But I'm not. Perhaps if I were one step more true to my own aesthetics, I'd look more like you."

"You can do that anytime," I begged with an insistent gaze. "Although I know just as well you'd like it if I became a tall curvaceous goddess. If I tried it now I'd bust out my little dress," I added with a chortle.

He chuckled at my pun, "You know me too well – we *shall* try *all* the combinations. Maybe later," he offered, but then just smiled and looked over the plan. "Planet Duncoff – are you serious?"

"My name, sorry. Like most, it would just translate to *Earth* again. I could call it Peon-1. It's the only living planet in their system," I said. "We'll have to learn their languages."

Still smiling he asked, "How many languages?"

"About two thousand," I pointed to an illustration of the planet's details. "But only a dozen or so cover the majority of the population."

Raising the paper, he looked over the statistics, "Third planetary body from their sun. Various billions of population, waxing and waning from wars and natural cataclysms. They have a tendency to build ridiculous banking systems where the currency is not properly backed by effort-based products of value. A planet with cyclical glaciation on a hundred-thousand-year scale – currently in an interglacial period. No other living planets in their solar system, the last having died out just twenty-two million years before from magma coil solidification, and concomitant loss of atmosphere. Obvious societies, each consolidating by styles, likely evidence of original souls' preferences – thus multiple creators. And the numerous languages suggest that too. Sounds like the fate of many planets – not unique at all. Um – a little heavy on the percentage of materialists, narcissists and socialists. It doesn't look like they are getting along very well."

"No – they're not. The toughest point for me, I guess, is that they don't realize that they'd created their own worst adversaries, they may destroy themselves before we even get started. It's so much like the planet I, as my primary soul divisions, just left."

"Don't tell me – nuclear capability?"

"Yes."

"Oh God! Even as a soul at the level that I am, I'm never pleased to walk into a nuclear-capable society with surreptitious, maleficent leaders," he said, firmly holding up the papers as if needing to reconsider.

"Well that's why they need our help – and they do have a concept of a God or Gods, an ineffective deism."

"So, they've at least hung onto that last and final clue that there is something other than chemistry in the makeup of a person… sounds pretty desolate. So, when they die they think they'll side-step directly to 'heaven?'"

I laughed, "Yes. They do – many of them do."

"Well *we* could – but I don't think showing them will help – they wouldn't have the capacity to perceive it." He looked about, checked a few more numbers on the planet's statistics sheet, then with a reserved countenance, "Well, okay. We can try it. But if they destroy themselves before we get much done, we'll just have to let them wallow in their devastation."

"No," I vociferated, half pulling up from my chair. "If I make a vow, I'll start with the first disembodied soul I can find, make a tractable idiot out of him, then a new spirit, then bring him on up through these transcendental states until I get him to his ascension. Then I'll start on the next." Settling back into the chair, I pulled up my lower lip. A little wetness welled up in my eyes. I knew the exasperation of being forsaken and aloof. I added one more thought, "Imagine my realization that I could have been the last person on a planet, only to find I may also have been one of the last few souls in the universe."

"You are so compassionate," he said softly. "But there's more than just a few souls left. It's still this same time-stained universe, the actualization of our arbitrary but consistent rules – patterned after so many predecessors. This plan – it's more precarious than sagacious."

I felt in danger of withholding an ulterior motive. "I know. But as I put my attention out into the present universe, this planet comes to mind. I – I think I might find her there – there's one like me. I've been getting new images and I searched the library – I think *Planet Duncoff* is it."

"I see," he said with a nod.

"Yeah," I said softly. "My 'spirit twin,' if there could be such a thing besides my six divisions – I must have lost track of her a long time ago – it must have been decided from the beginning. I feel it's my purpose to find her. I must be part of her ascension plan. If she doesn't ascend from this planet, I shall continue to search for her."

"And you should. So, *Planet Duncoff*. If we vow, we finish."

I readily nodded, "We finish."

"Okay," he said, throwing up his hands and adding a smile.

"Okay?" I smiled brightly. "To sneak our way in, we'll have to take flesh bodies again. At first, we'll even have to act like babies."

"Okay. We go as soon as our work is done here. To *survive* – at the biological doll level, that's the same as *to persist* at the spiritual level. I'm not sure how to eat or poop, I haven't done it in so long!"

"Well if forty years is 'so long!' They'll teach you," I offered cutely.

"As if they could teach me anything. Besides, those souls on that planet with your primary actors was also a place of my actors – not the truest me. I'm still here," he countered.

"Understood. So, it's a plan?" I begged.

"It's a plan – subject to modifications – but yes. It's a plan."

I leapt up with joy, throwing my little arms up. "That's great," I said. But I wanted to remind him of the graduation ceremony that night. "I'm going to sing tonight. It's already arranged – when I get my certificate for finishing the Identity Process."

"That's great, too. I haven't heard you sing in a while."

"I guess I hadn't wanted to."

"Well, you are *the angel* when it comes to vocals. I can't wait," he suggested.

"Can't wait? You've got forever."

"Lots of songs? One in particular?"

"Oh – the World song," I thought he'd remember.

"Remind me the lyrics?" he requested.

"It's the one that starts out with the *Weight of* the World, then changes in the next verse to *Way of* the World, and later to *Way to* the World," I said, following into sing-song with each phrase. I added the last line, softly singing it, "The Way to the World – it can make you laugh and make you sing."

"Oh, that one – fitting enough. How many times have you performed it?"

"Millions in this universe alone," I said.

"Well I'll see you at commencement," he smiled, pulling away from the table, giving me a little wave to which I responded in kind.

I was less concerned about the song as with the future plan. Other than my simple work here, I effactually had a discordant and adventurous game and someone to play it with, because tranquility and goodness was never the goal. Having superior ability to play a finer game was the goal. So, what if it was the same universe, as for years I had millions. As for myself – I'd remain *one*, though I could adeptly divide myself into my first-tier souls if I wished.

I walked across a plaza toward the dormitory where I had my room, enjoying the soft click of my little mock ballet shoes against the stones, feeling my perfect blonde curls caressing my neck and shoulders. You'd have to realize that the last thing I expected in that next moment was to hear a voice, but there it was, just as if it were originating right behind my neck...

EPILOGUE

Authenticity

When I'd recognized myself as *one*, in those moments of elation I could delightfully see beyond the borders of that contrived universe, as if a vestibule to heaven itself was directly within reach, a gate between universes just a step away. The realization wasn't trite, releasing the massive Leviathan whose tentacles had wrought about every concept of my multitude of incarnations, dragging *us* into the depths of a cavernous abyss of physical existence and existential philosophy, which itself is a created artifact to keep us within. Here we had slain Behemoth, who had perforce inveigled every nefarious twist of fate, conning us to become agnostic and spiritually forsaken, producing the incapacitation of even the faintest extant power.

And in doing so, I found my authentic self and my purpose.

I toiled to help others in that universe to lift myself above the state of despicable so that at the end of future universes I would not become so oblivious and disreputable. Though technically, there is no strict right and wrong in a universe (aside from fully losing oneself, for which there is no impunity), but per the definition requires consistency, whether identities and actions follow the arbitrary rules of the space, energy, matter and time that comprise it, as well as the expectations and agreements of others who joined the game. Of course, there are practical boundaries that one may exceed, sinfully as well as physically. I'd suspect that most don't know that physics itself can be exceeded when enough mass and force come together, allowing the uncontrolled release of all the energy, completely and totally, without harmonic interactions, a complete dispersal. Some souls are still the effect of such explosions, just witness the

Big Bang concept for the creation of the present universe, which I would contest never happened.

Among the many concepts in my spiritual edification was that my divided souls were those that played all potential roles. I had found that any person who had been my worst enemy, had been yet another incarnation, a spiritual clone, of myself, having been created with an opposing purpose to be a challenger, even my nemesis, all for the sake of playing out the games of the universe, all for adventure. As I had been so many characters, perhaps this tale could have been written from a multitude of viewpoints. It could have been from Purity. Though the viewpoint from my final lifetimes as Miranda and Dahilana, until becoming Purity, wasn't the most adventurous nor the darkest, it was instead one of the most beautiful as well as revelatory, and thus the story is worthy of transcription. I was a completely tethered and boring personality on some common planets, and a far more despicable, evil character on sequestered planets – either case eliciting exploits you would not choose to read, being mundane or egregious in the extreme.

The end of that universe came in due time, Michael, myself and the many souls that created it, including a girl I considered my spirit twin, found our origins as the creators. Armageddon is not a violent, tumultuous horror elicited by a single malediction from a God or Satan either one. It is not the condemnation of every man, woman and child to an infinite agonized desolation. It is simply us, cleaning up the mess we'd created for our own games, games we'd become completely lost within, in our own effort to create staunch reality. Armageddon is a triumphant end to any universe we authored.

Now, in this much later universe, I have found myself once again working through confession chains to handle my illusions and delusions and reveal my own self and truth. In fact, this story is derived from the 154th incident on just one specific chain and is many, many universes in the past. I don't know what else I'll find on this chain yet, as I'm still working on it. But I've recovered again the knowledge that I've been broken up into multiple identities, also based on the six primary personality divisions I'd found in this incident. Which am I? I'm Grace, and have my purpose as *connecting flows* of information and activities. In revealing this knowledge I've realized that I'm still a part of Purity, the greater combined soul with a purpose *to purify*. Thus, my greater purpose beyond that of Grace is to purify things, to whatever that can be applied, whether ideas, stories, designs of universes or something as simple as recipes, and of course, it can be applied to souls. Disappointingly, I don't have any evidence that there still exists a distinct and separate entity named Purity. It is only my hope that one day I will find a way to recombine all my broken selves into that one, and be able to once again, as a single unit, say, "I'm one." However, as with a coarse chunk of salt crushed into smaller pieces, all the elements retain the properties of the original, but the fragmented elements cannot so easily be mended together.

With my mind in a somewhat broken-up state, I believe I'm not alone. I believe that the other souls – the primary divisions of Purity – are here with me in this one body, acting out the role of a single person. I believe that each of us has our functions and misgivings and we play those out, attempting to be the best person we can be as broken personalities with broken memory. It's not entirely pleasant, but I don't think it is the most horrible state to be in, as it is far from complete oblivion. I don't think it is "multiple personality disorder" or some myriad other potential labels. Nor do I think it is a random occurrence, a happenstance of synchronicity. I'm certain, with regard to recovering my true identity and capability, it is a plan, such that I am not the last soul to exit the present universe. Though I may be a member of the condemned, I know I'm at least a fragment of the blessed as I search again for my authentic self.

It started when I heard a voice, much as a disembodied soul speaking directly into my consciousness, right into the back of my head. That's how I got my first clue. Perhaps this story is your clue.

Much Affinity,
True, Desire, Princess, Love, Joy and Grace

**Author Stephen Michael Ferree** grew up in a small town in Illinois and attended the University of Illinois studying Electrical Engineering. This education brought him to Columbus Indiana to work with Cummins Inc. Stephen is currently a single father with two good kids at home: Felicity is the creative and active teenager; Brandon the logical gamer.

www.ingramcontent.com/pod-product-compliance
Lightning Source LLC
Chambersburg PA
CBHW051933020726
47501CB00001B/107